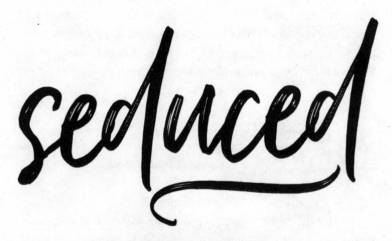

seduced

HONOR BOUND: BOOK THREE

ANGEL PAYNE

HONOR BOUND: BOOK THREE

ANGEL PAYNE

WATERHOUSE PRESS

For Thomas...for always

And special thanks to...

Charlie and Matt—I love both of you so much, as well as the beautiful love you share.

And to Hudsy—for being my first guide and friend down the rabbit hole. You truly have no idea how much it has meant.

To every single man and woman selflessly serving in our nation's military—

Profound and deep thanks for your service!

CHAPTER ONE

"Is this a dream?"

The words were whispered into Ethan Archer's ear by the forest goddess he was seconds away from kissing. Corny comparison? Roger that. Completely true? Double affirmative. She was mesmerizing. Thick mist rolled around the pine tree to which he'd pressed her, stroking the waves of her auburn hair, leaving droplets on the long lashes bordering her indigo eyes, caressing every inch of light-bronze skin the cowl of her sweater would allow. Lucky bastard, that mist.

"I was thinking the same thing," he murmured. "Maybe we'd better do some recon, just to be sure."

"Yeah. Recon..."

Her voice trailed away into a needy sigh, suffusing his chest with warmth and his cock with fire, as they leaned toward each other. He caught the end of her breath with a brush of his mouth to hers.

His gentle intent lasted two seconds.

The second he tasted her, he needed more. Strawberries. Mango. Sunshine. Sudden summer in this chilled bower. *Fuck, yes.* He used his lips to spread her, demanding deeper entrance. When she yielded with an eager mewl, he swept in, coaxing her tongue into a sensual dance. By raw instinct, he found both her wrists with his hands. With one sweep, he had them locked over her head against the tree's trunk.

He pulled away to lock his gaze on her. "My dream

includes this," he growled.

A slow smile curled on her lips. "Mine too."

"That's not what your eyes are telling me, sunshine."

Her lashes flew wider, exposing those indigo depths even more. "Wh-What do you—"

"What is it? What are you holding back? Tell me now."

"I...umm..."

"*What?*" he demanded.

"Tighter," she finally rasped, working her wrists against his grip. "I need it tighter, Ethan. Please..."

She had him at the throaty delivery and the subtle Spanish accent, but the request itself ignited his lust from a spark to a rager. With a snarl, he rammed her wrists harder to the tree. With a gasp, she gave him the full-access pass to kiss her again. Forget sweet preludes. He went to the depths of her mouth with passionate intent, spearing her throat just like he yearned to get his dick, now aching to the point of pain, inside her body.

A set of words echoed in his brain. They'd come from his Army Special Forces teammate, Garrett Hawkins, as glasses were raised to toast the guy's upcoming wedding.

Fate gives you the best shit when you least expect it, guys.

Ethan was way on board with that credo now. When he'd shown up to help with Hawk's last-minute ceremony, none of his wildest expectations had yielded someone like Ava Chestain, especially after he introduced himself by tackling her in Garrett's living room in a misguided rush of paranoia.

When she'd grinned and joined the banter in teasing him about the incident, he'd been intrigued. When she'd agreed to join him on a hunt through the woods for the bridal bouquet flowers, he'd been encouraged. When she'd given him that beautifully submissive whisper, he was a fucking goner. Just like that, a piece of his spirit plunked out into her gorgeous little palm—

And had remained there for the last seven months.

"Shit."

The self-directed oath blasted him out of the memory like an air horn. In an instant, he opened his eyes to the current suckage that was his life. The mist, the trees, and the once-upon-a-time forest were gone, leaving a Mexican desert sunset that matched the battlefield in his head. Orange, red, and yellow shot at each other past billowing cloud boulders. It was over thirty-eight degrees Celsius, which sounded a lot better than a hundred Fahrenheit. It was well over *that* inside his boots and BDUs.

He slumped against one of the unit's mud-caked Hummers.

Every minute of the last seven months suddenly weighed on him like lead.

Could it be because you've fixated too many times on that kiss, dumbass, and not enough on what came after it?

Oh, yeah. All *that*. Never mind that thanks to the criminal who crashed the wedding, he'd ended that day in battle gear and a debriefing instead of in his dress blues, hogging every dance with her. And the rest, what came after? He forced himself to remember that too. The phone calls she never picked up. The texts she never answered. Even the acknowledgment that never came after he sent her a goddamn florist's shop worth of birthday flowers.

"Fuck."

He muttered it before dropping his head between his shoulders. A glance in the Hum's rearview showed that he looked as defeated as he felt. Dust had transformed his nearly black hair into a weird blond. His blue eyes were bloodshot. His lips were as dry as a concrete gargoyle's.

He was tempted to laugh. If only all those talent scouts and modeling agents, always ready with their business cards and glam offers, could see him now. Because the best hunk of the minute was the guy covered in five inches of dirt, ten inches of rage, and fifteen inches of what-the-fuck-am-I-doing-with-myself, right?

Behind him, the creak of a rusty door sliced the air. The shack to which the portal belonged nearly collapsed from the movement, a strangely appropriate symbol of the interrogation that had taken place inside. Ethan grimaced. Nothing like the sound of a grown man's sobs to kill the lure of humor, appetite, or any hope of forgetting about the head fuck he'd just performed on the poor shithead.

"Bernardo, it's been a pleasure." Every word was dipped in Rhett Lange's mix of highbrow London and cocky New York. Ethan almost expected the man to whip out a party bag stuffed with plastic favors but knew better. A month back, Rhett had used the same tone before filleting a double agent's gut.

"*Chupa mi pito*, Captain America," wailed the guy who stumbled from the shack behind Rhett. His wrists were still secured behind his back with plastic cuffs. When he lifted his tear-streaked face and noticed Ethan, he shuddered and cried harder. "You too, *culero*. You and your devil word tricks. I curse you to the bowels of the hell you came from!"

Ethan parked his ass against the Hummer's front tire and, with a shitload of weariness, mumbled, "Bernardo, my man, you may be on to something there."

Pounding footfalls yanked his head up. The stomps also came from the shack, making the thing look like the San

Andreas Fault was opening beneath it, as a third man emerged. Daniel Colton, whom they'd nicknamed CIA Ken in honor of his flawless haircut, ducked to avoid whacking his trademark locks on the shack's awning before strolling free, thumbs hooked into his Dragon Skin vest, a chortle on his lips. "'Devil word tricks'? 'Bowels of hell'? Been catching up on your comic books between those heroin runs into California, *Señor Galvaz*?"

"Screw you, Colton. And your *puta* mother. And your whore of a sister."

"My mama's baking bread with the angels, *muchas gracias* for your concern. But I'll thank you right now to refrain from the sister references, *amigo*. They're not gentlemanly. Or wise."

Bernardo glowered. "Or what? You gonna come after me, big bad spy man?"

Colton let out a low growl. "*She'll* come after you, little narco."

"Bah. Just keep centerfold boy away from me."

Ethan kept his stare locked on the ground. The heroin dealer had laughingly given him the nickname when they'd started the interrogation this morning, and nobody had suggested a revision. The call was correct. When a prisoner thought he was nothing more than a set of dreamy blues, some lucky bone structure, and a well-worked pair of biceps, it made his mental scalpel that much easier to use. Less painful for everyone concerned.

And then there were the exceptions—like Bernardo. Guys who resisted every cut, making his job a sheer hell. He'd had to slice deep today, digging into emotional marrow he hadn't expected. By the time the dealer had finally spilled, weeping his way through the details they had needed to stop the truckload of heroin and illegal guns bound for the States tonight, Ethan had staggered to the shack's sink and scrubbed himself from fingertips to elbows. Not that it helped. You didn't wash the dirt of a man's soul off your own with rusty water. You barely did it with *holy* water. He should know. He'd tried.

Are you seriously pulling a pity party about this, dickface? You were the one who joined this machine to feel more valuable and connected to the world, remember? To feel like you mattered beyond your pretty face and your prettier checkbook, right?

Guess he'd just stepped into a pile of the world's biggest lesson-learned-the-hard-way. *Careful what you wish for, shit-for-brains.*

Colton's harsh *pfft* broke into his funk. "Damn, Galvaz. Why're you still all Bambi tears on me? We haven't touched a hair on your head, man. What the fuck?"

His pragmatic tone matched the gray matter under the government haircut. As spooks went, Colton was one of the better ones. He'd wisely listened to the advice of his peers—*let Archer do his prisoner whisperer thing and then stand back and reap the benefits*—and now his cocky swagger emulated his triumph in the decision. "It's time for you to grow a pair, man. You only have a few tiny scratches from where we cuffed you. Keep your wrists covered for a few days and nobody's going to suspect you're the one who surrendered the playbook on this shit for tonight. If it makes you feel any better, you saved some lives. Even without the smack on the truck, you know the family who paid the cartel to be hidden in the back would've never seen San Diego alive."

"Save your emo act for a fourteen-year-old who cares, *cabron.*"

Dan's answer to that was a soft *thwick*, the ejection of his pocketknife blade. "I'm cutting you out of these now, Galvaz, but try anything weird and we'll toss you right out of the transport. If you survive that part, you can play man against nature, Sonoran Desert style. Glad to see you don't like that option, because *I* sure as hell don't. Your return to the Aragon Cartel is of much better use. You're clear on that? *Sí, amigo?* You get back in there and stay alert. We may be coming by for a play date with you again soon."

Bernardo took advantage of his physical freedom to wipe the tear-streaked grime off his face with his forearm. "If you bring the centerfold bitch again, you can eat my shit. And I expect to be paid next time, spy man."

Colton rolled his eyes. "I'm not sure you're square with how this whole thing works, *amigo*."

"Oh, I am 'square,' *chingado*. Make sure your palms are growing lettuce next time, or stay home and let them whack you off to videos of your sister."

"Hell," Ethan spat. He pushed off the tire, expecting to pull Dan's fist out of Galvaz's face any second. But again, CIA man impressed him. Though Colton's chiseled features went tight as stone, all he did was swing his weary gaze back toward Ethan, like they wrangled an obstinate teen together.

Ethan shrugged during his approach back to the shack's porch. What mental poker would be the best to shove back up Bernardo's ass? He had a lot to pick from. A childhood of abuse and poverty. Teenage days capped by being blackmailed to make his first drug run, followed by getting tossed out by his grandmother when she'd learned of his involvement with the cartels. The girlfriend who left him when she discovered the same thing. Terrifying, what the mind believed once the heart lost its trust.

Silver lining? Galvaz was trying to do the right thing now. Too bad the dickwad was being a snot about the process, including the dramatic sob as Ethan got near. "Get away from me!"

Ethan turned up his hands. "Shit, 'Nardo. You need to chill."

"Don't come another step closer!"

"Not a problem." He let his left eyebrow kick up. "As long as you treat my associates with better respect." Squaring his stance sent up a small cloud of dust. "To be clear, that's an ongoing request. If I hear otherwise, I'll be happy to hop back on the helo and come for another visit. They know how to reach me real quick."

"Fine. *Fine.*" Bernardo's lips trembled as he inched a step backward. "Just stay the fuck out of my head. And watch out for my family. You promised you would."

"That we did." He exchanged an affirming glance with Colton. "And that we will."

"You fuck me over on that, centerfold boy, and I'll be up inside *your* head—with the barrel of my pistol."

The guy stalked away. Colton and Rhett grabbed him by the elbows and walked him toward the dry riverbed serving as their helipad. Soon a Black Hawk helo hovered into view, though the modified bird made as much noise as a pinwheel, allowing Dan and Rhett to exchange a hearty handshake and promises that they'd get together when Dan made his way through Seattle, where their battalion was based out of Joint Base Lewis-McChord. Colton tossed a wave to Ethan as well before joining more government Ken dolls aboard the helo, who'd already latched Galvaz in.

As the Black Hawk arced away into the sky, Rhett strolled back at a pace that suggested he was about to strip down to a Savile Row suit and whip out a perfect martini. Once they stood together again, he gave Ethan a solid clap on the shoulder. "You," he uttered, "are a bloody god."

Ethan feigned swatting at a fly to break the contact. Damn, he craved a shower. "And you're full of shit."

He went back into the shack. Wrong move. Bernardo's tears, sweat, and resistance clung to the air, uploading every hellacious minute of the day back into his mind. Rhett followed him in and started packing the recording equipment from the interrogation, which had fed all the data straight to the big heads at Special Ops Command. By now they were scrambling a team to seize that truck as soon as it crossed the border tonight at the time Bernardo had just supplied to them.

"You want to vent?" Rhett ventured.

"No."

"All right. Rephrase. You *need* to vent. So let it rip, asshat."

He sucked in a hard breath. Shot up half a sardonic smirk. "Seriously? You pulling rank on me, old man?" Rhett had three ranks and two years on him, though the difference was always used by either of them as a joke more than an operating procedure. He really hoped the guy didn't start that bullshit now.

"I'm pulling concerned buddy on you and nothing else." Rhett stilled halfway through closing the camera bag. "Look, mate...you were amazing this afternoon. You know all the work that brought us here. Two teams, three continents, and twice that many countries. You may not be digging lead out of your hide, but everyone knows what you did for the cause. You swam into the psychological thick of it with Galvaz so we'd get one step closer to the Aragons and hopefully to the bigger strings of this thing in Afghanistan and Somalia."

"Hurray, team." He swirled a finger in the air. And yeah, he probably should've said more after that, pulled out maybe one more stupid one-liner to reassure Rhett this wasn't the first time he'd been through this. It would've diverted the guy from guessing at the sick truth: that his sole attempt at the "venting" thing had nearly caused the brain bashers at Mental Health Services to slam a temporary disability card on his ass. *Not going to happen, assholes.* He hadn't defied his parents and given up a cushy ride to college with the promise of a Silicon Valley corner office to be told his head was too fucked up for living his dream. At the moment, he just needed to scrub it out a little. Some bleach, wax stripper, maybe a few lye pellets, and he'd been right as fucking rain.

"Fine," Rhett finally said. "Then how about I take you to get some Olympus-type nectar?" The guy curled a suave grin. "Or maybe just a truckload of *cerveza*?"

"No."

He bit it out harder this time. He was so damn tired. All he wanted was a transport home, along with the engine drone and earbuds full of an Incubus album as his lullaby.

The second he allowed that hope to blossom a little more, his radio crackled. The line boomed with the voice of John Franzen, their CO. "Double-O, Runway, got the word from Colton that's he's bugged with the target. You two pretty boys packed up yet, over?"

Ethan punched the comm button at his ear, connected to the speaker line that was formed to his cheek. "Just about. Advise rendezvous point for the exfil, over?"

Franz's answer carried a laugh. "That would be the

Twisted Iguana cantina, over."

Ethan frowned. "Repeat, please?"

"You heard me right, Sergeant. The Twisted Iguana. *La Iguana Torsida.* Double-O knows where it is."

Rhett nodded acknowledgment. But before Ethan opened the line back up, he cocked his head in puzzlement, almost pulling a physical double take. "Er...Franz..."

"Is there a problem with that command, Archer?"

"Uh, well, no. But you called me—" A glance down at the pin on his collar, displaying the double corporal stripes, emphasized how ridiculous the rest of it sounded.

You called me Sergeant.

Big fucking deal. Okay, it sounded nice, but that didn't make it true. Nor did pointing out the dick-up make any sense. Franz was likely—probably—just as tired as him and now compounded that with a very large beer on a half-empty stomach. Thinking fast, Ethan concluded with, "Never mind. We're nearly wrapped and ready and will be Oscar-Mike in less than ten."

"That's outstanding news, Sergeant. Franzen out."

Ethan didn't hide his confusion this time. Only the decrepit walls were witness to his reaction since Double-O was already outside, halfway to the Hummer with a load of equipment. It was only those walls that heard his quiet quip. "Right, Captain. And I'll just forget about that shit-eating grin you forgot to mask in your voice."

★ ★ ★ ★ ★

When Rhett pulled off the main road and guided the Hummer down a road as twisted as a dusty Candy Land board, Ethan cocked a brow at his friend. "Love the scenic detour, man, but even if there are waterfalls and fairies at the end, I'm not sucking face with you."

"Ha bloody ha."

"Okay, then. If you're thinking of doing the execution thing, I'll let you know right now that Hawkins has dibs on my books and Hayes gets my guns. The engraved pilsner glasses are still up for grabs—"

"Archer."

"Yeah?"

"Shut it."

Both words were underlined in arrogance. The next moment, Ethan saw why. They rounded a steep rock corner into a clearing with a parking lot—kind of—filled with every kind of vehicle from their monster military stuff and gas-guzzling clunkers to some new Ducati motorcycles and even a pair of beautifully restored classic Mustangs. The owners of those rides were packed onto about thirty picnic tables tucked beneath a massive lean-to shelter that was wedged between a gutted stake-bed truck and an old VW van with one side shaved off. Atop the stake bed, a DJ adjusted levels on the Pearl Jam tune that throbbed through the air. The van had been converted into a bar. A redhead with a great rack in a tight Godzilla T-shirt popped beers and poured drinks with saucy cheer. Strings of carnival lights were draped between the overhang and the nearby cholla trees. The décor consisted of every groan-worthy pop culture trend from the last twenty years, including Homer Simpson bobbleheads, a pirate ship with humping Jack Sparrow dolls, Victoria's Secret model posters, and a bunch of commemorative Super Bowl footballs that "flew" from the ceiling on fishing line.

Positioned in front of all this, with a grin that suggested he'd just screwed the poster models himself, was John Franzen. Flanking him were two of Ethan's battalion mates, Zeke Hayes and Garrett Hawkins. Their smiles also widened as he and Rhett got out and approached. Despite that, Ethan threw up his guard, keeping his face neutral. When the CO greeted you, in addition to the two guys who called the shots on most of the team's missions, it was either a really good thing or a really bad thing.

Franzen gave a fist bump to Rhett. "Nice work, Double-O. You got him here without rope or handcuffs."

"Damn good thing." Rhett chuckled and swung his gaze around. "The kinky shit is all yours, my friends. He even thought I was taking him to the wilderness to make out. I felt awful for busting his bubble, but—"

"Fuck you," Ethan drawled as Zeke and Garrett snickered. Franz didn't join them. With his newfound solemnity, he slammed a hand into Ethan's shoulder.

"You look like shit, Runway. You okay?"

Ethan didn't return Franz's scrutiny. A string of illuminated GI Joe heads became a perfect diversion for his gaze. "Lid's on fine, Captain. So, does Godzilla Girl have anything besides beer?" An inch or two of Scotch sounded really fucking good.

Franzen, damn him, didn't move his hand an inch. "No," he declared. "I don't think you're fine, Archer."

He slid a glare at his CO. "I'll *be* fine if everyone stops asking about it."

Franzen contemplated that before shaking his head and stating, "Uh-uh. You're still missing something."

"What the hell are—"

"You're missing this."

The man yanked on Ethan's collar, pulling the fabric taut so he could jam a pin into the triangle panel. Before Ethan could say a word, Franz finished off the business by detaching the pin that had originally been there, bearing the double stripes of his corporal rank.

Garrett cracked a bigger grin. "Now isn't that prettier'n a fresh drop of dew on a morning glory?"

Zeke rolled his eyes. "Hawk, you're a serious dork sometimes."

"It's okay," Ethan interjected. He stared at the new pin on his collar. Counted the stripes there for the tenth time. One, two, three. Sure enough, they were all there. "This time he's right." The pin was pretty. Better than pretty. It was perfect. So was the identical one Franzen placed into his palm.

"I'll let you get the other collar," his CO said. "And sorry we're not doing this on a stage in our Class As, Archer. Figured you'd appreciate getting the pay step that much faster."

"You figured right."

"Oh, yeah. That reminds me. You're buying first round tonight."

Ethan chuckled. "Sure thing. And thanks, Captain."

Franz busted out a wide smile, gleaming in stark contrast to the jet-black hair of his skull cut, before murmuring, "You want to thank someone, look in the mirror. You worked hard for this. Congratulations, *Sergeant*." He shook his head, his equally dark eyes glittering in amusement. "I can finally say that without worrying I'll fry your gray matter."

"I say we let Serenity take over that chore." Rhett nodded toward the bar and Godzilla Girl. While Ethan repeated his laugh, this time because he seemed to be the only one noticing the irony of a girl named Serenity with a fire-spewing lizard across her chest, the redhead noticed Rhett and gave him a soft wave.

"All right, everyone," Franzen announced, "pomp and circumstance is over. Shuck at least the tops so we can celebrate properly."

Three minutes later, after stowing their jackets in the Hummers, they reconvened at a long ledge, really a faded surfboard affixed atop cement blocks that formed one side of Serenity's workspace. Despite her preoccupation with Double-O, the woman had a line of five frosty bottles lined up by the time they got to the bar. After taking his first swig, Ethan jutted his lower lip in respect. Beer wasn't usually his thing, but the microbrewed lager from a California-based outfit was strong and smooth.

"Well, well, well." Franz tipped his bottle at the bar mistress. "Breaking out the good stuff for us now, Serenity? What happened between last night and now?" He flicked a glance between her and Rhett, clearly following the sparks zipping between the pair. "Or should I ask *who* happened?"

The woman snapped a towel at him. "Bugger off, Franzie Panzie. I'm tryin' to be nice."

"Franzie Panzie?" Zeke's face, normally the texture of a granite cliff, crumpled in humor. "Damn, why didn't I come up with that one first?"

Franzen eyed him. "Because you have to put up with me after tonight, and she doesn't."

Serenity jerked up her chin. "I noticed you wankers had some kind of special event goin' down, so I broke out the good swill."

"You figured right," Garrett offered. "Mr. Dark-and-

Chiseled over there is basking in his first hour as a full-fledged sergeant."

The redhead's face lit up. "Brilliant! Nice work!" She swatted the towel at Ethan too, though her intent was playful this time. In two seconds she was full of feisty fire again, arching brows back at Franz. "Though I'm happy to get the piss water back out for you, Panzie, if you fancy it?"

Franz held up a hand. "Nope, nope. This is just fine, sweetcakes." He dropped that hand in order to scoop up Serenity's, grazing her knuckles with a kiss. "Thank you for the thoughtfulness."

It escaped nobody, especially Serenity, that Rhett looked ready to punch their CO for the move. The redhead giggled before turning to load up the tabs on more of the bar's customers, which seemed to be a friendly mix of locals and American expats.

"Shit." Garrett examined the label on his bottle. "Never thought I'd say this, but some of these California beers are good."

Rhett huffed. Parts of the man would never acclimate to the rest of the world, and his booze preference was one of them. "Whatever."

"Hmm." Franz suddenly found the lip of his own bottle fascinating, though his tone was too contemplative for a place where an inflatable Batman in an evening gown was tied to the rafters over the bar. "I hear there's a lot of good things about California."

Without missing a beat, Zeke added, "I hear the same thing."

"Beer's damn tasty," Garrett said.

Rhett shook his head. "Hell. I give up."

"I do too." Ethan frowned. "What the fuck with the cryptic California tourism commercial?"

Franz cocked up one side of his mouth. "Because maybe I talked to the high-levels about how my guys grinded their guts to gravel to uncover a new international drug shipment stream and then tracked it across the globe to break the assholes' weakest links. And maybe after that, I also told them one of my boys was about to score his sergeant's stripe. And maybe after *that*, I convinced them that because of all this, my guys deserve a few days of fucking around in the land of beaches, babes, bikinis, and"—he held up his bottle—"really good beers."

Rhett shifted forward. "Are you bloody serious?"

Like they'd choreographed it, Franzen took a step back to let Zeke move up. "And maybe *I* talked my sexy bird of a girlfriend into meeting us in LA so she could arrange a friendly visit with her cousin...on the set of the TV show she works on."

That got a fist pump out of Rhett. "Oh, yeah! Hollyweird, here we come!"

Zeke chuckled, accepting Rhett's offer to knock bottle necks. Franzen and Garrett joined the toast. When the four of them swung expectant stares at Ethan, he somehow got his muscles to function at returning the *chink*. The action validated his new belief in miracles. How he functioned at all, considering how every blood cell in his body hit a red light at the same time, had to be divine intervention at work.

"Shit, Runway," Garrett drawled. "Don't let the excitement eat you up at once, okay?"

Zeke released a knowing snort. "Oh, he's excited."

Garrett seconded the laugh. "Figured your mention of a certain cousin might do it."

Rhett grinned. "You mean the one he tackled before

Hawk's wedding, thinking she was Hezbollah in heels? Or the one who did a personal GPS trek in lipstick across his face? Oh, wait. That was the *same* cousin, wasn't it?"

"Goddamnit," Franz snapped. "I missed all the good shit."

"Not all of it." Garrett scowled. "We finally got the vows in, but Sage isn't settling for the courthouse thing. Soon as the baby's born, she swears she's slimming down for the big dress and the Hollywood wedding production again. She wants to go *Nouveau Renaissance* this time."

"Hell." Zeke laughed his way around another swig. "Are goldenrod napkins involved again?"

"Not sure. But I told her if I'm wearing pants that button at my knee, I'd better damn well get a sword too."

The banter was background buzz in Ethan's mind. For the chance to see Ava again, he'd hop on a plane to goddamn Antarctica. Okay, Rhett was right; they'd first met because he'd let paranoia into the party and body-slammed her into a mound of wedding fabric—but even that had been perfect. No stupid pretenses. No feigned interest behind a social handshake. Just their gazes, meshed with honesty, awareness...connection. Every breath tangled. Every touch a tiny fire. Every second a new beginning. It was the core of what he craved from being a Dominant—hell, what he was searching for in *life*—yet seemed his personal Atlantis, a lost nirvana never to be realized.

Until Ava.

Fuck.

He took a long gulp of his beer, medicating his frustration. Summoning the memories back only reconfirmed that everything he'd felt seven months ago was so damn real. And damn it, those kinds of sensations weren't possible without return ammo. Like the way she'd lingered near him even after he'd pulled her upright from his tackle. The way her eyes danced like the rarest, darkest sapphires when she'd invited him into the forest for those flowers. The way she'd followed him through the trees and then begged him to grip her harder when he pinned her against one of them...

None of it added up to the way her radio had gone dark on him since. After Garrett and Sage's wedding had gone down in a blaze of disaster—including Zeke being zapped with a neurotoxin and Rayna getting carried off by a psychopath with a huge ax to grind—Ava stayed long enough to be sure that Ray was officially out of harm's way. Then she headed straight for the airport, telling everyone she'd been summoned back to Hollywood by her whack-a-diva of a boss. He hadn't bought the line for a second. Said diva had only been in the third week of recovery from an extensive nose and lip job. He doubted Bella Lanza was conscious enough to dial the phone, let alone capable of a text or email. Ava had fled Seattle for another reason. In the following weeks, the crickets that greeted *his* calls and texts were ample proof of that reason.

Would seeing her again explain anything? Prove anything?

At first, the hollow walls of his beer bottle were the only response he got. But suddenly, something replaced that fucking uselessness—something besides the anger, the exasperation, the loss. Resolve. It started in the core of his chest but spread out fast, making his extremities flex and his spine straighten. Once it got to his mind, it met up with a new friend: the Dom deep inside who now issued a surprising update. He hadn't given up on the goddess in the forest. He hadn't white-flagged it on a second of the desire in her eyes, the need in her kiss, the urgency in her voice when she'd begged him to pin her down harder. He hadn't let go of the hope that she wanted more from him...had more to give him in return.

And he wasn't giving up unless she told him to. With her own lips. Standing face-to-face with him.

He grinned. Somehow he found that harder to envision than their Hummer turning into a Lamborghini.

And once he had Ava in front of him again, he'd get to the truth—even the naked version, if she forced his hand—of why she'd decided to go AWOL on him after what they'd shared in that Washington forest.

"Serenity." It was more a command than a call, bolstered by his first real hope in seven months. The bar mistress wheeled, cocking brows in a silent you-did-*not*-just-summon-me-like-that, but softened when he twirled a finger toward the table and said, "Round two, please? The good shit again. On me."

Franzen kicked up one side of his mouth. "You know, Runway, when your morose silences lead to stuff like this, I'm okay with it."

"Copy me in on that." Zeke held his fresh bottle high. "So what're we toasting to, Archer?"

Ethan turned to his battalion mates and leader. His stare was as level as a sniper's crosshairs. "What else, man? To California."

"To California!" the other four men bellowed.

After they knocked bottles and took deep drags from their drinks, Franz's smile grew into a wicked grin. "This should be an adventure. And I'm sure as hell not missing it this time."

Ethan stepped away from their huddle and paced back out toward the cars. The lights and music of the bar faded a little. He looked up into the sky, where twilight lingered in a special strip between the horizon and the stars. It looked like the universe had scooped the color right out of Ava's eyes and painted it there. The indigo hue, a perfect mix of deep blue and purple, held his stare long after he should've walked back.

He drilled his gaze hard into that sky and gave it a small smile of his own.

"Adventure," he murmured. "That might be one way of putting it."

CHAPTER TWO

"Ava! Damn it!"

The outburst didn't just pull Ava Chestain out of her mental cloud. It yanked her down, slapped her hard, and then hurled her around, making sure her self-esteem got slammed against all four walls of the costume-dressing trailer. That included the sides with the mini-movie theater and the built-in kitchen.

Fortunately, her self-esteem had learned to laugh this shit off as the usual.

*Un*fortunately, there was nothing usual about today. And not in any of the best ways.

"Bella," she mumbled. "*Ay. Lo siento.* Let me fix it."

One of the world's most famous faces, a perfect Sicilian oval centered by a newly sculpted nose, aimed one glaring brown eye at her in the vanity mirror's reflection. The other eye was covered by the chunk of hair Ava had just teased, prepping it for the woman's normal style, an updated version of Sophia Loren froth. Trouble was, even Bella's hair wasn't the standard order today, and forgetting it was on the same par with unleashing locusts over LA. It never escaped Ava's mind that though her paycheck was direct deposited from Victory Cat Productions, the real ruler of her professional world was the petite woman who sat in the styling chair with posture that suggested a curling iron had just gotten jammed up her backside.

"Yes. You *will* fix it." The woman had carefully picked the burrs from her tone, leaving only the poison-dipped velvet beneath. "Must I remind you that Raven is in grief today? She's likely not even showered for forty-eight hours. The hair must match."

The woman shuddered. Ava waited, knowing she'd do it again. Bella often spoke about her character on the show as if Raven Ryder sat in the room with them or even like she was Raven herself. Ava actually liked the acting exercise. It was a hell of a lot easier to talk to Raven than Bella.

She was pretty sure that'd be the only time "easy" entered her vocabulary today.

She stole a glance at the clock. Whew. It was barely eight a.m. Rayna, Zeke, and the guys weren't due for their visit to the set for another hour. She had to shave an additional fifteen minutes off that because they *would* be early. And though she already had Charlie, work bestie extraordinaire, on standby for the set tour and introductions duties, she wanted to make sure her alibi of having to pick up something from Bella's house at least looked authentic. That gave her thirty minutes to make Bella's lustrous hair look like it hadn't been washed in two days.

She turned and started yanking every tube of product from the hair cabinet. To make sure she wasn't in the same room again with Ethan Archer, she'd dump a whole salon on the woman's head.

Because if she was in the same room with him again, she'd want to be in his bed tonight. Correction. She'd want to be tied up in his bed tonight. Yielding to him. Giving herself to him. *All* of herself. The On switch the man always tripped in her would be *on*, and this time, she wouldn't have the option of hopping on a plane before turning it off...if she'd even want to.

You've come too far, Ava. Worked too hard to get here. You're not going to let another cruise dog in camouflage turn your head inside out and your heart upside down just for three hours of passion, a couple of orgasms, and another dead-end hunt for a connection that isn't possible with a man. Don't let him in. You can't *let him in.*

To water down the panic that threatened a mutiny on her bloodstream, she decided to try to calm Bella at the same time. "So tell me what Raven has to deal with today."

Bella's eyes had already fallen heavy. She blinked up at Ava with matching torpidity, a signal that she'd clicked into her method by cloaking herself inside her character. "The CO has come to tell her that the insurgents have taken Jace hostage."

Jace, Raven's fiancé, was played by hunky Trent Lake, who'd just been named on a half dozen Hot Young Hollywood lists. He was also in two studio tentpole movies this summer and was "considering" his renewal offer for the show's next season, which translated into *give me more money or I walk.* Which was why Jace was currently in a Middle Eastern prison, fate undecided.

"So they don't know if he's alive or dead?" Ava asked as she combed in a conditioner with an olive-oil base. When Bella washed her hair tonight, the strands would be soft as a baby's butt. Or fall completely out. Sometimes a girl had to gamble.

Bella's brow furrowed. "No, they don't. Because of this, Raven is unbearably lost. Rudderless. What will she do without him? She...she wanders through their house. She unzips the wedding dress she still hasn't worn for him, and she thinks about all their plans for their big day, perhaps never to become real now. She thinks about the babies they wanted to have, the family they wanted to raise, the life they dreamed of sharing..."

Ava stilled her hand. Swallowed hard. "Shit. That's...um... really good, Bella." It was the perfect thing for her to hear this morning too. Nothing like a little make-believe grief to remind her of what real life would be by falling for another military man. A Special Forces warrior, at that.

"You think so?" Bella's smile trembled a little.

Was the woman actually nervous about this?

"Oh, yeah." She gently squeezed the actress's shoulders. "It's going to be really good."

"Yessss." Bella pumped her fist. "Emmy nomination, here I come."

So much for nervous. Ava was saved from trying to figure out the proper reaction to that by a brisk knock at the trailer's door.

"Enter," Bella called.

Of all the faces Ava expected to appear, Charlie Jenkow's was *not* on the list. Though the man dutifully nodded toward their star first, his gorgeous aquamarines locked fast on Ava. Her stomach reacted with a backflip of dread.

"Chaaarrrlie."

Bella extended a hand, wiggling the ends of her fingers as she finished what Chaz called the "Bella Lanza Broken Vibrator Remix" of his name. But he got no pity from Ava about it. He'd been the one to turn up the wattage of delight on his handsome perfection when she'd first used it. *Reap the oats you sow, my friend.*

Another look at her friend's face made her mentally take the words back. Charlie's gritted grin conveyed that her own "oats" were tumbling hard down life's payback chute. The casual offer she'd made to Rayna last October, inviting her and

Zeke Hayes, her new boyfriend, to come visit and tour the set, had ballooned into today: the PR bonanza the network smelled once they realized Zeke was the same Special Forces soldier who'd become Seattle's famous street vigilante hero from last fall. When Z asked if he could bring along some members of his battalion, the execs were as giddy as ducks around a kid with a loaf of bread.

By the look on Charlie's handsome face, the ducks were now circling tighter.

"Good morning, Behhhlllaaa." He tossed the broken vibe song back at Bella like it was the cutest thing in the world. Ava lasered a glare over the head of their giggling star at him. He simply smirked in a wordless version of *chill out, wench—method to my madness here.*

"What do you want, you shameless tease?" Bella demanded.

Charlie stepped all the way inside and leaned against one of the leather couches. "Well...now that you mention it... the boys from the big office are here for the promo op with the Special Ops team. They got here early, and you know how Cameron hates it when they hang and gawk over his shoulder." He pulled out his best Rico Suave stare, complete with pouting lips and tropic lagoon eyes. "If I bribe you with a skinny caramel latte, perhaps with a daub of whip and chocolate sprinkles, will you come out and dazzle them with your resplendence until the soldier hunks get here?"

Bella *psshh*ed at him. "Resplendence, my ass. I'm supposed to look like I haven't bathed in two days."

"You're resplendently filthy."

"*Porca Vacca.*" The starlet threw up her hands. "You could talk the Pope into bed, couldn't you?"

"Sweetie, Matt Reave is in my bed. The angels sing every night without the Pontiff's help."

Ava joined Bella in groans of retaliation. Matt was a smoldering model and witty entertainment show host, making him and Chaz one of the industry's hottest couples in every sense. That didn't mean every straight woman for ten miles couldn't grieve the permanent loss for the team.

But as soon as Bella grabbed her green tea and left the trailer, Ava dropped the humor. She spun on Charlie and grabbed his shoulder. "What the hell's going on?"

"Your soldier boy friends are here already, that's what," he countered. "I had to think fast."

"Huh?" A look at the clock showed that Z and the guys were nearly thirty minutes early. "*Mierda*," she muttered. "That's just rude."

"No, hon, that's Special Ops—yummy, overprepared studs that they are." The Rico Suave face made an encore. "You really sure you want to dash out? I got a nice peek at your Ethan before dashing here. Baby Jesus wept, Chestain. He's perfect."

"He's not *my* Ethan." She grabbed her car keys off the vanity. She hadn't taken anything else in with her. "He can't be anything except a really good memory from a really weird day, okay?"

"He looks like a spectacular kisser." Chaz's mouth curled with sensual intent. "His upper lip's got more curves than Mulholland Drive. Then there's that quiet-but-deadly thing in his walk. You *know* what that turns into under the sheets. And those *eyes*. And those *lashes*. Don't get me started on shaming the angels for wasting that beauty on a straight boy."

"Don't worry, I won't." Why had the trailer heated up by

ten degrees? Ava shoved past her friend and bounded down the trailer's steps. "Where are they now?"

"They're waiting for me on main set. I'm supposed to give them the fly-over there first."

"The tour and PR bullshit?"

"Roger Dodger."

"And after that? Still out to the grassy knoll for the photo op with brass?"

"Yep."

The studio had "grown" a rolling lawn in the middle of the lot for the show, with backdrops that could be changed out to transform it into everything from the hills of Afghanistan to a military base picnic lawn. But the show's crew had spent so many exhausting hours there that the area got permanently nicknamed after the hill made famous by the Kennedy assassination.

Ava mentally mapped out the lawn's location in relation to theirs before putting together a fast plan. "*Bueno*," she finally said. "I have to make a run over to Wardrobe to check the colors of Bella's outfit for tomorrow. That means I can cut through the hallway in back of main set and bust out the side door. I'll take the alley behind the New York street mock-up when I'm done."

"Sounds perf." Chaz did some tapping of his own. With one finger patting his chin, he drawled, "Especially in light of the massive favor you owe me right now."

Despite the hammer that'd gone to work on her heart for the last five minutes, she chuckled. "Let me guess. You want that Prada tux as a loaner for the gala with Matt on Saturday?"

"Have I told you lately how smart *and* gorgeous you are?"

She shook her head. "Save it for Bellllaaaa, you dork."

As they reached the spot where they needed to part ways, she added, "I'll see what I can do. Wardrobe owes me a few after they left pins in Bella's gown last week."

"You're a gem."

"And you're still a dork."

She nudged Charlie toward the entrance of the soundstage while she made her way toward the back door. As soon as she entered the building, she became part of a beehive. It took a lot of people to make a show like this into a success before the camera lights flashed green. Audio and video engineers. Set decorators and prop handlers. Technical directors and floor managers. For every one of those departments, there was a full crew too.

The bustle, translated into controlled chaos, always invigorated her. Today it accomplished more. It made her feel anonymous and safe in that concealment. From the second she heard Charlie approaching on the other side of the set walls, guiding their visitors in his most charming tour guide lilt, the plywood and foam core barriers might as well have turned into woven scrims for the protection they gave against her awareness of the group on the other side.

The group containing Ethan Archer.

Stay on task. Just get to the hallway and get out of here. Don't think about him. Don't think about how wonderful your heart feels against your ribs simply because he's in the same building. Don't think about how perfect it would be to see him again, to bask in the intensity of his eyes and the magic of his smile. Soldiers are bad for you, Ava—and he's a super *soldier. Special Forces. Not going to happen.* Can't *happen.*

"What the hell is that?"

She froze. *Shit.* Why did it have to be Ethan who tossed

35

out the query, his tone so melodic yet so electric? His baritone zapped her nervous system like a spark on charged air, wrapping around her...pulling her feet the wrong damn direction. Toward the set.

What could the harm be in indulging one fast, secret peek?

"Oh, dear fuck."

She recognized the sneer before even getting visual confirmation of its source. Sure enough, Zeke Hayes was the one who stood there rolling his eyes at Ethan. Ava smiled to see him tug her cousin, Rayna, into the crook of his shoulder. Ray giggled and circled her arms around her man's muscled waist. Next to them stood Z's best friend, Garrett, and his wife, Sage. Their hands were twined on top of Sage's prominent baby bump, and Ava wouldn't be surprised if the pair glowed in the dark with happiness. On the other side of the couple were Tait Bommer and Kellan Rush, often referred to as the battalion's "Bullet Ninjas" because of their sniper abilities. Tait looked like a surfing idol from the Rincon shore, while Kellan represented a dark-eyed god of the Sunset Boulevard club crowd. Grinning along with them were Rhett Lange and Rebel Stafford, respectively the brains and brawn of the team. Rhett liked to blow out computer systems; Rebel liked to blow in doors. Like everyone else, they chuckled at Zeke's rejoinder.

Actually, everyone seemed to be having a great time... except Ethan.

The electrical storm whipped harder through Ava as she stepped closer to the window in the set and looked at him. With his brows tightened and his lips twisted, he looked supremely miffed at Zeke, though she could tell his tension hadn't started there. It had been a part of him for a while now. It stiffened the planes of his shoulders, banded the breadth of his torso, hardened every muscle down his impossibly long legs. Throw a set of BDUs and a battle vest on him and the man would be ready to march into the thick of a battle to the death. The deadly warrior image certainly wasn't hurt by what he had on now, either. Skintight black T-shirt, dark jeans, and biker boots were topped by a scuffed leather jacket, officially turning her quickie peek into a transfixed stare.

"What?" he barked at Zeke. One side of his beautiful mouth curled up. "It's a legitimate question."

Tait sauntered forward, gold eyes glittering with mirth. "It's...uh...called a microphone, Runway. I know growing up in Silicon Valley must've been hard; you probably weren't exposed to many of these newfangled technical gadgets, but— follow me, now—they use it to record the actors' voices. That's how you can hear them talking when you watch them on TV."

The group snickered. Ethan glared harder. "Shut your hole, assmunch. I know what it is."

Tait chuffed. "Need those knickers twisted a little tighter, Runway? With your panties gone, the whole world can watch your cute ass a little better while you moon over—"

"Shut. Up."

Tait looked ready to smack Ethan from pure frustration, and Ava backed up the desire. He was "mooning" over someone? That was practically a rhetorical question. The man was wound up about something—or in this case, someone. But who? And if it wasn't her, did she want to know?

You have no right to know.

She'd ignored every one of his calls, messages, and attempts at contact since getting back from Seattle seven months ago. She'd made the right choice for her life. Whether

Ethan believed it or not, for his too. So if he'd moved on to getting his "knickers twisted" for someone else, she needed to be happy for him. She could do that, couldn't she?

The answer got stuck in her throat as she watched him cock his head, spearing Charlie with a curiosity that edged on innocence. It made his adjoining question all the more adorable.

"Dude, why is the microphone wearing a condom?"

Sage spit out her gulp of water. Rayna giggled again. Garrett and Zeke let out matching groans of the F-word. But Tait's expression actually changed to a glance of respect. "Huh," he said. "You're right." He looked at Charlie. "Why *does* it have that thing on it?"

Chaz's stance changed, too. He straightened from polite to commanding. As he launched into the advantages of foam microphone covers, reveling in the attention he got from a bunch of hunks who also relied on high-performance equipment to accomplish their jobs, Ava recognized her chance to slip away. *You've had your peek. And your stare. Now back off from the window, Chestain, before—*

"Hey, Ava! Do me a favor and move that tree about a foot to your right, would ya? The light's hitting it wrong."

Before someone like Blake, the set-decorating lead, called to her just like that.

"*Shit.*"

She spat it as she tugged the prop over, not pausing to acknowledge Blake's thanks. Or maybe she did. It was very possible, since every muscle in her body turned to ice as soon as she watched Ethan's head whip around at the mention of her name. Time didn't help matters, congealing to sludge that dragged every step she attempted—and made it possible for his gaze to stab into hers before she launched into motion.

Keep moving. Keep moving. Don't look back. Keep moving.

The order vibrated through every shaky gasp she made while whirling and hurrying through the maze of flats, cords, ladders, wires, toolboxes, and chairs. *So many chairs.* Damn it. Nobody ever sat around here. Why did they need so many chairs? And why had she worn three-inch boots today? And why did *everyone* pick this exact second to tromp in her way?

"Ava."

His call severed the air, shattering the ice beneath her skin into freezing shards through her bloodstream. She didn't alter her pace. She couldn't. The door was just a few feet away. Past it was a restricted-access zone. His visitor's pass would get him stopped faster than a gatecrasher at the Oscars. She'd be safe again.

"Ava."

She fought the pull of his voice. Resisted the urgent command of it, the fierce need. *No, damn it.* She was weaving meanings that weren't there. All they'd shared, all those months ago, was a kiss. After that, she'd all but told him to shove off. If anything, he was here to ask her for a reimbursement check for the birthday flowers that had filled her living room in February.

Keep moving. Almost there.

"Ava!"

Long fingers, steel and flesh certainly fused together, twisted around her elbow. Inside a second, they hauled her into the props and greenery prep room. Inside another whoosh, she was pinned against the wall while the door was booted shut.

And then her world became only him.

Ethan, burying a hand in her hair. Ethan, sealing his lips over hers. Ethan, tangling his tongue against hers as his body, so hard and big, fitted perfectly against the apex of hers. Consuming her senses with his leathery, dark pepper scent. Filling each heartbeat with his passion. Like the mist in which he'd first done this to her, blocking everything but his force, his strength, his desire.

So much for breathing.

As soon as he released her, she struggled to do so anyway. Once his stare impaled her, that cobalt intensity piercing straight to her center, she flew a white flag on the effort. A million words blasted through her head. Not a single one found its way to her mouth. Her lungs and her heart crashed against each other as he slid a rough thumb over the stinging pads of her lips.

"Hello, sunshine."

His murmur slunk through her body like smoke, the tendrils turning the ice into simmered drops. They pooled into the layers of her sex, soaking her panties, finally making her throat work again. A high-pitched gasp spilled from her, humiliating and liberating at once.

Crap, crap, crap.

"Ethan." Why did it sound like a prayer instead of a protest? Why did he confirm the mortifying fact by letting his eyelids grow heavy, his thick lashes brushing his burnished cheeks as he observed every movement on her face and every breath on her lips? Life bustled by just three feet away, beyond the door, but his focus made her feel like they'd jumped to another planet.

"It wasn't a dream." His whisper fanned her face. "Was it?" He swept his thumb beneath her chin to tug her face up, pulling her deeper into his hold, his presence. "*Tell me,*" he charged, capturing one of her wrists beneath his other hand, flattening it to the wall. "I want to hear you say it, damn it."

A sigh clamored up her throat. "No," she finally relented. "It wasn't. It..." *It was wonderful. And I've thought about it every day since. I've thought about* you *every day...*

Though she confined the words to thoughts, she couldn't keep them from playing across her face. As they did, his eyes dilated and his lips parted. With a harsh grunt that made her vagina clench, he bore down on her with another kiss. His lips demanded more now, taking every corner of her mouth, every ounce of her passion, every drop of her obeisance. She was helpless to give him anything less. She was in sheer heaven because of it.

She was in deep trouble.

She knew it even before the door to the room opened again—but even more so as soon as it did. Ethan tore his mouth from hers while a man as big as him strode in, sporting a dark skull-crop cut and a smile that descended into a gawk. "Runway?" He took in their positions, with their crotches locked and Ethan's hand bolting hers to the wall, and clearly filled in the blanks for himself.

Ethan gave a curt nod. "Captain."

"Captain?"

Ava answered herself with a groan. Of course. She'd seen the man at Sage and Garrett's wedding, albeit briefly and without his full clothes on. He'd barged into the ceremony in a T-shirt and shorts, having been drugged and then abandoned in Vegas as part of the plan for the bastard who'd nearly recaptured Rayna into white slavery that day.

"Hi." The man swung his gaze at her.

"Uh...hi."

"Ava." Ethan directed her name toward his captain,

though his tone was more explanatory than introductory. The next moment, she saw why.

"Ohhh," the guy exclaimed. "*That* Ava?"

Ethan nodded. "Uh-huh."

"Wow. Ava."

"*Ava?*" The outburst came from Charlie this time. He rounded the door with a scowl, but after his own inspection of her and Ethan, he joined Ethan's captain on the lascivious grin duties.

Hell.

She squirmed against Ethan's hold. "Charlie—"

"Franz?" The game of musical names was taken up by Zeke, who stepped into the room with Garrett and a couple more guys from the team. "And look! Ava!"

"What?" The jolt of her cousin's joy filled the air. "Where? Oh, my God, Ava!" Rayna surged in but stopped short, repeating Charlie's assessment. "Oh, my God. Um...*Ava.*"

Ava sent a pleading gaze toward the ceiling. The next person who stammered her name was going to get a knee to their gut.

"Ava?"

The distinct stress on the second syllable was only ever used by one person. Because of course, fate had decided to make her its bitch today.

"Ava?"

Bella stepped fully into the room. She tossed a dismissive glance at Charlie and the battalion boys before sweeping her attention toward the wall where Ethan still had her pinned.

"*Mierda.*" The groan surged from the depths of Ava's stomach. With a couple of urgent jerks, she wrenched away from Ethan. "Bella, listen, I can ex—"

"Ethan?"

Normally Bella's interruption would be situation normal. In this case, it would've even been a relief—except for the name the woman had picked for her interjection. And the smile, broad and enthralled, she tagged onto it. That look had charmed fans, journalists, and critics across a shitload of demographics in eight countries. In short, her I-want-you-in-the-palm-of-my-hand-*now* smile.

"Huh?" Ethan blurted it more like a chore than a word. Whether she wanted to let it go or not, Ava gave him another snippet of her heart in that moment. He was still genuinely impervious to most of the mob in the room, with his stare still transfixed on her.

Bella stunned them both by stepping forward and shoving his jacket and T-shirt nearly all the way off his left shoulder. In doing so, she exposed the silvered line of a nasty scar that bridged his collarbone.

"Oh shit," Ava blurted.

"What the..." Ethan uttered. "How did you know about—"

"Ethan!" Bella cried again. "Oh, my God, it *is* you!"

Ethan looked from the scar to Bella. His brows hunkered as his gaze sharpened. "Brenda?" he mumbled. "Brenda Lanzani?"

"Oh, yes! Yes, yes, yes!"

As Bella topped that with a long squee, Ava glanced to Charlie. They mouthed the same words to each other. *What the hell?*

"Ohhh, Ethan!" The woman's breathy elation got worse. "I can't believe it!"

Ava's gut sounded with a dozen alarms. But she didn't defend her heart in time. A chunk of it got hacked off and got wedged in her throat while watching the star's weirdness morph into a full Bella Blitz on Ethan. No, that wasn't right. "Blitz" implied that the target didn't have a clue. Ethan was *not* clueless. As Bella pressed herself against the man, she did so with the confidence of a woman who'd been in his arms before. He braced his hands to her waist with the same familiarity. And as she tilted her lips up, catching his at the perfect angle for a full-press kiss, it was clear the woman had been in that territory, too. Lots of times.

Damn it.

CHAPTER THREE

What. The. Fuck?

It set a good tempo for the thoughts going balls-for-batshit at each other through Ethan's brain. This wasn't how he envisioned the day, or even the hour, playing out.

Three minutes ago, he'd been kissing the woman of his fantasies. Now he was locking lips with the ex of his nightmares—or at least that was who the creature claimed to be. Two minutes ago, he was plotting how to keep the door to this room locked so he could seal the deal on Ava never ignoring him again. Now, he couldn't wait to get the hell out of here.

And one minute ago, he'd thanked the Creator for finally smiling on him. For the first time in seven months, not a shred of ugliness had crawled into his waking mind. No picking through the resistance of some drug dealer or terrorist, no dissecting some asshole's body language to detect signs the guy was lying, cheating, high, or just stupid. For once, he'd gotten to let the suspicions down and bask in something pure. Something good. Something exactly what it was supposed to be. Passion. Warmth. Sunshine.

What the hell had happened?

With a growl, he grabbed the wrists Brenda had thrown around his neck, using the leverage to thrust her back. Franzen was still in the room, so he didn't do anything more than plant the woman a step away. "It's...uh...been a while, Bren," he stammered. "You look...really different."

Somebody was dialing the understatement cops for that one. Brenda's face, which still possessed the same brilliant bronze eyes but had been topographically changed in every other way, quirked in what seemed a soft smile. He couldn't be sure. She didn't smile the same way. Her teeth were bigger, her chin was smaller, her nose was shorter, and her cheeks were higher.

"Thank you, babe," she said smoothly, "but you know it's not *Brenda* anymore, right?"

So much for sweeping tension out of the way. The second she said *babe*, he watched every vertebra in Ava's spine go tight. *Not acceptable.*

"Hmm. Sounds cool. So I'll drop the *Brenda* and you drop the *babe*, and we'll be squared up, all right?"

He looked up in time to catch a meaningful glance fly between Ava and Charlie Jenkow. They were obviously friends. That explained the subtle once-over he'd gotten from the guy when they'd arrived. Looked like his bluntness to Brenda, or whatever the hell she was calling herself these days, had earned Jenkow's approval. It clearly didn't sit so well with Brenda, who tipped another weird smile.

"Uh...right," she finally replied. "Though you do know what everyone calls me now, yes?"

A long silence took over the room. He was clearly supposed to confirm that, but the words would be a lie. He was officially lost here. Forcing his gaze away from Bella, Ethan locked a gaze onto Charlie, openly bumming some help off the guy.

Thankfully, Charlie believed in the friend-of-a-friend honor system. With a convincing facepalm, the man stepped forward and exclaimed, "For the love of Peter, Paul, and Mary. Where did my manners go?" Charlie lifted Brenda's hand with a gallant sweep. "Gentlemen, though I'm certain most of you are familiar with this icon, I'd like to officially introduce Miss Bella Lanza, the star of *Dress Blues.*"

This time, Ethan didn't have to fake his reaction. His grin was genuine. "Wow. Star, huh?" He looked over the expensive details she rocked besides the plastic surgery, from the diamonds on her manicured fingers and the trendy shoes on her elegant feet, and couldn't believe this was the cute theater major with whom he'd shared Friday night pizza and bike rides across the Stanford campus. "You're really all grown up," he murmured. "Good for you, Bren—" He borrowed the facepalm move from Charlie. "Shit. Sorry. *Bella.*"

The woman giggled. "It's all right. And understandable. Memories aren't simple to shirk, especially ones like ours."

She finished by winding a hand around his forearm. Ethan let his brain report to the office of Officially Uncomfortable. He didn't miss how Bella's claim, in verbal and physical form, made Ava's tension expand up her spine, working into her tight lips and aching eyes. He hated this. Every second. Goddamnit, if he could only order everyone out of here and get Ava back against the wall, back to where nothing or nobody mattered, back to that connection he'd waited seven fucking months to have again.

"Hmm." The interjection came from an openly smirking Tait. "Unshirked memories. Shit, Archer. That sounds like a lot of interesting bribery material to me."

Kellan added a knowing lift of brows. "It'd come in handy, now that he's a big bad sarge and all."

Bella's stare, as intense as her grip, got more penetrating.

"Sarge? As in *sergeant*?"

"Newly minted, ma'am," Franzen offered. "Gave him his new stripe after we finished a dick-whopper—err, a difficult mission—down in Mexico. Figured we'd make this little side trip as part of the celebration."

Another potent silence passed. Bella maintained her unyielding attention. And her damn C-clamp of a hold. She finally murmured, "You're one of the Special Forces visitors."

He flashed a lopsided smile. "Would appear that way, Miss Lanza."

Bella's eyes turned the color of brown sugar. The warmth flowed into the rest of her surgically perfect features. "Looks like you're really all grown up too," she replied. "You did it, babe."

Fuck. There it was again. But could he ream her for using the old endearment when he identified the awkwardness she masked with it? His decision to join up with the big green machine had been the beginning of the end for them. Wasn't like he was subtle about dealing the blow, either. He'd dropped it into the middle of a halfway pleasant date toward the end of their first year in college, even making Brenda—*Bella*—laugh at him, thinking for once he was pulling a bad joke. But he'd never been good at joking, and she couldn't see why he'd throw away the corner office at Dad's company, already reserved for him, along with the cushy starting salary and his choice of Jag, Beemer, or Mercedes as a signing bonus. Poor Bella had been stunned to the brink of tears, especially because he hadn't tried very hard to explain himself. What would've been the point? She thought of her freedoms as part of life's path, not treasures that had to be honored and defended.

Her outrage had been shared by most of the world.

His Stanford advisor labeled the decision "reckless and irresponsible." A blunter assessment came from his frat drinking buddies—their term was "stupid as shit pie." Mom hadn't used any words. She just chose to disappear into her greenhouse for four days. Shockingly, the worst reaction he'd expected had never come. Dad's support, and best of all his understanding, had made it possible to grab at the army's big brass ring. The Special Forces needed good men, and he'd set his sights on becoming one of them.

He concluded that thought out loud. "Fate smiled," he murmured. "Yeah, I really did it."

Behind him, Tait's laugh tickled the air. "Doing it's never been a problem for you, Runway."

"'S long as it's with his palm and fingers," cracked Kell.

"Gentlemen," Franzen growled, "we aren't on Uncle Sam's clock right now, but keep it up and I'll make you hate your sorry life when we are again."

"Roger that, Captain."

Tait's respectful reply still shook with humor. Ethan didn't care. He almost turned and thanked the ninjas for the interjection since it forced Bella to take her hand off his arm to cover her giggling mouth.

"All right," she finally declared, "I can tell that a silly little set tour isn't going to be enough time with all of you. You're all officially invited to my place for dinner tonight. We have a short shooting schedule today, and my chef should be able to do something casual. Do you all like lobster, shrimp, and bruschetta?"

Zeke chuckled again. "Honey, does a Wookiee like Cortyg brandy?"

Bella frowned. "Huh?"

49

"*Star Wars* geek," Rayna explained. She shook her head and then stood on tiptoe to kiss Z's jaw. "Nothing an Indiana Jones marathon won't fix."

"In your dreams." His countering mutter was thick with affection.

Franzen saved them all from the couple turning their smoochy moment into a puke-inducing PDA by stepping forward with his hands spread. "Miss Lanza, your invitation is kind but unnecessary. We're not nitpicky Hollywood eaters. We're soldiers with the manners of hyenas and the appetites of elephants. And this isn't even all of us. Corporals Lange and Stafford are still lurking around here somewhere, and—"

"Captain." Bella pivoted at him, showing off the same determination she once used to get into closed classes and private frat parties. "I have a five-thousand-square-foot villa that's tailor-made for entertaining, which I don't do enough of, especially when the crowd *isn't* a bunch of stuffy Hollywood eaters."

"Look, the offer's sweet, but—"

"It's on the sand in Malibu."

Franzen choked his next words into silence.

Hawkins laughed and spoke for him instead. "What time do you want us there?"

It hadn't escaped Ethan's attention that Ava's posture had gone stiff again. When Bella turned to Franzen, he focused all his attention on grabbing Ava's, but the woman kept riveted on Bella like a goddamn lady-in-waiting for Anne Boleyn herself. He was certain she'd filed him back into the ignore-and-he'll-go-away category.

Think again, sunshine.

The queen herself helped him out with that resolve. Bella

turned back, twisting more screws of tension down Ava's spine. If Ethan was a betting man, he'd lay sure odds on what would go down next.

"Ava darling, I won't need anything here for the rest of the day besides a few powder touchups, and Faye can handle that. Can you be a love and supervise preparations at the house?"

Yep. Fucking shame that Vegas was just an hour away by plane. He could've just made a mint.

Ava squared her shoulders and stated, "Bella, I don't think I'm the right—" She huffed when Bella's eyes narrowed and conceded, "Fine. Sure."

Bella's smile was a sweep of practiced goo. "You are *such* a champ."

Ethan recognized an opportunity when it hit. He scooted forward, smiling carefully. "Sounds like it's going to be a lot of logistics and shit. I can go along to help."

"No." Ava's rebuttal was fierce. "That won't be necessary, Sergeant."

She tried to push past him. Ethan didn't move. "It's no trouble." He grinned down at her. "Really."

Bella actually squirmed a little. "Uhhh..."

"He's really good at logistics."

Ethan made a mental note to thank Z for the well-timed insertion.

"I'm good at them too." Ava seethed it this time. She tried to get past him again.

Ethan almost laughed as he slid around for the second block. *Get it through your head, woman. I'm* not *giving up.*

Their cat-and-mouse dance wasn't lost on Bella. With a flirty toss of her head and another perfect smile, she ventured, "You...don't want to stay and watch me act, babe?"

Ethan scooped up her hand. "I've already seen you act, *babe*. Lots of times." He tapped his head with his other hand. "You just said it perfectly. Some memories aren't easy to shirk."

"Thanks," she muttered. "I think."

Zeke slammed his hands together. "Cool beans. It's settled, then. We'll see you at Bella's house tonight, Runway. Toss me your room key. Ray and I will run past the hotel on our way back to Ava's, and I'll grab your swim trunks."

Bella went even more quiet, which made him sense that his victory was near. "You *were* always so sweet about helping out on things." She wrapped her hand around his arm again and pressed herself close. The smell of expensive perfume made a full frontal on his senses. "Thank you."

"Welcome." Surprisingly, he got it out without a sneeze or a grimace. The smile that followed wasn't so hard. In an hour, he'd be miles from that perfume. He'd have Ava alone again. For the whole day. That made all the sneaky tactics worth it. Sometimes a guy had to bend the rules to achieve the mission objective.

Now, all he had to do was convince Ava that her aim was the same. Judging from the glower on her face when they met at her car ten minutes later, that was going to be easier said than done. The woman was clearly passionate about *all* her feelings, including total ire about having her day upended and her job description hijacked, not to mention Ethan's involvement in both. That was okay by him. In his own line of work, patience and tenacity were side-by-side partners. He was ready for this.

Including, if he had to, a little bit more than "bending" the rules.

CHAPTER FOUR

Ava forced in a deep breath. Another. Like they did any damn good at diminishing her ire at the man this time.

Actually, she was shocked she hadn't lost it sooner with the bastard. She'd sure as hell punched herself enough times for lingering too long at the set, inviting disaster to happen—an offer disaster certainly hadn't refused. It happily obliged by plunking her here, alone in her boss's villa with the man who'd pulled the audacity card in a move that still had her jaw heading toward the floor in shock. Yeah, the same man who shared a past of "unshirkable" memories with Bella—and with whom the starlet clearly wanted to create a few new ones tonight. That hadn't stopped him from charming himself into an invitation for the whole *day*, had it?

Ay! The ass! It seemed the Special Forces were giving their soldiers some extra training in balls-out boldness these days.

That was as far as she dared go in thinking about Ethan's crotch. As for having a face that could make even the most jaded casting agent stop for a second look? Probably not a Special Ops job necessity, though the man knew how to work that angle when he wanted as well—to perfection. For the last five hours, she'd been close to hurling more at him than her glower. Every time, he'd stopped her cold by flicking a charming wink of those piercing blues or lifting one side of his mouth in a deliberate grin. Knowing what he was doing to her with the looks. Watching every drop of her blood heat from livid ice to aroused flames because of it. Taunting her with what she couldn't have and shouldn't crave—especially now.

That wasn't even the worst of it. The hardest moments had been ones like this, where she walked into the room, this time the dining area between the open-plan kitchen and the sprawling living room, and caught him unaware of her stare at all. The rapt look on his face was beautiful as he listened to the lively chatter of the villa's two housekeepers, as well as the lead maintenance team man. The maids went on in rapid-fire Spanish, though the dialect was thicker than the Spanglish Ava had grown up with so she couldn't follow completely. Isko, the engineer, seemed to share her impediment, though he understood enough to insert some comments to the exchange. He used another language completely, but Ethan nodded and chuckled in comprehension of the man's insertions too.

Ava curled a hand to her chest, acknowledging the somersault of her heart. When he laughed, he went from beautiful to breathtaking. His eyes sparkled like the ocean outside the open patio doors. His thick hair fell forward, teasing his high temples. Subtle crinkles formed at the corners of his mouth. Her chest made room for the somersault to become a full floor routine.

What the hell was wrong with her?

"Seven months," she whispered. "That's the only thing wrong with you, *chica*. It's been seven months, and you're just... not used to this." *Not used to* him.

And if it had been only seven days, would she be? Seven hours?

Getting "used" to Ethan Archer...to his effect on her skin, her nerves, her libido. *Right*. And California was going to slide

54

into the ocean next year. And an animated movie would win the Academy Award for Best Picture. And somebody would make a sexy heel that didn't double as a torture device. Some things belonged permanently on the ridiculous list.

Suddenly, he looked up. Directly at her.

Ava retreated, mounting the half dozen stairs to a landing that overlooked the area, pretending "dust" on the wrought-iron rails had become the most fascinating thing in the world. She waited for one of his brows to lift in question, or his knowing smile, or his brash sideways smirk...

None of which came.

He simply stood, gave a quick *gracias* for the staff's time, and then put those long legs to work on a path straight toward her. Once at her side, he scooped both her hands into his. His gaze left no inch of her face untouched by its power. As it did, his mien did a slow burn from surface casual to deeply concentrated.

"What is it?"

Clearly the question he'd put on the phrase was a formality. The words were a demand, plain and simple. Ava squirmed, feigning interest in that dirt again, trying to break from his hold...from the piercing force of his eyes. "Besides the fact that you're gawking like I'm going to vanish into thin air any second?"

"Wouldn't be the first time." He readjusted his hold to weave their fingers into each other. The struggle to get free of him was officially stamped with *No Dice*. "You still didn't answer the question. What are you thinking?"

She gave him a long moment of contemplation before rendering a quiet reply. "Honestly? I'm thinking that those three have been working in this house for two years, and in that time, Bella hasn't talked with them as much as you just did."

The revelation didn't seem to surprise him, though dropping Bella's name darkened his gaze. Whether that was a good thing or bad thing, she couldn't determine.

"Pity," he said at last. "They're good people. Paloma's daughter graduates from high school next week. Valedictorian. Dory wants to get back to El Salvador to see her grandmother before the woman dies."

"And they've been having problems with a goose in the swimming pool?"

That set free a new chuckle from him. "Not a goose. Just a duck. Apparently Bella hates the thing, but it really likes her. She's ordered Isko to kill it, but he doesn't have the heart."

She let a smile rise. "He's a good guy."

"Sure is."

"He wasn't speaking Spanish."

"No shit." He beamed a teasing grin. "It was Tagalog. He's from Batangas, in the Philippines. Wants to move back too, but he's come to the States for a woman. Doesn't know if he wants to put a ring on it, though."

Her smile dropped into a surprised gawk. "You got all *that* out of him?" After he shrugged and nodded, she pressed, "How many languages do you speak?"

"Fluently? Four. Working on five, but fuck, Chinese is hard."

Ava gazed at him with renewed fascination. She wondered how many other secrets the man was hiding under all that beautiful hair—and, more prominently, if she'd really uncovered a person who charged at their goals more passionately than her. She wasn't just allured. She was aroused.

Lethal thinking. She couldn't do this. Not with him.

Especially not after what she'd learned this morning—and what she'd seen. The certainty in Bella's grip on his arm. The possessive flecks in the woman's almond-shaped eyes. *Pendeja.* Lusting after the boss's new toy was *Stupid,* capital *S.* Technically, "new" didn't even apply. Bella had played with this one before and now wanted another turn with the improved model. This Ethan was bigger, bolder, and more beautiful thanks to the very job that should have Ava stamping a skull and crossbones across his forehead to remind her of a few things. *Danger. Poison. Stay away.*

"Hello? Earth to Ava?"

Of course, it was easier to push toys away when the damn things cooperated. Like *not* kicking up a lopsided smile that made a girl want to kiss them and punch them in the same moment. "Ethan," she blurted, "I still have a lot to get done, okay?"

Her renewed effort at escape got a tighter squeeze of denial. "And you'll accomplish it all better if you take a break."

"No. I'll accomplish it all if I *do* it all."

"Shut up."

Despite the crack, he got benevolent and let her have one hand back. No, not benevolence. Ulterior motive. He used her free hand to pull her toward a small outside balcony. Ava sighed but didn't protest. What would be the use? Besides, it was a beautiful early June afternoon. The typical coastal haze had been burned off early. The breeze was sharp, with a hint of summer's approaching warmth. It was nice and bright out here. Sunny and safe.

She turned her face up into the golden rays before asking him, "So, did you give Isko any advice? About the woman and the ring?"

Amazingly, Ethan let her have her second hand back. He leaned an elbow on the rail and gazed past Bella's Italianate terrace, peacefully taking in the slope of Catalina Island toward the south and the larger silhouette of Anacapa Island toward the north. "I told him to go home."

She felt her brows jump. "Just like that? After only knowing him a few hours?"

He cocked his head back toward her. The sun flashed in his eyes, and the wind danced in his hair. Just like that, all traces of his casual mien were gone. "I could've told him that after a few minutes." At the are-you-nuts glare she refused to hide, he asserted, "A man usually knows what he wants, sunshine. If he has to question wanting it, then it's not worth dicking around about."

The words dropped between them like grenades, bursting open with plumes of new meaning and thick resolution. *His* resolution.

A gulp thudded its way down Ava's throat. "Oh."

Ethan took her hand again. He guided her fingers up, sliding them beneath his hair until they pressed against his nape. He circled his other arm around her waist, dragging her close until her body was locked inside the frame of his unflinching muscles. His grip was as fervent as the sun but as merciless as the sea wind, urging her closer until she saw nothing but him.

"I'm not dicking around about you, Ava." With steady surety, he slid his hands until he cupped the swell of her ass. A gasp erupted from her throat before she could control it. Another followed as he squeezed her there, sending a thousand jolts of awareness into every tissue between her thighs. "I never was," he went on. "Since that first moment I saw you, both of us tangled in all that wedding shit at Sage and Garrett's..."

"When you thought I was a terrorist?"

Her attempt at levity didn't work. "I would've been less scared if you were," he uttered. "I... Fuck, I was in such deep trouble. It's been a long time for me, doing all this...feeling all this. That day, just from rolling with you on the floor like that..."

His face tightened as if he were in pain. She ached from watching his brow furrow and his lips twist, until he lowered his beautiful mouth to her cheek, brushing her skin with heat as he continued in a harsh whisper. "That night at Hawk's bachelor party, all I could think of was how many ways I wanted you in my bed." He worked his way to the edge of her ear. Ava dipped her head back, giving him better access to her neck. "Yeah, even the kinky ways," he whispered. "Christ, I tried to be good...and I was...until we were in the forest the next day, and you begged me to pin you tighter to that tree, and—"

"And it felt so right."

Shit.

Why had she let the words slip out, instead of letting him be responsible for them? And why, oh *why* did she finish them by scoring his scalp with her nails, urging his mouth harder against her skin, letting him bend her back over the balcony's edge so he could plunge his tongue lower, into the *V* of her shirt, leading down between her breasts? Why didn't she stop him from twisting buttons loose and pulling the fabric open, exposing the lace-edged cups of her bra to him? Why wasn't she pushing him back instead of moaning from the searing pleasure of it, reveling in the feel of him against her? *Ah Dios*, his body was so big. His mouth was so urgent. His touch was so electric. Her skin sizzled. Her senses reeled.

So much for the damn balcony being safe.

He didn't stop unbuttoning her at a few holes. The pearl discs fell free beneath his fast twists until her shirt fell open, revealing her waist and the top of her hips. He smoothed the flesh with his long fingers before following the same path with his lips, nipping at her skin, wetting it enough so when the wind moved in after, delicious tingles washed through her. She swallowed hard, struggling not to be riveted by the sight of his dark head against her bare flesh, fighting not to love it.

Before she could get a grip on herself and move, he rose and covered her again. His body fitted to hers. His mouth delved into hers. He didn't waste time on subtle pretense with the kiss now. His assault was full and consuming, a hot barrage designed to melt her mind. The next moment, she knew exactly why.

"It's still right, sunshine." He grated it against her mouth. "Goddamnit, it's so right." He lifted a hand and gripped her cheek, compelling her to stay focused on him...to witness the steel blades of determination in his beautiful gaze. "I refuse to let you deny it this time."

Her breathing faltered. Conflict whipped at her soul. Saying no wasn't going to be as easy as deleting a text or ignoring a phone call this time. Or, God help her, even thinking about Bella and her implied claim on the man. Bella wasn't here right now. She wouldn't be for hours. The caterers were prepping the meal in the kitchen. The terrace was pristine. The house was being readied. There was nothing to think about, to surrender to, but this stolen gift of time with the man who'd stalked her thoughts and haunted her dreams since last fall. Ethan. *Ethan.* His effortless strength. His single-minded passion. His primal need for control.

I refuse to let you deny it this time.

She sifted her fingers in his hair and gazed deeper into his eyes. "This time," she repeated, "I don't want to deny it either."

His mouth twisted in sinful satisfaction. She struggled to dredge up the slap he should get for the look, but all she felt was joy that she'd pleased him so. His shadowed stare swept to her lips again, as if considering another brutal kiss. Instead, he dragged her back inside without a word. The second they cleared the door, he made a sharp left into the villa's wine room. The space was Bella's idea of a tribute to her name, with décor that looked like Caesar's Palace had been invaded by Bernini's ghost: marble statues, velvet couches, dark-tile floors, chilled air—not that Ava even noticed the latter. She burned for his touch again already. Yearned to get her hands on him in all the same ways too.

He couldn't pull her in, slam the door, and trap her back against it fast enough. The dim lighting of the room, compared to the brilliant sunshine on the balcony, temporarily blinded her. She didn't care. She found him with her hands. Learned his sculpted beauty in a whole new way as she scraped her hands beneath his T-shirt and over his back while he fused their mouths again. When he groaned in approval, she traveled her fingers around, sliding down over every hard ridge of his eight-pack. By the time she got back to his waist, he had let out a harsh grunt before simply tearing off the shirt. The silencers on his dog tags clunked as he tossed the shirt aside and then advanced on her again.

His hands, rigid and tight, felt amazing on her shoulders. His kiss, hard and consuming, turned everything outside the door into unreality, unimportance. He shoved her shirt off next, unhooking her bra as he did so it fell to the floor too. In the aftermath, she stood still, letting her lungs heave, watching the shadows of the room play across his face as he took in her bare, erect nipples.

"Beautiful," he finally grated. "More incredible than I could have imagined."

"You too," she whispered back. "Oh, Ethan..."

He stopped her by pressing a thumb against her lips. "I need to be clear. I want you, Ava. I want to be inside you. I want to watch your face when I command you to come and your body shatters around mine. I haven't had anyone else, haven't dreamed of having anyone else, for seven months." With his other hand, he guided her grip to the front of his jeans. Her fingers stretched around the black fabric, which was hot from the press of the flesh beneath. "If you stay in here with me—"

"I'm staying."

She didn't give him a chance to say anything else. With a whip of her head, she captured his thumb and sucked it into her mouth. He hissed as she rolled her tongue around the length of it. The sound became a growl when he finally yanked it away from her.

"I should spank you for that."

"Promise?"

"God*damn*." As his breaths escaped in heavy huffs, he pulled her close and sank his mouth to hers again. Her breasts mashed against the broad planes of his chest, rubbed and teased with friction that shot straight to the center of her body, now soaking wet with sexual need.

He set her free but only far enough to lock his gaze with hers again. "You have quite a sassy mouth, sunshine. I should put it to good use."

Ava slanted him a tiny smile. Sassy? Yeah, he'd pretty much nailed it—which was damn weird for her to admit. She'd never pulled shit like this on a man before. But no other man in her life had dared to trap her against a tree the second day they knew each other. No other man could dissolve her ire with the magic of his subtle smirk or make her want to throw back that arrogance just to see how *he'd* react, hopefully with that spanking he'd just threatened. No other man made her long to unlock the hidden side of her sexuality for him...because she knew he'd savor it, stroke it, make it soar.

And after this magical hour, none of it would be hers again. None of him *could* be hers. She needed to make every second of it count.

"Gee. You're *should*ing all over yourself this afternoon, Sergeant Archer. Plan on doing anything about that?"

That got his brows to jump. And his lips to part. And his fingers to curl into the clothes she still wore, unbuckling her belt and then yanking down her pants zipper. Without a word, he circled an arm around her waist and slammed her against him, lifting one of her thighs against his waist. With his brilliant stare still fixed on her, he yanked at the laces of her ankle boot, jerked the thing off, and then tossed it to join his shirt somewhere in the shadows. He lowered that leg and pulled up the other to repeat the action. When he was done, he rebalanced her on both feet, still not looking away, still radiating with dark sexual energy.

A thick moment passed. Neither of them blinked. With his arms at his sides and his shoulders held high, his torso was more breathtaking than the golden marble Adonises that peeked from the alcoves. Ava ordered herself not to stare at the twin ridges of abdominal muscle that arrowed down, leading beneath his pants...an impossible feat. *Ay dios mio*, he was breathtaking.

"Take them off, Ava," he ordered in a low, sleek tone. "Take off everything. I want to see every inch of the beauty I've been fantasizing about. All of it."

If she opened every bottle in this room and drank the contents, her senses wouldn't whirl this madly. She was achingly aware of every approving growl he issued as she shucked her formfitting jeans and the black thong beneath. But he saved the best sound for last. When she straightened, totally nude before him, a sound curled from him like a plume of smoke from a magician's pyre, redolent with approval...and arousal.

Out in the living room, one of the maids turned up some music. Ava almost wondered if the woman could see through walls and knew what was going on, because the selection, midtempo and belted by a Spanish soprano, was recorded for one purpose alone. A lusty, sweaty purpose.

As she walked to Ethan, that heat was carved into every inch of his perfect features.

"Good girl." It rolled out of him as he pressed closer. He was huge and hard and warm, consuming her vision again, a welcome domination this time. Without a second thought, she dipped her head into his chest. As her forehead pressed between his dog tags, she felt at once connected. Content.

Confused.

Don't get used to this, Ava. She had to be diligent about the reminders. This was a bite of sin only meant to be savored in this moment alone. There could be no "getting connected." No being "content." No letting him into her spirit or her soul. No *anything* except one beautiful lick of man candy. One. Period.

The mandate made her feel a little stronger despite the shivers he induced by raking both hands down her spine, continuing around the swells of her bottom, drawing his fingers together in the crevice between her cheeks. But as he glided farther in, parting the sensitive wings of her sex from the back, the tremors turned to liquid—and so did any rational thought.

"Ava." His voice was like a rich cabernet against her neck, a silken caress backed by unmistakable command.

"Y-Yeah?"

"You're already wet for me."

"Yeah..."

The dark thunder vibrated through his chest again as he moved his grip back to her buttocks. Like lightning had struck his inner storm, he kneaded her flesh with increasing urgency. He openly bit her nape. The pain made her gasp in surprise, which rocketed into excitement. As she mewled against the base of his throat, she wrapped her arms around his waist and clawed ten deep, slow tracks across his back.

A feral groan ripped out of Ethan. Even when he'd trapped her in the forest those many months ago, he hadn't sounded like this. But that was it, wasn't it? *All those months ago.* Lightning stored in a bottle for over two hundred days was an explosion in waiting. She experienced the truth of that now in every skin cell he marked, every tremble he induced, every inch of her body he claimed in sweeps and squeezes that burned and branded. His fervor boiled her limbs to the consistency of applesauce. When he shifted his hold from her ass to her shoulders, her knees gave out, and there was no way to go but down.

Oh damn, it felt good. Better than she'd imagined or hoped. Here at his feet...*yes*. It was natural. Perfect. Meant to be.

"Fuck." It left him on a strangled choke. When she pressed

her cheek into his thigh, his muscles bunched and tensed. She nudged him like a kitten seeking approval. He answered her need, bunching his hand into her hair, gathering the strands until they were tight between his fingers. Ava moaned, again hating him and adoring him for the brutal pain...and the magnificent mental journey into which he guided her deeper.

"I've had fantasies too." She confessed it as she rubbed her nose against his zipper. The bulge beneath her face pounded for release. He held her there for a long moment, grunting in pleasure as she bit at the denim. She'd never done anything like this before, and it was...wonderful. Naughty. Forbidden. Completely wanton. The world always demanded that she be calm and temperate, the graceful daughter, the sensible friend, the poised stylist. For once, she longed to be wild, wicked, and lost in sexual decadence with this dark, primitive warrior...and his hot, throbbing spear.

"Show me." Ethan's order made it clear he shared that mindset. He pulled her hair harder. "Show me exactly what you fantasized."

His choppy breath finished it, a sound Ava savored as much as the musky scent of his arousal as she unzipped his pants. As she pushed them down, a tattoo was revealed down the length of his right leg. The design was rendered entirely in black ink, depicting a chain of matching circles, each with a smaller ring attached inside, that were hooked together with the same Chinese symbol. She fingered it for a minute, wondering if the angels themselves had given it to him since the ink was such a perfect match for his dark beauty, before realigning her vision with the tight cotton that covered his clamoring lust.

With a careful tug, she freed his shaft from the fabric.

"Oh!" she blurted.

"What?"

She looked up into his face, its classic angles crunched in concern. A smile bloomed on her lips. "My fantasies weren't as good as this."

His apprehension darkened into desire once more. As it did, she ran her cheek along his erect length, letting her tongue trail in its wake. Ethan's groan filled her ears as she explored him even more, tasting, licking, kissing. His cock was as perfectly formed as the rest of him, sleek and long, velvet skin stretched over solid muscle. It was trailed with hard veins that pulsed as she made her way along his erection. Finally she closed her mouth over the bulb at the end, savoring the tangy residue of his precome before she drew him in by an inch. Then another.

"Fuck!" His reprise of the word came from the depths of his gut. He brought his other hand around, sifting through her hair again before bracketing her jaw. With his thumb, he traced her lips as she sucked him over and over, deeper and deeper. "Oh, sunshine," he finally grated, "I don't think mine were, either."

She pulled back for a moment, daring another gaze up at his lust-shadowed face. "Please...tell me I was here in your fantasies."

His brows hunkered. "Here?"

"On my knees for you. Serving you...like this."

It felt so good to say it. To reveal her darkest secret to him, this dream of being at her warrior's feet, naked for him, ready to please him in any way he craved, in any manner he ordered...

No. She needed to stop thinking like this. Weren't the tags that hung from his neck reminder enough of the fire with which she was playing? *Military men are* not *good for you.* If that wasn't dangerous enough, she tossed kerosene onto the mix by opening the closet on her kinky needs again. What the *hell* was wrong with her?

As soon as he spoke again, the answer to that didn't seem so important.

"Goddamnit." His voice was husky in all the right ways. He slid his grip beneath her chin, tilting her head in order to lock her gaze with his. "They sure as hell did, baby."

An insane, hot sting surged behind her eyes. She swallowed it back...and then threw open the damn closet and let her kinkster dance. "What else happened?" she asked in a whisper. "In your dreams...what else did I do for you?"

A hard gulp plummeted in Ethan's throat. Her spirit jumped. As she'd guessed—and hoped—it seemed he had a kinky closet too. But he was fighting it.

"Some parts of my fantasies are best left locked up."

She lifted her chin by a notch. "Unlock them."

His pupils dilated. His erection twitched. "Ava, listen—"

"*Unlock them.*"

With one hand, she palmed his penis again. With the other, she lifted a pleading hand to his ribbed stomach. Ethan issued the F-word again beneath his breath, echoing the conflict that crunched his face, bunched his shoulders, and even jerked his thighs.

It was time to stop doing this silly dance. If she had to pull open defiance on him, so be it.

"This is called topping from the bottom, right?" She gripped his shaft and squeezed. With her other hand, she scratched into his abdomen. "Doesn't a girl usually get paddled for this?"

Ethan's anatomical earthquake went still. Without

preamble, he grabbed the wrist against his torso and cinched it tight with his hand. When he answered her, there was no more forbearance in his voice. Or trembling. "Usually she does—unless that's the brat's goal." He cocked his head. "In that case, alternative punishments are considered."

Her mouth popped open. Her hand, still trapped by his grip, went still.

"Al-Alternative punishments?" *Shit.* She knew about those, of course—but always skipped those parts in the novels she read or clicked off those pages on the kinky community chat rooms to which she belonged. Thanks to Bella, her free time was rare, so she always wanted to get to the good stuff. The spanking scenes. "I...I thought paddling was the preferred—"

"I prefer lots of things, Ava." His left brow jumped up. Damn, he stole her breath *every* time he did that. "Are you still interested in finding out?" He gentled his hold and started stroking her knuckles with the tips of his fingers.

"Yes." She rendered the answer without hesitation—realizing she'd been waiting seven months to do so. "Yes, S—Ethan."

His lips quirked. "Sunshine, was that the beginning of a 'Sir?'"

Yes. "M-Maybe."

"Have you ever said it to a man before?"

"N-No."

"But you want to."

She swallowed. "God, yes."

"Then right now, you will." His teasing tone had vanished. "And you shall."

She let him see her grateful smile. "Yes, Sir."

"But *no* still means no," he emphasized. "And you'll still

stop me if I push too hard." He guided the shiny head of his cock back to her mouth, nudging it in enough that she wetted the hot purple surface again. "Because God fucking help me, I want to push."

His admission made her stomach jump and her senses leap. She opened her throat, longing to take him deep again, but he backed away, leaving only his heady masculine taste on her tongue.

"Stand up, sunshine." His tone turned brisk as he wheeled away, beckoning her deeper into the wine room with him. The tasting area had a pair of plush couches that faced each other, upholstered in red velvet. He pointed to one. "Sit there. Arms out to your sides, along the top of the couch. Keep them there until I tell you otherwise."

"Yes, Sir." The words flowed through her like honey, coating her mind with delicious warmth. As she scooted onto the couch, the velvet tickled her bottom and thighs. Ethan didn't make a sound. He didn't have to. The sensual strength of his stare flowed over and around her, joining with the next song in the housekeeper's mix: a thrumming, rock-influenced tango.

When she was in position, she looked up. Her gaze took in the firm brace of Ethan's feet before catching on the bottom edge of his tattoo wrapped around his right ankle. She followed the elegant circles and symbols back up to his torso, with his insanely perfect abs and arms. But even they weren't enough to distract her from fixating again on his proud, long cock, even more erect than before, practically pulsing in time to the music that throbbed in the air.

The guitars calmed, dipping into a musical bridge. His quiet but determined command filled the air instead. "Spread your legs."

Slowly, she complied. Nervously, she waited. His stare was like a physical force, burning across the tender crevices she opened to him, casting a beautiful haze over her mind. She'd never let a man gaze at her like this. It was unnerving. It was exhilarating.

"Your pussy's glistening, Ava."

"Yes, Sir."

"It's beautiful."

"Th-Thank you."

"Open wider, baby."

She licked her lips, obeying by a few hesitant inches. As she did, Ethan lowered to the floor in front of her. He braced his hands to her thighs, just above her knees—and, without a word, shoved them farther back. A high cry tore off her lips. She was stretched shockingly wide, no inch of her sex a secret to him now. Ethan might as well have finished a crossword puzzle for all the serene satisfaction on his face. She didn't know whether to hate him or adore him for it.

"Better." He trailed his hands upward. Higher, higher... intent on getting to the trembling layers he'd opened. "You're stunning, sunshine."

"So are you, Sir." Crazy as it was, especially after the liberty he'd just taken, it was true. If a casting director for the industry's next sex god project were here, his naked magnificence would earn him the gig in a second. Yet he sat there looking as if *she* was the world's hottest pinup. "Dear God," she murmured, "am I dreaming?"

A smile lit up his perfect face. "You're fond of that question." Tenderly, he thumbed the lips guarding her most precious entrance. "Just like I'm fond of proving you wrong."

"Ahhh!"

She cried it as he slipped one, then two, of his long fingers inside her. Her head fell back. Her eyes rolled the same direction. He quickly set up a rhythm of thrust and retreat, taunting her exposed clit every time he moved in until she whimpered and gasped for him. Despite that, she tried to maintain some shred of composure. She should've gone for roping down the sun while she was at it. The feeling of his flesh inside her, awakening her...was exquisite. Incredible.

He made it feel even more amazing by using his free hand to stroke the tops of her thighs. When she answered with a long keen, he growled, "Fuck, you're beautiful."

"Mmmm," she whimpered. "Uh...uh-huh..."

"Do you enjoy submitting to me, sunshine?"

"Y-Yes," she managed. "Yes, Sir."

"Excellent." The pressure in her vagina intensified as he pushed in a third finger. A moan erupted from her lips. He kicked up the pace of his plunges. "And you like being fucked by my fingers?"

"Yes...yes!"

"You want them to make you come?"

"Ohhh, please, yes!"

She dug her fingers into the back of the couch, expecting him to intensify the erotic assault. Needing it...*ay*, needing the completion so bad...

He pulled completely out.

She pried open her eyes. Stared at him through the fog of her arousal, past the air that heaved in and out of her chest. Looked down to the hand he'd just been using to pull her to heaven, now resting on her thigh. His fingers were still shiny with the evidence of what he'd done to her. She whimpered from the emptiness he'd left behind.

"Wh-What's wrong?" she pleaded. "What did I do?"

Ethan shook his head and gave her that damn Dalai Lama smile. "You're perfect. So fucking perfect." He rose to his knees, still between hers, and moved his hold to the sides of her waist. "It's about what you're *going* to do...for me."

She frowned. "I don't understand."

"Hmmm." He managed to make cryptic and smug look completely gorgeous. "Not yet."

"Shit." That made him chuckle, which tightened her scowl. "*No* still means no, right?" she challenged.

"Uh-huh." He surged a little higher, bringing his face even with hers...aligning his cock with the entrance of the tunnel he'd just emptied. "But you're not going to say no."

She managed to laugh. "Is that so?" As he glided his hands over her ribcage and brushed his thumbs over the tingling tips of her nipples, she rasped, "What do you have in mind, Sergeant Sir?"

Tee hee. How coy and cute was she? When the midnight skies of Ethan's eyes gained new silver stars of arousal, she gave him a wriggle of supreme confidence—

Which froze as soon as he uttered his reply.

"Alternative punishment."

CHAPTER FIVE

He was going to hell. If Ethan wasn't sure of it before, he was now, because his delight in her little shiver, the perfect mix of alarm and anticipation, wasn't something a pillar of virtue would feel. Like he could stop himself if he tried. She was stunning, beyond anything his imagination had conjured over the last seven months, when he allowed his mind—and his body—to indulge in a mortal's thoughts about corrupting a goddess. Her hair was fuller, sexier. Her eyes were more mesmerizing. And her naked skin, like honey poured over cinnamon...*damn*. He soaked in as much of its glory as he could, certain Mount Olympus was going to notice she was missing any second and skewer him with lightning to get her back.

No lightning came. He smirked in triumph. In that case, the punishment was on.

He savored the sight of her heavy gulp and the way she wet her lips in open trepidation before muttering, "I'd...much prefer knowing if you have anything *else* in mind."

He slowly shook his head. "That would be a *no way*, beautiful."

"Shit."

He let his grin spill into a chuckle, ending it with a tongue-twirling kiss on her sweet, acquiescent lips. "You're going to *like* this punishment," he promised. "Eventually."

Her chin jutted and her eyes narrowed. "What the hell is

that supposed to—*ohhh*!"

The cry sprang out of her as Ethan tugged one of her nipples and squeezed. The tactic worked at quieting her sass but bit him in the back bumper too. Dear fuck, the woman's breasts needed to come with warning labels. *Pinch at your own risk. Nipples will stand up like the peaks of Macchu Picchu and may result in painful swelling of the balls and cock.*

Despite that, he transferred his touch to her other breast and pulled it just as hard.

"Ohhh, shhiit!" She started to pant and tremble, making him look forward to the next moment even more. When he lowered his mouth to her distended tip, replacing his pinches with worshiping licks, those breaths turned into stunned sighs. She took it up another octave when he shifted back to her other breast.

"You like this too, baby?" He began to play with her nipples, taunting them with tiny scrapes of his thumbnails across their reddened crests.

Ava gazed at him with heavy-lidded eyes. "Yes...yes, Sir. It's...nice."

Ethan stilled his hands for a moment. Gazed intently at her. "It's just the beginning."

"Th-The beginning? Of what?"

"Of giving your mind to me." He began to rub her breasts again. Slowly this time. Reveling in watching how she absorbed his voice and his touch...how her skin pebbled for him, how her breaths synced to every move he made. "And most importantly, your imagination."

"I...I don't understand."

He lifted one hand to her face. "Just trust that you will." He didn't have to ask if she understood or had thoughts of rebelling. The woman still had her arms stretched along the back of the couch. Even when he'd crunched her nipples so suddenly, she'd kept both there, locked in the position he'd specified. The woman may have streetwise sass and a hellcat's mouth outside this room, but right here, right now, she didn't just want his control. She yearned for it.

Who was he to deny the goddess anything she wanted?

She just didn't have to know that if she asked him to bring her the moon, he'd find a way to make that happen too.

He captured her mouth beneath his again, melding their lips and tongues until tantalizing mewls danced up her throat before he released her and quietly ordered, "Close your eyes."

She sent her long dark lashes down, pulling in a deep breath to prepare herself for his next phase of punishment. Though uncertain tremors racked her body, she gave him every drop of her trust, of her surrender. Ethan felt it in the molecules of the air, sensed it to the marrow of his bones.

Fuck.

He drew in a breath of his own, hardly daring to believe what was happening. This wouldn't last. It never did. The conclusion was rooted in years of experience. He had Max Brickham, the owner of his regular BDSM dungeon back home, to thank for that. He'd witnessed the connection Max had with his own submissive and felt like Columbus discovering the New World. But after the horizon had opened up, it dried up. He'd fast learned that what Max and Megan shared was incredible, rare, perhaps one of a kind—and not meant to be for him. He'd been bitter about that for a while, until life handed him an attitude adjustment on a freezing day in a Paktika Province pass. He'd back-burnered the quest for his own Megan in favor of being grateful for his life.

"I'm all yours."

Life was picking a funny moment to throw him a new curveball. Her words, again such a priceless gift of trust and openness, slammed gates open in his psyche. Okay, maybe this wouldn't last—but goddamnit if he wasn't going to enjoy this perfect union while he could.

That resolve added a thick undertone to his reply. "Mmmm. You sure are, sunshine."

He lifted away enough to graze his knuckles over the tips of her breasts again. They were still stone-hard, her areolas puckered, her flesh vibrant.

"Ohhh..." It was a sigh of bliss, though it wobbled on her lips. She was certain he was going to clamp down his fingers again...a trepidation that turned him way the fuck on. He had her mind right where he wanted it...

"Ava?"

She bit her lip. Still a little scared. Still so damn mesmerizing. "Yes, Sir?"

"I want you to pretend something for me."

Her face wriggled in unspoken curiosity, but she nodded. He deliberately shifted back up, hovering over her once more, not moving his fingers.

"I want you to pretend those aren't my fingers anymore. Imagine I've brought nipple clamps in with me. Now I've got them out, and I'm screwing them tighter onto your beautiful tits."

Her sighs vanished. Her whole torso tensed as the air stuck in her lungs. Though he still only grazed her breasts with the tips of his knuckles, her face contorted like he'd really clamped her.

"That's good." The words left him on sparse rasps. "So

fucking good."

Her lips, bitten to the color of ripe raspberries, hinted at a smile. "What else?" she pleaded. "Is there...more?"

He'd never been happier to hear that word.

"I've attached a chain that connects the clamps," he went on. "In the middle of that chain, I'm attaching another chain." He freed one of his hands to draw a line down the middle of her body, stopping only when he got to the edge of her soft pubic hair. "It leads straight down to your sweet, tight cunt."

"Mmmm..." His naughty language yielded the exact result he wanted. But instead of a simple observation of that effect, he put it into words...with a few embellishments.

"Your pussy is dripping as you wait to see what that chain is for. The passage inside of you, where you're the wettest for my invasion, sends more moisture for the cause. You want my cock deep inside you." He enforced the image by nudging the bulb of his dick against the throbbing lips of her sweet pussy. He shook a little himself. Holy fuck, she felt good. Hot. Wet. Waiting for him. Open for him. "But you know I'm not done with my playtime, right?"

Her chest rolled with the force of her breaths. Her skin gleamed. Her mouth was parted, red and sweet as a pomegranate, in desperate longing. "Yes," she answered on a gasp. "Yes, I know, Sir."

"Good girl." He flattened his hands, fingers wide, as he slid his touch up to her hips. Ava writhed, silently begging him to close in on the petals that gleamed with her need. "Uh-uh," he told her. "If you want me to touch you there, then make it happen...here." He gently tapped her forehead.

"H-Huh?"

"You heard me, Ava."

"Are you seriously kidding—"

"Do I sound like I'm *seriously kidding*, sunshine?" He gave that to her in a voice he usually saved for submissives pulling the brat card. She was far from that but had hit a mental spike strip in their journey, making her spin out into confusion.

Luckily, his verbal force at least got her attention realigned. Her features eased and she took a long breath. "Help me," she implored. "Tell me what to do."

Her surrender, so sweet and complete, hit him like a damn grenade. Ethan bent and kissed his way down the middle of her body. When his lips touched the curls that were parted at her core, he lifted a little, denying her the direct contact. Instead, he blew steady air into the area, enjoying the tiny shivers he observed on her inner thighs, along her labia, in her clit itself. In response, Ava keened as her whole body quaked.

"You're already doing it," he assured her. "So perfectly."

As he returned to his original pace, grasping her hips and taunting her pussy with the tip of his cock, she bit her lip harder, clearly fighting back tears. "*Dios*," she whispered, her voice ragged. She was headed toward the spike strip again, trying to cling to self-control though her body had peeked over the cliff to which he clearly was driving.

"Let it go." Ethan lowered his voice, dug in on his touch. "All of it. Everything outside this room...it can wait. In here, right now, you'll give it all to me, Ava. I'll keep it safe, I promise. For now, think about those clamps on your beautiful nipples again...and the chain that joins them..."

"Shit," she rasped. "Okay."

"Now remember the second chain..."

"I hadn't exactly forgotten."

Her sarcasm made him smile. "It happens to have its own

clamp at the end."

"Shit!"

"You know where it's going, don't you?" He watched her lips wobble and her eyelids twitch. "Pretend it for me, sunshine. Imagine my fingers pulling back the lips of your perfect pussy, so slowly, teasing you. Finally, I reveal your clit, already so hard, like it knows what's coming. Then it comes... that grip of such sweet pain as I secure the clamp..."

Her chest pumped up and down, letting him see exactly how the scenario affected her. Ethan clenched his jaw for a long second, letting her beauty wash over him. Dark, erect nipples. Nostrils flaring, greedily drawing air. Skin shimmering with arousal. All were begging for his kisses and suckling.

No. Make her work for it.

"Imagine me licking up the column of your neck, distracting you from the sting," he went on. "You want to grip me harder, to keep me locked on that place just behind your right ear that makes you shiver and moan for me, but you can't."

"Wh-Why not?" It bordered on a whine and made him harder in a dozen new ways.

"Because, sunshine...you're tied down."

"Oh, dear God."

No more whine. The words slurred with her guttural inflection. Her head fell back. He continued to watch her, gauging every speck of her rising desire, though he forced his hands to remain where they were. Ordering his dick to continue hovering at the entrance of her core... That was a different ball of pain altogether. It was torture. It was rapture. She was so open for him, so full in her need and hot in her desire, that he could barely think of anything except being inside her. Gritting everything in his jaw and clenching every muscle in his thighs, he managed to hold back. Barely.

"Feel the ropes," he encouraged. There was a quarry full of gravel in his tone, but he didn't filter it. He wanted his lust woven into her fantasy. "They're probably rough hemp, because I know you want the burn...to feel every tight scratch against your skin."

She flung her head from one side to the next. "I do. *Ay*, Ethan. I do!"

He let out a savoring snarl. "Twist against the bondage for me, baby." He stared in fascination as the muscles along her arms clenched, and she jerked her wrists as if fighting full knots. "Yes. That's good. You like this? Being helpless beneath me? Knowing I control everything your body does right now?"

"Yes," she exclaimed. "Yes. More!"

"Exactly what I had in mind," he replied.

"Tell me," she pleaded.

"That comes after you *show* me, baby." With her confused grunt trailing him, he glided his hands together, joining them atop the silken skin of her lower abdomen. He pressed down. "Here," he said. "Clench hard here."

Her brows knitted. "I...I don't under—"

"Do it," he insisted. "Tighten everything hard. Harder!" When he felt her muscles squeeze, he ordered, "Now release it." He grinned, even more delighted when her lips popped open and her eyes, alive with indigo arousal, followed suit. "Again. Harder this time."

Ava obeyed without question this time. She winced when he made her stay tight a second longer this time but let out a laugh on the release. "Oh...my...God."

He cocked a brow. "Good?"

"A little better than that." She swallowed. "Again? Please?"

Ethan nodded. "Again."

"Yesssss..."

He compressed his hands harder, now as giddy as her. He'd read plenty about the Kegel muscles and exactly what areas they stimulated when employed, but the idea of coupling such a workout with a thorough mind fuck was a complete crapshoot on his part. So far, he wasn't disappointed with the results. Didn't look like Ava was either.

"Keep doing it," he instructed, loving the rhythm of her body beneath his touch. "Don't stop." Unable to resist, he slicked a hot kiss across her lips. "With every contraction, imagine that clamp on your clit, stimulating you."

"Ohhhh." Her head lolled to the side, her eyes closed again. "Yes...okay."

He hesitated a second before issuing his next command. Would he be able to say it without doing it?

"Now imagine me fucking you, Ava."

Barely. Oh shit, only by the thinnest thread of control did he resist turning that image into reality. Only by tightening his own muscles, nearly every one, did he hold back from plunging into her hard, letting her muscles squeeze him, her body surround him, her tunnel take him. Her utterly sexy whimpers didn't make the ordeal any easier—but when she began to rock front to back, her pelvis thrusting as if he was really driving into her, he couldn't leave events to chance anymore. Within thirty seconds, he fished the condom from his pants, tore apart the wrapper, and sheathed up.

Now he only had to decide one thing. Keep dominating her mind or start claiming her body?

Another look at her made the decision for him.

She was still lost in the fantasy. Immersed in the sinful

simulation of his creation. Every detail of her dream, of her mind, was still his to guide and control. If he took her now, reality still wouldn't suck for her—but the fantasy would be over.

Time for your happy ending, sunshine.

"I'm deep inside you now," he growled. "Driving hard and fast, my cock kissing your cervix with every thrust."

She pitched her pelvis faster. Damn, it was all he could do to keep her from impaling herself on him from the force of the motions. "Yes!" she cried. "Harder, Ethan! Oh God, I've dreamed of this since the forest. I've wanted this for seven damn months."

Despite the agony gripping his dick, he smiled down into her face. "You have?"

She nodded frantically. "Yes. *Yes.*"

The confession, so sweet and real, made him swell against the latex. His balls began to throb, threatening to send in the bullets whether he had the damn chamber loaded or not. He gritted his jaw. *Not* until she gave it all to him. Not until she came from the sheer force of his control.

"Ava, listen carefully now."

"Mmmm. Yes, Sir."

"I'm going to bury my dick all the way in, baby—and I'm going to stay there while I pull the clamp off your clit."

"Ohhhh," she moaned. "Okay. Oh, yes."

"The blood's going to rush back in. I'm going to touch you... once. Then you're going to come for me. You're going to come hard." When she only emitted a little mewl, he demanded, "Do you understand the order?"

"Yes...I understand."

Christ, she moved him. So committed in her passion. So

complete in her submission. He kissed her again, gently this time, before asking, "Are you ready?"

She nodded. Smiled. And kept thrusting those beautiful, curvy thighs like he was really inside her...like he yearned to be inside her. "Yes. Do it. Make me come, Ethan—please!"

CHAPTER SIX

She was seriously messed up. She had to be. In a recess of her mind, Ava knew much of this, *most* of this, wasn't real—but right now, reality was her enemy. Right now, the illusion was all she wanted, all she craved, all she needed. The way Ethan wove his words into her mind and his scenes into her imagination had her breasts thudding with dual locks of pain, her arms flexed against invisible ropes, and her pussy dripping as it ached for final release. Every cell of her body simmered and strained, quivered and clenched, reaching for the fulfillment only he could give.

That settled it. Ethan Archer didn't just look, smell, and sound like a beautiful, wicked warlock. He *was* one.

She felt his fingers tracing the top of her pubic line. Her heartbeat stuttered. Was his touch real this time? As he trailed two fingers lower, parting her swollen labia as he did, she wondered if it was worth questioning...even as the tips of those digits closed over the center of her clit and squeezed.

"Ohhhh!" she cried. *Ow.* And yet *yum* too. His pleased growl enforced the latter.

"One," he murmured. And pinched her even tighter.

"Damn!"

"Two."

Yeah. Harder again. "Ethan!" she screamed. "Seriously?"

"Three."

It was barely a breath above her lips as he pressed a thumb

along her clit. When he spread his fingers back, the heat was unlike anything she'd ever felt. She screamed as her body broke into a million shards of blinding, beautiful sensation. And her mind? It was collateral damage from the blast, annihilated into ecstasy-filled mush. Nothing mattered or existed but the white ball of fire she'd become—and her longing to engulf Ethan in its flames too.

"Please!" She managed beneath desperate pants. "N-Need you, Ethan. N-No more just in my head. You. *You*. Please!"

She was making as much sense as a bimbo who'd had too many shots in the party limo. But somehow he understood. The rough sough from his chest told her so. His insistent kiss showed her so.

The slide of his cock into her core told her so.

"Ahhh!"

How the *hell* could he have asked her to imagine this? Nothing she'd dreamed came close to what he really felt like, stretching and filling her, driving her toward a second detonation of light, lust, flames, fulfillment. When he grunted and gripped her hips, sealing her body completely around his, she abandoned her grip on the couch to throw her arms around his neck. Their slick torsos slammed together. His approving snarl gave her the impetus to hold tighter. So close. Oh hell, she was so close...

"Now, sunshine. *Now!*"

His demand, coarse with control but silken with seduction, spoke to every drop of blood in her body. The walls of her control toppled, the shreds of her reserve were gone. Her pussy was flooded by a second wave of scalding sensation. Her scream of release tangled with Ethan's harsh groan. Deep inside, she felt his cock pulse over and over again.

They rocked against each other for long, lingering minutes, heartbeats hammering at each other through their pressed bodies. With a heavy sigh, Ethan finally rose, peeled the condom off, yanked a sommelier's wipe off the roll on the marble tasting table, and then tossed them both into the trash.

As she rose and walked toward her clothes on wobbly legs, Ava tossed him a wry laugh. "Guess that was a damn good vintage, right?"

He didn't take her up on the joke. Instead, he caught her around the waist, his bicep tightening to hold her back. "What the hell are you doing?"

She pushed away. "Getting back to work."

She winced, instantly regretting the glacier she tossed in the wake of his sexual tsunami. With a guilty pout, she turned back and pulled his head down for a tender kiss. The move delivered on the payback. His hair, short yet so thick, felt wonderful between her fingers. "Thanks for the concern. I just don't require huge cuddle time, okay?"

Ethan unleashed a full glare. "The fuck you don't." Beneath his breath, *way* beneath, she heard him add, "The fuck *I* don't."

It was a ripe opportunity for another teasing giggle. Instead, as Ava bent to retrieve her bra, the heavy sting of tears assaulted. She froze, horrified by why her emotions ratted her out like this but achingly clear about their reasoning too. She'd had a glimpse of heaven, and it had been good. Really good. Everything, *everything*, she'd ever longed to share with a truly dominant man. *This* one was so good at the helm, he'd commanded her into an orgasm damn near with his words alone.

But it was done now. The sole bite of Ethan Archer decadence had passed her lips. She had to put the fork down and be thankful for what she *had* enjoyed. *If you indulge any more, you'll be puking by tomorrow morning.*

It might be too late for nausea anyway. She let out a sniff as the conclusion pummeled her full force.

"Ava."

His orgasm hadn't erased an inch of his Dom streak, reinforcing both his voice and touch as he cupped her shoulders from behind. Shit. Didn't he understand that only made this worse? Couldn't he get the message that she couldn't do this stuff? The hardcore "lifestylers" even had a name for it, didn't they? "Aftercare." Right. *Not* happening. If it did, he'd aftercare her into a gigantic ball of needing him again. Yearning for him. Wanting him like a gooey, fresh honeycomb, complete with all the little buzzing buggers who'd created it, without an epi pen to be had for miles. It would kill her.

"*Ava.*"

And yet she allowed him to curl her back against his chest, engulfing her in his hard, wonderful warmth.

Ohhhh, no.

She lost the battle against breathing him in. Her senses filled with his scent, a mix of leather and sex...and her. His deep breath conveyed it wasn't just her smell he'd taken in. His embrace alone—capped by him tangling one hand in her hair— told her he considered this just the beginning.

The beginning. She laughed at the words through her tears. The beginning of what? Of giving her heart to this knight in camouflage, letting him ride off into battle with her favors tied to his "lance" of an M4, only to wait for the day when there was a knock on the door and the notifications officer stood there with the stare that meant only one thing? Or maybe it was the phone that rang and it was camo knight himself, calling drunk from Vegas to tell her he'd found the "soul mate" she'd never been and had just decided to marry the woman?

Those were just the scenarios life had punched her with firsthand. There were thousands more. So many more ways to define how she could make the mistake of falling for a too-good-to-be-true military man again.

She pushed away from him again. Wrapped her arms around herself. "What?"

Lovely. She'd traded one-liners with TV stars, rock idols, and even Prince Harry during his set visit, and the best she could do was a tearful *what*?

Ethan clearly agreed. His eyes darkened to the color of midnight. "*What?* Is that really where you're taking this now?"

He spread his arms, making a damn good case why Michelangelo got it wrong with the original model for *David*. Ava forced herself to look away from his naked beauty, now matched in intensity by his frustration.

"I'm sorry," she rasped. "It's...PMS, okay?" *Good save.* That one always worked. Guys pretty much started for the exits once that three-letter card got played. "I'll be fine in a few—"

"Bullshit."

She lifted a glare. "Excuse me?"

"You know what I said. But just so we're clear, I call bullshit." He shifted closer by a steady, noiseless step. Another. He didn't try to hold her again, though the proximity of his body, with the bottom of his rib cage hitting her elbows, had her again feeling swallowed by the force of his focus and the power in his stance.

She wetted her lips in lieu of backing up. "Ethan, I don't think now is the right time—"

"Now is the perfect time. I've waited seven damn months for now." He took her bra from her and tossed it onto the tasting counter in one motion, and in the next, swept an arm around so he could brace her jaw, forcing her face up. "And something tells me you have too."

He emphasized his meaning by brushing her tears with the tips of his fingers. Like his voice, the sweeps were soft but ambitious...emotional ninjas. She had to fight back. She had no choice, despite the sorrow that still welled and the tears that still came.

"It was worth the wait," she finally murmured. She tried lightening the air with another laugh but gave up when his face didn't change by one solemn inch. "It was amazing, Ethan. But you...you're...and this..."

"Is pretty fucking awesome." Despite the earnest words, his features steeled. "You going to squirm away from that one too, sunshine? Go ahead. I've got the juice to go a hundred rounds with you on why I'm right." His mouth quirked in humorless triumph. "But something tells me you'd be lucky to last three."

"Something tells *me* that's pretty accurate." She gazed up at him, smiling softly with the confession. "Fucking awesome is a pretty good way of putting it. I don't think I'll look at that couch the same way again."

"You make that sound like a bad thing."

"I'm making it sound like a *real* thing," she clarified. "Ethan, look—"

He shifted his thumbs to lock on top of her mouth. "You want to know about real?" he growled. "Fine." For the first

ANGEL PAYNE

time, he dipped his gaze—making her know, with better-than-high-def clarity, that she was really in trouble now. "*Real* is what I felt, for the first time in a long time, the moment you smiled at me from Sage and Garrett's living room floor. *Real* was the way my spirit got zapped when my lips met yours in the forest the next day. *Real* was the thing my life missed for seven fucking months before I saw you again on the soundstage today. *Real* is this, Ava. It's rare. A treasure that's been given to us. We should—"

"Whoa." She finally jerked from his hold. "Okay, stop. Just stop." *Stop before I break every promise I've made to myself over the last three years and let you shred my soul into pulp for your nobility smoothie.* "A *treasure*? Don't you mean *your* treasure? The kill you chased and finally shot down?"

It was brutal. She knew it. Ethan's face reflected it. His lips twisted as if he were nauseated. "Is that what you think? That you were some kind of conquest for me?"

She didn't say anything.

His jaw went the texture of steel. Ava bunched her hands into fists in order to control herself from negating him, from running back into his arms and blubbering that of course that wasn't what she thought. That in the first second of his hold on her in the prop room, she'd felt the agony of every moment he'd waited to see her again and the torture of plodding through life without knowing he ever would.

Treasure. He had to have found the perfect word for it, hadn't he?

But sometimes treasure was cursed. Especially if the wrong person found it. Especially if they weren't the one meant to have it. The treasure always knew that part, didn't it? And then it turned to dust.

With a heavy gulp, she pivoted and picked up her bra.

"I have to get back to work." She deliberately picked panties and slacks next. That made it easier to keep her gaze down, away from where he'd be able to see it. To probe her in that way where he could read her thoughts in 3D. Her thoughts weren't his business now. And her heart sure as hell wasn't his "treasure."

He finally moved. The very air seemed to shift around him as he did, like afterburn of his ire. With two violent sweeps, he scooped his own stuff off the floor but made no move to get redressed. "Fine," he spat, "but this is far from over, Ava."

She didn't give him a response. Oh, she had one, but the chasm between thinking it and saying it was unbridgeable— and painful. As she jammed her top back over her head and picked up her boots, that didn't stop the retort from blasting open a few tormenting holes inside her head.

The hell it isn't, Sergeant Archer. The hell it isn't.

CHAPTER SEVEN

Ethan had only steadily dated one woman in the four years since breaking up with Bella. Fallon was an airline flight attendant who didn't just understand his insane life but often had a wackier one. As luck had it, her routes often landed her close to him if the team was forward deployed to a major city, making conditions ideal for enjoying each other's humor, fondness for foreign food, and passion for hotels with four-poster beds and thick walls.

Though Fallon topped too damn much from the bottom to be his longtime submissive, Ethan never sidestepped her aftercare. Yeah, including the cuddling. Letting Fallon watch *Sex and the City* reruns always assured he'd get to shower her with more than ten minutes of it, too. He even tried to understand the show, though that cartridge never clicked in his chamber. Did women actually talk like that? Did women actually *dress* like that? And his gut clenched at watching the scenes where the women sneaked away in the morning light, in such a hurry to get home and regret what they'd done that they couldn't bother to put on their shoes.

Ava left the wine room without putting on her shoes.

Even through a wardrobe change, exchanging her work jeans and blouse for a classic black sundress with a matching bikini underneath, the shoes were neglected. He knew it because he kept track with a stare that was likely a cross between an evil eye and a fuck-off glower. And he knew *that* because everyone made distinct efforts to steer clear of him.

Normally, that would be okay. After so many years of being put on display at Mom and Dad's soirees, paraded into jokes about early marriage offers to someone's sweet Diana or Lizbet or MarySue, he valued his solitude at things like this. But tonight was different. Tonight, he wanted to be in the middle of the room. Right next to Ava. Telling her to put her damn shoes on and stop looking like she'd killed someone this afternoon, instead of making him the most fulfilled man on earth.

All right, so Bella lived on the beach. And once she and the guys arrived for the party, swimsuits and cocktails made shoes an afterthought for everyone. *Not* the thought to make him ease on the demonic stare. He wasn't going to settle for hopping back into Ava's "afterthoughts" basket, a truth that would start with making the woman talk to him about the real reason behind her cut-and-run this afternoon.

From what he could see, a palm tree would work as well as a pine for pin-down purposes. After that, it was just a matter of creatively guiding the conversation. Thanks to his hook-up with Bernardo Galvaz three days ago, he was scalpel-sharp on that skill too.

All he had to do was wait.

Just a few minutes longer...

He'd watched her carefully from the juncture of the terrace to the living room. He was dry, having gotten into his trunks but too tense for a dunk with the guys. Her swim outfit went unused too since she hadn't ventured past the terrace herself while handling the party logistics. About a half hour ago, she'd stopped for a plate of food plus a glass of white wine and a bottle of water for balance. She was breaking into the second water now because Tait had dared her to a spicy-shrimp-eating contest. The result ended in a tie, but her cheeks were adorably red and her eyes watered as she chugged half the bottle. A trip to the bathroom for relief wasn't long off.

"Two minutes tops," he muttered to himself.

She barely lasted one.

The second Ava turned from Tait, who now had ten shrimp tails on his fingers and choreographed them to an off-key version of the latest Lady Gaga hit, Ethan was ready. As he expected, she headed for the palace-sized bathroom off the living room's upper landing. Perfect. He moved as well, starting down the terrace in a deceptively calm stride. She glanced at his new course—part of her I'm-avoiding-you-but-tracking-your-every-move thing with him now—but the glass between them did its job. After she realized he was outside, her stride visibly relaxed.

As she closed the bathroom door, she had no idea he'd be past the slider on the far end of the terrace, through the den beyond that, and on the landing waiting after she'd washed up with Bella's gold-flecked hand soap.

But as they often said on the team, a funny thing happened on the way to the ambush.

Clearing the terrace was an effortless hump. The glitch came once he hit the den—and found the room occupied. Sage Hawkins and Rayna Chestain were relaxing on the plush furniture, looking like new recruits to host one of those midmorning girlie chat shows. Their giggles had a naughty bite, as if they were discussing trendy sex positions or new condom flavors. But for all he knew, the subject could've been repurposing dryer lint into Christmas ornaments. Didn't matter much. They hushed the second he entered. A second later, the edge in Rayna's laugh climbed into her gaze, gaining a determined light.

Hell. Maybe this was more than a glitch.

"Ladies." He nodded and attempted a cordial smile. "Good evening."

"Well, hi there, Sergeant Archer." Sage lifted a hand off her rounded stomach to wave. "Damn. It still feels good to say that."

"Ethan." Rayna issued it with a little more purpose. "You're just the guy I was hoping to see."

Way more than a glitch.

Shit.

He spread his hands. "Ah, well...here I am. Now you see me"—he started toward the door—"and now you won't. Sorry I interr—"

"You're not interrupting. We were just catching up. We have lots of time to chat again tomorrow." Rayna shot one of *those* glances at Sage, comprehensible only if someone had matching chromosomes. "Can't we, sweetie?"

"Damn straight." Sage nodded and started scooting off the couch. "Best that I go check in with Sergeant Hawkins anyhow before he gets paranoid and sends a drone to scout for Little Hawk and me."

Ethan offered his arm so Sage could rise all the way up. After he helped her toward the door, Rayna motioned for him to shut the door. "You want to sit down?" she asked as he walked past a flat screen and sound system that practically begged for his drool.

"Do I have a choice?"

Rayna answered the smirk he gave it with a little laugh as he lowered into a leather easy chair. If he wasn't so sure what was coming next, he'd groan his thanks to the thing for making butter-soft love to his ass, but Rayna was the closest person on earth to Ava, and her scrutiny told him she wasn't here to banter about the genius of Bella's interior designer. Realigning his features into a determined stare, he leaned forward, elbows on his knees. He was ready for this conversation. Had been ready for seven months. *Let it rip, woman.*

"So, hey, Runway." Her bright tone was a sham, and they both knew it. "Did you and my cousin have a fun time this afternoon?"

He let half his smile linger, enough to tell her he'd clearly understood her meaning behind "fun." Since he hadn't noticed Ava exchanging more than a fast hug or two with Rayna tonight, he also assumed the query was an informational fishing expedition.

"Ava worked," he said. "I helped." He purposely didn't put anything on the hook but that. If Rayna wanted to make this the share-and-care hour, that was fine, but she'd be the one sharing. He had the caring part covered. After this afternoon, more than he wanted to admit.

"Hmm." Rayna tilted her head, her dark-green eyes probing toward him, her dark-red hair falling over the shoulder of her swimsuit cover thing. "She works hard."

"Yeah, she does."

"Nothing got handed to her on a platter. The career she has is all because of her efforts. And it's important to her."

The talk show banter had progressively vanished from her voice. Though its newest inflections of accusation were slight, Ethan combined them with the woman's battle-ready body angle and chose to speak his impression out loud.

"Is this where we cut through the bullshit, Rayna?" He

squared his shoulders. "Because I'm ready if you are."

The woman's lips lifted. Her pose straightened. He'd expected as much. The collar at her neck declared she was Zeke Hayes's sole submissive, a distinction requiring a woman of guts, fortitude, and brutal honesty. His statement conveyed he respected her for all that and more.

"Fine." The word was snippy, but her tone was warm. "It was clear to me, after I caught you with my cousin on Sage and Garrett's wedding day, that washing Ava's lipstick off your face wasn't going to get her off your mind."

"Smart woman," he murmured.

"Thank you. That makes it easier to reveal that I did a little reading up on you."

Ethan didn't shift his mien. Instinct told him she was making this interview a part of that "reading." He'd learned, not long after donning the Special Forces beret, to obey the hell out of his intuitions. "Hope it wasn't too boring."

"On the contrary," Rayna returned. "Pretty interesting stuff. Let me see if I have this straight. Ethan Aaron Archer. Turned twenty-six last month. Only child of Penelope and Robert Archer of Atherton, California. Played soccer and baseball until high school, and then switched to polo after that." Her features caved to a full *what-the-hell*. "Polo? Seriously? Does anyone on *this* side of the world play that?"

"In Atherton they do." He fitted his hands together, fingers-to-fingers, while trying to maintain his game face. It was his job to dig out shit like this about other peoples' lives, not have his own exposed. *Table in the back for one, waiter. Last name* Uncomfortable, *first name* Very.

Rayna tilted her head on a playful slant. "So which one did you like the best?"

"Chess."

"Huh? Never found anything about you playing chess."

"Of course you didn't." He purposely cocked a brow. "Not something the parental units wanted out in the open. Chess players didn't make interesting conversation pieces at the summer gala or elegant dance partners for daughters at the winter cotillion. Neither did video game geeks."

"What? Say it isn't so!" Her scandalized giggle made him grin, despite the awkwardness still parading in his veins.

"My polo coach was a douche, so I'd cut practice and go hang with my friend Parker. Thanks to his software-guru dad, who was also a gamer, we got advanced beta copies of all the big ones. Half-Life, Halo, Grand Theft Auto, all the Marios..." He laughed softly. "Even all the Minecraft updates."

"I love Minecraft!"

"Who doesn't?"

She sobered a little. "So is that what got you starry-eyed about joining up? Playing the shoot-em-up military games?"

He rolled up on his posture. Stamped her harder with his gaze. Much harder. "The only stars that came near my decision were the ones on the flag I defend, Rayna." He expected the skepticism that tightened her features. It was why he continued with, "I'll tell you about the day that decision came. I wasn't five. I wasn't fifteen. I was twenty-one. It was June, and I was almost done with my sophomore year at Stanford— and I could barely face the day because I was so hung over. I stumbled in to a convenience store after a fraternity rager. It was six in the morning, and I hoped to consume enough coffee and doughnuts to force my liver to forgive me so I could make my way through a hairy midterm that morning."

He caught her gaze narrowing but expected it. Relaying

this story was never easy, but it was critical that he never forgot it.

"Poor little rich kid, right?" he went on. "Had to interrupt the party to do something like school? Well, that's what I was standing there groaning about, when the door opened to the store and a guy strolled in. Wasn't much older than me, even looked about the same as me. Difference was, he didn't stink like a bottle of Patrón, and he was actually lucid. And smiling. And excited about the day. He told the clerk about how he was going to hear about his scholarship application that day, about how hard he'd worked on the damn thing, and how much he'd dreamed of getting into Stanford since hearing about the engineering program. Seemed he wanted to design and build better prosthetics for veterans." He shook his head. "Man, I yearned to be that guy. I wanted to know what it was like to have a dream about something more than me, about the slot I was already guaranteed in the family empire. I wanted to work for something. To care about something. To connect to something...bigger.

"That's when I looked down. And I saw that the guy had made that happy entrance on two prosthetics of his own. I also noticed the tats on both his thighs, above his attachment sockets. One was the eagle, globe, and anchor of the Marine Corps. The other was just one word. *Kandahar*."

Rayna shifted a little and cleared her throat. "So...what?" she queried. "The little rich boy had a sudden epiphany?"

"Yeah." He shrugged again. "I know it sounds lame, but... yeah." He rose and crossed the room, looking out at the beach and the waves. "I looked into that marine's eyes, at his pride in where he'd been and his hope in where he was going, and realized I'd never seen that same light in the mirror. I also knew I never would, if I kept skipping down the pretty crystal path in front of me."

"So you just dynamited the path?"

He gave a wry snort before turning back. "Pretty much."

"And your parents were cool with that?"

"They got over it." He jammed his hands into his pockets. "Eventually."

Rayna studied him in silence for a long moment. "Pretty gutsy, Mr. Archer."

"No," he rejoined. "Not gutsy. Pretty fucking selfish, actually."

"I don't follow."

He twisted his lips. Letting Rayna in on the basics was one thing, but letting her further in, admitting this really tough shit? He had to be a goddamn head case. What was with these Chestain women and their gift for filling the air with some subsonic, give-me-all-your-secrets siren song?

"I had the silver spoon, Rayna, but it wasn't enough. I wanted more. I wanted to be more, to stand for something more. Things were happening fast in the world. Afghanistan was still a crazy scene. Terrorists were still infiltrating the Philippines, and Korea was—*is*—a giant pot of insanity." After the adrenaline wore off from saying all that, a beam of understanding hit bull's-eye in his mind. He spoke it in a troubled mutter. "But yeah, maybe I did have a few stars in my eyes."

Her response came equally soft. "There's nothing wrong with that." She shifted again, coming forward to lean her forearms on her pressed knees. "And now that I know this about you, it's much harder for me to say this."

The siren's song hit a nerve-racking discord. Ethan

gripped the lining of both pockets with coiled fingers. "To say what?" The words, low and taut, came from the pit of his gut.

Rayna twisted the hem of her cover-up. "Those stars, Ethan...they need to stop before they get fixed on Ava."

Nice. The second he decided to reconnect with his gut, she sent in *that* bomb of bile. He would normally order the shit into submission and tell himself to get a grip on the melodrama, but Rayna wasn't a weepy megaphone. The stare she wore now was a hundred percent sincere.

"Is it someone else?" After this afternoon, he highly doubted that, but diving for the usual suspects was all his mind could maneuver right now.

"No." Rayna let out a long sigh. "If it was, that might make things easier."

"Great." He pivoted back toward the window. The coastal fog layer, a nighttime fixture this time of year, crept over the water like a Radiohead song. Moody, resigned. "And you didn't think to share this with me back in January?"

"Because it's not really my shit to share, okay? Besides, I thought you'd get the picture, dumbass. It seemed like you did, too. You finally backed off—"

"It was temporary." He swore one of the clouds scowled at him. *Same to you, buddy.* "Sometimes retreating is the best option. Helps for strategy. And stamina."

She groaned. "Did you get that one from Zeke?"

"No. But I'll take that as a compliment."

She nested her head in her fingers and shook it. "So I take it you've made Ava aware of your...newfound stamina?" One of her fingers shot up. "Don't answer that. I forgot about your unique reunion with her at the studio this morning. And your creative self-invite out here, too. And the way you've been guarding her—oops, I mean *watching* her—since we all got here."

He braced a hand against the window. It anchored him from whirling and pinning the woman with a justified glower. "I'm a goal-oriented man. Sometimes my means are...vigorous. But the end to those means is Ava's happiness." The statement acted like an affirmation, calming him enough to turn around. "Ava's had a pretty good day, Rayna. I can promise you that."

Good-scenario reaction? She'd smile, nod, maybe tack on a couple thumbs-up.

Best-scenario reaction? She'd rise, hug him, and officially give him her "Chestain Cuz Blessing."

Greatest-scenario reaction? All of the above plus her help in getting Ava away from the party again.

There were a few more setups in his head, but none included the woman's huffing lurch to her feet. They sure as hell didn't include her piercing glare or twisting lips. "Good day?" she charged. "Yeah, I'll bet. Like a heroin junkie has a *good day* when they can ride the horse for hours on end."

He felt his whole face tightening. "What the hell are you—"

She silenced him by grabbing his hands, gripping with pressure that went beyond anger. She was scared. The tremors beneath her fingers verified it. "She couldn't help herself, Ethan. You're everything she craves, okay? And everything she's terrified to want, ever again."

Voicing his confusion about that wasn't going to help. He stepped toward and sat on the couch, wordlessly beckoning for her to do the same. That gave him time to pull in a much-needed breath.

After Rayna settled, he directed, "Start by defining

everything."

She matched his inhalation before speaking. "She's like a sister to me. I think you know that already. We grew up together. Subsequently, we hit puberty together. And when a girl starts noticing boys in a city like Tacoma—"

"That includes the guys from the base."

She popped a finger to her nose, confirming his direct hit. "We drooled over the army and air force hunks together for years, but by the time our dads allowed us out on dates, I'd had it with the chest-beating shit, thanks to those seven clods who call themselves my brothers."

It wasn't the time or place to point out that the woman's collar had been bestowed by the world's biggest chest beater. This was about Ava and the fact that every instinct in his body was a rocket of anticipation in staring at her cousin. He knew, with burning certainty, Rayna was about to give him a huge key of revelation about Ava's turf-ripper exit today—and likely the glacier she'd been giving him for the last seven months.

He considered himself a patient guy. But telling her to get the hell on with it was a bark that begged to be unleashed off his tongue.

"Ethaaaaannn. Ohmigod, *here* you are!"

The delighted squeal, coming from the freshly opened doorway and the woman who filled it, cranked his tension even higher. "Bella." Screw the bark. He went straight for the snarl. "Look, it's really not—"

"A good idea to avoid your party hosteth." She snaked onto his lap while moaning at her slur, giving him a face full of her barely covered chest—and her vodka-laced breath. "Umm, hosteff. *Hostess.* Yaaayy, I did it!" She waved her fingertips at Rayna. "Hiiii. Are you havin' fun?"

Rayna gave her a polite smile. "Yes, Miss Lanza, we are. Thank you so much for the invitation. Your home is beautiful."

After flashing a "grateful" smile that looked as natural as the lacquer on her nails, Bella swept her gaze back to him. "Do you like it too, my golden arrow?"

"Golden arrow?" Rayna smirked in curiosity before Ethan could hit her with his don't-go-there glare.

"He's the Archer, right?" Bella shifted so she could run a hand across his chest. "Which means he has to have an arrow." She skated her caresses lower. "A long, hot, solid-gold one." Her fingers closed over his crotch.

Rayna wisely stowed her snicker behind a hand. Not that she had the ammunition for long. Ethan snared Bella's wrist and surged to his feet, meaning she had no choice but to follow. "It's time to take this outside, *Miss Lanza.*"

"Mmmhmm," she singsonged. "Whatever you say, Sergeant."

Once he'd hauled her to the terrace, he plunked her onto a padded deck lounger. The sky and the ocean had gone dark now, making electric sconces turn on. Their golden light made Bella's skin look luminous, even in her well-juiced state. Why wasn't he surprised?

He paced to the edge of the terrace and back before looking at her again. "You want me to get you some water? Maybe a pot of coffee?"

"Negatory, sergeant gorgeous." She swung her legs open, one on each side of the chaise, and patted the cushion between them. "I want you to come here and sit with me."

"Not a great idea."

She pouted, again a look rehearsed to perfection. "You used to fink—think—it was a good idea." She slid down until she was prone, hands roaming over her toned, poster-ready body. "You used to like fucking me outside."

"Once," he clarified. "It was once, during spring break, on a beach in Cabo, at two in the morning."

"And it was wonderful."

"It was long ago. We're different people now."

"Uh-huh." She licked her lips. Rubbed her inner thighs. "We certainly are." Her gaze climbed up his form. "*You* are." She stopped at the front closure of his swimsuit. "Sweet *madonna*, Ethan. Have you gotten bigger...everywhere?"

It might be a good thing that she went for the celestial plea. He considered seeking out the saints to boost his own fortitude now. The woman had persistence for a middle name, especially when she'd been drinking. He might need a miracle to get out of this one without pissing her off. A hungover Bella was already going to worsen Ava's day tomorrow; she didn't need a diva who screamed at her every two minutes as well.

Seemed Bella decided not to wait on the screaming. A shriek erupted from her, shattering the festive mood in the villa—and damn near the windows.

Ethan huffed, wondering what toe she stubbed or nail she splintered. When he saw she'd sat up, scooted back, and curled into a trembling ball, instinct drove him to drop next to her. "Bella, what the hell is—"

Her second wail was more ear-piercing than the first.

He was about to run a mental list of what drugs, when combined with vodka, did this to a five-foot-three, ninety-pound woman. But then he heard the boot steps. A lot of them.

What the fuck?

He twisted to glare toward at least ten men who seemed formed from the dark sea itself. They were dressed completely in black, including hoods only exposing eyes. They held their rifles in well-trained grips and advanced on the villa with coordinated precision.

Acting on raw instinct, he jammed Bella behind him. It was the only move he could make before three of the ninjas converged on the chaise. The largest of them stepped forward, wielding a pistol instead of a rifle. He was likely the leader, needing mobility for other purposes. As if that mattered. At the moment, the SIG in the guy's hand was just as dangerous to Ethan.

The bastard verified that himself a second later. "Not another move, my friend, or I'll blow your balls off."

CHAPTER EIGHT

Let the fun begin.

It was Tait Bommer's go-to phrase at the start of any crazy mission or insane infil, but right now, he let the words bounce around in his head only. Because right now, he didn't know what the fuck was happening.

One second, Kell and Zeke had joined him in the dancing shrimp tails act and they were taunting Franzen with an obscene rendition of "All That Jazz." The next, they were backed into the kitchen at the wrong end of mismatched rifles and a couple of assholes taking the basic black Bob Fosse theme to whole new levels. Two more gunmen cornered Rhett, Rebel, and Garrett against the double-wide fridge. Bella Lanza's scream had ripped across the terrace. Her stylist, the woman with whom they'd found Archer in hardcore lip-lock training this morning, was nowhere to be seen.

The other two women in the room, Rayna and Sage, were silent as they got forced into a corner of the living room. The two of them, having spent a year on the run from slavers in Africa and Asia, knew the value of staying calm in a situation like this.

Tait clenched his jaw. He *really* didn't feel like staying calm.

"What the hell is this?" Franzen bellowed. Guess he agreed with the *fuck calm* approach too.

"Shut up." Fosse ninja number one aimed his weapon at

the center of Franz's sizable chest. He didn't shift his focus, even as the trio of attackers from the terrace came in with Ethan and Bella under guard, though he jerked his head at the stockiest of them. "Guess I was right to insist on a full team, after all."

The guy puffed his barrel chest. "I have no fucking idea what happened. I triple checked this. They had a short day on the set. They needed the lot for some special event the suits are throwing. Lanza was going for a wax. She has a standing appointment every two weeks."

Though Bella had traded sloshed-up for terrified, she tossed up a glower. "That's *not* knowledge for public consumption, you ape."

"Says the one who skipped her wax appointment." He snickered.

"Skipped? Really? I'm Italian, moron. I fit it in on my lunch."

"Enough." Another ninja pushed forward. Though he didn't wield a rifle, the heat in his hand was sweet. A SIG, clearly custom, likely untraceable. Damn, it was beautiful.

Cut the gun boner and open your observation deck, Bommer. What kind of details will you be able to relate about this asshole—if you get out of this alive?

As the guy moved into the living room, he hooked a hand around Bella's elbow and dragged her with him. He moved with confident purpose, which meant two things. One, he knew the villa's layout. Two, he'd done shit like this before. A lot. There was a seasoned serration to his voice that Franzen had too, an edge that came with experience. But for some of his men, the assurance was a thin front. They'd been expecting to find Bella alone here. Her impromptu party had turned into their not-so-little mission hitch, whatever the hell their mission was. Unless Bella was hiding half the Louvre somewhere in this place, the force was excessive for a home-invasion robbery.

Again sharing his mental page, Franzen mumbled, "What the fuck is going on?"

"What part of *shut up* did you *not* understand?" barked their guard.

"Yo, Hulk?" SIG man called it from the living room without diverting his attention from Bella, whom he dumped on an ottoman without ceremony. "I believe the gentleman has a good grasp of the situation, as well as our control of it."

Ninja minion huffed. "Damn it, Mag. We have orders to restrain any trouble—"

"That's not trouble, buddy. That's just a question." The guy flicked an almost respectful glance at Franz. "A question to which he won't get the answer, but just a question all the same."

"Magneto, I don't apprec—"

"Shut. Your. Hole. And kindly bring your friends over here." He nodded at minion number two. "Rorschach, grab his six."

Tait barely held back his eye roll. The asswipes might be packing pro-level firearms and using all the right terminology, but superhero mission names? Mixed between the DC and Marvel universes? Arrogant idiots.

They were all guided into the living room and directed to park their asses on the room's two long couches, upholstered in a trendy shade of light blue that was likely named after a mythical bird or tropical resort. Sage and Rayna were brought over as well. Knowing Garrett and Zeke would have their attention dented by the women's presence, Tait focused harder on picking out the weakest links in this weird gumball gang. His vantage point gave him the chance to scope out the remaining pair who kept watch on Runway, while his teammate returned the favor on the two guys assigned to him. He ran a visual on the remaining soldiers too. Their tail man had stayed on the terrace, sticking to a shadow behind some palms to watch over the beach access to the villa. But that couldn't be all of them. He suspected Magneto had already waved in two or three more men to search the other areas of Bella's home.

Magneto. Seriously? And I'm Professor X, asshole.

"Okay, l-look." Though Bella's words wobbled, she crossed her legs and folded her hands to look like she was simply being grilled by a nosy talk show host. His impression was intensified by the woman's charm-drenched smile. "You boys seem nice, so I'll be straight-up. I don't keep a lot of valuables at the house, but there's a safe in the library and another in the bedroom. They're both controlled by double passwords, but I can go with you and—"

"Dear fuck," growled Hulk. "Can I work on shutting *her* up now too?"

Bella glared like he'd farted. "I beg your pardon?"

"My pardon isn't what you need, diamond diva. It's my mercy."

"Spare me, *pompinara*. At least I earned every one of my diamonds, instead of sneaking into someone's house like a rat cocksucker and stealing them!"

Hulk snorted. "Honestly? You sticking with that, babe?"

Bella tossed her head, dramatically swinging her thick black hair. "What the hell is your problem?"

"You're fiddle-fucking around, Miss La-La Lanza. *That's* my problem." He advanced on Bella by a step. "Stop pretending you're mortified that we're here and tell us where he stashed the codes."

That seemed to seriously stun her. "He who? What codes?"

"Enough." The roar came from leader man. Hell. At least the guy had the Magneto boom down pretty well. "H, you're trying my patience."

The guard huffed. "And she isn't?"

"I said *enough*."

Tait swapped a knowing glance with Ethan. In it, they acknowledged a couple of things. Number one: big bad call sign or not, Magneto had trouble controlling his team. Even without Hulk giving him this grief, the guys who'd gone out to recon the house hadn't radioed in or returned yet. Two, was *anyone* in this band of bastards in agreement on what the hell they were doing here? He didn't care about the answer to that. Runway's piercing blue gaze, double blinking in return to the identical move from Tait, said he didn't either. They were both ready to surge when Hulk decided to get pissy again. The wait likely wouldn't be long.

Unnervingly, their bulky guard fell into a brooding silence. He decided to actually watch them for once too. Tait fought his impatience by gritting his teeth and watching Magneto kneel next to Bella. As the man lowered his body, he did the same with his gun. With the hand that had been fitted to the SIG's grip, he now held the star's hand with the gentleness of a lover. Tait knew better and tensed because of it. Fuck. No way to flip the bitch of fate on these guys as long as Mag Man had his paws directly on Bella.

"Miss Lanza." The man's tone was a respectful request—on the surface. The underline of force was undeniable, even to Bella. Tension shoved its way along her shoulders. He continued, "I apologize for my associate. He can be uncouth. But he's also right. We're not here to take your jewelry or your art." He lifted his hold from her hand to her chin. "You know what we're here for, don't you?"

She tried to tug away. The man held her firm. Even from where he sat, Tait watched her pupils dilate in deeper fear. "No," she finally rasped. "P-Please. I have no idea what you're talking about."

Magneto sighed. Lowered his hand. And picked up his pistol again. He stroked the barrel along the outside of her thigh. "Let's approach this a different way."

Bella whimpered. "What the hell do you want from me? I really don't know what—"

"Ssshhh. I just want to talk. To ask you a few questions. Answer me honestly, and I won't have to use this on your kneecap, all right?"

Bella managed a jerky nod. A couple of years ago, Tait would've added a chuckle right along to it. The guy he'd been back then was even more a skeptic than he was now, hardly believing in the validity of shit like intuition, let alone someone's ability to discern a true lie. After all, he'd lied to his own father since the age of five and gotten away with it. But twenty-one years after that first fib, he'd met Ethan Archer and the man's mental polygraph machine. For all he knew, Mag Man was one of those hyperintuitive freaks too.

"Wh-What do you want to know?" Bella stammered into the man's long silence.

Magneto leaned back a little, again conveying the appearance that he was just here for a friendly chat. "You did some entertaining here last night as well, didn't you?"

Tait traded another glimpse with Ethan. This time, puzzlement consumed the guy's face. He saw the same thinking in Franz and the rest of the guys. Hadn't Bella proclaimed to them all this morning that she didn't invite people over to the villa enough?

Bella squirmed, now that her exaggeration had been caught. "I wouldn't call it entertaining," she justified. "I...had a friend over. For a fast drink."

"Which turned into a little slumber party."

The woman flashed apprehensive eyes at Runway. Part of her invitation to all of them tonight had been rooted in her desire to rekindle old flames with him. There was no secret about that, though the same didn't seem to apply toward her drinking buddy from last night. With an awkward smile, she explained, "Well, we had more than one drink. And we got to talking late. And I do have three extra bedrooms here."

"But Mr. Lemare didn't stay in any of those rooms, did he?"

Her anxiety hitched into blatant alarm. She compensated for it by going for a haughty sniff. "Mr. Lemare and I are required to be close. It's essential that we're on the same page, creatively and strategically, for *Dress Blues* to work as well as it does. Besides that, we share the same heritage. He is my friend as well as my producer."

"And your lover."

"That's none of your damn business."

The guy shrugged. "Not usually. And quite frankly, sweetheart, I don't care if he fucked you sideways doggie style while swinging from the chandelier. I just need to know what the guy gave you for safekeeping between tossing out the condom and sharing your morning shower."

Buh-bye, terrified starlet. Hello, enraged diva. It would've surprised no one if Bella grew full claws before spitting, "You're repugnant. I refuse to dignify a word of that with—"

"Oh, for fuck's sake." He jerked his head at Hulk and one of the guards who covered Sage and Rayna, the one Tait had pegged as a skittish colt. Didn't seem so skittish now. He surged forward to help Hulk in pinning Bella's wrists back. "What you find repugnant is of no damn interest to me," he went on, as breezy as if discussing whether LA would ever get its own football team again. "I just want to know what Enzo Lemare gave you after he slept with you. And of course, where you're hiding it for him."

A gasp from the atrium was loud enough to silence him. Since the atrium was directly behind their couch, Tait couldn't see the source of the sound, though the pitch of pure shock made him guess that the recon team had just found Ava Chestain.

Sure enough, the woman was dragged toward Magneto by a couple of his ninjas. She fought their clutches with rebellious little yanks, making them both grunt—and screwing a grimace onto Runway's face that Tait had never seen before. Shit. The guy's lips curled so tight over his locked teeth, Tait wondered if Ethan would chomp right into the jugular of these guys if either of them gave Ava so much as a broken nail.

He didn't have to wait long for that answer.

As the goons pulled at her, Ava fought them again. Her mass of dark hair fell back, making her whole face visible, including the shiner that bloomed beneath her left eye.

Ethan shot up like fifty rounds went off in his ass. Forget that. All fifty blazed in his eyes, wild and incensed, even after one of the ninjas slammed him back.

"What the *fuck* did you do to her?"

One of Ava's guards jerked his head over. "Crazy bitch did it to herself. Did a pinball bounce on the wall and bathroom floor after I found her hiding in the master shower."

Ava's face sparked with victory. "After I took you down with me, asshole."

The guard growled as he searched for a good response for saving face.

He got cut off by the wails of angry sirens. And right after that, the approaching thunder of a helicopter over the ocean.

Bella took her own turn to gasp. Sage and Rayna locked hands. Tait looked at Ethan, who still stared at Ava like her whole nose had been sliced off. But Ava kept *her* gaze glued on her main guard. With a smirk growing across her lips.

"Did I forget to tell you I did that *after* I called the cops?"

"Damn it." He grunted it in unison with his partner.

Magneto slowly rose to his feet. Tait appraised the movement in curiosity. The guy looked like he was the damn water heater inspector and Bella simply the pilot light that gave him grief. "Well, this puts a dent in things," he muttered.

Bewilderment made camp in Tait's psyche. Looked like the other guys on the team commiserated. Fifteen minutes ago, these wannabe superheroes had materialized out of the night and infiltrated the villa with, he reluctantly admitted, damn fine precision. But now their leader was twirling a hand in the air, finishing it by jabbing a finger back toward the beach, like they were all supposed to just cut and run?

"Huh?" He muttered it as the ninjas did just that, hustling out one by one. He recognized the disappointment in his voice, thickening as he repeated it in Franz's direction this time. "Are we really just watching this? Captain, aren't we gonna do *anything*?"

Franz tossed a dark stare. "You want to run that risk with innocents present, T-Bomb? Especially when *armed* support is on the way? I'm frustrated as hell too, but maybe you know something I don't. Maybe that's your twenty-two millimeter thug stopper in those swim trunks and not your dick. If so, then go get 'em, cowboy."

He huffed. "Damn it, we're trained for this."

"And so is the LAPD."

Fuck. He hated it when Franzen was right. For the second time today, his mind flicked backward in time, to summer days of nearly twenty years ago, when he and Fire Hamilton were feeling ballsy. They'd sneak into Old Man Stromberg's orchard and concoct epic alien battles from a hay bale fort. They'd just be set to launch their *big attack* when Fire's mom would call him in for dinner. Tait would trudge home, knowing dinner *wouldn't* be waiting, which was no biggie to his deflated stomach.

He felt the same way now. It sucked ass enough that the ninja assholes had ruined a once-in-a-lifetime invitation to a celebrity's Malibu beach house, but they didn't have the decency to make the whole thing about something exciting like drugs, jewelry, money, or even sneaky paparazzi shots. Now *that* would've been cool. They would've been the shit back at base once those pictures broke, showing them kicking back in Bella Lanza's fancy digs, eating grilled shrimp with the glamorous star...

He was about to give these whack-offs another heavy snort when one of the minions bumped him in the haste of their retreat. And damn it if the shithead didn't smell a lot like salon-quality hair conditioner. And *fuck* if the guy didn't have the most perfect, heart-shaped ass he'd ever—

"Gaaahh!"

He was so far over the cliff from shock, he couldn't even swear right. Apparently fate wasn't sticking it and twisting it enough at that, because the ninja stopped and froze—letting him gawk longer at that beautiful backside. Letting him gaze up over hips and a waist that now, under second and third consideration, were too damn sleek for a guy on a team this well-trained.

Tait blinked. How had he missed this bozo before now? And why couldn't he stop staring at the bastard, unable to control the sparks of strange recognition that popped through him, a case of déja vu set to his mind's own speed metal song?

And why, as the guy turned back to stare at *him*, did he imagine that the space between the ninja's hood and jacket parted enough for him to glimpse a ponytail—a coiled braid of black, lavender, and silver hair?

"Holy fuck."

He rushed to his feet. Stumbled forward. Déja vu? Screw that mystical shit. He recognized that ass from solid, real memories—because he'd seen it before. Completely naked. Getting Dommed into a thousand beautiful shades of red, in a dungeon a thousand miles away, on a cold autumn night that felt thousands of *years* away. The Dom had been his buddy Zeke, and he'd been the scene monitor who'd never forget that submissive as long as he lived. He'd jacked off a few hundred times to mental replays of that scene. To thoughts about that woman and her daiquiri-in-a-bottle hair shit, and the way that tricolored hair wove around her breasts like dark seaweed on a pale mermaid. He even fantasized about hurting her the way Z had, just to make her smile like she had after their session...

just to give her soul everything it so clearly needed from all that. And yeah, he thought a lot about holding her again too. About curling her against him like he had when Z had to leave so suddenly after the session, feeling like fucking Zeus when she'd let him.

But that woman had been hauled off to prison ten days later. She'd aided the criminal who'd almost murdered Zeke in a revenge-driven zeal to capture Rayna back into white slavery. She'd finally had a surge of sanity about all that and was able to use her proximity to the monster to aid the police in bringing him down, but sometimes a right couldn't cancel a wrong. Tait had walked her to the police van. It had been a freezing, miserable day, but crazily, the sun sliced through the clouds as she'd turned to tell him goodbye. It had haloed across her head and glimmered in her eyes, stunning him into silence with their brilliant purple light. Sadness yet peace, resignation yet despair... It was all there, a goddamn universe in her gaze... and they'd locked it away.

Two states, seven months, and thousands of miles later, a masked soldier turned and looked at him—and hit him with that universe again.

"Holy *fuck*."

There was no hesitation to it this time. Only his laugh of raw joy.

The soldier gave him a desperate shake of his—*her*—head. Right before she spun for the door to the terrace and raced through it.

Tait didn't think twice about giving chase.

He caught her a couple of feet past the terrace's light. Now that he had her secure, he let his mind give way to the full, phenomenal reality of this. Of *her*.

"Luna." He breathed the word. "God*damn*. Luna."

He got to rejoice in that for about a second. After she *thwacked* a hand across his face at full strength, he got busy dealing with his stinging skin, his bleeding pride—and the violet glower that bore into him with the subtlety of a power drill.

"Stay where you are, Weasley. I don't want to hurt you."

As he watched her trudge down the sand and blend into the night, he failed to erase the music of her voice from his head—especially as she'd wrapped it around the nickname that she'd given him that night he'd held her in the dungeon. *Weasley.* He'd laughingly accepted the title, reminding her that in the world of teenage wizards from where she'd pulled the name, Weasley was the one who finished off the tale with the beautiful genius witch on his arm.

He laughed again now but had no idea why. As he turned and got ready to face the curious gapes of the other guys, he muttered, "It's a little too late for that, woman."

CHAPTER NINE

Ava crossed the threshold from her garage into her kitchen and peered around in bewilderment. Turning the light on over the sink didn't help the confusion. She ran fingers over the folded dishtowel, the coffee cup she'd scrubbed and put in the drainer this morning, the miniature herb garden that grew in a wood box on the windowsill. Though Zeke and Rayna had gotten up after her and had still been snoozing in the guest bedroom, everything was exactly as she'd left it sixteen hours ago, at six a.m.

But nothing was the same.

She folded her arms around herself, feeling like she hugged an alien. When she'd left this morning, she'd been sore from pushing it hard at the gym. Now she ached in newer, stranger ways. Her face throbbed from her face-plant during the struggle with Bella's strange intruders. Her arms carried bruises from where the jerks had grabbed her. But below her waist, the pain took on a different edge. It had been months since her last date, let alone one with a man she'd allow in her bed. Technically, that wasn't where Ethan had been either— but her body, with its most tender tissues aching in the most intimate ways, sure as hell didn't know the difference.

And neither did her heart.

That had to explain the nervous jolt of her stomach as Ethan entered in her wake. His footsteps, though mellow, were loud thumps in the silence of the house. Rayna and Zeke wouldn't be home for a while, as a bunch of the guys were still ravenous after their dinner was interrupted at Bella's. He pressed against her from behind, ensuring the dervishes in her stomach now formed parades through the rest of her body. Without a word, he offered back her car keys, which dangled from one of his impossibly long fingers. She murmured her thanks for him driving her home, the only words she could seem to get out while her pussy throbbed from the memory of that finger exploring her with deep, dominating thrusts.

So much for the dervishes being fair about this.

Ethan didn't move for a long moment. *Dios*, he felt good there, so large and strong behind her. "You doing okay?" he asked quietly.

"Uhhh, yeah." She forced the casual tone as she turned to face him. "I'm...just wiped. After the cops asked all those questions, and after Bella—"

She chopped herself short. One side of Ethan's mouth quirked as he drawled, "Go ahead, say it. After Bella added more bling to the tragedy queen crown? Spread on a new layer to the melodrama pie? Made Sarah Bernhardt roll over in her grave and barf worms?"

She covered her mouth and giggled. "Something along those lines."

Through another thick pause, he simply stared at her. When his study dropped to her mouth, her lips tingled with excitement, awareness. Oh God, how she wanted him to kiss her...

He pushed away instead, pacing to the dining nook and bracing his hands on the back of a chair. "That welt on your face really makes me want to punch a hole in the wall, but it gave back a little, at least. Punched my ticket out of *Casa de*

Drama. So now *I* owe *you.*"

"Oh, shut up."

She finished rolling her eyes in time to catch the teasing glint of his smile. But as their gazes locked, his lips sobered. There were no other lights on except the little one she'd just flipped, making his eyes look like a pair of sapphire crystals. His nostrils widened, taking air deep into his chest. He looked like he wanted to pounce on her any second. Ava's breath burned in and out of her lungs while she imagined him doing just that. Like breathing was doing her any good right now. The air between them now felt like soup. The hot, thick, stomach-warming kind.

"I'd better call for that cab," he finally said. "Franz said something about going to the La Brea Tar Pits tomorrow."

"Y-Yeah," she stammered. "Sure. That's a good idea."

Neither of them moved. Their silence was so potent, a wave crashed on the beach and sounded like it was a foot away instead of a block. And the soup pot went right back to simmering.

"Ava?"

"Huh?"

"I need to use your phone." He held his cell up. The screen was black. "Mine's dead, remember?"

"Shit." She attempted a little laugh. "Sorry." On knees that felt like rubber, she crossed to her bedroom door and pushed it open. The creak sounded like cannon fire. Normally, she loved all the eccentricities of the classic Hermosa bungalow but tonight, everything felt new and strange, dipped in a bath of Ethan Archer's presence. "It's...errrm...on the nightstand, under the magazine." She felt safer hanging out in the doorway as he lifted up last month's *Vogue* and toppled the fabric swatches that were resting on top of it. "Sorry," she repeated. "The, umm, other magazine."

She forced herself to dash in, fish the phone from beneath the latest issue of *W*, and jab it up at him. Ethan accepted it though didn't do anything with the device. Once more, he barely moved. Once more, the corner of his mouth tugged up. And once more, he looked dangerously fascinated with her. And so beautifully kissable.

Shit, shit shit. She tore her gaze away, refusing to put together the facts—*this man, my bedroom, hours until dawn*—into a conclusion that gave her any action plan except getting her ass into bed as soon as the cab came for him. The fallen swatches were a good distraction. She dropped to her knees and began piling them back on top of each other.

Ethan still didn't get the hint. There was no telltale dial tone overhead, no beeping 4-1-1 to ask for a connection to the cab company.

Instead, he crouched next to her. Because *that* made a lot of sense. Ava kept the grouse to herself and finished reassembling the stack.

"What is all that?" he asked.

"Fabric samples of the dresses Bella's wearing to the haute couture shows in Paris in a few weeks. She needs makeup and hair looks for each ensemble."

"Which you're supposed to design."

"Duh."

"In your spare time."

"Well, yeah." She rose to set down the squares on the nightstand again but made the move too fast, giving herself a head rush. Wisely, she kept that tidbit to herself as she plopped onto the bed, next to where he lingered on the floor, shaking his head with a peeved glower. "Okay, what?" she snapped, wondering if she'd regret it.

"You seriously have to ask that?" He stressed the point with a growl. "C'mon. Custom-designed makeup? For some stupid oats show?"

Regret was definitely crossed off the reactions list. Laughter, full and bright and consuming, was another thing. She flopped backward, unable and unwilling to stop the mirth. "Not oats." She giggled. "*Haute*. It means *high* in French, as in *high fashion*." She flicked her knee, gently clipping the side of his head with it. "I can't believe foreign language fanboy doesn't know that."

He snorted. "Paid my dues to the couture crowd during my polo years."

"Hmmm." She smiled at the ceiling from the image that bloomed in her head. Ethan's ass, hard and high, shown off to perfection by a pair of those tight white polo pants. His long legs tucked into a pair of rugged black boots. His sculpted abs hugged by a shirt in royal blue, complementing his eyes... "I'll bet you were good at it."

After a second, he answered wistfully, "I liked my horse."

She rose and rested back on her wrists. After nudging him again, she flashed a little grin. "I bet he liked you too."

Ethan turned his face forward. His profile went tight, the noble lines only more beautiful with the new definition. When he spoke, that quiet determination branded his words too. "I don't want to talk about polo."

"Okay. I can just teach you some more French words."

"I want to talk about tonight."

Tension shot its way back through her muscles. "Wow. You know how to throw bombs of all kinds, don't you?"

That did nothing to loosen him. "Ava, when those asswads found you in Bella's bedroom, they didn't...try anything, did they?"

His tone, which clicked from unswerving to unsettled in twenty seconds, at first confused her. When his intimation finally registered, she blurted, "Oh, *no*. God, no." She wanted to laugh again but saw he was nowhere near the same mindset. "They were on a mission, Ethan. That goal definitely didn't include a sloppy-seconds quickie with Ms. Lanza's stylist."

She waited for his relieved sigh. It never came. His scowl darkened as he snapped, "You're not a sloppy second. Do *not* say shit like that around me, Ava."

She scooted back against the headboard. "Yes, Sir."

That earned her a sharp uptick of his left brow. After another moment of consideration, he pushed up onto the bed with her. Ava tucked her knees in front of her chest, hoping it bought her an instant to come up with a line of such perfect wit, he'd have no choice about dropping his moody scrutiny. But her brain had officially hit the Pause button, and the user's manual had come with an extra warning: *Engaging button will induce endless fidgeting and suck all the air from your lungs. Use with caution.*

Her head actually did swim a little. Here she was, in her most personal space, watching him fill it...as she'd dreamed of him doing so often. Here *he* was, dark and glorious, a fantasy fulfilled against the backdrop of her very real life in its yellow-and-aqua normalcy. How many times had she thought of him with her head against these pillows...and touched her most sensitive folds while imagining his hands on her skin and his long, thick cock inside her core...

"Those words roll so easily off your tongue, Miss

Chestain."

There was no moment needed to interpret his meaning this time. She dared to look into his eyes for her response. "You're the first person I've ever given them to, Sergeant."

He pivoted, tucking in a knee to face her more fully. "Because you want to respect me with them?"

She nodded slowly. Thanks to her thudding heart, it was all she could muster. Dear God, what was she doing? She couldn't dance on this edge again with him. He'd invaded her head once today. Filled her body. Made her scream with exquisite pleasure. He'd given her incredible new fantasies for nights in this room...to be revisited alone.

Alone was good. Was what she'd fought for. Had moved two states and over a thousand miles from that damn military base to achieve.

"But I don't feel respected."

She gave him a double take. A real, utterly lame double take. Luckily, she was too pissed to be embarrassed. "Excuse me?"

"I'd rather not." His features took on the texture of golden marble. Smooth. Entrancing. Beautiful. But deadly if used for force. Imagine *that*.

"Rather not what?" she demanded.

"Excuse you." He curled his hands over the tops of her knees. His fingers, long and confident, spread and stretched like flesh cages. He planted his chin on top of them, which brought their faces within inches of each other. "I'd prefer to keep you right here so we can easily move to the next subject."

Before she could sputter a syllable of protest, he reached and stroked her jaw and then her cheeks. He used just the tips of his fingers, with such soft purpose...the exact touch he'd used to catch her tears in the wine room this afternoon.

Mierda. Why hadn't she seen this coming? Remembered it likely *would* be coming after his growled promise as he'd let her get dressed? *This is far from over, Ava.*

"M-Maybe we really should call it a night."

"Not until we discuss this afternoon."

"Ethan—"

"You said some troubling things, Ava."

She yearned to jerk away. And damn it, she would have if he'd used any weapons other than those caressing fingers, that intent stare. It was genius and devious in the same move, and she was helpless against it. She fought a furious flush at remembering the shit that had gone down after the magic in the wine room.

"You said some troubling things too," she retorted. "And it wasn't fair."

"Why?"

She squeezed her eyes against the new intensity in his stare. Sucked in a sharp breath. Her chest hurt. Her head hurt. He was storming her heart's fortress with a titanium battering ram, letting in light to corners that didn't want it. Making her cringe from the blaring heat and paralyzing fear. She couldn't let him do this. *I'm sorry, Ethan. I can't.*

"You know why," she whispered. A weak laugh escaped after it. "I made you feel 'real'? I 'zapped your spirit'? We've been given a 'treasure'? *Qué no?* What universe are you living in, Ethan?"

Whew. She'd said it. Now she just had to brace for his enraged male huff, followed by the wounded kiss-off and the flight to the next room, where he'd make that call for the cab before stomping out to the curb. Then she'd be able to curl into these pillows, bawl her eyes into puffy slits, and start the disgusting process of pulling up her heart's drawbridge again.

A moment passed. Another.

He didn't move. Even his damn fingers stayed put, catching the tears she couldn't hold back anymore.

"What happened, Ava?"

Just three words. They said nothing. But they asked everything. "What the hell are you talking about?" she retorted.

His tone was like his touch, tender but unyielding. "I'm pretty sure your spirit didn't always have such a huge wall around it. So what happened?"

She gulped again. The sting in her eyes was worse than a thousand bees. "Don't." The sound of her plea was mortifying. "Please don't."

His silence wasn't reassuring. A moment later, as he curled his knuckles against her skin, he proved her instinct right. "Maybe the better question is...*who* happened?"

A crater opened in her chest. It filled with memories dredged like slime from the bottom of a swamp, making her clutch his forearms for purchase. Stupid...so stupid. He'd caused this agony. How could he help drag her from it? But he did. His skin was warm, his grip didn't waver, his muscles were filled with surety. Of course they were. They'd been trained to take down the baddest of the bad guys, to keep this entire country safe. They'd keep *her* safe, right? They'd take care of her, hold her, never leave her—

Never demand what he just had of her.

"No." She shook her head desperately. "I...I can't..." She stopped and blinked at him. "How the hell did you even know..."

"I didn't." He tilted her face up to scan every inch of it. "Not for certain. But I do now."

She tried to jerk away. "Good for you, Nancy Drew. Proud of yourself?"

His lips pressed into each other. "Not particularly. Not yet."

She squirmed again. And, once more, didn't get very far. "Let me up and go call your damn cab, Sergeant."

His lips slanted in challenge. "Not until you answer my question."

"*Not* happening." She nodded toward the door. "If you're really not leaving, then have fun sleeping on the couch."

Without a word, he slipped his hands back to her knees— then pushed them apart. He kept them spread by shoving his own against them and then locked her down by twisting his ankles around hers. She grunted in astonishment. He'd kicked his flip-flops off at the door just as she had, freeing his toes to dig into her insteps with irrefutable force. Did Special Forces training now include toe calisthenics, too?

"Fun?" The word was a growl, his punctuation a dark chuckle. "I like playing, sunshine, but not like this." He stretched his hands to brace her again, though this time he caught her by the wrists to lock her against the pillows. "And right now, playtime is officially over."

The tears evaporated. In their place, she seethed at him with hard huffs. Several yanks of her arms and legs brought the realization that he was serious about keeping her here. Flat in her own bed. Trapped against her own pillows. By a soldier with muscles like boulders, a grip like steel, and even toes that were recruited for his cause.

Terror should have been declaring siege on her bloodstream, but she was too furious for that. Her rage grew to include even her own body, which acknowledged the intimate weight of his with a horrible betrayal. Her inner thighs ached and clenched. Her vagina started to pulse and drip. Even her nipples started to throb, awakening for him, stretching for him.

"Ethan, what the hell are you—"

"Don't you mean *Sir*?" He charged it from lips that barely moved, again hovering inches above hers. "Two minutes ago, you were all about that, Ava. Eight hours ago, you freely tossed out the same words. And seven months ago, you begged me to trap you against a tree and control every move you made." He dipped closer, so near that she could see the flecks of black smoke that fought with the cobalt fire in his eyes. His voice glided around her with the same sinuous intent. "Your need for submission is beautiful, breath-stealing. And god*damn*it do I want to be the Dom who delivers for you, but..."

She wanted to scream when he cut himself off with a harsh growl. Her lungs sawed on air, caught in her body's civil war: her soul and her sex against her head and her pride. He'd just given her the perfect opportunity to save the latter, too. She just had to stay silent, continuing the charade that what he'd just done hadn't been the emotional equivalent of dangling solid-gold Gucci heels in her face. No, worse. She'd longed for a Dom longer than the shoes. A man who took the word seriously, who would accept her submission with that same reverence, who would use their exchange to unlock a connection like no other...

That connection doesn't exist, Ava. Not with a man like Ethan Archer. Not even with a Dom like him. He wears camouflage to work, remember? Delete him from the list. Delete him from your life.

"But what?"

The civil war had its winner. Her lips had fallen in with

her lust. She heard a disgusted sigh echoing in her psyche as she urged Ethan on with the only method she had available: a pleading gaze. She watched him absorb it into the depths of his own before dipping his face toward her, wrapping her deeper in his power with every inch he closed in.

"You want to open the door, baby, but you're missing the key." His murmur was still molten, mesmerizing. "You want to call me 'Sir' and mean it and know the power that comes from it? Then you have to earn it...with your honesty. By talking to me. By letting me in." He brushed his lips against her forehead. "I know you somehow think I can open this up and read it, but I can't. Not what you lock away from me. Not what you won't let me see."

His feather-soft kisses loosened chunks of conflict through her mind. She shuddered as every piece fell. "I know," she told him in a whisper. She'd never meant two words more. "I know. You can't give me anything more than what I give you."

His brows hunched. "So why do you say that like it's a deployment to Siberia?"

She gave a dark laugh. "Good comparison. Damn accurate, actually." As she finished, their gazes tangled again. Her heart slammed against her ribs. Looking at the man was like getting hit by a blue laser. "Ethan, I can't lie and tell you that submission isn't my dream...but I can't go back there. I *cannot* dig all of it up again. I worked too damn hard to bury it, to leave it and make this life in its place. So unless you want to step up for a mission...to...Siberia..."

Her syllables slowed and then stopped as the man pushed up, releasing his hold on her arms so he could yank off his T-shirt with a pair of hard tugs. He stripped off his dog tags too and then wrapped the shirt around them and hurled the whole wad out into the dining room.

Ay dios mio. Every rippled inch of his torso was no less resplendent than this afternoon, when she'd had just the dim light of the wine room to help her gaze. The slice of light from her kitchen helped now, making it more impossible to reclaim her pulse from her bloodstream as he braced his hands to the tops of the dual ridges that dipped beneath his shorts.

"Let me make something clear." His posture alone told her to interrupt him at her own peril. "Missions are what I do for a living—and that doesn't define this." He emphasized that by pinging a finger between his chest and hers. "It isn't even in here anymore." He swung the finger toward the door. "It's out there, okay?"

Exasperation surged. She'd heard enough. She *had* enough. "Damn it, Ethan." She tried getting away from him again but only got in a hard jab to his chest. "It's *not* 'out there.'" Was he seriously living that high in the clouds? Or maybe he'd eaten some amoeba in the Mexican seafood that gave him crazy delusions. "It's never 'out there' with you guys. Your survival depends on it being right *here* and *here*"—she pointed at his sternum and forehead before sweeping her finger toward the room—"which turns *this* into a pretty convenient op target, right?" As the words spilled, so did her bitterness, stemming from the truth of every word she blurted. "I mean, why not?" Her breath wobbled. "Easy insertion point, yeah? Simple exfil too. After you're done, you can just compartmentalize it all to a back drawer in the brain, and soon, it's easy to forget it ever happ—"

The torrent of his lips, wild and consuming, didn't just drown her words. He drenched every thought in her head and sensation in her body. Surely the flood had been forged by a volcano, for his mouth was as scalding as a surge of magma from a burning core. He was everywhere, fusing his tongue and lips to hers with rolling waves of sensual invasion.

Ava mewled in protest. It didn't stop him by a beat. She raised a hand to pummel his shoulder. He seized her fist and slammed it into the mattress. Her mind ignited in fury. Her blood detonated in white-hot arousal. Maybe that was why she tried the same move with the other hand. Maybe it was why her stomach flipped when he handled it in the same way, adding a harsh growl this time.

No more than a minute passed before he lifted his mouth from hers.

Sixty seconds in which everything had changed.

The man who'd joked with her during the drive from Bella's? Gone. The Dom who'd silently brooded at her during the party? Disappeared. Even the half-panther lover from the wine room, who'd just popped in for a cameo in her own kitchen, had fled the building. This creature was someone new. Some*thing* new. Her breath snagged, caught on thorns of confusion and even fear as she struggled for a definition that fit him now. Impossible. Anger didn't begin to describe the ferocity of his gaze. His focus had reset to the power of a thousand, every degree zeroed in on her.

On a ruthless grunt, he shifted his body so her feet were freed from his—because he pinned her lower body with his crotch instead.

"*Ay, Dios!*" She gasped in punctuation. Even through his shorts and her jeans, his cock pulsed with enough force to tease the swollen ridge of her clit. It was bliss and torture in a single second.

"My thoughts exactly." Ferocity clawed every note of his

voice. "But I'm not sure God can save either one of us right now."

"Wh-What the hell are you—"

"I tried to do this the decent way, sunshine." His jaw tightened in proportion to his grip. "I asked nice. One word, one name, was all I wanted. We were going to sit here and just talk about it. I stripped the tags off, threw them out the door. I wanted you to have nothing but me, committed to knowing more about you. But you wouldn't let it go. Apparently I wear those sergeant's stripes on my fucking forehead, because that's all you see. It's all you *want* to see."

She slammed her head to the side and gritted back more tears, accepting every word of the accusation. And why not? They were true. "Some things can't be changed." She prayed he heard the apology in her voice. "Some windows can't be opened, damn it. They're sealed shut, and that's how people are doomed to see things."

His angry breath seemed to fill the room. "Yeah? Well, that's what hammers are for."

CHAPTER TEN

Ethan watched Ava wrestle with that threat, licking her lips in hesitant curiosity but still not looking back at him. That was for the best right now. He couldn't remember a time when he'd been in a woman's bedroom, just a sundress and bikini away from having her naked and screaming *Yes, Sir* nonstop but too enraged to make a single move.

Damn it, he hated mental smoke screens. In prisoners, the maneuver was maddening, but at least those poor shits had an excuse. From Ava, it was an insult. A bomb launched for maximum damage, intended to drive him back, generated from panic that rivaled any he'd felt from the poor morons they captured on missions. Fear that pushed at the realm of dread.

Of what?

Of *him*?

How? Why? Damn it, she'd been in that wine room this afternoon too. She'd had the same hours as him to remember every one of those incredible minutes and every second of the connection they'd forged. To realize the enormity of the trust she'd given him and the explosion they'd created because of it. And now she was talking about super glue on her windows?

Well, there was more than one way to open a goddamn window.

He didn't give her any time to deliberate on his meaning. Or, more importantly, to develop a defense against him. While she still blinked in analysis of the hammer reference, he reared up and planted on his haunches—and took the bodice panels of her sundress with him. The little buttons made like buckshot all over the room, backed by her high gasp.

"*Caramba!* Ethan! What the hell are you—"

She stopped herself with another choke as he continued ripping down the middle of her skirt. He was glad she kept sputtering for a couple of seconds, because the sight of her light-bronze curves, tucked to perfection inside a halter bikini top and a string-tie bottom, had his tongue struggling for coordination too. Thank fuck his brain wasn't stopped at the same red light. It hit the gas pedal right toward Domination Highway, and he enjoyed every second of the ride.

"Ethan?" He looped a sarcastic edge on it. "Who's that?" After pushing away the torn sides of the dress, he leaned and caught her dropped chin with a thumb, redirecting her eyes back at him. "You're going to call me *Sir* for a while." He slid his other hand back to stroke the valley between her ear and her nape, a place he'd rapidly learned as one of her sensual hot buttons. "If you have a problem with that, tell me now."

A ragged breath shuddered up her throat. "Bastard."

He let his lips quirk up. "No. It's *Sir*, remember?"

"Sir Bastard."

He chuckled. The laugh came from relief as much as amusement. She wasn't going to toss him out. Not yet. That gave him hope that this might work...that a taste of what they could physically be as Dom and sub would crack open her emotional ramparts too.

"Hmm." He drew back again, dragging his hands over her breasts, stomach, and thighs as he went, letting his fingers play at the ties of her swimsuit. "For that, sassy baby, you won't get my help getting out of the rest of this."

Her nipples turned to small stones through the bikini top, though stubborn fires still flared in her eyes. "You mean I may actually get to wear it again?"

His hands were positioned beneath her thighs. Perfect. Two sharp pinches to the flesh just beneath her ass elicited a lovely little yelp as well as her renewed attention. "Take off your clothes, Ava," he ordered evenly. "Now."

He watched another skirmish cross her face. Part of her, that scared shitless girl who'd shed those tears on his fingers ten minutes ago, clearly clamored to give him the kiss-off to hell and beyond. But the other part, the woman who'd been longing for submission since well before their forest kiss, responded to the command like a kitten shown to a cream waterfall. She didn't just want this. She needed it. The rapid rise and fall of her breasts, which she bared so beautifully for him by untying her bikini top, betrayed that. She was more demure about revealing the treasure beneath her bikini bottom, but he caught a long enough glance at the shimmering tissues to know cream wasn't just flowing figuratively here.

The conclusion, beautiful as it was, laid down a conundrum. How did he give her what she needed without just handing over what she craved? How did he bash through her window without breaking her completely? And how did he do it all without giving in to the lust to simply spread her wide and fuck her so deeply, she wouldn't remember anyone's name except his? But that was no different than feeding a buddy the answers to an exam. No lesson learned. No trust bonded. No connection forged.

Connection. He couldn't believe the word now echoed in his mind. It had been a long damn time since he'd even hoped for such a thing. Years since he'd met a woman who seemed perfect for it on all the levels for which he longed. It seemed unreal that he took in the naked splendor of such a woman now.

Yeah. He needed to do this right. For both of them.

Which added another hurdle in the challenge course. Her bedroom wasn't a dungeon with play toys on the walls.

Or was it?

Available resources. It was a key directive of any soldier's training, especially once a guy was going for his beret. It came in handy now. Draped over the footboard of her bed were a dozen scarves in various colors and weights. He leaned back and scooped them all off, fast selecting the one he planned on using first. It was made of soft but strong fabric, meant to stay in place once tied. And it was all black.

"Perfect," he murmured.

"For what?" she queried, though one glance into her eyes, brilliant with attention, proved she'd formulated some guesses. The look was pretty damn adorable, not that he was going to let her know that right now.

"Tell you what," he offered. "I'll let you pick the start square." He extended the scarf between his hands. "Wrist tie or blindfold?"

Her breath audibly snagged. "What if I say no and ask you to leave?"

"You can do that anytime you want, sunshine. Call a red light and we're done." He leaned in to capture her gaze more securely in his. "But I don't think you want to be done."

The amethyst glints in her eyes got darker. She pulled in a long breath. "And what if, after everything, I still refuse to talk? What happens if you don't get the information you want out of me?"

He unfurled a slow smile. "Oh, I'll get it."

She volleyed with a little smirk. "We'll see."

Fuck, it was good he still had his shorts on, not that they helped much in hiding how her spunk fired his spirit—and his cock. "Well, one of us will." He inserted enough wry command to assure she got his meaning. Not that he had to worry about that. Before he'd even kissed her the first time, he'd seen that the woman's mind shined as bright as her beauty.

Sure enough, Ava's mouth dropped open again. "You said I got to pick, *Sir*." She stomped on the title hard enough to suck any trace of respect from it. "Wrists or blindfold, right?"

"I said you got to pick where we *started*, mouthy girl." His blood surged with exhilaration as he hooked the scarf behind her neck and pulled, making her eyes spark again. "But that little line just cost you the privilege." He tugged her an inch closer, lowering his face so she didn't miss an inch of how deeply he desired her. "Now up on your knees, with wrists presented up front."

It was a pleasant surprise to watch her comply so fast. He left the first scarf draping from her neck, the sheer black fabric playing at her breasts like the magical mist from the forest where they'd first touched lips. The image fit. This was an important first for them too. Though this afternoon had been incredible, he hadn't been dominating her, pushing her. Not as he would now.

The longest scarf in the pile, a knitted crimson thing, was his choice for looping around her wrists in a figure-eight pattern. He had to improvise on the technique since this wasn't typical bondage rope, though he was able to finish off the knot with a nice circle wrap between her wrists, ensuring she wouldn't squirm her way free anytime soon. With what he had planned for the things he'd seen on her nightstand, that was a good thing.

Ava sighed as he tugged at the improvised cuffs to test his work. He double-checked the space he'd left to give her proper circulation but didn't give her any sound or response in return. Still without speaking and keeping the scarf's lead in hand, he swept off the bed in order to make her lean forward, extending her hands toward the footboard. Her bed was a sturdy piece of furniture, heavy wood embedded with wrought-iron cutouts that looked inspired by a church in one of the missions that dotted the bottom half of the state. When he secured the scarf to one of them, her torso angled down and her flawless bronze ass shot straight up. *Glory Hallelujah.*

He lifted her face toward him with a thumb and forefinger. Her gaze was cloudy with deep indigo smoke. She'd been biting her lips, because they were plumped and crimson with the rush of fresh blood. "Beautiful," he growled.

"Thank you, Sir."

She whispered it with quivering reverence. After that, the dark-cherry planes of her lips parted, all but roping him in for a kiss—and calling every swollen inch of his dick to come out for a long dip between them too. He locked his teeth in resistance and instead rubbed a rough thumb across them before offering, "One more chance to do this easy, sunshine. Right now, all I want is his name. We don't have to dig any deeper than that tonight. One name, and—"

"What?" she interjected. "You set me free?" She pushed out a playful pout. "After all your hard work?"

"Didn't say *that* was happening." He used the same urbane fluidity to pull the black silk from her neck. After wrapping the material twice around her eyes, he fastened the knot hard against the bridge of her nose, ensuring she knew that his glib mien didn't cancel his serious purpose. "Just thought you'd appreciate knowing the options again. There's a fun side of being bound and fucked and a not-so-fun side. Your choice." He smoothed both his hands down the column of her neck and then over her shoulders. "One name gets you the fun, baby."

She released an unsteady breath. Dipped her head. For one moment, Ethan thought he'd get to disregard the stuff on the nightstand and get right to claiming her body in all the ways his mind could conjure and his cock could stand.

That was before the next second, when her muscles stiffened beneath his touch. A tight whimper emanated from her throat. "You're like a damn dog with a bone, aren't you?"

He sighed and dropped his hands. "Let's hope you're a dog lover, Miss Chestain."

She snickered. He let her have the defiant moment. It was the least he could do, considering what the shit on her nightstand was mandating for the evening. He stopped there on his way back to mounting the bed again, making no effort to mask the sounds of his search from her—including a nice long slide of the drawer. That gained him the sight of a gorgeous shiver up her spine, no doubt inspired by what she knew he'd find in the compartment. With a smirk, he pulled out the handheld vibrator and joined it with the other items in his hand.

After he dumped all the items onto the bed, she treated him with another long quiver. "Ethan, why the hell are you raiding my nightst— *Oww!*" She writhed as he let the hard plastic teeth of a hair claw dig into her left buttock. As he grabbed her hip to hold her in place, he balanced it by securing one to the other side of her ass.

He hummed in satisfaction. Those things held firmer than he'd anticipated. They looked pretty cool too. One was embossed with zebra stripes, the other with leopard spots. "Wild thing," he murmured, "you make my heart sing."

"Shut. Up. Oh, *shit!*" Her scream pierced the air again as he got a smaller tortoiseshell clamp into the skin below the zebra clip. Holy hell, could this woman let out an expressive wail.

"You want to try for number four?" he taunted. "Forget my proper address again, and I'll be happy to make it one of the big ones too."

She snorted. "Don't you know how to just spank a subbie like everyone— *Oww!*"

He made it a big one anyway. This clamp was giraffe print. It blended nicely next to the leopard colors and slid into her skin with beautiful perfection. "Are you still obsessed with swats, baby?" His chastising chuckle lasted until he leaned deep enough to get his lips on her shoulder, taking care not to hit the clamps on the way. "That's so cute. You're actually trying to change the rules, aren't you?" He gently bit into her shoulder. "But the thing is, they're my rules. My way. You want to help call the shots again? Just give me his name, Ava."

Her head slumped. "Why?" she moaned. "Why do you even care? It's over. In the past. *Far* in the past, okay?"

"Then it shouldn't be such a big deal to talk about it, right?"

She didn't say anything for a long moment. "Damn it."

He shifted back to his position behind her thighs. "I'll take that as a sign to carry on."

She fumed again in response. Ethan sat and gazed at her for another moment. Her upper thighs, as bronze and breathtaking as the rest of her, spasmed in anticipation of him pulling off the clamps. When he left the wild-patterned torture tribe right where they were, she seethed with a little more gusto—right up to the moment he slipped the vibrator between her thighs and turned it on.

"Ohhh!" she cried. "Oh...mmmm..."

While she slipped from pissed to blissed, he took the four jumbo paper clips he'd also found on the stand and expanded them to fit the tops of his fingers. A quick tug on each one transformed the innocent office utensils into small but purposeful spikes. If his instincts were tracking right, Miss Spank-Me-Please wasn't going to like the sensation of the four sharp tines marking her skin.

His intuition was right. She yelped with surprise at first but settled into an exhilarating shriek when he started the spikes down her right thigh—especially because he timed the move with shutting off the vibrator.

"Aggghh!" She threw back her head, unknowingly turning him on in at least ten new ways. Her blindfolded face thrusting in the air...her lips open and straining on that scream... The sight was achingly similar to how she looked this afternoon on the wine room's couch, in the throes of the orgasm they'd reached together. Again, thank fuck for the board shorts. If he was naked right now, this would be torture for them both.

He pressed the tines against the back of her knee. And scraped his way up to her ass.

"Shit!" she cried. "I...I don't like this."

"And yet you're trembling for me, Ava."

He let his hand continue, spreading his fingers over her ass cheek, weaving them around the hair clamps still fastened there. He let the vibe drop from his other hand long enough to swipe those fingertips through the slick layers of her sex.

"And your pussy is dripping for me."

He scooped the pleasure stick back up. Started it back up on the low setting, brushing it over her dark genital curls.

"And I haven't heard you call red light."

He switched off the vibrator again. That, along with the deliberate arrogance he laced to the words, made her spine stiffen in anger.

Ethan steeled himself for anything. Though the woman played the Hollywood game with success, it was clearly never at a price she wasn't willing to pay. She maintained her pride like most starlets in this city took care of their fingernails, but tonight, he'd been yanking it out piece by agonizing piece. He'd tied her up, rendered her sightless, and now controlled more and more of her body's reactions. It was a power for which she was either going to hate him or thank him when this was done. At the moment, he couldn't predict either outcome. She'd let her head fall back between her shoulders, but her fists were still balled against each other, and she let out huffs like a she-bull preparing to charge.

"Well?" he prompted.

"What?" she seethed.

"Where are we at, Ava?" He flattened the vibe back against her clit but didn't turn it on. At the same time, he pushed the paperclip spikes into the top of her other buttock. "Red light says you're free and I'm gone. Stubbornness earns you another spike bath. But a name gets you more pleasure and my cock deep inside you."

Her breathing got rougher. "You don't get it, do you?" she finally bit out.

He didn't alter his position. Was this actually a crack in

her window? Without having to pull out the sledgehammer? "Enlighten me."

"You think that I simply won't talk. But the truth is...I can't." Her head weaved as if a huge weight rolled inside it. "I can't."

"Why?" He lifted it just above a whisper.

"Because it hurts." There were tears in her voice now. "I can't. It hurts. It *will* hurt. I—"

"Ssshhh." He cut her off after flicking off the paper clips and lifting his hands to trace the length of her spine. "That's what I'm here for."

He got the reaction he was seeking. Her lips fell silent as her whole body quivered. A tiny whine shook in her throat, full of question and confusion. He smiled at the sound. Oh, yeah. There it was. The crack.

"Let *me* take care of the hurt, Ava." He repeated the long drag down her back, using his fingernails this time. Her ass rolled in visceral response; her hips clenched in blatant need. "Fuck," he murmured. "You are so beautiful." She moaned, juicing him to go on. "Give me more, sunshine. I'm not worth a damn without your gift...without your choice to give everything over, be it your passion, your pussy, and yeah, your pain. Just for now, let it go. Put it in my hands to give to you"—he pulled the smallest of the hair clips off her ass, making her yelp—"and to take from you." He soothed out her sting with a gentle sweep of his palm, but just as she relaxed, he yanked one of the bigger clips. She yelled louder, reacting as more blood rushed back to her skin, but again he smoothed the burn, turning her cry into a whimper. "It's all mine now, baby. I'm going to control it so you don't have to. You're safe, Ava. You're safe."

She shrieked again as he took off another clip. She sighed

again as he rubbed the pain into warmth...and admired the crimson slashes left on her dark-gold skin as well. But even after all the clamps were gone and she undulated beneath him in a bath of raw sensation, her lips remained tight. Her resolution hadn't changed.

Ethan growled low. "Does the cat still have your tongue, Ava? Damn it, I thought we were turning you into a dog person."

She pushed her bottom against his hand. "M-Maybe if you did that longer...or turned the vibrator back on..."

He had to steel his own resolve. "Devious minx." He meant every syllable. How the hell did she know he'd crawl on glass for her right now? How had she figured out what the sight of her was doing to him? How had she discerned that her stunning response to his domination was flipping every fucking switch of elation inside him and that now, all he wanted to do was slam into her body until they both screamed with completion?

But he had her on the brink. There weren't just cracks in her window now. Full fissures showed in her composure, and he couldn't stop just because his dick gushed precome and his balls pounded with demand.

He squeezed her hips and loomed over her once more. "Are you red lighting on me, Ava?"

"No." Her answer was immediate. "God, no. Ethan—Sir—please, I need more. Please...m-more!"

Her breath hitched. Her whole body gleamed with need. She hadn't stopped undulating her hips or biting hard on her lips. She began to babble as her senses started flying, ascending to a space of pure, hot desire. God*damn*, it was incredible to watch. To experience. To feel her giving in to him, inch by hesitant inch, and experiencing such bliss because of it.

He knew what had to happen now. What had to be

implemented so that she released her last bit of resistance. The last piece of the arsenal he'd snagged off the nightstand. And ironically, the smallest weapon in the stash.

The crackle of the plastic candy wrapper would've been as inelegant if he'd pulled the stunt in the middle of an opera. This occasion definitely trumped the middle of *La Bohème* for sinful satisfaction. The payback potential didn't suck either.

Ava's thick curls bounced against her back as her head tugged higher. "Wh-What is... Are you seriously eating a damn peppermint—"

"Ssshhh." He issued it as a full command this time. To drive the point in, he took advantage of having all that hair so close. With one well-placed jerk, her soft curls filled his hand and her aroused gasp filled the air.

It was the calm before the storm.

"We're almost there, sunshine...but you haven't turned it all over yet, have you?" He slipped his hand from her hair, skating it down again, stopping when he had his palm flat against the top of her ass. What a sight. The full globes of her raised backside. The symmetrical ladders where each clip had marked her skin. And, as his prodding fingers revealed, the perfect whorl that led into her body's back entrance. "You need to be pushed just one more step outside that comfort zone, don't you?"

Gingerly he spread her rectum a little wider.

"E-Ethan!"

He maintained his grip. "Wouldn't recommend that screaming stuff, baby. The tighter you clench, the harder this is going to be."

"This...this isn't going to *be* anything. You... I can't let you just—"

"You can." He slipped one finger in, teasing the ultrasensitive flesh just inside her tight tunnel. "And you will." He pushed a little deeper, making her whine again. "Because you won't be able to stand not knowing what this is like. Not knowing what it is to give me everything...even this, the naughtiest kind of pain I can inflict."

Her body squirmed. Her hands bunched back into fists. "You really are Sir Bastard."

"And you're ten versions of sexy when you whisper it like that."

"*Vete a la mierda.*"

"I'm sure hell would be thrilled to see me. But I plan to fuck you right here—just as soon as I turn your sweet ass into a *really* sweet ass." Ignoring her skittering whimper, he took the red-and-white candy out of his mouth. Lowered it to her puckered entrance. "Relax, Ava," he murmured. "Surrender it all to your sergeant."

He felt her suck in a breath. When she blew it out, he pressed the peppermint into her tight little back hole.

Oh, how she fought it. She bucked and shoved and bore down against the finger that held the candy in as he waited for her body heat to start dissolving the candy, and—

"Ohhhh...*caramba*..."

Ethan withdrew his finger. He used the sanitizer he'd also brought over before caressing her back with more long, lingering strokes. The muscles beneath his touch were the texture of noodles, though she still wiggled her hips, reacting to the mint that awakened every tissue in that dark, naughty tunnel. As she did, he watched the depths of her pussy get shinier with her need to be filled there too. She was swimming in new sensations, and it was breathtaking. Damn, she was so open, so hot...so ready.

It was time.

As he pressed his body against hers, letting her feel the length of his aroused dick through every hot fold of her pussy, he snarled in her ear, "Did *he* ever make you feel this way?"

As he expected, she tensed. Gulped hard. And set free a sorrowful moan before she whispered, "Colin. His name was Colin."

He turned the snarl into a kiss. "Thank you, sunshine."

"And Flynn."

He kissed her ear again. "It's okay. I don't need the middle name too."

"It wasn't a middle name."

He stilled. Released a huff against her neck. *Dumb shit. Dumb shit.* "There were two."

Her jerking nod came a second before her full sob.

"Ava." He trailed soft kisses along her neck and over her nape, into the valley between her shoulder blades. "Ava...oh, sweet Ava..."

He needed to bring her back to him. Back to *them*. Back to *this*, here and now. He started that by jerking on the circle tie on her wrists, setting her free. As her arms separated, he flattened them to the bed, his own framing them, his hands atop her wrists. He sank his teeth into the curve of her ear as his cock seemed to move on its own power, nearing her sweet vagina. The air smelled like peppermint, coconut, and the sea. Her body felt like golden satin. Her sobs, now coming through the hole of the window he'd shattered inside her, officially crashed through the triple panes of his.

He seriously needed to be inside her.

He fumbled first with the ties of his shorts and next with

the condom he'd stashed in the Velcro pocket. Thank fuck he'd had high hopes for where this would end tonight, though the journey had possessed more twists than the road to Serenity's bar down in Mexico. But there was no stopping him now. Without even kicking off the shorts, he lined himself up to her tight sheath.

"Colin and Flynn," he said into her ear. When she stiffened again, he scratched his nails into her forearms. "We're erasing them tonight, Ava. Stay with me so we can do that. We're drowning them with this, with us. They're not here anymore. I am, and I'm not going anywhere. Tell me you understand."

Her head bobbed beneath his. "I...I understand, Sir."

He slid a kiss along her neck. "Good girl." His dick swelled a little tighter. It had been so long since he'd spoken those words. It had been even longer since he'd relished speaking them. "Now...tell me who made your ass hurt so good tonight."

"You," she whispered. "It was you, Sir."

"And tell me who you want here now...at the entrance of your perfect, sweet cunt."

"You." She released a high sigh. "Please, Sir!"

"Who do you want to fill you and fuck you?"

"You." She trembled and pushed against him. "God, Ethan! I need it! I need you inside me. Fuck me now!"

With a triumphant growl, he slid into her tight, ready channel. He was fully seated within delirious seconds—not that he rested there long. It didn't just feel good physically to fuck her hard. It fed the reaches of his Dominant's spirit. It opened a dungeon inside him that had been dark and neglected for so damn long. Tonight, the dungeon was still there—only now, it was alive with her passion, illuminated by her beauty, vibrant with her cries as he thrust into her over and over again.

Soon, her shrieks resonated with his name. "Ethan—Sir—I can't last much longer."

"Same page, sunshine." He reared back, letting his hands trail into the juncture of her thighs. His gasp escaped with hers when he slid a finger over the hard knot of her most tender nerves. "Give this to me too, Ava. Every screaming second of it."

She complied in glorious detail, arching her head back, unleashing a groan that threatened to blow off the roof. Every muscle in her passage utilized its Kegel workout from this afternoon, squeezing down on his cock. Electricity sizzled in his balls, zapping the way for the hot milk that shot from him like liquid fireworks.

"Fuck! Ava!" He grabbed her by the hips and rammed her back hard on his shaft, needing to give her every last hot drop. Like the act of claiming her, there was more than carnal fulfillment to it. He'd asked her for so much. Despite her fear and despite the pain, she'd given it to him. In return, she deserved every measure of his passion too.

He gentled his hold as his limbs went slack, anticipating she'd pull away too. It wasn't even midnight yet, and the day had been one for the unexpected. As soon as he let go, Ava turned around and reattached herself to him, arms around his neck and legs around his waist. Though the move dislodged his cock from her, he smiled and wrapped her back up in his arms.

Instantly, his senses were blanketed in peace. *Fuck. Peace.* When was the last time he and that word were on speaking terms? But for this collection of moments, there was no other term to encompass this complete connection of his mind, body, and spirit.

Because of this incredible woman.

On that thought, he forced himself to shift far enough away to see her face. Her high cheekbones were still stained with tears, but she had the heavy-lidded happiness of a satisfied subbie.

Nevertheless, he asked, "You okay?"

She slowly nodded. "Thank you."

He frowned. "For what?"

"For helping me to start what I should have a while ago. Getting rid of the ghosts. Colin...and Flynn."

He shook his head. "I told you, we don't have to talk—"

"I know. And we won't. Not tonight. But I promise, you'll hear about them both...soon." She tilted her head. "Okay?"

He brushed her nose with his lips. "Deal."

She had the cutest nose. The tip had a tiny dent in it. He wondered what other nuances there were to learn about her.

"So." She issued it with an impish curl of her lips. The quirk deepened her left dimple. Another nuance. "Do *I* get to ask a question now?"

He shot back a playful glower. "Am I going to enjoy answering it?"

She squared her shoulders, which made her breasts undulate in a way that turned *distracting* into an understatement. "Am I *ever* going to get a proper spanking... Sir?"

Well, that did it. His cock lurched, his chest flipped, and his pulse jumped. Screw the Tar Pits. If she was ready for round two tonight, then he sure as fuck was. He lifted a hand, buried it in her hair, and tugged her head back, exulting in the shaky little gasp she emitted as he did.

"I think that can be arranged, sunshine."

He should have remembered it wasn't midnight yet. That

this day, full of as many crazy game changers as any twenty-four he'd known on the team, couldn't possibly give up the ghost on midnight without a fight—a fight that sounded a hell of a lot like his phone, chirping with the special ring that every guy on the battalion knew all too well. It was John Franzen's version of the bat signal, and it meant only one thing.

Drop everything. Now.

CHAPTER ELEVEN

Tait wasn't sure what to expect when he and Kell got out of the cab in front of the Foxfire Room. A North Hollywood dive bar wasn't Franzen's normal scene for a battalion rally-up, especially because most of them were staying at the Hilton in Universal City.

Okay, so none of them had actually *been* at the hotel thirty minutes ago anyway. In light of the throwdown at Bella's place tonight, nobody had been ready to turn in. He and Kellan had made for the Whisky on Sunset for a kick-ass local band and some ribs, while Garrett and Zeke headed someplace quiet with their girls, in light of Sage's condition. He'd heard Franz talking to Rhett and Rebel about checking out the famous Pink's Hot Dogs joint, but after what happened on the beach tonight, he'd needed heavy booze, heavier rock 'n' roll, and a place where he had to address his best friend in a lung-busting bellow. What he had to divulge was best done that way.

Their captain's urgent text had preempted his confession.

"You good?" Kellan asked while shrugging into his faded leather jacket. His friend's inflection and the expectant set of his jaw translated into a longer message. Something along the lines of *You okay, ass face? Because you never drink four beers inside an hour without starting commentary on everything in the room that moves, so I know something's up. Probably something big. And now you can't tell me because of this code-red call from Franzen. So is this gonna wait, or do we have to stand out here and hash it first?*

Tait shoved some money at the driver and then gave his friend a nod. "Yeah." He tugged open the door that was set into a flagstone wall that hadn't been trendy since Kennedy was sworn in. *You're right. It's big. Too damn big for the sidewalk between a hair salon and an imports store with mugs screaming "Kiss Me, I'm Irish."*

"Later, okay?"

"Roger."

After they stepped inside, they had to let their eyes readjust to the dark, even after the murky street they'd left behind. The place was crowded for a weeknight. There were at least twenty stools occupied with customers of all kinds, including some guys who looked like they'd stepped out of a trendy magazine spread, some burly types in T-shirts from the local stage employees union, two girls with purple hair who flanked a third in blue tattoos, and a multipierced couple with their tongues down each other's throats. A TV played a silent repeat of tonight's Dodgers game. The ceiling-mounted speakers pulsed with one of Tait's favorite Dave Matthews songs, though he wasn't sure that was enough to officially bring the place into the twenty-first century. Could've had something to do with the yellowed rope lighting tacked up around the perimeter of the room.

Seventies Christmas kitsch aside, the strands came in handy for guiding them to the back corner, where the place's sole booth already held most of their battalion mates. Franz, Rhett, Rebel, Zeke, and Garrett were present, along with a new guy he didn't recognize. Wouldn't be surprised if they called him Ken, though. Dude looked like a supersized version of Barbie's famous boyfriend, complete with perfect haircut, square jaw, and muscled shoulders that pushed against a T-shirt emblazoned with Jack Kerouac's face.

As they settled into the booth, he looked around to flag a bartender. There was only one, and the friendly old guy was laughing at a joke made by a customer at the other end of the room. Shit. That fifth beer was going on hold for a while. Might have been a good thing, if the terse look on Franzen's face was an accurate indicator of the theme for this powwow.

After another head check around the table, he threw out, "So Archer's in the head?"

Rhett waggled his brows. The rope lights picked up the red tints in them, making him look like a demon king from those bow-and-arrow computer games he played. "Archer isn't here yet."

"What?" Kell got the rejoinder out before he could. "*We* beat Ethan?"

Zeke smirked. "Twenty says Mr. Time Clock was busy getting laid."

Nobody took him up on the bet. Ethan was always the first one in the door at team meetings. An exception could only involve a woman or a natural disaster. Best as he knew, the only disaster tonight had been what the Dodgers had wielded on the Mariners.

They didn't have to wallow long in curiosity. The door opened and the rope lights illuminated the dark head of their party's last arrival. Runway hurried to the booth and scooted in across from Tait, next to Rhett. "Hey." He nodded in deference to Franz. "Came as fast as I could."

Zeke made sure that didn't get ignored. "Aw, we sure hope not, Runway."

"Huh?"

Z snickered. Garrett backhanded the purple-and-gold Hawaiian print that covered his friend's huge torso and gave Ethan a diplomatic smile. "Dude, it's always a good idea to check in the mirror before dashing out the door."

"What?" Ethan looked down. "Why?"

"Your shirt's inside out, your fly is open, and for the record, a little hand sanitizer or olive oil is great for getting lipstick off your earlobes."

"Shit." Runway joined the rest of them in chuckling at his expense. The moment was temporary. Ethan's grin fell to a shocked gape, aimed right at Malibu Ken, who'd been hidden from him by Zeke's bulk. "Colton?"

The guy jabbed his chin up. "Pleasure to see you, Archer."

"Likewise, but what the hell are—"

"You're getting on the tracks in front of the train, Runway." Franz sliced it in before jamming his elbows to the table and circling his stare over all of them. In the dim light of the room, he looked like Don Corleone had gotten a makeover from the Scorpion King. "Gentlemen, thanks for circling the wagons even on your vacation, which I'm afraid is being cut short." He paused for a second, smiling a little when nobody at the table so much as flinched. "I know it's not the first time you've heard that from me, nor will it be the last. The fresh factor here, as you've all surmised, is the pretty young thing sitting to my left."

The Ken doll snorted. "Pretty young thing who whipped your ass last time we were at the firing range."

"Eight months ago," Franz sneered.

"You're still buying my Scotch tonight."

Good luck with that. Tait glanced at the bartender, who'd headed back their way but stopped halfway. It was like someone else was tending the second half of the bar, a ghost only that old guy could see.

"Now you're talking," Ethan added to Ken doll's comment. They bumped fists in front of Zeke's rolling eyes.

Franzen chuckled. "Clearly some of you are familiar with Agent Colton already." He glanced to Rebel and then Tait. "For those who aren't, allow me to introduce Daniel Colton, one of our best guys currently serving the Central American region of the CIA."

Ken doll muttered, "And South."

Franz frowned. "Huh?"

"Central *and* South America, shit-for-brains."

"Oh, yeah. That's right." He added under his breath, "Overachieving spook."

"Adrenaline-whore ground-pounder."

Tait exchanged perplexed scowls with the other guys as Franz and Colton snickered like they'd slung the last decent insults in history.

Archer was the next to speak. "Sorry to break up the riff, Captain, but what the fuck's going on?" To Colton, he queried, "What're you doing on this side of the border? You didn't let the Aragon truck get away, did you?"

That caused a ripple of tension at the table. The entire team had nearly ground their nuts to dust in helping the spooks track the Aragons from one side of the globe to the other. Raids, searches, surveillances, interferences...an undercover op that had included Rebel in drag...Ethan practically going comatose from questioning dirtbags from Abbottabad to Zacatecas... They'd pulled out all the stops on the fuckers, leading to Bernardo Galvaz finally spilling about the massive heroin shipment due for the border three days ago.

But confiscating the smack was only part of why that goal

was important. Several families had paid the Aragons for safe transport into the States on the truck, not knowing the Aragons would never allow loose ends like that in their business. If the CIA had let the *Especiales* "handle" that truck into invisibility, Agent Colton might find himself resembling Mr. Potato Head instead—with the parts in the wrong places.

"We didn't lose it," Colton stated.

"Thank fuck," Rhett and Ethan muttered together.

Tait threw an assessing look at the spook. "So why do you still look like you're going to tell us Bin Laden is really alive?"

Colton went still as all eyes at the table riveted back to him. Franz leaned and muttered, "Sergeant Tait Bommer. He's half of my sniper team."

"He's the spotter?" Colton returned.

"Oooo, you *can* be bright when you want to be."

Despite the banter, Colton's mien didn't change. He steepled his fingers and stared over them back at Tait. "You have good instincts, Sergeant," he stated. "Our interest in the Aragon Cartel has gotten a whole lot more urgent since we stopped that truck." He swung his gaze to everyone at the table. "No. Fuck *urgent*. This is sticky. Peach pie on the sidewalk in the middle of July, being eyed by a thousand flies, sticky. Got it?"

Garrett emitted an admiring groan. "That was impressive, man. Shit, I may need to borrow that."

"No," Zeke interceded, "you will *not*."

"Toss out that shirt and I'll consider it."

As the friends grunted into a truce, Tait directed his attention back to Colton. "What's going on? And what can we do to help you, Agent Colton?"

If it were possible, the agent's posture went stiffer.

Everyone pressed in by another inch.

"The takedown on the truck got...messy," he muttered. "Dark and messy. The guards had heat. We expected that, of course, but it was serious heat. High-end semiautomatics and a shitload of handguns. They were well-trained to use it all too." He jutted his jaw and huffed. "Just listening to it on the radios was a nightmare. It was like a goddamn Michael Bay movie. There must have been ten or twelve of them too. We caught eight. The rest took off into the desert."

"Probably maggot food by now," Rebel commented in his Louisiana drawl. "In one way or another."

"But ten or twelve?" Kellan added. "For a basic heroin shipment and a handful of innocents? Doesn't add up."

Garrett dragged a hand across the blond mess atop his head. Tait could practically predict what the soon-to-be new father would ask. "Casualties?"

"Only one," Colton supplied. "A passenger in the truck."

"Shit."

"An adult," the agent clarified. "And *not* an innocent." In response to their puzzled frowns, he explained, "A courier."

After they digested that in perplexed silence, Ethan asked, "A courier for what?"

Colton laced his fingers. "We don't have the answer to that yet. It's the blank in the middle of the crossword puzzle, missing all the key letters. I can sure as hell tell you want the feeder words are, though."

"Lay 'em down," Franzen encouraged.

"Secrets. Layers. Lies. And danger."

Rebel had the guts to spit out the laugh they were all feeling. "You stirrin' gumbo up in that gray matter, Colton? *Maudit*. Sounds like a bad movie ad."

The agent shrugged. "Agreed. But the guy had himself handcuffed to a laptop."

Franz's brows jumped. "Handcuffed?"

Colton nodded. "With no key on him to unlock it."

"What's on the thing?" Ethan asked.

"That's the billion-dollar question," Colton replied. "Everything on the computer has been encrypted behind the nine cyber-circles of Hell. That's why we reached out to the bureau here in LA for a helping hand."

Rhett gave that an approving nod. "The LA-based FBI guys are some of the best. A lot of them helped implement the city PD's RACR war room, which is goddamned impressive. A bunch more have been drafted from the security teams at high-list terrorist targets like Disneyland and the Hollywood hub. Their people know some good shit."

Colton turned a cryptic look at him. "Yeah. Their team is an interesting melting pot."

Garrett grinned. "Something tells me this plot's about to thicken."

Zeke snorted. "You forgot your flappy hat, Arthur Conan Doyle."

"Holy shit," his friend returned. "You read that book I gave you!"

Tait threw an evil eye at them both. "You two clowns wanna let the guy finish?"

"The courier also had a cell phone on him," Colton continued. "There were a number of California-based numbers stored on it, though none with any names attached. One was definitely the guy's favorite."

"And you tried calling it?" Rhett questioned.

"Fifteen minutes after we confiscated the thing." Colton

shook his head. "No answer; no voice mail."

"Which means his calls to the bastard at the other end were set for prearranged times." Rhett's mouth went tight. "I'd bet both nuts it was disconnected the next time you tried calling."

"Your gonads are safe, *amigo*." Colton tapped his folded hands atop the table. "Which brings me to the reason why the LA bureau was a gift from the gods."

Rhett smiled. "They knew the number?"

"Instantly." The agent took a deep breath. Tait watched the guy, and the tension that still laced his posture, with even more care. "It belonged to a target they've been watching with increasing interest. His name is Ephraim Lor. But he's better known as Enzo Lemare."

For a group of guys trained to remember everything from license-plate numbers to GPS coordinates in a single mission, summoning the man's name from three hours ago, when Magneto ninja invoked it in Bella's living room, wasn't a hard jump. Still, Tait clarified, "The producer of *Dress Blues*?"

"And the guy who played hoochie target practice with Bella Lanza last night?"

Kellan stole his follow-up, but Tait was grateful. It let him focus on Ethan's reaction. Wasn't every day that a guy discovered his college girlfriend had grown into a knockout TV star with a Malibu villa—and Bella had made no secret of her desire to rekindle a connection with Ethan. Had they done that tonight? If so, how would he feel about knowing the man who'd been between Bella's sheets *last* night was now connected to a mysterious courier with the Aragon crime cartel?

"Yes and yes," Colton answered to the queries. "And now that we know a great deal about Lor, thanks to the agent who's stuck to him like moss on a cypress, we're ready to start connecting dots."

Nobody said anything. Ironically, Archer himself finally spoke up. "All right, I'll bite. The dots to what?"

Colton pulled out a tablet. He woke it up and then opened a slideshow containing pictures of a sophisticated man with black hair, eyes that were too pretty for a dude, and a lean but rugged build. The first shots were clearly from the man's younger years, showing him in ornate European settings. "Lor was born and raised in Rome. His father was Palestinian, his mother one hundred percent a *Roma* girl. She was a devout Catholic who worked as a cleaning lady at the Vatican. It seemed a love match until Daddy had to return to his motherland, where he apparently reconnected with Allah. When he returned to Rome a year later, he became deeply involved with the Red Brigade paramilitarists. He was in charge of a secret plot to take down Vatican City from the inside out."

Zeke emitted a low whistle. Other than that, everyone was quiet as Colton advanced to more photographs, grainier shots depicting Lor as a boy of ten or eleven, outfitted in soldier gear with a rifle over his shoulder. "According to our source, the guy grew up idolizing these rebels. They were his Avengers, his Luke Skywalkers, his Jack Reachers. But when the brigade dismantled in the eighties, he was lost. His parents divorced, and though he remained with *Mamma* in Italy, he kept close contact with his father. He ran away on the day he was supposed to go to his First Communion and quickly found his way to Cairo, where he hooked up with his father. Near as our bureau contact can figure, he was fully radicalized by the time he hit his fifteenth birthday."

As newer pictures lit up the tablet, now showing Lor as a teenager in militant regalia, Rebel spoke up again. "After all those years of goin' to Mass in Saint Peter's Square?"

"Time can change a lot of things, Master Sergeant Stafford."

The bottom fell out of Tait's gut before he finished looking toward the source of the interjection. Sweet God. That voice. Silken enough for fantasies but rough enough to say *don't fuck with me.* Or other things, like *Stay where you are, Weasley. I don't want to hurt you.*

"Holy crap." Garrett spat it as Luna planted herself in front of the table, flipping her long ponytail and bracing her hands on hips that looked poured into dark-red denim pants. Hugging her torso was a short-sleeved black T-shirt, a fitting visual lead to the tattoo of angels and demons that ran down the length of her left arm. On her feet were black combat boots that were caked with beach sand.

Zeke looked like he'd been strangled with barbed wire and sounded like it too. "What the *hell* is she—"

"Calm down, Zsycho." Franzen issued it in a growl. "That's an order."

"She's supposed to be in prison!"

"I feel you, okay? I was there for all the reasons why."

"Oh yeah? You sure about that? Maybe you need to be kidnapped, drugged, and abandoned in Vegas again as a refresher. Or watch me almost die because of the neurotoxin unleashed in my blood by the monster she aided and abetted. You remember *those* reasons, Franz?"

"Yeah. And I also remember that Rayna would be some foreign asshole's sex toy by now if this woman hadn't stepped up and done the *right* thing in the end."

Zeke slammed back against the leather seat with a glare the temperature of an inferno. "This is bullshit. Unbelievable, un*fucking*real bullshit."

Tait leaned forward. He balled his hands to prevent himself from doing two things. One was reaching for Z's strained neck. The other? Grabbing Luna, hauling her next to him, and announcing to everyone that the next dickwad who contributed to the Luna Lawrence slur campaign could do so with his fist in their mouth. That helped him gain enough control to say, "Z, maybe it's a good idea to hear her out. If the bureau has trusted her—"

"Then the bureau's a bigger bunch of imbeciles than I thought."

He slid his hands off the table. Atop his thighs, they shook in rage. Z's hands were still as steady as an idiot preacher who'd sentenced an adulteress to hell. It wasn't fair. Yeah, Luna's crush on Z had been a tad zealous and hadn't wound up how she'd wanted after their intense scene in the Bastille dungeon all those months ago, but the woman had owned up to her misstep. She'd come clean and been responsible for saving Rayna's life because of that. Had Zeke just tuned that part out from Franz? Didn't that matter?

A glance up at Luna said the answer to that might be an ironic *no*. She dipped her head at Z in contemplative scrutiny. "To be honest, Sergeant Hayes, I don't give a shit what you think anymore. Our heads can't be there right now. Our job is bigger than that. Way bigger."

Even through the vacation scruff on his face, Zeke's jaw turned the texture of a granite wall. "Isn't your 'job' supposed to be washing orange jumpsuits?"

Screw it. Tait shoved his elbows backward and prepared

to lunge. "That's *more* than enough, asshole."

The only thing that held him back from Z now was Luna's hand, cream skin accented with lavender nail polish, pressed against his bicep. "Chill. It's okay." Her profile was regal and gorgeous, even in the bar's crappy lighting and even as she continued to endure Zeke's glower. "Your panties are in a wad, Zeke. It's understandable. Hopefully the episode recap on this will hold you for now."

Zeke grunted. "This should be entertaining."

She pulled her hand back from Tait and folded her arms. "The night we dropped the net on Mua, my arresting officers were sweet about noticing what they saw as slick crisis-management skills. Guess I'm a natural-born fast thinker. Imagine that.

"Fate helped me out a little the next day. A girl locked up with me in the prisoner processing cell flipped out, managed to get a gun off one of the guards, and threatened to kill everyone in the room." She shrugged, almost as if confused. "I talked her off the ledge. Didn't think it was a big deal, when the alternative was a shitload of people getting bullets through their brains. The bureau didn't agree. They reviewed my case, along with a bunch of personality tests I thought were a part of normal prisoner processing, and determined I might be a good choice for joining the field team on tracking our friend Lor. And since the government owns my ass for another year and a half, I'm free labor."

Though Z no longer looked like the walking Grand Canyon, he cocked his brows and murmured, "A 'good choice,' huh? And the thinking behind that was...what again?"

She waved a hand at the room like a game show model unveiling a car. "Behold Enzo Lemare's regular late-night stomping grounds. You know any normal spook that'd fit in here?"

Tait answered that one with dawning comprehension. "You work here. You're the missing bartender."

She tilted her head with just enough of an impish grin to make his chest tighten—and his cock surge. "You thirsty, soldier?"

Oh fuck, yes.

But the next moment she was all business again, turning to the rest of the guys. "We caught a break tonight. Lemare is attending the TV Critics Association gala. Normally I'd be nursing Enzo through his third gin and tonic, listening to another rant about how the capitalist assholes of America are ruining the universe." She patted the third earring up on her multipierced lobe. "And my homey Walter, somewhere in that big-ass building over on Wilshire, is getting every word of it. Hi, Wally!" She tossed a shrug at Zeke. "See? I'm free *and* fun. Maybe now the bureau can give Colton a raise. He needs the flow for a decent haircut."

"Screw you, loony tunes." The agent grinned as he said it.

"No thanks, Dan the man." Her answering smile descended fast, and she shook her head. "No time for extracurricular anyway. After tonight's mess at the Lanza villa, I'm afraid we're back to square one for finding the codes to crack the intel on that laptop."

A ripple of shock moved around the table. Tait dialed in his bearing at a careful neutral, hoping nobody would notice his own jaw hadn't plummeted along with theirs.

Franzen threw a narrowed stare at his bureau buddy. "Mother of a fucking sand flea. That was you guys pulling the ninja hoedown earlier?"

Colton smirked. "I was the cute one next to the door."

Franz pounded his shoulder. "Asshole! Why didn't you say anything? Pull me aside? We thought you were some high-end thievery ring with balls for brains and—"

"The audacity to mix Marvel and DC characters." Tait felt morally compelled to get it out.

Colton threw him a conspiratorial grin. "I was sickened too, man. But we had a Spiderman camp and a Batman camp, and neither was backing down."

Franzen's glower got darker. "You haven't answered my question."

Colton swung back an equally menacing look. "Okay, listen. We had no idea what we'd encounter at Lanza's villa. We were hoping the woman would be out, maybe on Lemare's arm at that gala. We came prepared for an army, just in case Lor was onto us somehow. We didn't plan on finding *the* army, let alone one of its finest SOF teams. We had to maintain some kind of edge on you guys, just in case—"

"What? We were all on Lor's payroll or something?"

"Stranger things have been known to happen. You know that as well as I, cock noodle."

The guys chuckled. They'd gotten a hidden surprise tonight, hearing someone give their captain lip like that and live to tell about it.

Franzen rebutted, "A second ago, I was the leader of one of the finest SOF teams."

"Yeah, but you're still a cock noodle."

Franzen's parry to that was to ignore it. "So you were hoping to find a memory stick the guy hid at the villa."

Colton's face tightened, producing lines around his eyes and mouth that instilled Tait's respect for the guy. Pretty boys didn't stay that way for long in their line of work—except for Ethan, who had to be working an Oil of Olay regimen when the rest of them were asleep.

"It was a wild hope, but yes," Colton said. "It's unlikely he's had the thing directly on him since the courier was killed. We immediately pumped sources at the man's dry cleaners, car detailer, private spa locker room... Nothing's been found."

Garrett leaned forward. "And you can't get into his house?"

Luna answered that one. "He hasn't been anywhere near his house. On the night they took out the courier, Lor worked late at the studio and then checked into a bungalow at the Beverly Hills Hotel." She winced. "Made it a garden view too. We were blind for two days. The guy didn't even order room service. Who gets a bungalow at the BHH and doesn't order room service?"

"What did he do for fresh clothes?" Franzen questioned.

"Bought them new off the rack, down the street on Rodeo Drive," she answered.

Zeke emitted another whistle. "So you're saying the fucker's rich."

Franzen snorted. "I think she's saying he's paranoid."

"Agreed," Colton said. "We still don't know where he's bound tonight. The TCA gala was at the Langham Hotel in Pasadena but concluded an hour ago. Our eyes say he's been at the hotel bar ever since, pounding G and Ts like they're the last he'll ever drink."

"So he'll likely check in there for the night," Z offered.

"And then what?" Garrett directed his stare toward Luna. "That's where you're going with this, isn't it? Lor's clearly lying low, but not for good. Even Rodeo Drive will start to get suspicious of his ass."

"So he's waiting," Zeke supplied.

"But for what?" Garrett scowled.

"Something on a time frame." Tait's statement came from the tightening knot in his gut. "Something like orders to abduct someone...or attack something." The tautened faces of his battalion mates confirmed their thoughts had steered the same direction. "Shit," he muttered. "Without that stick, we have no idea what we're dealing with."

Colton rolled his knuckles atop the table. "It's big enough that Lor is working with scumsuckers like the Aragons on it."

Franz sucked in a harsh breath. "Yeah. Scumsuckers with ties all the way over to the Balkan drug-trafficking routes."

"Which means Afghanistan," Rhett put in.

"Fuck," Zeke spat.

"We need that stick." Garrett clawed a hand through his hair. "But I guarantee you Lor's planted it in a furrow close to the barn. When it comes time to jump, he'll need it handy."

Ethan had kept his gaze down, rotating a cocktail napkin on the table with his pointer fingers. When he lifted his head, it was to state the inevitable. "Then the stick's at the studio."

Tait watched Luna and Colton trade glances. They shared a telepathy that seemed purely professional but still chapped his hide with a fucker called jealousy.

"The bull's-eye goes to Sergeant Archer," Colton declared. "And leads to how you guys have now become our best friends."

Rhett gave voice to the confusion making its way across everyone's faces. "Runway may have just hit the target, but we're all still in the forest, my friend. How do we figure anywhere in this? We were visitors on the set of *Dress Blues* for one day only."

Colton gave him a Ken doll smirk. "Not if the showrunners decide they need real-world military consultants for the show's upcoming episodes."

Luna dropped her gaze to Ethan. "And not if one of those consultants won't have any trouble scooting closer to its star and producer."

Ethan stopped circling the napkin. His fingers visibly tensed. "How much closer?"

"As close as you can, Sergeant. In any manner they'll let you."

Tait couldn't help it. His snicker spilled out on top of Zeke's and Garrett's, though it was Rebel who put words to the moment.

"Aha! *C'est bon. C'est trés bon*, I think."

"*Bone* it certainly is, man." Zeke sputtered the phonetic equivalent of Rebel's French. "All the way."

"This is gonna be awesome," Garrett agreed.

Ethan lifted his head, saying nothing. He didn't have to. Tait had seen that look on a man's face before. It had been in the sports bar on base, back at home—when a guy was told he was being deployed to Iraq for the sixth time.

★ ★ ★ ★ ★

An hour later, they had a solid plan. Their "new role" on the *Dress Blues* set would be announced at a table reading for the new week's script tomorrow afternoon—technically, later today—with Cameron Stock, the show's director, to be the only person actually aware of the charade. Orders were strict; nobody else on the show's team could be told of the ruse since there was a good chance Lor wasn't working alone.

Stock advised them the "consulting team" shouldn't realistically exceed three guys, although nearby backup teams were okay. Ethan was the obvious choice for the first inside slot. Grabbing his six in the trenches of the assignment would be Rhett, invaluable because of his tech skills, and Rebel, who could sweet-talk a nun out of her granny panties if he had to. The rest of the team would take up tactical positions atop neighboring sound stages at the studio, in order to record anyone meeting with Lor outside or engaging in unusual behavior. Tait had joined Kellan, Zeke, and Garrett in groaning about that one. What defined "unusual" when spying on a TV and film production lot?

As soon as the logistics were hammered out and lot badges issued, it was time to get to bed. Since Franzen had the rental van, everyone started filing out toward the street, grateful for the easy lift back to the hotel.

Everyone except for Tait.

"T-Bomb?" Kellan lingered at the back of the pack to call it out. "Come on, man. We're rolling."

He watched Luna's backside disappear into the bar's storeroom. And stopped in his tracks. More accurately was jerked to a screaming halt there. The center of his chest throbbed. His palms broke out in a sweat he hadn't felt since sixteen.

For fuck's sake.

He wasn't superstitious. Spiritual? Sure. You didn't confront the possibility of your own mortality on a regular basis without squaring up your shit to the power who created you, however you defined that. But chest-grabbing *signs* from that power? Honestly, did God have time for this?

The answer to that was apparently a big affirmative.

Because she walked out again, lugging a tray full of extra drink garnishes, and he could've sworn the woman glowed.

"I'll get a cab back," he told his friend. "Think I want a nightcap after all."

"Because the half keg you sucked down at the Whisky wasn't enough?"

He gritted his jaw until the ache matched his chest. "Just go, would you?"

Kell's stare went the shade of a thunderhead. He probed it deeper back, beyond Tait, to where the only sight of Luna now was the top of her head as she bent to restock the garnishes. "Be careful." His storm-dark tone injected the words into the special translator they shared again. *Be careful, asshat, and think about this woman with your big head as well as your small one. The FBI may trust her, but I still don't.*

"Thanks, Mom." Without another word, Tait made his way back toward Luna.

She'd just shut the mini cooler and pushed up to her feet when he slid onto the stool in front of her. Her pupils dilated, and her lips parted, even hinting at a smile, before the bureau programming took over and her cavalier façade slammed back down. She didn't even greet him until after a bar rag was in her hand and she'd taken an order from the only other guy left on her end of the room.

"You're missing the train back to Hogwarts, Weasley."

His grin likely made him look like an idiot, but he didn't care. "Appears that way."

She spread her arms and braced her hands to the bar. The rope lights played across her tattoo like divine light that couldn't make up its mind. Angels or demons? He smirked a little. Maybe it was possible to be both.

"So what's up?" she finally asked.

He shrugged. "You asked if I was thirsty. The answer's yes."

"Okay." She tossed out a napkin. "What's your poison?"

He locked his elbows to the dark wood between them, determined to hold her gaze this time. Success, though his nervous system paid the price. Every inch of it sizzled like rice in hot oil as he took in the depths of her eyes. Goddamn, how had he forgotten how mesmerizing those purple depths could get, especially when she started to shed the feline detachment that the world saw most of the time? How had he forgotten what it did to him? How he longed to throw himself over the bar, hike her ass onto that cooler, and fuck her like a caveman with his tongue rammed down her throat?

You. My poison is you. And I can't think of a better way to die.

"A beer is fine."

She cocked her head, seeming a little surprised by that, though she pulled out a bottle of a dark import, popped the top, and set it in front of him. After he took an appreciative swig, she ventured, "So you're not scared of catching cooties from crazy Luna?"

"Never was." He pushed the beer aside and went for her hand, which she'd left on the bar after sliding the bottle out. "You know that."

For a second, she returned his clasp. But a heavy swallow went down her slender throat. "Tait...look..."

"That's what I'm doing, flower."

He didn't try to hide the tenderness from it. Or the protective longing. She'd hissed like a ticked adder when he'd first called her that nearly eight months ago, ordering him never to use it again. But he'd never been one for following orders that didn't make sense.

The woman didn't hiss this time. She broke into a little laugh. Sweet. Musical. Incredible. "You've got a pair of those stupid Victorian poet pants stashed underneath those shorts, don't you?"

He tossed back more of the beer for fortitude. "Let the op report show that *you* introduced the subject of what's in my shorts."

"Let the report show that you noticed."

"Just willing to do my part for the success of the mission."

Her gaze darkened to the color of the sky over Rainier before sundown. "Tait, we can't."

He shifted off the barstool and reached for her again. Too slow. She'd already stepped out of range, breathing hard against the arms she wrapped around herself.

"Why not?" he demanded.

"Because officially, I'm still the property of the Washington State penal system."

"So we're living dangerously. I'm sort of used to that."

"You didn't let me get to the unofficial part."

It hung in the air between them, weighted with a thousand times more meaning than what those nine words contained. Tait watched her lips work frantically against each other, took in the violet intensity in her eyes. The desire there. The need.

"I'm letting you now."

She swallowed again. Shifted from one foot to the other. "Maybe that wouldn't be so—"

As soon as she started the words, he surged into action. He'd been sitting near the end of the bar, so one swoop and a couple of steps got him behind it and then seizing one of her hands. Without a word, he stalked toward the storeroom. On the way, he steeled himself for her sputtering protest, for some colorful sentence strings comparing him to an ape, an asshole, or worse, but Luna didn't utter a peep. She actually kept pace with him.

All those facts confirmed an instinct that had grown over the last two minutes. The woman had to maintain a tigress's front for the world without a break. Perhaps the last time she'd let everything go was the hour she'd let him hold her in that private room at Bastille. Now, she definitely remembered what she craved but had lost the nerve, perhaps even the words, to ask for it. Her vacillation was likely worsened by the last experience she'd had with Domination. It wasn't Zeke's fault. It wasn't *her* fault. It just *was*. But now that truth would change.

Now, it was time the tigress got reminded how good it was to get devoured.

An affirming growl raged up his throat as he pushed her against the walk-in cooler. A moment later, he had her hip-to-hip and mouth-to-mouth. She moaned as he spread her lips and thrust in his tongue, claiming her with feral intent. He kept his grip on her hand long enough to fling it around his neck and guided her other arm to do the same. She tightened her hold as if instinctively knowing, maybe begging, for what he'd do next.

He clawed both hands into her thighs and lifted them around his. Dear fuck, she felt good. As the apexes of their bodies slammed together, his blood roared and his cock surged. He groaned and grunted before sliding his grip around her ass.

"Now what were you saying?" He gave her the taunt as his lips hovered over hers. Yeah, that abstinence wasn't going to last long. Their tongues were tangled again the next second, urgently mating as he began rocking her body against his. Tait gulped hard and gritted his teeth as he increased the pace, watching the ecstasy start to bloom across his flower's perfect features. He loved watching her brow knit. Her nostrils flare. And her lips, now stung from the pounding of his own, release harsh gasps of arousal.

"We...we can't—"

"We can." He kissed her again, letting another growl escape as she enhanced the pace by engaging her hip muscles, working with him on each crash of their bodies. "*You* can. Yes, Luna. Yesssss."

"Help me," she pleaded.

He pulled back enough so their stares met. Her eyes were hooded, heavy pools of purple lust. "You mean hurt you," he said.

Her answer took three seconds to come. "Yes. *Yes*. Make me forget...everything. Make it hurt. Please!"

He nodded. Slowly set her down. As soon as he was certain she could stand again, he grabbed her and turned her toward the kitchen's little chopping block. It smelled like a citrus grove. This is where those fresh drink garnishes had been prepared. How convenient that someone had left behind a whole box of those cute toothpicks with the colored swizzle tops.

He actually grinned as he pushed her over the block, facedown. She writhed and sighed in pleasure. He let her squirm in that state for close to a minute as he paced around the block, making sure she saw him stroking the growing mound at the center of his thighs. Only then did he speak again.

"Unbutton your pants, flower. Shove them down to your knees along with your panties." He broke the seal on a new box of toothpicks and let the contents flow out along the block in front of her face. "I'm going to give you what you need, Luna. I'm going to hurt you, and then I'm going to fuck you. I know you've got a few issues with safe words, but it's been a while for you, so call that red if needed."

"Yes," she whispered. "Yes, Sir."

He repositioned himself behind her, stroking her spine in appreciation for this stolen, perfect moment of time. Fuck, what a night. It had gone from crazy-good to crazy-bad at Bella's, then just plain crazy in the team's meeting, and now escalated to crazy-ecstatic.

He never should have underestimated the power of crazy-bad.

"Laudia?"

The shout came from the old bartender, now standing on the storeroom side of the swinging door. It was a good thing half Tait's brain was still in hyper-response mode, because he got Luna yanked up and turned around a second before the guy's gaze landed on them.

"Harvey!" Her voice was overly bright, though Tait doubted Grandpa Simpson noticed.

"Laudia?" He shot it at her in a teasing mutter.

"Cover name," she whispered back.

"Yeah, but *Laudia*? You didn't have time to bother with one more letter?"

She elbowed him as she gave Harvey a smile that likely raised the man's blood sugar by ten points. "Sorry. You need me? I was catching up with an old friend. I'd like you to meet... errm...Abnuss. Yes, this is my friend Abnuss."

Grandpa gave him a brief wave. "Nice to meet ya, Ab." He glanced back at Luna. "Sorry to break it up, but we got a rush.

Was there something goin' on at the Bowl tonight?"

"Likely." She was still more falsely cheerful than the first runner-up in a beauty pageant. "It's summer, and they *are* the Hollywood Bowl."

"Hmmppff." Whether that meant the guy agreed, disagreed, or just had bad gas, Tait couldn't tell. After "Laudia's" assurance she'd be out in a second and the guy finally left, he turned and pinned her with a playfully dark glower.

"Abnuss?"

She smirked in feline defiance. "That'll teach you to hate on my cover."

He moved in on her again with two prowling steps. "Yeah, about covers. Or as I prefer, no *covers* at all..."

He kicked up a new grin. Just as hers descended.

"A-Actually...Harvey probably saved us."

He gritted against the renewed ache in his chest. "Why does that sound like the Luna Lawrence version of *we need to talk*?"

She tipped her head, again regarding him with that strange mix she'd given him out at the bar. Part curiosity, part needy, with a giant slather of sadness on top. "There's nothing to talk about." Their hands touched. She laced her fingers into his, one by one. "You know it as well as I do."

He breathed hard, waiting for the pain in his chest to explode into fury. Didn't take long. He broke from her clasp to grab her face with both hands, ravaging her lips with an angry, biting kiss. He needed to brand her, make her feel—

What?

He jerked back, stunned by the charge that came from a corner of his mind. What *did* he want from her? What had he wanted from being with her tonight?

The answer burst at him immediately. Straight from the depths of the gut she couldn't stop wringing like a goddamn towel in a floodplain.

He didn't want anything.

He'd only wanted to give her what life itself couldn't.

Freedom.

In the depths of her mind, at the heights of her soul, with the submission of her body. If only for a few precious minutes... he'd wanted to set her free.

But gazing at her now, with the shutters back over her eyes and the tension rewrapped in her stance, divine revelation smacked him again. *A tigress can leave her cage only if she wants to.*

He heaved a leaden sigh. Kissed her again, this time with gentle resignation. But he didn't let go of her hand. He only did that after he grabbed a pen off a nearby clipboard and wrote the number of their hotel into the center of her palm.

"Just in case the cage closes in on you."

He turned after he whispered it, leaving the bar via the back door, treasuring the tiny gift she'd given him to take with him. The single tear he'd just thumbed off her cheek.

CHAPTER TWELVE

It was five a.m., and Ava's cell came alive with the strains of Britney Spears's "Piece of Me." Six months ago, she'd linked the song to one special person as a good-karma move. The day after, her sister had packed up and moved to Las Vegas after landing one of the most sought-after gigs in the city. She'd been chosen as a backup dancer in the star's sexy Planet Hollywood Resort show.

She rolled over in bed and scooped up the phone, almost stunned to observe that her hand looked normal against the device. After what Ethan had done to her body last night, she thought she'd be glowing. "Mmmm, *buenos dias, mi hermana.*"

For a long second, Zoe didn't say anything. "I think I'm going to call back and ask for the real Ava Chestain to pick up the phone."

"Laughing out loud...not."

"It's five in the morning. You're supposed to bitch at me that you were trying to catch ten more minutes of sleep. Then I'm supposed to argue that this is the only time you'll pick up the phone. Then you're supposed to tell me how my diva is doing, and I'm supposed to ask how yours is doing. Then I'm supposed to tell you that I just got moved up to lead on the dance team, and you're supposed to—"

Ava cut her off with a joyous shriek.

"Something like that," Zoe finished with a giggle.

Ava laughed in return and lowered her voice to a rasp.

"Oh, shit. Rayna's in the guest room with Zeke. They came home later than me too. Bet *you'll* become her favorite cousin now."

"What? I wasn't always her favorite?"

Ava scooted herself up and propped against the headboard. "Wow. I'm so proud of you, *hermana*. You worked your cute little ass off for this."

"Awww. *Te amo, cariña.*"

There was a telling pause. *Uh-oh.* Ava could feel her sister's assessment even through the miles that separated them. She needed to fill the gap fast with a chit-chatty question or comment, but nothing entered her mind except the man who'd filled this bed six hours ago. Who'd filled *her*... made so many of her forbidden fantasies come true in ways she never could have dreamed. In the hands of Ethan Archer, her submissiveness had become a gift as much for her as him. Even his abrupt departure, leaping to the call of his team, somehow added to the magic of being with him. The way he'd gotten dressed inside a minute, followed by his rough kiss and a growled promise to call so they could meet again before he went home, all imprinted his raw masculinity even deeper on her body and psyche. Even the lingering scent of him in the sheets, musk and midnight and pure man, made her blood sing and her body clench, wanting more...

"So, errrmm...what else is new in the city of sin these days? You still seeing that cop who gets mistaken for Chris Hemsworth every time you go out?"

Zoe laughed. "Yeah. Sorta."

"Sorta?"

A discomfited whine trickled over the line. "He's a little weird."

"Weird?"

"Yeah." Zo sighed. "I don't know. He looks at me strangely sometimes. Like he's appraising me for an estate sale or something."

She put Ethan on the back burner for a second and straightened in alarm. "That doesn't sound right."

"Meh. It's probably just a cop thing. I probably need to end it. We're just not on the same page. It's great to have a guy who understands my working hours, but other than that, we're not..."

"Not what?" Ava prompted after Zo's trail-off became a long pause.

"In sync," she supplied. "You know what I mean?" Her frustrated groan filled the line. "Aggghh. Maybe it's asking for too much, to have a guy who just...reads you right, you know?"

Ava couldn't help it. She smiled. It flowed up from her soul and into her reply. "It's not asking too much."

One long moment passed. Another. "Wait a minute." All three of the words were drawn out with Zo's older sister knowingness. "I know that tone."

"What tone?"

"You've met someone." When Ava feebly attempted a scoff, Zoe persisted, "You *have!*"

Discomfort set in. Was Ethan now a "someone"? In the roughly two hundred and one days since their forest encounter, she'd kept him firmly in the *Man Moments Best Forgotten* file. In the space of *one* day, he'd not only jumped out of the folder but was tempting her to torch the damn thing.

That left the question of what file he went into next.

"I don't know if I'd call it that," she muttered.

"What, so you didn't *meet* him? Does he work on the set?

Or was it one of those cute things, like you slammed grocery carts and his bread got mashed against your Ding Dongs?"

"My *Ding Dongs*?" She giggled.

"Don't diss the Ding Dongs. They're one of the main food groups."

She took advantage of Zoe's aren't-I-hilarious moment to slip in her revelation. "I met him when I went back home to visit Rayna before the holidays. At Sage Weston's wedding. Well, almost-wedding."

"The day that crazy convict held everyone hostage and nearly killed Garrett's friend?"

She purposely kept her voice light. "It was a memorable day, for sure."

"Wait." Zoe's tone took a fast turn into apprehension. "Weren't a lot of the guys at that thing from the base? Garrett's friends?"

Ava took a long breath and let her sister hear it. "I can tell where this conversation is headed."

The line went loud with Zo's huff. "*Estás loca?* Have you not learned anything after the shit that flew after Colin and Flynn?"

She punched a pillow. "*Mierda*. You don't even know his name."

"I don't need to. I don't *want* to. *Dios*, Ava! Soldiers are to your soul what bees are to your body. They suck you dry and you happily let them!"

"This isn't like that. Ethan is—"

"Different?" her sister shot back. "Really? How? He doesn't have the body that's hard in all the right places? He doesn't have the stare that makes you all gooey, ready to throw away every scrap of dignity you have just to feel that way again? He hasn't growled all the right things in your ear, kissed you until you can't think beyond wanting to be with him all the time, until you can't think *at all*? Am I wrong about any of that, *cariña*?" She stopped to let out a girl growl. "Am I wrong about telling you, as the person who helped scrape up what was left of your heart after Flynn's bullshit, that you're a jewel who doesn't deserve to be crapped on by these animals?"

"Stop it." She spat the words. "These *animals* sacrifice their lives for us! Ethan's team has spent the last seven months on a mission that was so dangerous, he can't even talk about it."

"His team?" Zoe practically stammered it. "A mission? *No me digas*, is he Special Forces, too? Ava, are you out of—"

"Time," she snapped. "I'm out of time, Zo. We have a long day on the set, and I need to get going. So save your breath."

She listened to her sister swallow back a lump of emotion. "I love you, Ava. That's all. It's only you, me, and *Papí* now. We need to take care of each other."

"I know." She sighed. "I know. But I'm twenty-four years old. I need a sister now, not a mother."

Zoe's thick silence told her all about the raw nerve she'd just struck. Feeling like crap, Ava picked at a thread on the pillow. Zo hadn't asked for the burden on her eleven-year-old shoulders when Mom came home from seeing *Giagia* in Greece and was dead from tuberculosis a week later, but she'd accepted her new role with grace and generosity, and she'd always been there to show Ava the way. But now it was time for her to let go a little. Now it was time for her to see that her *cariña* was full-grown and capable of learning from her mistakes—and qualified to make better decisions because of them.

Ethan was a better decision. She felt it in every thought he filled, in every window he'd smashed inside her lonely heart.

"Have a good day." Zo said it with as much cheer as Eeyore.

"You too, Ms. Dance Lead."

Her sister's comeback had a renewed smile in it. "Go make some people beautiful, wench."

"Got it, baby."

She laughed as she disconnected the line, and then looked at her phone for another long moment. Biting her lip nervously, she scrolled to her text-messaging screen...and tentatively typed the beginning of Ethan's name. Though she'd been diligent about deleting every message he'd ever sent to her, the device recognized his name and automatically filled it into the Recipient field. The blinking cursor waited for her to fill in the message part.

With a chastising grumble, she closed the window.

"Do this the right way," she ordered herself. "He told you he'd call, and he will." She nodded with determination. "Show Zoe she's wrong. He'll prove he's the different one. You know that. You *know* that."

Maybe he'd even prove he was the right one.

With a smile she felt down to her toes, she hurried to take a shower, taking care to keep the phone nearby.

★ ★ ★ ★ ★

A text came in on her way to the studio. She heard it ding when she was three stoplights away from the studio gate but dutifully left her cell in her purse until she'd parked. That officially turned those blocks into the longest she'd ever driven.

Her heart sank when she picked up her phone. The message was from Bella.

Exciting cast + crew mtng this am. Meet me on main set.

After the disappointment ebbed, the curiosity set in. Bella never went to the set without makeup. But her message distinctly said "exciting." It was a dichotomy worth witnessing, at least.

When she arrived at the soundstage, the air buzzed with activity like it was nine a.m. and everyone was ready for the first take of the day. Ava checked her watch. It was barely seven thirty. She gravitated toward the area they all referred to as main set, though it was actually a composite of four smaller areas that represented the main characters' homes and domestic base workplaces. The show had a couple of other permanent sets, including a huge "Middle Eastern forward operating camp," affectionately nicknamed Camp Cameron, and a scale representation of a Chinook helicopter with part of its side carved away for camera accessibility. Though the crew called that one "the shithook," openly borrowing the real army's slang, Ava had heard rumors it had a more secret pet name, as well: Bella's Bodacious Bird.

The real Bella wasn't looking terribly bodacious yet today, though Ava admitted the woman was more put together than she'd anticipated. Since the studio sent a car each morning out to the villa, Bella's usual MO was to roll out of bed and into the car, relying on Ava to tame everything into place for the day's shooting schedule. Right now, Bella had actually changed out of the sweats and T-shirt in which she normally showed up, favoring a soft caramel-colored sweater that was belted so as to show off her bust to its fullest. Her skinny jeans were tucked into suede ankle boots. Her hair was piled on top of her head in a purposeful mess, with tendrils framing a simple, self-applied makeup job. The only exception to the *Bella au naturel* look were her lips, perfectly adorned in the red she'd made so famous, MAC Cosmetics had renamed it "Bella's Kiss."

The title seemed appropriate this morning—in a way that made Ava's stomach turn over.

She entered just in time to watch the woman transfer at least an inch of that lipstick onto a defined, noble jaw...on the face that had filled her dreams last night. "Ethan?" she queried beneath her breath. "What the...?"

It trailed into nothing as her lungs clutched. Even in his dress uniform, he let the lipstick just stay there. Revision. He broke into a dazzling grin as Bella wiped it off for him. He murmured something, making her laugh louder as he tugged at the curls near both her cheeks. When she leaned her face into his palm, his smile vanished...as he tunneled his long fingertips deeper into her hair. They looked like a pair of teenagers dancing around the are-we-gonna-do-it-or-not elephant.

"Oh my God." She had a weird urge to laugh. Though she hid the burst behind a hand, it was the comfort she needed to push down her nausea and apply some common sense to this alternate universe into which she'd clearly stumbled.

That logic returned some indisputable facts. Ethan had been at Bella's last night but chosen to go home with her. He'd done those magical, carnal things with *her*. He'd commanded *her* to call him Sir and assured she'd never look at a peppermint without smiling again. And he'd helped her to start putting Colin and Flynn where they truly belonged. Far in her past. She was ready for the future—and his parting kiss from seven hours ago had told her he wanted at least an immediate part of that. Oh hell, that kiss.

He hasn't...kissed you until you can't think beyond wanting to be with him all the time...until you can't think at all?

"*Basta*," She spat it at a nonexistent Zoe, jamming her hands into her jeans pockets so she didn't have to watch them shake. There was a sensible reason why Ethan was back here today. And letting Bella paw him like they were rehearsing a sexy tango for one of those celebrity dance shows. And continuing to smile like he enjoyed every second of it.

Cameron to the rescue.

She let herself breathe as their director and unspoken leader entered. Cameron Stock was as big as a UFC champion but gentle as a high school guidance counselor, a combination that served him well during the show's production. By the gleam in his eyes and the eager grin on his square face, Ava judged he was working on his fifth or sixth cup of coffee for the day. Despite that, the man lifted his voice in its normal blend of statesman and quarterback.

"Good morning, everyone. Thank you for prying yourselves out of your normal nooks and crannies for the early call time."

As everyone chuckled, he turned to give a nod to one more person who arrived on the set. Though Cameron's motion was small, the effect was significant. The person he greeted was Mr. Lemare himself, dressed in his usual open-necked shirt, casual-but-custom suit, and luxurious Italian boots that were worth three months of Ava's salary. Everyone bolstered their posture and silenced their phones as Cam continued.

"As you can surmise, we've got a significant piece of news to relay today. Several, in fact. First, we have decided not to renew Mr. Lake's contract with the show. I know this part doesn't come as a surprise, considering how avidly Trent's been pursuing a film career. We wish him the best in his endeavors."

The bitterness in the man's eyes betrayed the opposite sentiment, but that wasn't a shock to anyone. His smile became a savoring smirk as he continued, "On that note, I'm ecstatic to say that we'll be killing off Mr. Lake's character in a big two-hour special taking place on our normal broadcast date in ten days." After the excited ripple from the declaration abated, he went on, "When I say big, people, I mean it. Mr. Lemare has gotten the studio's green light to contribute his own backing into this endeavor. We're buying up our own advertising slots so as to present the episode commercial-free. We'll be able to write it as a two-hour movie instead of a ten-part television episode, with the last half hour to be a live broadcast of our scripted content.

"Because of this, the story will be bigger, the action more intense. We'll be double-checking every detail of the plot, with the help of some real-world consultants generously on loan to us from the army. I'm happy to introduce Sergeants Archer, Lange, and Stafford, whom many of you met during their set visit yesterday. I'd like to thank you all for continuing our *Dress Blues* hospitality during their time with us."

Cameron basked in the excited applause that filled the building. Thirty seconds later, the production crew swarmed him in full interrogation mode about how the live broadcast was going to work. Everyone else turned to each other, chattering about the challenge ahead. It wasn't rare for reality shows to broadcast live, but in scripted television, the decision was a move that could either fly high or fall hard. At the moment, everyone concentrated on the more pleasant of those two options.

It was all background buzz to Ava.

Cameron's news had filled in the blanks about why Ethan

was still here. She'd been so riveted on him, she hadn't noticed Rhett and Rebel were here too. Of course, neither of them had Bella practically sitting in their lap with the flirtation jets on full, leaving them free to toss Ava a pair of good-natured waves. She slapped on a brave smile in return but quickly made her way outside, deciding she needed several minutes of air and solitude.

There was a corner outside that she'd secretly claimed as hers. It was located steps from the Wardrobe department, a benefit since Bella enjoyed making sure the team there earned their paychecks with her last-minute changes. Ava could always scoot there fast if need be. But the location was also dark and private, thanks to the hydraulic lift that seemed permanently parked there.

Today, she decided to take advantage of the equipment. After scooting up onto the platform of the lift, she rested her arms and chin on the lower railing and stared at the soundstage wall in contemplative silence.

Ten days. Ethan's stay had just been given a huge extension because of this gig as one of the show's advisors. The decision about the script direction must have happened late last night and explained why he'd gotten the drop-everything text from Franzen.

It was a gift. Wasn't it?

If asked back at midnight, she would have danced naked on the beach in thanks to the Hollywood marketing gods for it. A big part of her was still crazy proud of him and girlishly excited for herself. Just knowing he was in the same geographic vicinity, instead of two states and thousands of miles away, made the air itself feel a little more special.

But she couldn't deny what she'd just seen. The giddy

smile on Bella's face. The cavalier grin on Ethan's. And damn it, if Noah were loading up his ark today, they'd be the pair picked as the most beautiful creatures on earth. Bella looked like she belonged on his arm—and was fully acting the part too.

Which means what?

The question—to be accurate, her utter lack of an answer to it—had rolled her gut into the aching ball at which she winced at now. The spur to her heels, getting her out of there as fast as she could.

She instantly squirmed in retaliation. "You don't cower, Chestain." She ordered it from grinding teeth. "Cowering is in your past, damn it." Her shoulders straightened on a surge of determination. "You can handle this, whatever it is. He was in *your* bed last night, not hers. He kissed *you* goodbye until *he* broke away."

He was also the person she'd dragged out Colin and Flynn for. To whom she'd opened herself in ways she swore would never happen again.

"You told him their names. It wasn't a crime."

Just like it wasn't a crime for him to be holding Bella's hand and trading some jokes with the woman this morning.

She had to stop being a coward. To at least give him the chance to explain. *This time without Bella making like human plastic wrap on him.*

With head high and a confident stride, she made her way back to work. But once she was back on set, perplexity hit fast. Bella wasn't there anymore. That usually meant the star was in her trailer, which normally generated at least one frantic text with a demand of Ava's whereabouts, but the phone had been silent.

Charlie strolled in. "Hey, sweet truffle!" he greeted. "There you are. I looked for you during Cam's big pep rally. You didn't miss it, did you?"

She returned his hug. "I was in the back of the mob."

"Mmmm." Though his tone was encouraging, his gaze darted away. "Probably for the best."

Her throat turned into a solid lead pipe. "What's that supposed to mean?"

Charlie rolled his blue-greens at the catwalks overhead. "Dear Lawd in Heaven, I told her to jump fast onto the good bounty that is Ethan Archer, did I not? You heard me, heavenly fathah, didn't you?"

"Yeah," she retorted. "And so did I." Her face warmed. "And so I...did."

He plunged his gaze back down, eyes now wide. "Pardon the hell out of me, crème brûlée?"

"Have you and Matt been on another dessert obsession?"

"Don't you dare change the subject." He grinned as he grabbed her by the elbows. "You and Mr. Hunk of Decadent Goodness?"

Ava's whole face began to warm. "Yeah," she muttered. "Yesterday."

"Yesterday?"

"At Bella's place."

"At *Bella's* place?"

"In the wine room."

"Holy shit." He hauled her closer. "Does Bella know?"

"No!" She grabbed the front of his black D&G shirt. "And *you* are sworn to secrecy, Jenkow."

"Duh," he countered. But confusion crunched his features. "I only asked because..."

"Because what?" She dreaded giving the prompt. And if

Charlie gave the answer she expected, the feeling was doomed to get doubled.

"If Bella caught a whiff of the tour you gave him of the villa, that would explain a few things."

"What things?" She verbally stomped on the second word enough to make her friend hunch his brows at her. But before she could get any more information from Charlie, her cell buzzed. Bella's name appeared in the window, along with the string of exclamation points that formed the woman's version of a drop-everything summons. "Guess you lucked out, sweetie."

Charlie tugged her into a hug, his face still conveying that strange pensiveness. "And I hope you do too, creamsicle. God knows, nobody deserves it more."

She snorted. "You're just saying that because you still want that Prada tux."

Her joke worked. He grinned and drawled, "I'm just saying that because I love you." With his old snark intact again, he pulled back. "I also happen to be the new president of your fan club."

"Huh?"

"Fornication in Bella Lanza's wine room." He said it like the explanation was obvious. "There's no mountain you can't climb now. Go get him, tiger butter."

★ ★ ★ ★ ★

The trip back to Bella's trailer took her past the show's on-site production offices. Ava watched Cameron walking toward them, head down in what looked like an intense conversation with Rebel Stafford. Rhett waved at the pair from the window, sitting at a conference table that looked like a war room already, giving her the impression Ethan was likely nearby as well.

The observation, along with the boost of knowing she had a fan club with a president and everything, made her laugh as she walked the last thirty yards to the trailer. She berated herself for the conclusions to which she'd jumped when scrutinizing Ethan and Bella earlier. Bella herself would likely provide the logical explanation for their overtures, citing how they were remembering old times and couldn't keep their hands off each other for a few minutes. She'd respond by listening patiently, knowing Ethan would call soon...confident they'd find a way to see each other again during his stay.

Her heartbeat sped. Maybe they could even revisit the prop room. Just flashing on a memory of their kiss from yesterday, with the wall at her back and Ethan's body fitted to hers in all the right places in front, provided deeper assurance that whatever happened between him and Bella on main set—

Was now the main attraction they'd taken to the dressing trailer.

"*Dios.*"

The adrenaline she'd been enjoying two seconds ago turned into a congealed mess at the base of her throat, preventing nothing more from coming out. Not a sound. Not a choke. Certainly not a breath. But her eyes worked just fine, damn them, and were now seared with the image of Ethan, sans his uniform jacket, leaned back in Bella's styling chair, chuckling while the woman straddled him, playfully brandishing a tube of hair cream. Like she needed help from the product. Her red fingernails were missiles of seduction in his thick hair. As she deepened the invasion, Ethan's hands tightened against her bare thighs. Such a thing was possible when all somebody wore was a mini satin dressing robe, a red demi cup, and matching thong panties.

"Ava!" Bella's greeting was half buried in giggles. "Finally. *Per amor di Dio*, where have you been?"

"I...uhhh...had to... Wardrobe had something for me to—"

"Did you make it for Cameron's meeting?" As the woman scooted off Ethan's lap, her tone clicked into a business mien, though that didn't stop her from sliding a hand down his chest as she went. Ethan's tight but discernible grunt, definitely a sound of pleasure on top of pain, assured that the knot in Ava's throat wasn't going anywhere.

"I..." she stammered. "Yeah. I was there." She couldn't bring herself to move. Or to stop staring into the mirror, where it seemed easier to look at Ethan now. If she confined him to the reflection, then it wasn't really him sitting here. It wasn't really his wrinkled clothes, with his dark-blue pants stretched into that hard mound where it most mattered. And it sure as hell wasn't his stare that stabbed through the dark discord of his hair, right at her, without a moment of softness or acknowledgment about what they'd shared yesterday. It wasn't him staring as if she might as well be just another pretty face in a land that ate pretty for breakfast.

"Good, good." Bella strolled to the refrigerator and pulled out a vitamin water. "*Porca vacca*, with all this excitement, I'm simply parched. Ethan darling, do you want one too?"

"Negative." He let that stretch into the most uncomfortable three seconds of Ava's life. "But Ava looks like she might."

"I'm fine."

She spewed the words more than said them. She could barely stand here breathing the same air as him right now, let alone be bothered with the sham of civility. Ethan seemed to understand at least that much, but Bella didn't. Her boss whipped over a look of such stunned fury, Ava was forced to drop her head. Humiliation joined her rage, pouring its scalding pain through the giant crack in her heart and into the center of her soul.

"Of course she is. Ava's always good to go. Aren't you, sweetie?"

"Oh, yeah." She threw a smirk full of Cinderella sweetness at Bella. "That's me. Ready for...anything." With the smile still in place, she let her eyes throw Evil Queen daggers at Ethan. "But you know, I did leave some, umm, supplies back at main set. Be back in a jiff."

As she turned and stumbled to the door, she was all too aware of Ethan rising behind her. There was no way she couldn't be. Even now, with every cell in her body yearning to get away from him, the awareness of his size, his heat, his potent presence was like a drug on her helpless libido, pulling ruthlessly at her for another hit.

When would she learn?

When the *hell* would she realize that guys like him had special radars for women like her: the ones who got one look at their dog tags and one earful of their boot stomps and opened their legs while closing down their common sense...until it was too damn late. Like now.

"I need to get going too, missy," she heard him say to Bella.

"Awww." Her trademark pout permeated every note. "For real, arrow bear?"

Arrow bear?

She was strongly tempted to use that as an excuse to hurl when she got outside the trailer door. But getting away from

Ethan Archer, as fast as she possibly could, ranked much higher on this mission objective.

CHAPTER THIRTEEN

Ethan didn't bother shouting after her. It hadn't worked yesterday, and it sure as fuck wasn't going to work now. Instead, he skipped straight to catching up to her, hooking an arm around her waist, and hauling her into a nearby building that was thankfully unlocked. From the desks he'd glimpsed through the window, he guessed the place was a temporary production office. The assumption was right. The room also contained a bunch of filing cabinets, rolling chairs, and even a kitchenette with a single-cup coffee maker. As settings went, it was fine. He wasn't too sure about the seething fireball of a woman still locked in his hold.

"Let me go!" Ava demanded.

"Stop kicking and I will."

"I'll scream."

"Empty threat, sunshine. You're doing a fine job of that right now."

"Shut. Up. And take your goddamn hands off me!"

"Stop kicking first. Please." Ironically, he summoned some Dom mojo to emphasize the last word.

"Ethan, if you don't let me go—ahhh!"

He released her. And watched her fall right on her adorable ass. Because she'd been kicking so hard, she had no proper footing to stand.

Because of how you hurt her. How you're still hurting her because of this ruse with Bella. And have to continue digging that damn knife into her, until that memory stick is found.

He turned, unable to contain his grimace. He'd done shitty things for this job but this capped the list. He hadn't signed up to be lounging around a goddamn movie studio, playing James Bond games and earning himself a tormented glower from the woman he'd pursued across seven months and over a thousand miles. This woman he now had to treat like a possible suspect in this fucking thing, at least in the eyes of his team.

But if he went to Franz and came clean about everything, told him that Ava Chestain had passed his personal "body cavity search," the captain would toss his ass onto a plane for home faster than anyone could yell *Roll, mark, action*. He couldn't, *wouldn't*, let that happen, not when Ava was working every day for a man with tight ties to terrorists who'd been pulling some scary, shifty shit lately. If he had to endure Ava's hatred for that, so be it. She'd be pissed, but she'd be *safe*.

He held out a hand to help her up. Ava glared, shoved to her feet by herself, and then parked herself in one of the rolling chairs, pulling a hand through her hair in fury. *Hell*. She had to remind him of how the thick chocolate curls had felt between his fingers, didn't she?

It took every ounce of concentration he had to keep his voice even. "Are you okay?"

"Do you care anymore?"

He caught her stare, afire with fury and pain, and answered quietly, "After last night, is that fair?"

She let out a bitter laugh. "After last night, should I have expected to come to work and find Bella straddling you like a lap dancer? Of course, after the two of you warmed up at the cast and crew meeting—"

"Bella and I share a past." The words were tight with

his tension. The truth was, Bella—at the time, Brenda—was a mistake that never should've happened. Just being around her the last forty-eight hours had shown him that. What had he seen in her eight years ago? A sexual appetite that matched his own, that was what—not that he was going to drop that particular bomb into this conversation. "We're comfortable with each other. And this *consulting* shit is a whole lot of brand-new and weird to me. She's trying to help."

"Right. With her naked body in your face."

He hated this. Dancing on the line between truth and fiction...this wasn't how he did things. He was called in when the op called for someone to dig at the reality, uncover the facts. Bending them made him feel like a wolf in a bad sheep fleece. Sure, he'd pulled on the wool before, just never after one of the lambs had let him strip her, dominate her, and bury himself inside her until reaching one of the best climaxes of his life. Just the recall of it tempted him to pull the window shades, lock the door, and take her all over again, spread-eagle under him on one of these desks...

Fuck. That stick had better turn up *soon.*

Dwelling on that mirage wasn't doing squat to help him right now. *C'mon, asshole, you* do *remember at least a few things about the art of tact, right?*

"Okay, so her communication style is...unique."

"You didn't seem to be minding 'unique.'"

Ava deliberately dropped her gaze to his crotch. Crazily, he opened his stance, letting her look her fill of the engorged space between his thighs. The flush that filled her beautiful cheeks turned the moment into agony, every inch of his dick on fire, every drop of come in his balls boiling, but he didn't waver as he summoned the strength for a reply.

"I'm a man, Ava. Biologically, I responded to her—after she rubbed and stroked and dry-humped me for close to an hour. *You've* done this inside of twenty seconds with your eyes alone."

She didn't say anything to that. But her silence, tremulous and thick, was three times worse. She wrapped arms around herself and rasped, "Is that supposed to make everything okay?"

He looked to the floor. And was pretty sure he saw most of his gut mixed with the grime between a couple of loose floor tiles. "I can't tell you what's okay and what's not."

"Really? You had no trouble doing exactly that last night." She sniffed and there was no mistaking why. The sob that followed overlaid her next words. "And I thanked you for it. *Dios mio*, I adored you for it." She shot out of the chair and paced to the kitchenette. "*Qué tonta eres.* I'm such an idiot. Zoe was right, wasn't she?"

He moved toward her in a couple of silent steps. "Zoe?"

She started. His new proximity took her by surprise. Good. That was his intent. Keeping her off guard would keep her truthful. He didn't expect her to spill anything on Lemare, believing every instinct he had that she was ignorant of his Lor side, but maybe this was his way of getting all the way inside her emotional window and gaining her trust despite everything he had to hide from her right now.

"My sister," she explained, bracing hands on both sides of the little sink. "She called this morning before I came to work. I told her about you." Bitterness stamped her conclusion. "She wasn't happy."

"Because my carpool van is a Black Hawk and my negotiation suit is a set of BDUs."

She sliced another glare over her shoulder at him. He was used to getting such a look, that mixture of *how did he know* and *thank God he knows*. "A little bird named Rayna talked, huh?" Her fingers pressed against the counter, betraying how she intended to deal with her cousin about it.

"She was only trying to help," he contended. "Just like Zoe." One more step brought him to the kitchenette as well. As much as he ached to pull her close, breaching her personal space would shatter both their composures, so he maintained a stance against the other end of the counter. "I was starting to snap it together for myself anyhow."

That got him a longer look. It came attached with a wince. "You snap too much," she whispered.

He threw back a gentle smile. "Hazard of the job, sunshine."

The wince crumpled into another sob. "Don't pull out 'sunshine' on me right now. Don't you dare."

He held up a hand. "Fair enough. As long as you help me in return."

She only answered by rolling her eyes before shoving away from the counter. How was it that on any other subbie, that shit reeked of gum-smacking twelve-year-old, but on her it was a gorgeous invitation to harness her sass with the power of his tongue—or any other means necessary?

He gritted back the arousal to focus on her more carefully. She trembled from head to toe as she walked to the opposite side of a small round conference table. Yeah, she was still pissed, but a new epiphany hit as he studied her. Witnessing the new "closeness" between Bella and him didn't comprise all of her anguish. That had only hit the start trigger. If his intuition was running true, and there were few occasions when it wasn't, her torment was tied directly to his presence itself, to the fact that he still stood here at all.

In his dress blues.

Smacking her in the face with memories. Painful ones. Likely the stuff that Rayna was going to tell him last night before Colton and his team put their unique dent into things.

What the fuck had happened to her?

Half hating himself for the move, he pulled one of the chairs at the table and lowered into it. Yes, he knew the impact of what he was doing. Visually, it made him submissive to her. He emphasized the impact by opening his arms and laying them flat on the table. "Pretend I'm Rayna and Zoe too. Pretend I just want to help. Help me understand, Ava. Talk to me."

Silence fell. Outside, a truck beeped as it was thrown into reverse. A costume rack squeaked by. Leaves skittered in the wind. Hollywood clamored on. The world spun.

The woman who plummeted into the chair next to him didn't care. One look at her face, contorted in her misery, told him why. Her mind wasn't here anymore. It was in the past, facing the heartbreak that waited for her there.

He ordered his arms to stay where they were. *Grabbing her and holding her isn't going to help her through this. You can't help her climb a mountain if she's on your back.*

After several long minutes, she spoke.

"I had a few boyfriends from the base when I was very young." Her voice was a wobbly rasp. "They were fun, but it always ended once a long deployment came up or a girl came along who wanted to hitch up, get a little house, and start having babies and swing sets." A little smile twitched her lips. "I wasn't the girl who wanted all that. My *mamá*—my mom—

died when I was nine, and watching what my dad went through, to say goodbye to her...it broke my heart too. It broke *me* in some ways, I guess. Crazy, huh? One day you're a kid who cares about nothing except the next school dance. The next you're wondering if your dad will ever smile again. And it wasn't *Papi*'s fault. Things just get...broken. And so do people, right?"

Ethan wasn't sure if she wanted an answer or not. He chose silence. These were strange waters for him. Listening to people, even the things they showed instead of spoke, was part of his job, natural as breathing, because he was always behind a window of his own. But that neutrality didn't exist now. He felt the ache in each of her softly accented syllables. Burned with the sadness that clung to the indigo depths of her eyes.

"Oh God," she finally murmured. "Why am I telling you any of this?" She shook her head, pulling nervously at her hair. "You have to get to some meeting, right?"

"It can wait." Until next year if it had to. Especially because his instinct didn't want to shut up now. Despite that, he dreaded giving voice to it. "So who was it that didn't make you feel broken anymore? Colin or Flynn?"

Her head yanked up. Across her face, a race of emotions took place. First she gazed at him in fear. Hot on its heels was amazement. Then trepidation again. "How the hell do you know—" She visibly hauled back her thoughts from that gallop and confessed, "Colin. It was Colin."

He was a little surprised to watch a soft smile tug at her mouth. Surprised and jealous. Tying back both the useless sentiments, he ventured, "He was from the base?"

"Oh, yeah." She lowered a hand and scooted it toward his. As she curled their index fingers together, she went on, "I'd never met anyone like him. He was like a rock star with a yutcut. Bigger than life, so cocky and silly... He made me forget I'd ever been sad in my life. I think I fell in love with him inside a week. The day before he shipped out to Kirkuk, he proposed. We didn't have time to go find a ring, so he made me one out of some wire and pieces of a seashell we'd found on Alki Beach. He told me—"

She stopped herself with a hard swallow.

Ethan's chest clenched. "It's okay." He added the rest of his hand to their clasp. "Ava, you don't have to do this."

"He told me he'd come back," she bit out. "He promised... we'd buy a real ring." She pulled in a ragged breath. "A lunatic with an IED made sure that never happened."

Again, he didn't speak anything in response. He let her have the silence. The normal things people said with news like this...were just that. Normal. Standard niceties used to make a story from hell feel less horrific. He'd buried enough friends, grasped enough widows' hands, to know the silence was kinder.

After a few minutes, he took a chance on letting his instincts gain voice again. "And...you thought it would be different with Flynn," he said softly.

She gave a ragged nod. "Sure did."

"Was it another IED?"

Of all the responses he expected, her full-throated laugh wasn't anywhere near the list. As he arched a bewildered brow, she blurted, "It was one hell of an explosion. You got *that* part right."

"Officially lost here."

A blush actually claimed her face. She shook her head. "Flynn was just the mistake who taught me that boys in this"— she stabbed a finger into his uniformed chest—"are not a great idea for this." She pointed back at her heart.

With that, the energy in the air shifted. Her grief got clearly sidelined for antagonism. Once more, silence seemed the wisest plan for response.

"I'd been weeping in my wine about Colin for over a year," she explained. "My friends finally decided that getting me drunk and laid would help with that a little. Flynn was just in the right place at the right time. He was a cute, smart PFC who worked on helicopters with his big, rough hands—better than chocolate to a girl who'd gone without for a while."

He still rendered little else. The story about Colin had been easier to handle than imagining her in a girls-night-out dress minus a few inhibitions thanks to *Señor Patrón*, then going home with some asshat who only wanted one thing. For the moment, he ignored the realization that *he* probably appeared that way now too.

"I ended up giving him my number afterward." She blushed again. "Stuffed it down his pants to be exact, right after learning he'd never be shipped out due to a nasty high school football injury. In my mind, the universe was telling me the grief dues were paid and I'd finally won the jackpot. We got very serious, very fast. Well, what I thought was serious."

"Engineer Flynn wasn't on the same page?" The man must have been a damn idiot, but Ethan wasn't about to voice that.

Her gaze drifted out the window. "That's one way of putting it." She let out a raspy laugh. "The signs were all there; I just didn't want to see them. Flynn was like Colin in all the big ways—the sex, the laughter—so like a fool, I jumped straight to the next logical conclusion."

"That you two were connected enough for marriage." After accepting her grimace as confirmation, he ventured, "So you really are the cute house and swing set girl."

She swept to her feet in a furious rush. "People break, Ethan, remember? And who wants broken goods?"

Okay, no more Mr. Calm and Understanding. He surged up as well and advanced straight toward her. "And that's logical how? Just because Flynn the Fuckhead didn't want to walk down the aisle?"

She turned back before he got to her, stopping him in his tracks. Every inch of her face was possessed by raw defeat. "Because he didn't want to walk down the aisle with me, Ethan."

He scowled. "What are you saying?"

Another sad laugh spilled from her. "He went to a training meeting in Reno sponsored by a civilian contractor. On the second night, he called sobbing at me—in happiness. Apparently, he and a girl from the base workshop decided to come clean about a mutual attraction, and they'd just tied the knot. *That* knot. He'd called to ask if I'd go to his apartment and clean out my stuff so his new wife wouldn't have to."

"Fuck."

It wasn't eloquent. He doubted it was even comforting. But it was the only thing his fury could coherently create. It turned him into a slab of awkward uselessness, unsure whether to hug her, punch a wall for her, or ask her for Flynn's last name so he could hunt down the prick and turn him into a soprano for her.

Ava was somehow able to read all that across his face. "It's all right," she said with a shrug. "I should probably thank the guy. After Zoe helped me get my head and heart back together, I decided that after everything the Lewis-McChord boys had put me through, the Hollywood jungle would be a breeze. It's when I moved down here and took a shot at styling the big-timers."

"And here you are." He let her hear the encouraging pride in his tone. It seemed to surprise her. Then unnerve her.

"Right." She flashed a smile more falsely bright than her voice. "Here I am."

"Successful, confident, beautiful." *And never imagining that the corporal you kissed in the woods back home was going to be the sergeant who brought all that shit screaming back to your front door.* "I'm really proud of you."

He dared to lift a hand to brush some hair from her face. Somehow he had to make her see that he wasn't another Flynn, that everything from yesterday still meant something to him today, probably more. But in doing so, the curtains from the ruse with Bella had to stay up. He had to save face without tempting her to claw the skin off it. Easy-peasy, yeah?

While he deliberated what the hell to say and do now, she'd obviously been doing the same thing. From the sad vacillation in her eyes and the little bites she dug into her lips, he already knew he wouldn't like her outcome. "Ethan..."

"What?"

"You're still officially on duty, right? How do you guys say it? 'The op's in play'?" She asked it in a rasp softer than the breeze on the windows. *Damn it.* He could deal with her in pissed-off whirlwind mode, but this permeating sadness simply froze him in place.

"Yeah," he growled. "Right."

Though she ran reverent fingers along his lapels and name badge as she did, the motions were more *goodbye, soldier* than *hello, Sir.* "That means you're *working* with Bella more."

Ethan expelled a hard breath. He wrapped her fingers in

his, dragging the depths of his self-control not to grip until he had her hauled against him. "What does that have to do with us?"

The beginning of a new sob crunched her face, though she beat it back by defiantly jerking up her chin. "It has everything to do with us and you know it." The tears finally broke through, falling in thick, silent tracks down her face. "It always did, from the second Bella saw you again yesterday. I knew it and I ignored it...and I was stupid to do so."

His own teeth locked, barring his snarl until he spoke. "*Ava—*"

"I just hoped..." she stammered. "I...I just thought that maybe..."

When she couldn't finish, he decided to do it for her. Why the fuck not, when his gut-deep growl phrased everything so perfectly? It resonated through him as he dragged her against him. In a heady instant, her scent surrounded him. Oranges and jasmine filled his nostrils as her sweet nearness ignited his body. His skin blazed. His blood was liquid fire. His cock felt like a goddamn signal flare. He tunneled his other hand into her hair, positioning her face for his commanding kiss. In another second, he'd prove that her hopes weren't for nothing. That he hoped too. And wanted. And needed. And craved. And—

She'd be even more shattered than before.

Fuck. He couldn't do this. No matter how it got choreographed, taking her in the horizontal mambo now would be doomed to disaster. Even if he gave her a dozen screaming orgasms, it wouldn't redeem him from what had to happen when they returned to real life. The Don Juan veneer with Bella had to continue until he, Rhett, and Rebel cracked

Lemare's inner sanctum. Compounding that by getting naked with Ava again would officially ink him onto her *Flynn and Assorted Other Assholes* list.

But if he took her into confidence and revealed the true purpose of their on-set presence, he risked the security of the entire team as well as her own. They had no idea what the Aragons and their producer friend were actually up to. Letting her bite that apple of knowledge would only replace her fury with fear, exhuming Colin's ghost when she was blatantly reminded of how dangerous his work really was.

He stood in the middle of Hollywood, California, but he might as well be on the road between Ramadi and Fallujah. Screwed no matter which direction he chose.

He pressed his forehead to hers as he sucked down air in hard heaves. Her chest pumped with the same ferocity. Fuck. *Fuck.* Just another inch, a few millimeters, and he'd at least get to taste her once more. Drink in the nectar of her sweet, hot mouth...

With tight chokes, they pulled away from each other.

"M-Maybe," she whispered, "this all happened for the best."

The fuck it did. "Sure."

"Don't growl. I'm serious."

Serious was a few miles back, sunshine. I'm pretty much at miserable now. "Uh-huh."

"We...we have closure now, Ethan. Seven months ago, we didn't. We got it all out of our systems. Now we can move on."

She had the audacity to urge him into a "friendly" hug. But as he enveloped her back in his arms, breathed her back into his senses, let her warmth permeate him like a bath in the summer sun, only one blowback of thought blasted through his mind, charring the edges of his soul.

"Out of my system?" That's one place you'll never be again, Ava. Ever.

CHAPTER FOURTEEN

"I'm never going to complain about surveillance on hostiles again."

Kellan's remark, mumbled between a couple of swigs of energy drink, brought out a commiserating chuckle from Tait. They'd been parked on this soundstage roof from six in the morning until ten at night for four days now. Nearly sixty-five hours of watching nothing but rolling costume racks, trucks full of plants and props, carts full of electronics, and golf carts full of arguing people roll by. If gathering intel in the Mideast desert was tedious, spying on this rogue state of creative combustion was a goddamn soul sucker.

"Crap on a stick!"

A starlet below, outfitted in a formfitting gold toga for an episode of the superhero show that taped down the way, stopped and exclaimed it to her friend, who was outfitted in a turquoise-blue version of the same ensemble.

"Another broken nail?" Tait mumbled.

"Pffft." Kell peered through his hand scope. "She's looking the wrong direction. I'll bet the double-sided tit tape isn't working on that slick fabric again."

"We can only hope."

His friend hummed in surprise. "Not a broken nail. A broken heel."

"A *what*?"

"Shoe," Kell explained. "Her left heel snapped right off."

"That's new."

"No shit. I wonder if Wardrobe checks the costumes for issues like that."

Tait shoved back and leaned against a low wall that framed an industrial air-conditioning unit. "And I wonder if we'll ever have a conversation about something that really matters again."

"Fuck." It was Kell's way of agreeing. Not that he dropped the scope for a second.

They passed several more minutes listening to the buxom blonde and her leggy friend go over the options she had with the broken shoe while continuing to keep one eye apiece on the side door to the *Dress Blues* soundstage. While this entrance got used less by the show's cast and crew, they took an educated stab at this being the best area to observe Lor's comings and goings, since his on-lot offices were closer to this door. But so far, the only thing they'd seen the guy do was talk on his phone, fix his hair, pace to his office, talk on his phone some more, hit on gold toga *and* turquoise toga, and then talk on his phone even more.

At first, all that cell chatter had given them hope, but after accessing and translating both sides of the conversations, they had nothing except recordings of Lor talking about production deals, selling his mansion, and bawling out his nutritionist that, after taking thirty supplements every day, he wasn't gaining the muscles the guy had apparently promised. Tait and Kellan had started to throw down bets as to when the nutritionist would grow the balls to address the man's nonstop cigarette habit. So far, their joint ante totaled forty-two dollars and fifty cents.

"Okay, let's feed the kitty," Kell offered. "A buck says Aphrodite girl decides to go for the exotic look and barefoots it."

Tait snorted. "Are you serious? She's pea green over the bestie's height. Not a chance she's giving up the heels."

A voice from directly over his head drawled, "Sounds like you boys are having a grand time."

Tait joined Kell in whipping out his pistol and turning on the source of the quip. "Holy God," he spat, exasperated and relieved at the same time. Though he matched Kell's inhalation to try to regulate his heartbeat to normal, there was a slim fucking chance of success when Luna stood there outfitted to the brink like the studio accountant she was impersonating. Her dark-brown wig was styled in a demure bun that topped double pearls at her neck, a gray vest over a white dress shirt, and a black pencil skirt with matching black pumps.

"Somebody rang for God?"

She strutted forward, taking the saucy secretary image to a whole new level. Tait couldn't rip his stare off her. Holy fuck, what he wouldn't do for a three-piece suit and a desk with bondage hooks about now.

Kell broke into that wet dream with a line of blazing rage. "Are you fucking nuts?" he charged.

"Maybe," Luna returned. "Scratch that. Yeah, probably."

Kellan held up his pistol while he dropped back into position to scope out Lor's door. "These are called firearms, Luna. We pull them out when there's the possibility of hurting or even killing someone with them."

To Tait's shock, Luna dipped her head and kicked at the cement below them. "You're right. Sorry."

After Kell acknowledged that by throwing up his hands, forgiving her and ignoring her in the same gesture, Tait shifted closer toward her. Watching her even inch toward submissiveness with someone other than him was, he now openly admitted, a massive problem. "How the hell did you get up here? In *those* shoes? It's a twenty-foot vertical climb *after* you clear the soundstage catwalks."

"What?" Her eyes, covered by contacts that darkened them to midnight blue, narrowed in confusion. "They're platform heels, Weasley, not strappies."

"Well, shit. Now I feel so much better."

"Stop being a Neanderthal."

He grinned. The opening was too damn good. After making sure the toga girls had really secured Kell's attention again, he couldn't resist forming a hand around the perfect swell of her ass. He leaned down and grated into her ear, "You crave Neanderthal."

Her breath instantly hitched, igniting every inch of his body, before she countered, "You have no idea what I crave."

"I have *every* idea what you crave." He moved his hand around her body. "And every idea of how to give it to you."

She reached a hand to stop him but stopped it at his forearm, betraying her own need by gripping him tight there. Since they were working this op out of sight, he and Kell were dressed in camo tops and bottoms, but that didn't stop the magic of her touch from penetrating the thick cloth.

"What?" she murmured. "You going to wave your *magic wand* at me, Weasley?"

He ran his lips down the column of her neck. "Flinging long, blunt objects might have something to do with it, yes."

She dug her grip harder. The action pulled at his arm hair. The tiny rasps of pain fired his desire even hotter. "We...we have to...stop."

He groaned. "Did you have to pick the second I discovered your thong line to say that?"

A little laugh sounding like sultry music spilled from her before she stepped back and deliberately kept him at arm's distance. "This is business, okay? I'm up here, even in this getup, because Franzen and Dan sent me."

For a second, he was actually grateful for her no-nonsense stance. It helped him leapfrog over the observation that she'd said *Dan* again, with that little pitch of familiarity smoothed on top. *Nope. Don't go there, dude. Not now.*

He called back to Kellan, "Yo, Slash. Get your adorable ass over here."

Kell shoved to his feet and trudged over. "My ass is none of your business, dickwad."

Normally that would earn the guy another line of snark, but Luna now braced her posture like his, doubling his curiosity about her purpose in coming up. When she had Kell's full attention too, she started. "Bernardo Galvaz contacted Dan late last night."

Tait traded a glance with his partner.

"The guy Runway chatted up in the desert last week?" Kellan confirmed. "Colton reinserted him back in with the Aragons after the interrogation, right?"

Luna nodded. "He called on the private line for the branch. Wouldn't speak to anyone but Dan. Apparently the Aragons are planning quite a party, cartel style."

"Meaning?" Kellan prompted.

"The compound has become more lively than usual. Galvaz even said he felt like they were preparing to become a war zone. The two Aragons themselves, who usually appear publicly in nothing but pricey suits and designer shoes, were greeting new recruits in battle camos." Her brow furrowed and her full lips twisted. "The fact that they were greeting recruits

218

at all raises a flag. Mateo and Alex aren't usually ones for denting their manicures on the boys who run their smack."

Tait voiced the logical conclusion to that. "If the *guests* are drug hustlers at all."

"That was Galvaz's point." Luna raised her hands to her hips in emphasis. "He went on to tell Dan that these guys didn't seem like street dealers. They walked past tables full of new heroin bricks without blinking. Their goal was clearly something else."

Kellan leaned against the air-conditioning hutch, shoulders tight with concentration. "Professional mercenaries, then? But for what purpose?"

Aggravation pressed on Tait. "Damn it. We need to get into that laptop."

Luna took a measured breath. "That's why I'm here." She tossed a glance across the roofs of the studio lot then back to both of them. "They've sent out a *second* laptop."

"What?" He joined Kell in growling it.

"It left the compound after midnight in a Mercedes with California plates, with *four* of those new mercenaries inside. It was the main reason Galvaz called. The guy is wigged. He negotiated with Dan on the line for his family's safety because he's sure he'll be dead at the end of all this. He's also sure he won't be the only one."

"Fuck," Kellan muttered.

Tait was tempted to echo his friend's sentiment. There was something about the way Luna's face softened as she said that, almost like she commiserated with Galvaz, that made his arms clench with the need to pull her close again and keep her there this time.

He funneled his frustration into a tight-lipped outburst.

"Haven't these jerkoffs heard of the Internet? What's so important that they can't encrypt the shit out of it, press Send, and become the problem of the cyber-spooks in Langley?"

Kell didn't bite on the bait of his rant. The guy rarely did. It was why they worked well together. Instead, his friend lifted a nearly serene gaze back to Luna. "So you're saying we now keep eyes open for the second laptop."

She nodded again. "And radio straight to Franz if you see it."

It was the answer they both expected, so Kell didn't say anything at first. He swept an even gaze across the cityscape, raising it to include the iconic letters on Mount Lee—H-O-L-L-Y-W-O-O-D—before murmuring, "We're still only doing half the job if we don't get that data stick."

The comment made Tait wince on behalf of Rhett, Rebel, and Ethan. As much as this part of the op sucked ass, he and Kellan had a cakewalk compared to the world of glitz, glamour, and insanity through which their friends had slogged the last few days.

"I can speak for the spooks in saying we wholeheartedly agree with you, Sergeant Rush." As if to prove the point behind her tense tone, Luna squirmed against the confines of her outfit. Fucking great. Just when Tait's crotch had settled into a comfortable state of stand-down, she went and let all that fabric rub her body in all the places he wanted his hands. "And I'm glad to say we might be catching a break there too."

"Thank God," Kellan declared.

"You're welcome." She smirked. As Kell snorted and shook his head, she continued, "I'm not so sure Runway's concurring with your take, but he's being a good sport about things."

"A 'good sport'?" Tait let his eyebrows dance in amusement. "Please tell me this involves the guy having to put on some makeup. Some of that pancake stage shit?"

Luna's smirk became a little laugh. "Actually, worse."

That got even Kellan's interest. "Worse?"

"The network is the key sponsor of a small but pricey fundraiser event at the Loews Santa Monica tonight. Wounded vets organizations are sharing the proceeds. Ethan and Rhett are going as special guests at Enzo Lemare's table."

"What about Rebel?" Tait queried.

"He begged off with a sore throat."

Tait openly scoffed. "Sore throat, my ass. Rebel Stafford is half pirate. Even the devil won't touch him. Every virus and bacteria on earth swore him off ten years ago."

Luna shrugged and fingered her pearls, a pure feminine move that still didn't help the damn tempest in his pants. "Well, he's also a good actor, because it stuck. He's confined to checking script accuracy for the afternoon. Runway and Double-O are on their way to have manicures, scalp treatments, shaves, and hair styling while their dress uniforms are prepped."

He and Kell waited for a second of respectful silence. Then let their laughs explode.

"Scalp treatments?" He emitted a lingering snicker. "And manicures? And somebody's going to take pictures of the pretty little ponies when they're all done, right?"

Luna's gaze met his, sparkling with merriment despite the contacts. Damn, it felt good to give her some happiness. "With the entire Hollywood press corps invited and half the limos in town booked? Uhhh, yeah. You could say that."

Tait turned and bumped fists with his friend. "Epic."

CHAPTER FIFTEEN

An early season hurricane had hit Mexico last week. The debris from it, nasty balls of tangled seaweed and mud, had started to wash up on California beaches a couple of days ago.

Except for the wad that had made its way to Ava's throat.

She did her best to smile through the agony while she kept to the shadows near the Loews hotel's pool deck. While a small ensemble filled the air with a grandpa's jazz take on "Blurred Lines," flashbulbs popped to record the gripping, grinning, air-kissing, and flirting of upper-tier Hollywood. Nearly all the one-namers were present, including Brad, Angelina, Kerry, Channing, Jenna, Leo, and George. Diamonds sparkled. Evening gowns swished. Champagne flowed.

And Bella draped herself all over Ethan every chance she got.

The woman wasn't shy about making sure there were a lot of chances. Ava knew this for a fact because her whole body felt electrocuted with each occurrence. Every time the woman stroked his chest with demure possessiveness equaled a sixty-watt heartache hit. The knob got cranked to a hundred twenty if Bella rested her head against his shoulder, cheesy girlfriend style. That doubled any time the woman trailed her fingers along the firm line of his jaw. Thank God someone at the salon had convinced him to throw some product in his hair and slick it into a sophisticated neuvo-Euro look so Bella's grip couldn't get anywhere near the thick waves.

Thank God he looked like he didn't know whether to grin or puke from all of it. *Welcome to the club, Sergeant Archer.*

"Avvvvaaaa!"

Bella's interruption to her brood was a shock. She'd only diverted her eyes for a second, captivated by the last rays of the sunset over the waves, apparently one second longer than allowed.

"Shit," she muttered. "*Shit.*" The repeat happened when it was clear Ethan was right on the woman's heels. And that was surprising...why? The two had been the giggling, flirting golden couple on the set for four days. As thoroughly as Ava had fought to ignore the development, the rest of the world hadn't. The web leaks had likely made it to neighboring galaxies by now. Tonight's event was clearly doubling as their coming-out soiree.

Bella herself sealed the deal on that speculation, as well as Ava's heartache, by insisting Ava dig out a cocktail dress and shadow her with the styling bag for the night. Unless Ava came down with the plague, absence wasn't an option. It wasn't like she didn't know the drill, having been tagged as the woman's glamour secret service before. She was to be out of sight and out of mind unless there was a hair, makeup, or dress disaster that needed life-saving intervention. Apparently, one of those emergencies had struck.

As Bella paced closer, she performed a fast visual to try to spot the calamity. Her assessment yielded nothing out of place, but that didn't mean anything. Bella didn't give her any clue, gliding closer without a waver of her smile or champagne flute. That also didn't warrant surprise. The woman had once given a flawless interview to *Entertainment Tonight* on the red carpet as Ava crouched at her feet resewing two inches of hem that'd been ripped during the limo exit.

She forced her face into composure, ready for anything. Not an easy feat, considering Ethan looked even better up close. His dress jacket, which brought out the layers of cobalt in his eyes, was pressed and perfectly fitted on his wide shoulders. He'd also been treated to a manicure and professional shave and then dunked in something that smelled wonderful on him. Damn. No wonder half the women out here risked Bella's backlash by giving him lingering gawks. No wonder every cell in her body burst open in new awareness—followed by livid castigation.

Maybe this all happened for the best, Ethan.

She still believed that. She *had* to believe that. Her throat convulsed on the painful swallow she forced as affirmation. Not that simply looking at them couldn't accomplish the same thing. They were the most perfect couple on a patio filled with perfection. The noble soldier and the breathtaking starlet. She had no doubt half the producers in the room were already scheming ways to develop their story for the screen.

Mierda. Why was it suddenly so hard to breathe?

Thank God Bella didn't share the challenge. "Oh, Ava, Ava, Ava," the woman chirped. "Ethan needs you."

Seemed that shock therapy came in handy as a good warm-up. The thousand volts that hit her now were a little easier to handle, especially as she looked to Ethan for confirmation. His gorgeous face was etched in a mix of bewilderment and embarrassment that made her heart pinch until her brain retaliated. She couldn't forget he'd asked for this bed as much as she—for the last four days, to be exact. If he was uncomfortable, maybe he should've researched the linens a little better.

"What's the problem?" she asked as diplomatically as she could.

Bella giggled. It was the laugh she got after refusing to eat all day, resulting in half a glass of champagne flying straight to her head. "Me," she said, snickering again. "I'm the problem!" She wiggled her fingers in the air. "Oopsie!"

Ava deliberately swung her gaze out to the beach again. There were times when reacting to Bella's "humor" in any fashion wasn't a good idea. She wasn't sure if the woman was feigning the frivolity or if the bubbly was hitting her that hard.

A huff came from Ethan's direction. When she looked up, his irritated glare was tough to miss, even past the tumble of his hair. "Bella," he muttered, dragging the stuff backward with one hand, "honestly, this isn't—"

"*No!*" Ava's reflexes weren't clouded so she was able to get the protest out faster than Bella. She was also able to step to the man, grab his wrist, and wrench it down before he could wreak any more damage to the 'do. As he glowered, she charged, "Stop. Now. Fingers don't go near the head again tonight. That *is* an order, Sergeant."

"Amen, sister!"

She couldn't help chuckling at Bella's tipsy vote of support. Her mirth seemed to calm Ethan too. "All right, all right," he muttered. "This isn't a fight I'm going to win. Torture me, Mistress Ava, but don't expect me to give up state secrets."

Ava rolled her eyes while searching for a discreet alcove. The idea of having her hands in his hair both thrilled and gutted her, meaning she wasn't totally opposed to the sudden appearance of Enzo Lemare.

"Sister?" the man questioned in his rich Italian accent. He strolled up in a luxurious double-breasted tux—probably

Armani or D&G—that was impeccably tailored for his elegant build. "*Davvero?*" He directed his attention, full of smoldering green eyes and smooth hands, right at her. "Why did I not see the resemblance before? It is clear to me now. What a clever move, Bella, to hire your stunning sister as your stylist. Who better to know the family secrets and keep them that way, yes?"

Ava threw back an indulgent smile. "Thank you for the lovely compliment, Mr. Lemare, but I'm not—"

"Stunning?" Bella looked as puzzled by the statement as she did her empty champagne glass. "Sister? Oh, Enzo, you and that language barrier. Darling, I meant—"

"To have me take you inside." Ethan saved her from the embarrassing blurt by smoothly grabbing her waist, making sure the booze didn't deliver Bella face first into the concrete. "It's getting chilly out here. Your wrap is already at the table."

"Awww." Bella crooned it with adoring eyes while stroking his jaw with a finger. "You take such good care of me."

Ava could've sworn Ethan's whole body tensed at that but wrote the perception off to her own reaction, unplugging the electroshock in favor of old-fashioned nausea. But the moment she thought they'd finally leave, giving her five minutes to grab some water with a Pepto-Bismol chaser, their offside soiree turned into a full attention-getter. Bella's caress on Ethan's cheek was captured by a blinding photographer's flash. When Bella herself winced at the intrusion, Enzo stepped forward again.

"*Mie scuse, cara.*" He spread his hands. "I was so busy basking in your sister's beauty, I neglected to tell you I brought a friend."

Protesting the man's error seemed fruitless right now, especially when someone laughed at Lemare from the darkness beyond the flash. "Friend? That's debatable at the moment. Put your wizzler back in your pants, Enzo, before you get me killed. You told me Miss Lanza would be on the arm of an army man, not a bloody demigod."

Ava forgot about wanting to puke. For a long moment, she wasn't even cognizant of her stomach. A fast peek at Bella corroborated her awe. That cosmopolitan mix of accents, delivered in that unmistakable mix of snark, swagger, and sex, only belonged to one man on earth. She gasped his name at Bella now. "Grant Fulsom?"

"*Mio Dio*, Ava," she replied. "I think so."

Sure enough, the iconic photographer himself strolled up in a wrinkled polo shirt and khakis, his angular face weathered from years of capturing superstars everywhere from Athens to Montserrat to Zimbabwe. In the world of celebrity, being immortalized by Fulsom was one of the rites of passage into superstardom. It was one of the things on the "big list" to cross off. Memoir. Fragrance. Shoe line. White House visit. Grant Fulsom photo shoot.

"Mr. Fulsom." Bella's voice actually shook. Ava watched Ethan's arm tighten around her waist in silent reinforcement. "It's— What an honor to—"

Fulsom chopped her short by swooping her hand to his lips. He followed with a vigorous laugh. "By God, Enzo, you're right. She's an enchanting dish." The man wheeled an equally suggestive appraisal toward Ethan. "And so is he."

Ethan barely moved, though his growl sounded like a living beast in the air. "Kiss my hand and *your* wizzler is dust, assface."

"Ooohhh." Fulsom's dark-green eyes went wide. "Yes, sir!"

Mr. Lemare chuckled and backhanded Fulsom's shoulder.

"Down, *amico*. You'll need plenty of energy in the days to come."

"Oh?" Bella flashed her most charismatic smile. "Are you in town to shoot someone big?"

Ethan glowered at her and then the men. "What the hell?"

Lemare let out his own booming laugh at that. "She means a photography shoot, Ethan. How do they say it in your unit? It is all right to...stand down?"

"Not for too long," Fulsom asserted, still giving Ethan a workup with his gaze. "He's bloody fine in the standing position too."

While Ethan fumed and Bella threw Lemare a probing gaze, Ava kept an eye on Fulsom. She was pretty certain what he was thinking. She looked at Bella in the same way all the time, projecting elements like skin tone, hairstyle, eye brightness, and facial features into the future to determine how certain lighting was going to affect the look of each. By the time a full minute had passed, she could nearly predict what Lemare was about to say to his show's leading lady.

"He is in town as a favor to me, Bella." Enzo grinned like a dad about to tell his kids they were skipping school to go to the fair all day. "I think our live broadcast would be well-served with some of Grant's photos to accompany it." When Bella gave that just a tiny smile of hope, he went on, "Photos of you, *cara*—with one of our fine soldier advisors as your strapping alpha hero." He nodded at Ethan in conclusion to that.

Bella squealed.

Ethan paled.

"Okay, whoa," he mumbled. "Bella—oof!" He stumbled back a step as she threw herself into his arms. "Wait. *Wait.*" He glared back through her hair. "Look, Mr. Lemare—"

"Enzo." The man held out placating arms. "I already told you, Sergeant, you must start calling me Enzo."

"Great. Enzo. Look, I'm *not* a model."

"Now you are." Bella kissed his cheek long enough to leave an imprint that was only going to come out via remover wipe. "This is going to be wildly fun, Ethan! You'll see."

He set her back, his eyes getting darker. "The only thing I'm supposed to be *seeing* are the scripts, the set, and the route back to my hotel. Bella, we had to jump through a bunch of hoops just for Rhett and me to come to *this* thing. A damn photo shoot—"

"Has already been approved by your captain and his chain of command," Lemare filled in.

Ethan's lips twisted. "Yeah," he said, "I'll bet."

"And there will be plenty of us there from the show's production staff, myself included, to make sure you two behave...most of the time."

That drew another delighted giggle out of Bella. Ava studied her for a long moment. When the woman was truly happy, not just putting it on for paparazzi or acting it for the camera, the emotion transformed her from beautiful to breathtaking. She'd tried to make Bella see that, but the starlet was one of those stunning women who'd been told, somewhere in those important years of their girlhood, that they were ugly and always would be. Ava had met many such girls during the weekly beauty class she volunteered with through the inner-city church cooperative. Maybe, with the love of a good man or thousands of dollars in therapy, the star would comprehend her true worth one day—but right now, Ava was certain that Ethan's psyche was going to be her bigger concern.

The conclusion plummeted her gaze to the ground in self-beratement. *Mierda*. She'd tell herself not to take one more step down that path...if she wasn't already on it. If she didn't know, from the core of her spirit, that she was really concerned about how this bizarre turn of events would affect Ethan. During those two days in Seattle for Garrett and Sage's wedding, she'd seen why he wasn't the guy with the shrimp tails on his fingers. He'd grown up in a world where appearances were everything yet had given him nothing, leading him to take a leap of faith and dedicate himself to a job where nothing mattered but his mind and his mettle. Now he was being ordered to let one of the world's biggest image makers capitalize on the one thing for which he never wanted to be seen.

So yeah, despite everything they'd been through this week and what they'd never have again, her heart lurched for him. No matter what, he was a friend. If he needed a commiserating ear, then—

As soon as her gaze found his face, she blinked in perplexity.

Maybe it was just an anomaly, that his expression seemed tight but determined...and nearly as peaceful as the waves lapping at the sand a few feet away.

Huh?

Shouldn't he be seething and tense? Shouldn't he be looking for an escape to go call Franzen with a string of *what the fuck*s? Why did he just keep standing there, arm still dutifully around Bella, seeming damn near resigned about all this?

The party was awash in custom lighting, but she suddenly felt trapped in the dark. It wasn't a sensation that sat well with her, not since those days she and Zoe had spent wondering what had happened to Mom and not being told anything until it was too late.

On unwavering steps, she moved to the side of Ethan not occupied by Bella's clinging form. In a discreet murmur, she offered, "Should I get that hair fixed now?"

As she'd hoped, Bella gushed in gratitude. After shoving Ethan at her, the starlet moved away, phone in hand, determined to make the news of their sessions with Fulsom into a viral buzz inside of ten minutes. Ethan said nothing, becoming a silent shadow as Ava rushed inside, leading him down a deserted hallway.

She stopped when she was reasonably certain they wouldn't be seen or heard, though Ethan got the first word in.

"Hey, are you okay?"

She already had some fresh hair serum in her palm and rubbed her hands together with a briskness that defied her tone. "I'm fine, Sergeant. How about you? What's new?"

"I, uh—*ow*!" He exclaimed it as she worked the new product in with the old, making her fingers stick for a second. Damn it, even with all the goop in his hair, it filled her grip with a heady combination of strength and softness. "I think you know the answer to that one, Miss Chestain." He emphasized his formality with a sarcastic snarl.

"Really?" she shot back. "Do I, now?"

"What's that supposed to mean?"

She was about to give him a finishing sweep with a wide-toothed comb. Instead, she parked that hand against her hip and eyed him for a long moment. When she spoke again, it was with quiet conviction.

"What's going on, Ethan?"

He dipped his head. "I guess we're going to go take a lot of pictures."

"And you're really this calm about it?"

He jutted his jaw and looked down the hall. "Guess I have to be."

"Then why won't you look at me and say it?"

With an angry grunt, he lifted his head. But the second his stare tore into hers, his ire transformed to something else, an emotion she couldn't place, intense and conflicted. The force of it pulled at every muscle in her body...and reawakened every nerve in her sex. Holy shit, how could the man do this to her with one look? *Why* was he doing this to her with one look? He was with Bella. Belonged with her. End of story. Someone cue the dramatic music and the happily-ever-after sunset backdrop, please.

"Ava." It finally fell from him on a guttural rasp. His chest rose and fell, betraying more of his inner battle. "Please don't push. Not now."

For a second, his urgent voice rendered her without one. She blinked again, processing the realization that the tickles of her instinct were founded in truth—a truth that had made Ethan, a man who took orders from nobody except his superiors, pleading with her to back the hell away. "Don't push at what?"

The perfect cliffs of his features fell into deeper shadow.

"Ethan?" She took a step toward him, cocked her head, and glared. "Damn it, talk to me. Don't push at *what*?"

The next moment, as he watched someone appear around the corner, his features darkened into deep secrecy again. The moment was gone.

"My *dolce* Ava!"

She spun at Enzo Lemare's greeting. The man approached with a champagne flute in each hand, his deep-set Roman eyes sweeping over her. After a gallant bow, he offered her one of the glasses.

"Mr. Lemare," she murmured. "Errmm, thank you, but I'm working tonight and—"

"Not anymore." With the aplomb of Caesar, the man pushed her hand up, urging her to take a sip of the chilled Cristal. "I told Bella that since you'll be working very hard the next few days, you have the rest of the night off. *And* you're enjoying dinner at my table, as my guest."

She managed a smile, but there wasn't a shred of comfort behind it. "That...is so...sweet..." *Sweet? Did you seriously just use the same word on Enzo Lemare that you pulled out to turn down Bobby Weller for junior prom?* "But I'm...I'm not dressed correctly...and look at my hair..."

"All right." He stunned her into silence by deftly yanking out the two pins that held together her "style" and then combing his fingers down to bring it all tumbling around her face. "If you insist."

For some reason, every bone in her body longed to run.

One look at Ethan convinced her otherwise.

Though his lips were fixed in a cordial expression, his eyes betrayed a different objective. The potent desire to hurt Enzo Lemare.

Didn't take the man long to return with the mixed messages. Okay, despite Lemare's insistence that Ethan use a first-name basis with him, an underline of tension between them was a given. Bella had been with Lemare, at least for a night, before scooping up Ethan. That had likely been filtered by the Dominant side of Ethan's brain into a degree of protective jealousy. But the octane level of his glare was burning much higher. He looked like he longed to remove the man's spleen by hand. Why?

Mierda. She needed to go home, trade the champagne for a cup of chamomile tea, and call it a night. No espionage books. No more binge-watching her favorite spy shows. Straight to bed with the vow that Ethan was Bella's concern now, no matter how much she ached to do it...no matter how deep the certainty that the woman rarely coupled the word "concern" with anything past crow's feet and where she ranked on the latest best-dressed lists.

The same certainty that made her stomach fold over on itself.

Which was why she gritted a smile at Lemare and allowed him to tuck her hand into the crook of his elbow before guiding her into the ballroom for dinner.

★ ★ ★ ★ ★

She should have opted for the tea and her pillow.

Two hours and a crap-load of discomfort later, she was no closer to figuring out the purpose behind Ethan's cryptic words in the hallway. The man himself didn't turn over a single clue, spending the evening between his whispering love cocoon with Bella and his robust "man chat" with Enzo. That itself gave her eyebrows a nice workout. Ethan actually looked like he enjoyed hashing out the finer points of his first manicure, the nuances of a good chianti, and what shoe silhouette was going to prevail over the fall and winter.

When Ava wasn't biting back giggles, she was swallowing back tears. Apparently the interesting half of the table ended at Enzo. Despite the producer's attempts to include her in their exchanges, Ethan barely acknowledged her beyond a few polite nods. In short, he did everything he could to enforce his command from out in the hall. Whatever door she'd been pushing, he wanted her off the stoop for good.

It hurt. She didn't want it to. She didn't need it to. Damn it, wasn't *she* the one who told *him* they'd be better off this way? Then why was she the one who could only pick at her filet and prawns, appetite gone and apprehension on high? Why was she the one who couldn't banish the memory of that brilliant blue gaze, unwavering at her, filled with the same force of his words? *Ava. Don't push.*

It was finally time for dessert, though even the triple-chocolate ganache wasn't enough to keep her at the table. As Bradley Cooper, the night's master of ceremonies, got up to announce they'd be starting the program soon, she frantically looked for the door. Even a few minutes of respite from Ethan and his weirdness would be heaven.

"Needing some air, *mi dolce*?"

She smiled in real gratitude at Enzo. Though his overtones of gallantry were a little excessive tonight, she couldn't blame the guy for wanting to lick the wounds Bella had dealt by pouncing on Ethan two days after he'd left her bed. Enzo would realize that in the morning, after the wine had worn off. In the meantime, she appreciated him fabricating an excuse to take a phone call in order to escort her out to the foyer, where she scooted into the ladies room for some much-needed solitude.

The break helped freshen her lipstick, if not her senses. Like the tides hitting the beach outside, she was awash in confusion one second but bright with clarity the next. She didn't care what Ethan did but watched his every move through the night—and by doing so had gotten another huge lesson in puzzlement. Why did he fawn over Bella only when she was looking? Why did his regard of Enzo swing to such extremes, openly admiring one second but seething with animosity the next? And why did he stare at everyone else in the room like they were all potential suicide bombers?

She headed out from the bathroom with a growing headache.

There was no sign of Enzo anymore. A spattering of applause sounded from the ballroom, so she assumed he'd gone back inside so as to not miss the start of the program. She released a little sigh of relief. One last chance to get her shit together before returning to Awkward Central.

There was a small buzz from her purse. She smiled when pulling it out. A text from Charlie.

> *When the HELL were you going to text me*
> *about Grant Fulsom?*

"Oh, dear." She murmured it on half a giggle, making her way out to the patio to dash a quick retort. The glowing, empty screen taunted her. This message had to be a doozy. Something full of breezy yet witty remorse, ending with the kicker that she'd been unable to message due to being occupied at dinner with—

The man who stood on the patio now, pacing intently with his cell at his ear.

Ava backed up as quietly as she could. Wow. Enzo really did have a phone call to take. A hairy one, by the looks of it. "Duh, Chestain," she muttered while sinking into a chair just inside the door to the patio. "The man isn't at the top of all the industry lists because he only takes calls until six."

She settled farther into the cushion, wondering if she could just ask Housekeeping to bring her a blanket and tuck her in for a good night's sleep in the luxurious thing. "Focus," she muttered, redirecting thoughts back on her message back to Chaz. Shit, she was tired. The strain of the last four days piled on her like a truckload of bricks, dragging her eyes down.

Enzo's voice, raised and ruthless, stabbed the peace of her reverie.

"I am telling you that I have it handled, Mateo. You and Alex caused this mess; now you will let me clean it up with no more questions!"

For some reason, she kept her eyes closed. There was no way the man could see her from this angle, but the viciousness in his voice told her this was no ordinary business call. Her gut clutched. Her palms got clammy. She pressed herself back, wishing the chair would simply swallow her.

"Do not worry about that. I have them handled. Yes, all of them. Cameron's idea on that is proceeding perfectly. Of course he knows what he is doing. You know what they say... Keep your enemies close, *qué no*?"

She wanted to squirm but kept herself frozen. And the whole time called herself ten kinds of an idiot. Did she think production deals got negotiated over rainbow-sprinkle cupcakes and a round of wine spritzers? Men like Enzo were called the big sharks for a reason.

Of course, the second she entertained that thought, the man broke out with a warm and friendly laugh. "Now that is what I was hoping to hear. Perfect, perfect. We *must* work together, my friend. One hundred percent success is the only acceptable benchmark, one we can only accomplish together. Call Cameron Stock and me when you get into town. We shall want to know you have gotten here safely and are ready to proceed." After a long pause, he went on, "Stock has that handled as well. He is interfacing with the relevant specialists on a daily basis."

That comment made her indulge a small smile. Despite the mess it had created for her personally, it had been satisfying to have Ethan, Rhett, and Rebel on set, recognized for their expertise and service to the country.

"Yes, of course, of course. Thank you, Mateo. Soon, my friend, it will be next Tuesday night, and our mission will be complete. We shall celebrate our grand triumph together. Very well. *Buenas noches.*"

As he ended the call, Ava scrambled up and strolled out to the patio like she'd just gotten there. Though it was reassuring to know he was fighting for the success of the show's big night, her deeper instincts still told her it wasn't a good idea to reveal she'd been eavesdropping.

"Well, here you are." She plastered on a relaxed smile.

Enzo held up his phone. "The ball and chain." He pocketed the device and cupped her shoulders. "The fog is coming in. It is cold out here. You should be inside swooning over Mr. Cooper along with the other ladies."

She let her face tighten. The idea of facing Ethan and his antics again registered on the scale of having to run a marathon right now. "I'm getting a pretty awful headache." At least that wasn't a lie. "And we're in for a crazy ride up until the live broadcast next week..."

Enzo gave her a gentle smile. It turned his face into something that could be on the cover of European *GQ* in its handsomeness. "I understand. I will render regrets to the table on your behalf."

Ava forced herself to return the look. Damn it, why couldn't she truly feel the emotion beneath? What was wrong with her? Enzo Lemare was gorgeous in all the right ways, had treated her like a queen tonight, and probably toweled his toned bod in hundred-dollar bills every morning. He at least deserved a smile she hadn't ratcheted into place.

"You've been so amazing to me tonight." The awe in her voice was genuine. "I feel like Cinderella at the ball. Thank you."

She couldn't read his reaction to that. His dark stare traveled across her face before he lifted a hand to frame one side of it. Without another word, he softly kissed her.

Technically, it *was* a kiss. He brushed her lips with just enough pressure, pausing at just the right second to determine if she'd encourage him to do more, to qualify it as such. Ava searched deep, frantically begging her senses to respond, but came back with nothing. Compared to the heat Ethan brought with his mouth, this was more like a pleasant caress or a parting peck between friends.

Damn it.

She grabbed Enzo's hand and squeezed it, wishing it could be transformed into a mental chalkboard eraser. On the newly blank slate, she'd dutifully write a thousand repetitions. *I will not fall for another military man again. I will not fall for another military man again. I will not fall—*

"Ava." Enzo's voice, a satin cushion around her name, coaxed her mind back. "*Cara*, what is it?"

She sighed. *Just do it. One step and you're there.* His embrace offered strength, his eyes promised comfort. But that nagging intuition compelled her to let him go and back away. "Nothing a full night's sleep won't help. I'm...I'm just going to head home." With an impish tilt of her head, she added, "See you at the office tomorrow?"

"The office," he echoed with a chuckle. "Of course."

She took the quickest route home, south on Coast Highway. The fog that rolled over the road, thicker every minute, seemed an ironic fit for her mental preparation for the days ahead. She'd learned a long time ago that "expecting the unexpected" was an understatement in this business, and most of the time she even thrived on the mantra, but the strange unease in her stomach, introduced when she'd overheard Enzo on the phone, had only gotten worse as she had the chance to replay it. With Ethan's shit storm of confusing behavior stirred into that, she was surprised she was able to steer the car home correctly.

Her head and her heart had declared war on each other. And short of hitting the Delete key on her brain, she didn't know how to enact a truce. But doing that would mean eradicating everything, including every moment she'd shared with Ethan... every kiss, every smile, every connection that contained no sound or word because it didn't have to...

With a heavy sigh, she fell into bed, grateful for the weight of exhaustion that pulled her under the waves of sleep, into the dark hours of nothingness before the war started again.

CHAPTER SIXTEEN

"I'm still not sure whether to feel right at home or mildly freaked out."

Tait responded to Kellan's quip with a snort. "Mildly?"

They joined each other in stares mixed of astonishment, amusement, and plain what-the-hell-ment while watching Grant Fulsom and his crew set up for Ethan and Bella's photo shoot in the Desert Garden of the Huntington Botanical Gardens. The Huntington was located about a half hour from the hub of LA and offered an impressive collection of plant habitats that represented all corners of the world, including this area Fulsom had transformed into a Middle East oasis. Since the photo spread's theme was "Army Undercover," that apparently made sense to the man, even if he felt the need to hide a good chunk of the flowering succulents and cacti behind a Bedouin-style tent filled with fabrics, rugs, drapes, and pillows.

"Welcome to Marrakech," Kell cracked.

Tait gave that a light laugh. "Didn't think anything could best the backlot watch, but I could be wrong."

Kellan fiddled with the Nikon camera around his neck that they'd purposely banged up last night. They were here under the guise of being Ethan's photography-crazed battalion buddies. "I'll bet there's plenty of double-sided tit tape around here."

"Only thing I care about is if *Lor's* around here." While

muttering it, he peered around the garden and scowled again. There was no sign of the pretty-man producer, despite confirmation from Runway and Double-O that Lor planned on being around for most of these photo shoots. It was the reason Tait and Kell had been pulled off the roof.

Their new purpose was two-pronged. First priority: watch Lor for any behavior that told them he had the memory stick or new laptop here with him. Their second goal, just as essential, was to back up Ethan. With a team of stylists constantly following him, there'd be no way he could hide a wire or earpiece for monitoring his interactions with Bella and Lor. Yeah, the guy could read people more clearly than a voodoo shaman, but that talent was as good as a limp dick if his cover was made—or worse. Tait and Kellan would serve as his eyes and ears while remaining in contact with Rhett and Rebel, who were able to hang back at the *Dress Blues* set and get in more searches of "Lemare's" office.

With any luck, something would shake out soon. They were all patient men, used to waiting it out for long stretches to get the intel they needed to get their job done, but this stint in a land where even half the buildings weren't real was just damned exhausting.

Garrett and Zeke had lucked out. At least their women were around, making the nights and mornings better. The rest of the guys had learned the area around the hotel and even ventured to other parts of the city from time to time, but Tait had started bailing on some of those excursions, claiming the hotel's free HBO was too good a treat to ignore. He wondered if anyone actually believed him. Speculated if anyone except Kell had discerned his truth. Yeah, *that* truth. The hope, however ridiculous, that a certain convict-turned-agent would reconsider her self-imposed celibacy and come knocking on his door. And confirm that everything he'd felt in that bar's storeroom had been at least a little real...and a lot right.

Kellan's snicker yanked him off that emo-lined path. Tait followed his teammate's glance and instantly exchanged morose for snarky. Beyond his control, a chortle spewed off his lips.

Ethan, who'd just walked into the catering area where they'd been hanging, snarled as Kell raised his wrist. The live-stream camera taped beneath Kell's sleeve now broadcasted every inch of Ethan's attire to Colton's office across town.

"Lower it now if you value your fucking arm." Ethan punctuated it with a lethal glare as he grabbed a bottle of sports drink and ripped off the cap.

Kellan tempted fate by delaying one more second. Tait didn't blame him. The sight was just too damn fine to ignore.

Archer's head was covered in an all-black *keffiyeh*, with its long length held in place by a shiny gold version of the *tagiyyah* band. That was where the authentic portion of the outfit ended. A black leather vest was the only thing covering the guy from shoulder to waist, unless the accessories counted. A black leather hawking gauntlet was secured to one of his forearms, and a thick leather strip around his neck was supposed to be a—what *was* that? A scarf? Tait snorted again. Because *that* was practical if a guy was undercover in a real Bedouin camp, right? Didn't matter. The pants were even more ridiculous. Sheathing Archer's long legs were billowy black pajama bottoms, whipping up to expose the guy's bare feet.

"Sure." Kellan finally moved his arm. He swiped it across his body, folded the other on top, and then dropped his head fast against them both. "Whatever you say, Master Aladdin."

"Suck my dick, monkey lice."

Tait choked on his water. Sometimes getting in a chuckle was worth it. "You're taking a giant one for the team, Runway."

Ethan kicked up a brow. "Just one?"

"It won't be forgotten."

"Damn right it won't," Kellan jibed.

"Didn't I just tell you to suck my dick?" Ethan snapped.

"No, thanks." Kell's mouth threatened a small smile. Tait prepped himself to note the day and time, since the guy cracked a grin as often as the sun had an eclipse, but the moment was lost as Kell jerked his chin around. "But I think you'll have a taker in her."

It wasn't a brain-buster to see Bella walk out in a high-fashion version of a harem girl costume, complete with sheer ivory pants covering a barely-there bikini bottom and a halter top covered in gold rhinestones. She was also barefoot, with anklets that had gold bells on them. Her hair was long and loose, with strands of gold bells braided into it in a few places.

When the starlet saw Ethan, she let out a yelp of delight and hurried over. The *chings* of her outfit echoed across the garden. "*Mio Dio*, Ethan." Her gaze, heavy and sultry, didn't hide any secrets about what the woman wanted to do with him. "Grant is right. You *are* a demigod." When that acted like the permission slip for Tait and Kell to let their guffaws fly free, she chided, "If you two are jealous and want in on the fun, I'm sure Grant can find costumes for you too."

They both went silent.

Tait braced himself for Archer's version of a full retaliation, probably in the form of sucking face with Bella until they looked like murder victims from her smeared lipstick, but the guy's self-restraint was impressive. Though he still raked the area with an irked glare, he dutifully let Bella rearrange his scarf, or whatever the fuck that thing was, until she seemed satisfied with the artful angles at which it grazed his bare chest. Shit. The guy was whipped. Bad.

"Everyone ready to roll?" he finally asked Bella. Tait's ears did a figurative perk. Something in Ethan's voice was...off. No. Something was *missing*, which was baffling considering the man's norm of verbal minimalism. Was Archer okay? Damn it, was he falling harder than he should for Bella? Was his head still in the game?

Get a grip, T-Bomb. He wasn't the one who currently resembled a mash-up of *Lawrence of Arabia* and *Electric Boogaloo Goes to Morocco*. Maybe he needed to cut Archer a little slack.

Over at the tent, Fulsom began directing his assistants in positioning his tripod, the set floods, and the reflector panels, which helped illuminate a large bed and the seventy pillows piled on top. A moment later, Lor finally made his appearance in his typical tailored suit and silk shirt. Ava Chestain, Bella's stylist, was with him. Tait jotted a mental note. Pretty boy Lor seemed seriously into her. If the woman was woven into Lor's plots, even unknowingly, things were going to be messy. She and Rayna were tight.

He exchanged a nod with Kellan. The moment had come to move closer to the man. Ethan offered his arm to Bella and followed their path across the lawn.

As they neared the tent, Tait noticed the light wasn't the only thing that began to change. Ethan's mien, which had been so full of calm focus just a minute ago, now seemed as nettled as a panther that'd been awakened by a she-cat's mating scent. Trouble was...that cat wasn't Bella. Ethan followed every move

Ava made, completely locked as the woman helped Fulsom's assistant to put the last-minute touches on Bella's exotic look. Since that put Ethan's head and eyes in her general vicinity, Bella didn't pick up on the nuance. The actress was glad to be the center of attention in any way she got it.

Tait released a black laugh to himself. Maybe Kellan *had* been right yesterday. Watching camels spit and sand fly was a hell of an easier gig than this.

The shit got thicker when Lor finished up his banter with Fulsom and then walked over to the bed, where the crew now positioned Ethan and Bella for their first shots. While Kell engaged Fulsom in a battery of questions about crap like f-stops and digital tweaking, Tait was able to fully observe Lor, picking apart the man's behaviors for anything remotely suspicious...not to mention any wayward memory sticks that might conveniently fall out of his pockets.

The guy was smooth. Tait could confirm that much. Lor bantered with Bella with every speck of charm intact, pressing a kiss to the back of her hand like an admiring prince instead of the guy who'd been banging her in Malibu less than a week ago. When he turned to Ava, he simply squeezed out a bigger glob of the royal court formula, bussing her knuckles but turning her hand over and grazing the inside of her wrist with his lips too. He gave her a gaze filled with the same seductive intent.

Though Ava pulled her hand away from Lor right away, teasing that she was working and he had to behave, it was like tossing a cup of water at the forest fire of murderous intent now raging across Ethan's face. It was a good thing the only "weapon" the guy could conceal in those pajamas was his cock.

Tait looked at Kell, who'd caught the same bead on Ethan. Kell twitched just the top of his head toward Lor, but thanks to their Bullet Ninjas telepathy, that was the only directive needed. Tait made his way toward Lor. Time to creatively divert the target before their teammate killed the guy for kissing a woman's hand.

He got drop-kicked and sidelined after barely hitting the field. By a spook in a bun wig, a pencil skirt, and black platform pumps. And new for today, a pair of thick black glasses and a formfitting, pale-purple sweater set that made his palms itch to rip up a little cashmere.

"Mr. Lemare." Luna layered a Southern farm girl accent to her voice that surely revirginized her with the force of its innocence. "Hi! Ahhh, I'm Ronnie—from Accounting? I dunno if you remember me?"

"Not really," the man murmured, letting his gaze linger over the swells of her breasts, "but that is completely my fault, dear girl, not yours. What can I do for you?" Since he'd gotten away with ogling her top half, he openly admired her hips and legs.

Tait suddenly felt a lot more sympathetic toward Runway's jealous pain. The only thing that stopped him from lunging and clocking the guy was the supposition that Lor's lothario bullshit was just a half-plausible cover. If people fled from Lemare the skank, they wouldn't see Lor the terrorist, right?

Luna let her eyes go wide. She added a "nervous" little lip bite and a thoroughly convincing blush. That made it official. Once Tait had her alone again, he was going to throttle her—before kissing her until she never thought of turning that color for anyone but him again.

"I'm so, *so* sorry to bust in on you here," she declared to Lor, acting the part of a production minion to perfection. "I mean, everyone on set knows how important this photo shoot is. I normally wouldn't have left to come bother you like a stalker in the corn, but with the shooting schedule changing up to allow all this, along with the extra rehearsals everyone's attending for the live broadcast, I didn't know when we would see you on set again, and—"

"It's fine." The man had clearly reached the tolerance point for his accountant's babbling, no matter how stunning her rack. "How can I help you?"

"We just need these checks signed." She giggled and bobbed her head back and forth. "You know what they say. Gotta pay the piper, right?"

Lor obliged "Ronnie" by scribbling on a handful of checks. Luna maintained the chatter stream the whole time, commenting on everything from the weather to a "mighty fine wedding reception" she attended at the hotel up the hill a few years back. Tait couldn't keep his eyes off her. The way the woman committed to her cover identity... It was goddamned impressive, a skill at which even well-trained agents had to labor. She fascinated him even deeper. Made him want her even more.

Burned him up with the longing to protect her. Especially now.

He wasn't clueless about this shit. Luna had been sent here without previous notification to any of them, meaning it was urgent—and also required her to get so close to Lor, she could likely tell what he'd had for lunch just by sniffing his breath. It set Tait on a razor's edge of apprehension, especially when he watched her slip a hand into the man's *inner* jacket pocket.

Screw the pooch sideways. If Lor noticed her action in the tiniest corner of his eye, "Ronnie" would be caught and—

Caught at what?

Tait muffled a growl. From the grunt that came from Kell, who'd made his way back to his side, it didn't sound like he was the only one. "What the hell's going on?" his friend grumbled.

Tait gave him three syllables in answer. "NFC." *No fucking clue.*

Lor pivoted back on Luna just as her palm cleared the pocket.

The man's face darkened to a full glower.

For two seconds.

"Bee!"

Luna whacked at his coat and the air, adding shrieks to the mix. A loud *clang* from the tent compounded the chaos. Ava winced sheepishly in front of the prop hookah and copper urn she'd just toppled.

"What the hell?" Grant yelled.

"My thought precisely." Lor glared at Luna.

"It...it was a big bee," she explained. "Really. Willikers, it was huge!"

"I just need to know if it's gone." The interjection came from Ava. She was in the corner of the tent, visibly shaking now. "S-Sorry. I'm allergic. A lot allergic. And my epi pen is—"

"Where?" Ethan issued the charge, enforcing it by lunging off the bed and to her side. Fulsom fumed in impatience, Bella frowned in confusion...and Ava bowed her head in submission.

Comprehension slammed Tait now. Archer wasn't just playing with the idea of being with Ava. Hell, he'd already gone there—and was clearly burning to go back again. No wonder the guy's tension level was taking bites out of the ozone layer. Adding insult on top of that injury on this crazy anomaly of a mission was the target who'd made Ava *his* target. If Lor hadn't made that obvious before now, he did so by rushing to Ava himself, clutching both her shoulders in order to turn her totally from Ethan.

"*Mi dolce*," he murmured, "I had no idea about your condition. Perhaps it is not a good idea for you to be out here, *sì*?"

"She's not an invalid." Ethan exhaled, clearly trying to be diplomatic instead of defensive. "She just has to make sure her epinephrine pen is nearby." He hiked a brow at Ava. "And it is, right?"

Tait didn't know whether to slam his hands to his face or *whomp* them in applause. Had Archer just pulled an openly Dominant move on Ava while she stood in the arms of another man?

As riveted as he was by the *cojones* of his teammate, another sight took urgent priority. Knowing Kell had an eye on things under the tent, he took advantage of the chance to beat feet toward "Ronnie," who gathered up her folder and purse and then hustled her tight-skirted ass back toward the Huntington's main entrance.

He followed her into the next themed botanical area, a collection of palm species that formed a lush grove around winding paths. Despite tottering on the hard-packed trail in those damn heels, Luna picked up the pace, looking like she was fleeing a swarm of zombies.

He caught up to her at a spot where the path expanded into a little clearing that included a bench and natural rock waterfall. He would've chuckled at how incongruous she looked, missing only the pencil in her ear in a setting that warranted more a caftan and flats, but he was busy fighting off the alarms of apprehension she'd set off ever since her hand came out of Lor's pocket.

"Luna. *Luna*." After a burst of speed, he was able to pull her into an area submerged in deep shade. He expected her to struggle a little. He didn't expect the whack she sent across his face. "What the hell?" he seethed. "It's me, damn it."

"I'm aware of that." She stared back with eyes that were darkened by abject panic as well as the dreaded blue contacts. "I'm also aware that I don't have time for your drama right now, Weasley. Let me go."

Good thing for her he was an expert on shoving aside frustration in favor of rational thought. "Imagine that. I don't have time for drama either, especially after I watched you pinch something from Lor's jacket. Based on the determination that those checks are fakes and your real reason for getting here so urgently was whatever you took from—"

She silenced him by holding up one object. A black computer memory stick. "You mean this?" While he gaped at the treasure, she explained, "Rhett caught a break when he lingered after a script revision meeting. He saw Lor move the stick from his satchel into the jacket. We moved fast, not knowing how long he'd keep it there."

He clenched his jaw as his senses seesawed between elation and irritation. "I don't know whether to kiss you for the stones it took to do that or boot your ass for not letting us handle it."

"Right," she sneered, "because Lor's suspicions wouldn't have spiked with even one of you Tarzans pawing at him. And don't harp at me about how you would've tricked him out of the jacket by spilling something on him or whatever the new SOF trick is. Short of burning the thing off his body, none of you were getting close to it anytime soon."

"Okay. Point taken. But what happens when he notices the stick's gone? He tucked it in close for a reason."

"I'm new, not stupid. Slipped a duplicate in its place. With any luck, we've bought ourselves a few hours, maybe longer. Let's just hope the stick still works with the first laptop."

She finished that by peering around him, still breathing hard as if she expected those zombies to bear down on them any second. Tait gave in to the craving to nudge her face around with a firm hand, backing it up with an unwavering stare down at her. "So you headed back to the studio now?"

"No!" She forced down a long breath before repeating in a more subdued cadence, "No. *Ronnie* is leaving the Accounting pool and *going back to Arkansas* right away. From now on, I'm back to playing exclusive engagements at the Foxfire. Laudia the smart-ass bartender will keep mixing the G and T's while praying her buddy Enzo isn't into playing the *gee, you remind me of someone* game."

The words shifted into sarcasm, but everything about her face, from the evasion of her eyes to the trembles of her lips, betrayed what was really going on beneath her bravado. "Hey," he murmured, prodding her face higher. "Listen to me. Colton knows Lor's going to be jumpy. He also knows he can't have you at that bar without some backup in place, and—"

She cut him off by beating his hand away. "*Stop it!*" The thin veneer of her composure toppled. Her face crumpled and her body sagged, despite how she hugged herself so tight, she rocked from the effort. "Don't do that to me. Don't make me think everything's simply going to be all better." When she glanced at what must've been the mute perplexity on his face, she grated, "I'm the last thing on Dan's mind right now, okay?

252

Whatever this is—whatever the *hell* Lor and the Aragons are up to—it's a giant arrow dipped in some crazy-ass poison, and we still have no idea where it's coming from or whose ass it's aimed at. You know what that means? Collateral damage, that's what that means."

She stopped and forced herself to breathe again. Like that did any good. From the way she ground her lower lip into hamburger, Tait now realized the woman wasn't just skittish. She was terrified. His logic, born from years of instinct and field training, took the next step from there.

"What happened?" He asked it in a tone that conveyed he not only knew there was an answer but expected to get it. "*What happened*, Luna?"

She let out a leaden sigh. "Galvaz is dead."

He didn't gasp or groan. His knowing nod might have skated at the edge of callous, but it was also the display of strength she needed right now and hadn't gotten from Colton. Not that Tait could blame the guy. Losing Galvaz was a loss that couldn't have come at a shittier time, especially if the Aragons had dealt the blow. He had a feeling he could already solve that little mystery too.

"I take it he didn't go peacefully in his sleep?"

"Bullet through the forehead." Her voice was a rasp. Her forehead crunched and her eyes squeezed shut.

"Colton has proof?"

She dipped her head. "They...they took a picture. Dan got it as a text from Galvaz's number."

"That's certainly a way of telling the spooks you're onto them."

Luna fell into a taut stillness, which got him even more stressed than all the frightened fidgeting. "He...he knew it was going to happen." Her stare stayed riveted to the center of his chest. She raked him there with her fingertips, the motions awkward and needy, which clearly deepened her fear. "Weasley...he knew. When he called in two nights ago... remember what I told you? He gave us specific directions about all of it, about taking care of his family. He made Dan promise that his wife and kids would get US citizenship and witness protection. He talked about his little girl. He wanted her to get a college education. He told us she's really good at math. He was so proud of her." Tears shone in her eyes and then brimmed and rained down her cheeks. "He was so calm," she uttered. "He was so...resigned. He knew what was going to happen, and yet he did it anyway. He *thanked* Dan for the chance to do something right. Said he'd spent so many years doing shitty things but he wasn't a shitty person. He was just lost. Just...lost."

Tait slid his hand around the back of her neck. But instead of compelling her face back up, he tilted his down. He let her see that he valued every drop she cried and understood every word she spoke.

"And you told him you'd been lost once too."

She gazed at him. No. Not just *at* him but *into* him, slamming his soul with the shimmering force of her sorrow. "Yeah," she whispered. "I did."

"And today, you've done what *you* had to—but now you're afraid to feel calm about it."

She didn't answer him in words. He didn't care. As her tears turned into chokes and then sobs, he folded her into his arms and let her plummet into the emotion she needed right now. If the world was perfect, he'd be giving her this pain in the form of cuffs, clamps, and whips, but they were miles from perfection, and the best he could offer was a few minutes of safety so she could strip down her heart and give it release.

Incredible, intense woman. Her emotional nakedness was as stunning to him as her bare body and just as precious a gift. He still didn't know anything about her beyond the few details Zeke had shared about meeting her on the street when they were teens, but in moments like this, Tait didn't need her baby pictures and a life journal. Now, just like that night when he'd helped her through the subdrop at Bastille, she made him feel like a human skyscraper. A lion king. Her personal hero.

The guy who'd fallen hard for her.

After a few minutes that raced by too fast, she snuffled, swiped the mascara off her cheeks, and stepped back. "Damn it. I'm a mess."

He couldn't hold back from cupping the side of her face again. "A beautiful mess."

She shot him half a smile. "You seriously need your head ex—"

He pulled the rest of the word off her lips by dragging her close and kissing her hard. Reckless move? Yeah. Completely unavoidable? He gave that a giant check mark too. Ahhh, God... The sweet nectar of her mouth, the lingering salt of her tears, the lush taste of her lips... He'd never tasted such a wonderful ambrosia in his life. And doubted he ever would again.

"My head's working just fine." He said it when he finally let her go, still pressing his forehead to hers. "Both of them, as a matter of fact."

"Shit." She got it out between a couple of labored breaths. The action made that damn sweater set go tight in all the right places, which didn't help the protest she tried to stammer. "Weasley...we really can't—"

He handled that just like the other nonsense she tried to blurt. He simply meshed his mouth and tongue to hers again. When she finally tore away, he grated, "Come to the hotel tonight." He traced her eyebrows, her cheeks, and her lips with the pads of his thumbs. "Luna...come be with me."

He watched the *yes* enter her whole face, bringing a new sheen to her eyes and a slight part to her lips before the shadow of fear conquered it again. "I have to get the stick to Dan. We have no idea what this is going to unlock on that laptop."

"And after that? Don't you have to sleep sometime?"

"Of course." She guided his hand to the back of her neck again but made him press into her skin. His fingers hit a little ridge that felt like a staple under her skin. "In the bed where they can find me, via this fun little tracking chip." She sniffed and attempted a smile. "Karma's quite a bitch, huh?"

"Fine." She wanted to play this for the jugular? He could do that too. "Then I'll wait."

Her laugh wasn't surprising. "You'll wait," she repeated. "Right. Sure."

He squared his shoulders. Tightened his jaw. "I know exactly where you're going with that, Ms. Lawrence. Be my guest. I'm right behind you."

She folded her arms and jutted her chin. "For the next year? Because you realize, no matter what goes down with Lor and the Aragons, *that's* the crazy assignment you're volunteering for, right?"

He didn't alter his position by an inch. "I'm a smart guy, flower. And a patient one."

Finally, the words seemed to sink into her. Her generous lips curled a little. She gazed up at him, the darkness in her gaze beyond anything she'd ever hit him with before. He almost felt like she was looking at him for the first time ever.

"You mean that, don't you?" Her tone warmed him like someone had distilled the afternoon's sunshine and urged him to take a shot.

Tait swallowed hard before brushing his knuckles across her cheek. "Don't you remember what they say at Hogwarts, honey? The beautiful, crazy witch is always worth the wait."

She gave him the gift of another laugh. It filled his senses with melody and light, making him grin like an idiot in return.

In another two seconds, the moment was gone. She turned away, still teetering in those heels even though she reached more level ground after leaving the palm grove. As Tait watched the sway of her enticing backside, a jolt of something strange hit his chest. He rubbed his sternum, unable to recognize the shit at first. It had been such a long time since he'd felt it...but the connection finally struck. It was pure, unfiltered joy.

CHAPTER SEVENTEEN

Ethan was pretty sure he was going to hell.

There had to be some cosmic law against using a Sunday night for dressing up in Dominance leathers and a T-shirt laced with silver sparkle threads, pretending to top a starlet who was as submissive as Xena the Warrior, in front of ten floodlights, a catty photography crew—and the woman on whom he'd much rather be wielding the crop. Yeah, the same woman who'd been watching him for the last two days like a hen eyeing a fox outside her coop, while a filthy fox named Ephraim Lor kept slinking in through her back door.

Yep. Hell. He had no doubt it was already stamped on his mortal train ticket. Didn't have a problem letting the track take him there either, as long as he got to kill Lor first. Slowly. Painfully. Since tonight's photo session was taking place in Ricochet, one of LA's largest and best-equipped BDSM dungeons, he was sure he could find a stretching rack or a high-intensity electro-stim kit that would help him carry out the mission in style.

As Fulsom and his crew worked with the Ricochet maintenance team to pull a St. Andrews cross into an area that better depicted the "undercover kink club" theme for the shoot, Bella clacked away on her latex boots to swap her red leather skirt for a long black lace thing held up by Fulsom's fashion consultant. Sure, because that was more conducive to depicting a "naughty spy sting" in D/s land, right?

He quashed the thought as soon as it hit. He should be grateful for the costume change. It would force Lor to ease the suction cups on his octopus hold around Ava. She'd be called away to help toss Bella's hair, straighten an eyelash, adjust the cinch on the corset from which the woman's plastic cleavage was already tumbling... He didn't care what the emergency was, as long as he could take a break for even five minutes from the torture of watching the man conduct a hands-on topographical survey of her body, apparently with her full permission.

God*damn*it. The woman thought she'd been making crappy choices in men before? He was of half a mind to march across the room and tell her about the "prize catch" maneuvering to get between her thighs now. An imposter who'd been raised by a pair of zealots, politically radicalized at the age his hormones raged highest and now deceived the world into thinking he was Hollywood royalty while partnering with international criminals.

On second thought, maybe he'd skip the whole "talking to her" part of that plan and get to the section where Ava was in the next room from the bastard. Better yet, the next country. He wondered how he could arrange another planet.

Could this ordeal drag by any slower?

He flung the crop a few times, testing its *whir* to cut his tension while waiting for Bella to call out for Ava. But when the actress finally spoke up, it was to tell Ava that she and Fulsom's assistant could handle the wardrobe change themselves.

Damn it.

Now he formed a seething audience of one as Lor took advantage of Ava's black knit dress in ways clearly inspired by their kinky surroundings. With every inch of skin the man revealed during his groping, a new tendon in Ethan's body coiled straight past jealousy and into incensed.

By the time the crew turned the lights back on, he had grabbed at Bella like an unthinking ape—a comparison that didn't veer too far from the truth. After tearing off the bottom two feet of the useless skirt, he got to work on ignoring Grant's session directions, using his own instinct to pose her with animalistic fury. It was just his fucking luck that Fulsom didn't just approve of the behavior but was gleeful about it. The man started taking shots with a camera in each hand, shouting at them in wild encouragement. Bella, never missing an easy bandwagon upon which to climb, got into the act too. Her moans and sighs filled the room as Grant flashed away, finally collapsing and declaring himself "verklempt with photographic delight" before ordering a furniture and lighting switch for the next round.

Dandy. Fucking dandy.

Grant turned his monitor toward Ava and Lor so they could join him as he scrolled through the shots. Ethan wondered why the views that garnered the photographer's most triumphant crows, the steamiest ones of the shoot, were also the ones that drained the smile out of Ava's eyes—and sometimes off her lips too.

The same lips that gave you the grand kiss-off six days ago, Archer. Remember?

He grunted softly. Did he remember? The more apt question was, how did he make himself forget?

Did the tremors in her lips mean she hadn't forgotten either? And was maybe reconsidering her words...a little?

He decided to latch on to that hope, even if it was false, to get him through the second half of the shoot.

Thwack.

He grunted in satisfaction after rounding the corner into the next play area and testing the crop at full strength against the red leather pad of a full-bondage bed. The big, black-painted piece featured at least twenty rig points, as well as cups in the posts to hold extras like lube or clamps. As it had a dozen times since he'd even glanced at this thing, his mind filled with all the decadent ways he longed to take Ava in it, on it, next to it. Thank fuck Grant had decided they'd done the "sexy bed" theme to death during their Arabian reenactment at the Huntington and had taken this shoot in a different direction. He wasn't sure an ice pack jammed down the front of his leathers would sit well with the photographer but was damn sure it'd be the only thing hiding his erection if he and Ava were in the same vicinity of the bed.

"You've got a good arm there."

He looked up and smiled at the source of the sultry statement. The statuesque strawberry blonde, with curves that were *all* hers and a smirk that told him she really meant the statement, had already been pretty awesome to them tonight. As the owner of Ricochet, Hudsy Hawn had not only opened the club exclusively for the shoot but had a full spread of sandwiches and snacks ready for them too. The woman hadn't stopped the hospitality there, either. In the gracious style of the switch she was, every one of Grant's requests or needs were seen to personally—right before she gave the guy a minute-long lecture for spilling soda on the floor and not cleaning up after himself. Ethan had to actually admit agreeing with Grant when the guy called Hudsy "a helluva sexy ball breaker."

Finding himself at the receiving end of his own one-on-one time with the model, actress, singer, and club owner, he looked at the woman with sincere respect. "I'm rusty, but thanks." He offered the crop back to her. "You don't go wonky on your equipment, do you? Is it custom?"

Her smile inched up, conveying her deference in return. "Yeah. I have a guy."

Ethan chuckled. "Just one?"

She laughed. "Well done." After she took the crop, she refilled his hands with something else. The black T-shirt displayed a gray version of the club's logo: a bullet unpeeling from its casing in blatantly phallic symbolism. "While I'd love to stand here and trade one-liners until one of us caves, I've come to fetch you back to my office."

He narrowed his gaze. "Why?"

"Some guy called and asked if I could link you up with him on a video call. His name is Franzen? Says he's your CO? Built like Thor of Polynesia? Kinda hot? Okay, maybe a little more than kinda—"

"Shit." He weathered a hit of both relief and unease. Had they finally caught a break with the memory stick that Luna lifted off Lor on Friday? The USB key had at last unlocked the laptop, but the information on the device was gibberish, a combination of numbers, symbols, and pictures that seemed a more insane puzzle than the *Kryptos* sculpture that greeted the spooks out in Langley.

"*Shit*," he repeated after taking two steps. The dungeon's lights picked up the threads in his shirt and reflected them across the wall in a kaleidoscope that screamed *use this fashion disaster against me forever*. While that ball-wrencher was going to be inevitable once the photos were published anyhow, he wasn't about to give Franz, and whoever was on the call with them, any extra ammunition for the cause.

"Came to the same conclusion," Hudsy drawled. "Which

is why I brought the new threads."

After whipping off the disco magic shirt, he pulled the cotton over his torso and emitted a grateful groan. No more threads that felt like a thousand scorpions had turned his torso into their dance club. Unable to help himself, he gave Hudsy a mushy cheek kiss. "I adore you."

She whacked his shoulder. "Those are only pretty words to me, Sergeant." Her hand curled in except for one chiding finger. "Save them for the one you really mean them for."

As they started down a hallway that led past the club's kitchen and storerooms, he gave a dismissive snort. "Bella gets lots of adoration, each and every day, I guarantee—"

"I wasn't talking about Bella."

She tossed another knowing smile in emphasis before stopping at a door with a sign that read Bow to the Queen, Boys. On the other side of it was a small office, though not so tiny that an old-fashioned school desk and a spanking bench couldn't occupy one wall. The desk to which she directed *him* was clearly used for the real business side of the club. She pulled out the leather chair located in front of it, but Ethan didn't sit yet. Instead, he squared his stance to the woman and cut to the proverbial chase of things. She was clearly as good a Domme as she was a sub, which meant coy and cute were a waste of time here.

"Ava and I... Let's just say it's complicated."

Hudsy angled an elegant hand against her latex-clad hip. "The best ones usually are, honey."

He locked his teeth. "I'm not her Mr. Right. I'm not even her Mr. Right *Now*." He sank into the chair. "Not anymore."

She hitched her hip onto the desk and cocked her head. "And that creepazoid of a producer *is*?" When Ethan returned only a sullen silence, she scooted back to her feet with a huff. "Fine. Talk to your boss. I have some things to take care of."

Before she stomped out of the office, she hit a couple of keys on the computer to bring up the window to which Franz had obviously directed her. He wondered if Hudsy thought it odd that "Thor of Polynesia" had given her a Victorian home-decorating site to bring up as their conference portal but pushed back the concern as he navigated the triple firewall into the screen where Franz waited with Colton at his side. Neither of them jolted when his ping sounded on their end. They were ready.

"Runway!" his leader declared. "Good, you're on. Are you alone?"

Ethan frowned. Urgency soaked Franzen's tone. "Yeah," he replied. "I'm in the club's office. Can't guarantee how thick the walls are, though."

"Understood. We're going to be quick and general about this, anyway."

"Okay." He drew it out as half a question. Franz was a smart guy; he'd pick up on the subtext. If this call was classified as "quick and general," why had they called the club and brought Hudsy in on the exchange instead of just hitting him on his cell?

The answer punched him in the gut.

They didn't want anyone to know he was getting a call. At all.

Franz cleared his throat before continuing. "I'll get to the point. We've only scraped the fucking iceberg on breaking through this code. But somewhere between the cartoon conversation bubbles, the algebra questions in Dr. Seuss form, and the paragraphs that look composed by a toddler, your friend Rhett hooked up with a new friend from the FBI encryption team, and they hit what we think is a significant breakthrough."

He leaned back with a deepening frown. "How significant?" Was it good enough so they could pull the plug on this part of the op? Could he finally cuff Lor and his octopus arms and drag him in for interrogation? Best of all, were they telling him they had enough to authorize a kill order on the bastard?

"What do you make of this?" Franz clicked the mouse on their side, sharing an image from their screen to his. If the guy was thinking to dispel his confusion with it, Ethan had disappointing feedback.

"Looks like you had some playtime with those toddlers and told them to make a *C* with a pack of colored candy." The rainbow of dots was scattered into a rough representation of the letter, curving only slightly at the top and bottom.

"Good analogy. How about now?"

He clicked up another shot of the same dots. This time, the boundaries of California, Oregon, and Washington were laid on top of the mess. Some dots appeared in parts of Idaho, Nevada, and Arizona as well.

"What the hell?" Ethan muttered.

"The next view is where we're hoping to grab your help." Franz didn't waste any time clicking to the third version of the map. This time, each candy piece had an Asian symbol superimposed on it.

Ethan's pulse kicked up as he examined the images. The characters weren't exclusive to their own color. The assignation of the characters seemed random, but logic told him that wasn't the case. There had to be a concrete reasoning behind the coupling of a character and a color. But what?

"It's Chinese," he declared after a few seconds. "Korean has circles and sweeping curves. And Japanese has simpler strokes."

"We'd deduced the same thing," his captain replied. "We just don't know what the symbols mean."

"Give me a second." The language wasn't considered the world's hardest to learn for nothing. Every word had its own character, and many had more than one depending on the context. "Okay, one of them is *party*, as in a birthday or anniversary of some sort. The one that looks like an upside-down *pi* symbol with arms attached is *happy graduation*. The one with the duplicated characters is for *wedding*. There are a few more that are variants of the *party* theme." He shook his head. "What is all this?"

The map didn't disappear, so he couldn't observe Franzen's and Colton's reactions. He could only wait through their long, all-too-telling silence.

"Fuck." Colton finally snarled it. A second later, his face reappeared along with Franzen's.

"What?" Ethan countered, though another thorough study of their faces filled in a lot of the reply already. "Come on. You don't think this is a target grid, do you?"

Franz drilled a hard look into the camera. "Every single one of these events has terrorist catnip written all over it. High civilian attendance, happy occasions full of what's perceived as classic overindulgence."

"So they're going to drop a suicide bomber in on every single one of them?" He dropped a finger onto the desk. "That's a supersized bag of Skittles on that map, boss."

Franzen gave him a respectful nod. "Agreed. So what's

your take?"

"It's an elaborate drug-drop grid." He rendered the reply almost immediately. "Granted, I've never seen any hustler, even for the high-end blow and smack the Aragons are getting into, keep a delivery grid that elaborate—"

"Or encrypted," Colton inserted.

"Yeah, there's that." He shook his head. "But it still doesn't add up. I still vote smoke screen. That's a map for a party planner, not a terrorist. Not even one with ties to the big guns in the Middle East."

Franz glowered. "I should have Hudsy whip you for a pun like that at a time like this, Archer."

Under less stressful circumstances, he would've pressed Franz for details on how he knew the beautiful switch in ways that seemed more than "just business," but right now, his brain was racing, working to detangle the mystery that the grid introduced. "The symbols," he murmured, "are Chinese, not Arabic or even Italian. If Lor's behind this, why the different language?"

"Another smokescreen?" Franzen suggested.

"Or part of the code we have yet to crack?"

His leader dropped his head into both hands while Colton looked on with a dreary stare, torturing a paper clip in his own frustration. "Runway," Franz finally uttered, "I'm afraid this means we've got to move forward on the op at status quo."

"Roger." He would've summoned more enthusiasm if they'd said he was bound for a waterboarding.

"Get creative, man. Step up the bromance with your pal *Enzo* any way you can, all right?"

Terrific. Just the motivator he needed right now. Getting ordered to spend *more* time with the man who was operating under a fake name to cover a paramilitarist identity, while pawing the woman who still sucked a lung from his body every time he saw her. "Got it," he said through clenched teeth. There was nothing more to say and certainly no small talk he wanted to dawdle on, so he mumbled, "Archer out," and disconnected the line.

Fuck.

Back to work. And that meant back into the Satan-spun silver sparkle shirt too.

Barely tamping a growl, he shucked the cotton T-shirt but couldn't bring himself to put on the disco scorpions again. With the silver thing wadded in his fist, he wrenched the door open and stomped back down the hall toward the playrooms.

The air smelled like leather, and he smelled like a goddamn makeup counter. Outstanding. *Clear the way. Dickless wonder coming through.*

How the hell had this happened? Ten days ago, he'd smelled liked fuel fumes and desert dust, slinging trash talk with his teammates before fast-roping into the little complex in the Mexican desert where Galvaz was holed up. Two nights after that, Franzen had pinned on his new ranking and offered a ticket to Tinseltown in celebration.

That was the moment he should've remembered the word *no*. The instant he should've realized that fate only let a guy play so many risky hands before it bitch-slapped him in the face, reminding him who the boss was at the cosmic poker table. He should've cashed in his winnings as soon as those stripes hit his collar and left the game a content man. Instead, he got greedy. Wanting a woman he should have forgotten months ago.

Craving her exactly as he did right now...pummeled anew by her burnished beauty.

She sat beneath one of the dungeon's recessed lights. It had been tinted in a light flesh tone, making hers look like mocha ice cream poured over the most tempting body God had created. A lucky bar stool supported her, and she had one heel-clad foot hooked to one of its rungs, making her dress hike up and showing off her thigh beneath the smart pad she was tapping on. All of her hair was pushed over to one side, tumbling into the V of her cleavage like a sexy, soft waterfall.

And she seemed to be alone.

In the same room as the Cadillac of bondage beds.

Not a great thing for him to notice. Or hope for. Not with the solid case of pissed-off-at-the-universe decimating his gut right now. No sense in beating around the bush about it either.

"Where the fuck is everyone?"

She looked up at him with a grin—*a grin*—that formed an adorable dimple in her right cheek. "That must've been one hell of a bathroom break, Sergeant. Do I get to ask if someone was doing the nasty in the next stall, or has a more personal problem dragged out your inner asswipe?"

He peeked around the corner, into the room where they'd been setting up for the next half of the photo session. Grant and his crew, along with their floodlights and reflectors, were packed up and gone. "It's a crime to ask a question?" he flung back. "Especially one that clearly needs an answer?"

She gave him a look that made him feel like a kid who'd pushed his mother too far. He didn't like it one damn bit. Her conciliating tone didn't hit the happy spot either. "Enzo got a call from the writers' room. They had a brainstorm and wanted a huge script change for Tuesday night. He approved it, which means he and Bella are needed back at the studio for new rehearsals. Grant rolled up his own crew and was out of here five minutes ago."

Hudsy picked that second to drift in behind him. "Didn't that all work out conveniently?" she murmured for his ears alone. Before he could throw back even half a glare, she lifted her voice to call to Ava. "It was great meeting you, but one of my boys is taking me to dinner at Opaque. We're dining completely in the dark. I'm *certain* he won't be late picking me up." Her green eyes danced with naughty glee. "My maintenance guy is in the back fixing some equipment, so yell at him when you leave and he'll lock up behind you."

"Will do." Ava sent a warm smile at the woman. "Thanks for everything, Hudsy."

He felt oddly rooted in place while the woman's footsteps grew faint and then were replaced by the *whump* of the back door. Lingering in the air, silent and potent, were the words she'd issued to him like a kinky gauntlet. *Didn't that all work out conveniently?*

He took a heavy breath. There was nothing convenient about this. There was nothing about this that was easy, lucky, auspicious, or advantageous—because there wasn't a goddamn thing he could do in this place, with this woman who looked at him with her magical indigo eyes and her luscious lip caught in her teeth, that wouldn't haunt them both in the end. The only thing missing to this ongoing torture session was the itchy silver T-shirt, which he gladly ditched in a trash can.

I'm not even her Mr. Right Now.

The words had come out of his mouth, yet he hated them. He turned his hands into fists with the longing to crush them out of existence. And fought back at them with the vicious snarl he threw at her.

"So what the hell are *you* still doing here? Lemare didn't

offer a lift back in his Lamborghini? Or was he slumming it in the Rolls Royce today?"

Her eyes flashed, but he couldn't tell if she was peeved or hurt. "I came in my own car. And I was waiting on you."

Hmm. Peeved *and* hurt. Where was the Chinese symbol for *I'm a jerk-ass* when a guy needed it? And why did he care? She clearly didn't. The path he'd yearned to take to her heart had been blazed and shit on twice already, so she roped off the lane before he had a chance to start. The best thing he could do now was his goddamn job, to get Ephraim Lor out of her life before she decided to let down the barrier for his slick, smarmy ass.

"Why?" he finally challenged.

"Because..." She let out a petite, and damnably cute, snort. "Because I'm concerned about you."

"*Why?*"

"I'm not fucking Lemare."

He was both troubled and grateful for the relief that flooded him. "Thanks for the status update, but you still didn't answer my question. Why are you 'concerned' about me?"

She dropped her gaze to the floor. "You've seemed sad."

The confession stopped him cold. And for some reason, made him want to laugh. "Sad?" His voice went quiet as he took a step toward her, though it was a compulsion more than a decision. He was fascinated by why she'd said it. And by why there was such a melancholy note in her own voice.

"Uhh...yeah. Like your head's not all here most of the time."

Hell. Was she actually worried about him? God, not now. He fought against the husk of her voice, the somber oceans in her gaze. "I'm not your concern anymore Ava, remember? You told me it was for the best. We had 'closure.'" He bracketed the last word in sardonic air quotes.

She straightened her spine. "So that means I can't care at all about you? That we can't still be friends?"

"We're not friends!" He hurled it back the second it left the incredible curves of her mouth. "From the second we knocked noses on the floor at Garrett and Sage's, we weren't friends, Ava. You know it as clearly as I do, and don't you dare put it into pretty words to make yourself feel better. This"—he raced a finger between his chest and hers—"*isn't* words. And it sure as hell isn't 'friends.'" As much as he longed to let that serve as their finality, the tears that gleamed in her eyes were like beacons, pulling him closer until the curves of her jaw were fitted between his hands and her cheeks were warm, wonderful, and soft beneath his combat-roughened thumbs. "I know it's hard for you. I know you still carry the ache from what happened with Colin and Flynn and that you don't think you can handle a third blow. So don't. Let me take the hit instead. But goddamnit, don't cheapen it by slapping on a label that isn't true and never will be."

She drew in a shaky breath. He felt every shudder of it. "I won't use the label," she whispered, "but you can't take all the pain." She squeezed her eyes. The salty drops fell and puddled against his fingers. "It's impossible."

Against every instinct of survival he possessed, he shifted closer to her. The smart pad on her lap slipped to the floor. He stepped in again, pressing their bodies together. Dear God, she was so sweet, so silken, so right. "I'm Special Forces, sunshine. We specialize in impossible."

Her eyes darkened even more, pulling him down like dual whirlpools of her raw emotion. "You can't take away something that's already sewn into my heart."

Her words heated the few inches left between their mouths. As Ethan bent to close up that space, he let his senses cave to a single, inexorable certainty. If his heart was killed tonight in her hands, then so be it. It wasn't a bad way to commit suicide.

He didn't say a word about the decision. He let her see it in his eyes—in the two seconds before he crushed her mouth in his conquering kiss.

CHAPTER EIGHTEEN

Yes.

It was the only word, the only thought that filled Ava's being as Ethan filled her mouth, ignited her blood, accepted her tears...consumed her heart. With a surrendering sigh, she gave it all to him. Opened herself for him. Rejoiced in the completion of his embrace, the rightness of his kiss, the heat of his passion. One moment, this perfect moment, and the world fell away. It was as if they stood in a magical forest again and he was touching her for the very first time. Just like that misty morning, she lifted her face and offered him one word in supplication.

"Tighter." She guided his hands down, against the small of her back, before wriggling her wrists inside them. "I need it tighter, Ethan...please."

A growl rolled out of him in degrees that matched his constriction around her wrists. He dipped his head and sank possessive teeth into her throat, chopping her aroused sigh in half. "What else do you need?" He spoke it against her jugular before lapping away the burn of his bite with the flat of his tongue.

Her head fell back and her lungs struggled to keep up with her racing pulse. "You...you already know," she uttered. After a purposeful pause, she added, "Sir."

He squeezed her wrists harder. "If you're going there, sunshine, then you'll go the rest of the way—and you'll tell me, clearly and proudly, what you need from me."

Every syllable he issued sent a new wave of arousal through every inch of her pussy, unfurling ribbons of fire down her legs. But gee, it all still found ways to lend some of that heat to her face, which flamed anew from his command. She flushed deeper as he brushed his mouth across both her cheeks, gazing at her with unflinching purpose, unmitigated desire.

"I need the words, Ava. Six days ago, you called us *closed*. I'm not going back in unless you open the door."

She lifted her gaze to look fully into his. She had to see in there what she'd heard in his voice. The visceral need. The brutal honesty. That "going back in" wasn't just a physical action for him. He wasn't just summoning the obedience of her body. If she opened again to him, he'd demand access to the bridges of her mind, the connections to her soul.

As if she could give him anything less.

She longed to preface her next words by stroking his strong, perfect face. With his hands binding hers, she did it with her eyes instead. "I've never been able to fully close it. And I think you know that too...Sir."

For a long moment, nothing in his mien changed—until he let out a long breath through his nose. Its cadence told her he'd not only heard her honesty but absorbed it, cherished it.

Ava smiled as he slowly lowered his lips to hers again. Her heart crashed against her ribs. The last time he'd kissed her with this tenderness, they'd been picking wedding bouquet flowers in the woods. Just like then, his embrace filled her with a thrill of awakening...and desire old as the ages. Also like then, his muscles coiled from the pressure to keep the pressure chaste. It was all too easy to remember what she did next...the tiny cry she'd released into his mouth, telling him the gentleness wasn't what she craved, wasn't what her body and soul needed. That in his arms and beneath his control, she longed for more. So much more.

She didn't let out the cry for him now. She gave him a full moan.

Ethan responded with a harsh growl—before ramming her mouth wide and plunging his tongue in.

She gave him access to everything. And he began to take. As he incinerated her with his mouth, he unlocked her hands to tear his hands beneath her skirt, feverishly searching for her panties. Ava took advantage of the chance to touch him in return, scraping the massive plateaus of his naked shoulders, gripping his biceps at the moment he coiled them to tear off her underthings. Her mouth fell free from his as she gasped in shock and panted in lust. That didn't stop her from watching the mesmerizing tension of his face while he slid a hand beneath her shirt, seized her bra clasp, and twisted it apart in one ferocious move. Inside a second, her breasts sizzled with the same hot exhilaration as the rest of her body. *Dios mio*, nobody had made her feel like this before her clothes even left her body.

She drew in a breath, shivering in anticipation of the kiss that was sure to follow, but found herself trembling instead. He'd pushed her back by a step and now raked her from head to toe with eyes that held fathoms of cobalt hunger. He'd dropped his arms but flexed his fingers. His mouth parted to reveal the feral lock of his brilliant teeth.

"Take it off," he ordered in a rough, low voice. "Every last stitch."

Another shiver washed over her. Instinctively she wet her lips, causing him to pull in a harsh hiss. It made her feel gorgeous and powerful, even while she acquiesced to his order, pushing away her dress and her bra until they tumbled to her feet.

"The shoes too," he instructed. After she stepped from her pumps, he released another rasp. Softer this time but longer. So much longer. "Dear Christ," he murmured. "I really am bound for hell."

The exigency in his voice made her brave again. She gave him a tentative smile. "Why?"

He stopped flexing his hands. With his long fingers extended out instead, he advanced on her by a step. "Because of everything I just imagined doing to your beautiful body." With one of those hands, he pulled at her hair, guiding her head up. "And your incredible mind."

Right. Some "incredible" mind. Only one word pulsed through the neurons beneath her skull, screaming at her for release. She set it free once more, turning it into a desperate plea this time.

"Yes...*yes.*"

Ethan's face tightened. His wolf-bright eyes searched her face. "Yes what?"

"Do them," she returned. "All of those wicked things." She swallowed hard. "If you're going to hell, then take me with you."

His grip curled harder against her scalp. He leaned in closer, now pressing the prominent ridge in his leathers into the space between her lower ribs. "You need to know everything you're asking for, sunshine." He firmed his jaw and locked his gaze with hers. "I haven't fucked Bella this week."

He acknowledged her surprise with a sweep of his free hand, grabbing hers and pushing it against the erection that throbbed heavier with each minute. "But if you beg me to dominate you again, if the word *yes* leaves your lips one more time"—he turned her to make her look at the bondage bed, with its hooks and chains and shadows—"then I *will* be inside you tonight...probably in several different ways."

His promise filled her with as much fear as it did arousal. Looking at the bed, practically seeing the scene his mind painted for her in it, was daunting, terrifying...and wholly irresistible.

He'd control her. And she'd let him.

He'd penetrate her. And she'd permit him.

He'd hurt her. And she'd adore him.

Her mind spun. Her body trembled. She took one last breath of sanity and then let it out, giving into the madness with a grateful whisper.

"Yes."

For a long moment, Ethan didn't move. He kept one hand braced on her hip, the other wound in her hair. His body remained a powerful but motionless tower behind her.

Ava gulped, unsteady and unsure. Was she supposed to do something else now? Drop to her knees? Call him *Sir*? Say some weird submissive oath of fealty?

"Ssshhhh."

His admonishment came so softly, she almost thought it was a rush of wind against the building. She frowned and tried to pivot her head around. "Wh-What?"

He seized her harder, keeping her locked in place. "Sssshhh." It was a harsh slice off his lips now, released into her ear before he ran his teeth along the length of her lobe. "Quiet it all down, baby. Your thoughts are so loud you can't hear your feelings." His hands finally relaxed, the top one kneading her head, the bottom caressing her stomach, her breasts, her hips.

Again into her ear, he coaxed, "There's no right. There's no wrong. There's only you, surrendering to me. Everything. All of it."

He curled his fingers, scoring her skin with his nails, dissolving her insecurities into dust. "Yes, Sir," she finally said with a sigh.

He clawed her harder and charged, "No. I don't expect your *Yes, Sir*s tonight either. I expect your obedience, without hesitation or argument. Call a red light if we hit one, but other than that, you will simply *be*."

While her mind was a tornado in her attempt to comprehend that, she managed a little nod. "Yes, S—"

He bit into the flesh just below her ear. "That protocol begins now, sunshine."

It was the hardest damn thing in the world to simply still herself, to let him take over. And *mierda*, he did just that.

Though maintaining his position behind her, he widened his stance and pulled her tighter back, pressing her into the frame of his leather-clad legs. The ensuing minutes were torture and paradise combined. There wasn't an inch of her arms, breasts, stomach, or thighs that he didn't explore with worshipful slides, glides, and strokes, setting her skin ablaze with steady purpose.

That was the utopia part. The damnation came every time he got anywhere near the juncture of her thighs—and passed over it with nothing but feathery touches to her pubic curls. By the time he did that for the tenth time, she nearly bucked against him in frustration, chewing her bottom lip to stay dutifully silent.

Ethan's beard stubble grazed her nape as he settled his lips against her ear again. "Go to the bed now," he directed. "Get in the middle, facing the headboard, and kneel for me there."

At this point, she would've done it even if the bed was lined with hot coals.

After eagerly climbing onto the firm red leather, she took the pose he'd ordered. Through enough of her dabblings into the nature of submission, she remembered that subs often honored their Doms by turning their hands upward, resting atop their thighs, signifying their willing acquiescence to the dynamic. Doing it now made her feel strange yet peaceful... exactly where she was supposed to be, with the man she most wanted to be here with.

More of her doubts slipped away. She focused completely on listening to Ethan, who now shifted in the room behind her. He opened the cabinet against the wall and gave a number of approving hums. She heard items clinking together, the *whoosh* of leather through the air. She visibly shivered, and he audibly chuckled. Gorgeous, sadistic bastard. Did he think he could mess with her mind by making her listen to him play with the toys behind her back?

It was working.

Her heart thudded harder. Her womb clenched tighter. Her pussy dripped wetter. If she could draw any reassurance from the horny mess, she realized that at least he couldn't see any of those things—or take advantage of them.

Or so she thought.

He moved up behind her again. Climbed right up on the bed, grazing the back of her head with the ridges of his abdomen, nudging her neck with the tight mound at the front of his leathers. She barely resisted the temptation to turn her head, press her lips against that prominent swell, and beg him to unzip so she could taste his flesh once more.

In hindsight, maybe that was exactly what she should have done.

Ethan reached around and took hold of both her forearms, totally ruining her pose. He pulled until she was in an upright kneel instead of the butt-on-ankles position in which she'd just been. More significantly, he didn't stop lifting on her arms until she looked overhead, suddenly realizing his purpose. A two-in-one leather cuff dangled from a chain suspended between the bed's support beams. He didn't hesitate about cinching her into it, the middle strap serving to tighten the clasps for both her wrists.

Her mind immediately went for some snarky Spanish slang, countering her massive uneasiness at being so suddenly exposed for him. With a deep inhalation, she quelled the outburst. Though she was still unnerved, she also found herself immersed in a strange peace. She made her living being worried about how things looked all the time, about how elements got placed, lighted, presented. She couldn't remember the last time none of that was a concern. It freed her senses to actually experience details instead of analyzing them. The cool air against her nude skin, tickling the insides of her thighs as she widened her knees for better balance. The smell in the air, redolent with steel and smoke and sex. The rough soughs of Ethan's leathers as he moved again, swirling his hands across all the planes of her body as he examined her from every angle with those dark, wild eyes.

"Goddamn," he murmured, tracing the edges of her ribcage with the tips of his fingers. "You're so beautiful like this. So perfect." He bent and kissed the hollow between her breasts. "So mine."

She hoped he heard the heartbeat that crashed beneath

his lips...the *Yes, Sir* she yearned to exclaim until it filled every corner of this room. She willed the force of it into her gaze as he looked back to her face, his own features gripped with such intensity, he made her pussy wetter just by looking at him.

Of course, the man discerned that fact nearly before she did. With a rogue's quirk to his lips and a demon's glint in his eyes, he glided a hand to the tissues that were so available for his touch now. A slow hum prowled up his throat as he explored her soaked folds and then finally slipped a finger into the depths of her vagina.

"Ahhh," she keened softly. It didn't count as a word, did it? Dear God, how she wanted to say more. Beg him for more. Plead for more of the tantalizing strokes he gave to her intimate walls, drawing out more of her moisture and heat. She kept it all back by clenching her teeth, a visible battle that earned her his wicked half grin.

"Somebody likes bondage," he murmured. "A lot."

She narrowed her eyes, showing him the taunting touches were fast moving past arousal and into sensual torture.

"Your body feels like it wants to come, sunshine." After she managed a jerking nod, he went on. "But I want to see it throb for its reward." Though he kept teasing her tunnel with his finger, he rotated so his body bracketed hers from the side and he could start exploring her spine, ass, and thighs with his other hand. "I want to turn it pink and then red. I want to mark you with stings and screams...to hold your thoughts and your will in my grasp until I give them back, letting your body take mine."

Vaguely, Ava felt her head rolling forward. It was almost like she nodded but felt more like falling under a beautiful, sexual spell. But a wince fell from her when he pulled his finger free, robbing her of the steady pressure that her deepest caverns craved. He trailed her own nectar up the midline of her body until letting her breathe in her own arousal as he tucked that finger beneath her chin and lifted her face toward his again.

"I need to know you want it too, Ava." His stare fell to her lips like a starving man beholding a feast, but he sustained his distance. "I need to know you're ready for this part of my Dominance. I'm not going to put fancy words on it either. I've wanted you like this since the first time I kissed you. That means I've been thinking about it for damn near eight months now. I can't guarantee how gentle I'll be or how—"

Unable to use words, she shut him up with a kiss. Just lunged her face up, sealed their lips with hard, needing urgency, and prayed it would be enough to prove he wasn't the only one who'd been dreaming about this for all those months.

From the way he bared his teeth in a look that was half grin and half snarl, it looked like he finally got the point.

The moment after that, he slipped off the bed and into the shadows.

The immediate effect of that was a shocking hit of weirdness. For a moment, pure fear washed over her. She was suspended, nude, and alone. No...not alone. As if they were bound to each other with invisible filaments of energy, she felt Ethan's presence flow back to her, into her, his silent acknowledgment of the trust she'd placed in him. He verbally communicated as such too, letting her hear his approving growl when he came to stand directly behind her.

"You're fucking exquisite."

She looked up a little. His shadow played across the wall, framed by the bed's heavy posts, as tall and carved and defined as his magnificent body. As she took in the sight, her stomach twisted and her breath stopped.

At the ends of his shadow hands, there were now shadow floggers.

Before she could start breathing again, he gently draped the leather falls of one down her spine. "Ohhhh," she moaned. The thin strips were supple and cool, making her pussy tighten as he swished them over her backside and upper thighs. He repeated the treatment with the other flogger. She duplicated her blissful exhale.

Until he sliced it short by bringing the first flogger back down on her.

Hard.

Okay...*wow*. She blinked, trying to gauge if the heat across her skin was pleasure, pain, or both. Before she could sort it out, he wielded the second blow. Then the third. Then at least a dozen after that, each just a few seconds apart, until her eyes drifted shut and her body began to fall into a strange, syncopated rhythm with the strikes. This was actually a little relaxing...

An extra-hard smack reared her out of the reverie.

"*Mierda!*" she protested. "*Hijo de puta!*"

He did it again.

"Ethan!"

She heard him rest the floggers. Of course, that also gave him the chance to lean in and rub a hand across all the skin he'd just enflamed, ending with the tender flesh that dipped between her thighs. "Is that your version of a red light, sunshine? Are we stopping now?"

His tone was only half-serious. He'd reserved the other section for that self-sure man in the dress blues who'd first pinned her to a tree in a Northwestern forest—and knew she'd like it. The sadist in him was openly baiting the masochist in her, knowing that girl wouldn't give up the game this early.

"No," she snapped. After a deliberating breath, she added, "No, Sir. I...I want to go on."

His own assessing pause made her tense back up. "Even though I'm going to switch toys?"

She gave a scoffing snort. "What, as *discipline* because I spoke?"

"You spoke up because you had a genuine concern. Why would I discipline you for that?" If his temperate tone wasn't a hard enough pill to take, he moved next to her again, bracing a large knee just inside her left one. "When I ordered you to silence, it was because I knew you wouldn't comply any other way. I was also sure that once you tried to let go, you'd like the mental freedom."

She flashed a penitent glance as he brushed the hair from her face. "Oh." And *ugh*. He was completely right. She'd liked it. A lot.

"Your smart-ass attitude right now, though—that's a different issue." He shoved his leg in harder, stretching hers out, so his thigh rubbed directly on her pussy. She shuddered as waves of heat and arousal flowed from the contact, tightening her thighs, clenching her abdomen, flooding her body in waves of heat and need. The torment got worse as he reached and palmed her right butt cheek. He wasn't as tender with his touch this time, gripping her with the same ferocity that had reclaimed his face. "Baby, if you were really my subbie, there *would* be a lesson involved for that. A nice, healthy chunk of that—what'd you call it? Hmm, yeah—'discipline.'"

She had no idea, aside from the man's quadricep grinding

her kink curiosity into overdrive, what possessed her to lick her lips and blurt out, "Discipline...like...how?"

He gentled his grasp on her ass but bore his gaze into her by several ruthless degrees. "Like doing something that pleased me more than you."

Despite the position in which he'd trapped her, she huffed. "That's impossible, then."

He cocked his head. "Oh?"

Despite her state of hot, bothered, and beyond agitated, she gave him a soft smile. "Because if I pleased you, I'd be happy."

"Happy," he repeated like she'd just told him the earth was square. "So happy and discipline don't go together?"

"That's the point, isn't it?"

He adjusted his position a little. Not only did he ram his thigh harder against her crotch, he angled his hand deeper into the crevice of her backside...now running a slow finger around the delicate rim of the forbidden entrance there. "It's an interesting theory. Perhaps it needs to be tested."

All the air in her body shorted out. Ethan filled the taut pause by pressing his finger into the first sensitive inch of her anus. She mewled and pulled a little at the cuffs, alternately panicked and enflamed. Being touched there was so sinful, so intimate, a border she'd never wanted to cross with anyone... before now. "Per...perhaps," she finally uttered.

Ethan's reply was just as rough yet thoroughly male. "Your ass has filled my dreams since I first laid hands on it in that wine cellar." With his stare locked to hers, he eased a second finger in, stretching her illicit opening even more. "And it would make me very happy to claim it in every way I can."

Her senses careened. Her skin cells were a million bursts

of electricity. Her muscles bunched and quivered, struggling to keep still beneath burst after burst of arousal. Her nose filled with the leather-and-pepper smell that was only Ethan...this man who'd torn into her spirit like no other, who made all her erotic fantasies come true...including the one he proposed right now.

With that resignation, she returned his gaze, pulled in a long breath, and whispered, "Tell me what to do...please, Sir?"

CHAPTER NINETEEN

He was going to hate himself for this. Some crazy protester marched through his brain still screaming that, but Ethan wrapped a mental fist around the asswipe's neck and squeezed hard. He was tired of the screeches. Exhausted from the voices that kept pep-talking him through a pretense he hated, in the name of an op that had just gotten even crazier.

He was weary of the logic that decreed the insanity of caring for Ava Chestain, let alone touching her...especially like this.

But right now, the only thing that felt sane was her. The only thing that felt right was this. He had no idea what was going to happen in the next hour, much less the next day, but if fate was offering one more moment with her like this, he wasn't going to insult the bastard. He was going to grasp this with every grateful bone in his body and make it incredible for her too.

Her beautiful plea clung to the air between them. *Tell me what to do.* After giving her a reassuring kiss, he decided to show her instead. Wordlessly, he unclipped the cuffs from the chain overhead. This kept her wrists bound, which he guided downward by hooking a finger in the leather loop between them. He pressed on the space between her shoulder blades to indicate he wanted her upper body to follow. It took little effort to find a rig point in the headboard, to which he clipped the cuffs in order to hold her in that position.

He let a hand slide over her bowed head and lowered shoulders, then up the sleek line of her back, and finally atop the buttocks that were now raised and ready for his pleasure... his use.

"Perfect," he murmured.

Ava responded with a deep sigh. "It's all yours," she said, her tone so silken and sweet, he knew she was headed into a nice subbed-out zone again. He almost hated shattering that. *Almost.*

"It's stunning," he told her, swiping both his hands across the golden-skinned globes that topped the graceful curves of her thighs. Christ, he could spend days in veneration to her ass alone. But he had maybe an hour here at best. Time to get on with things. "I love the pink we've already painted across this canvas. But now it needs something more. Are you ready for my new paintbrush, baby?"

He watched the chocolate waves on her head glisten in the light as she nodded. "Yes, Sir. Ohhh, yes."

He'd brought over a nice leather dragon's tail from the toy closet but then noticed Hudsy had left the crop from the photo shoot in a convenient hook on one of the bedposts. The woman, being the perfect hostess she was, also left the cup next to it stocked with lube and a beginner's anal plug. And people accused *him* of being part psychic?

After making a mental note to send Hudsy a long thank-you note and a good bottle of Columbia Valley cabernet, he positioned himself behind Ava, steeling himself for the glorious view her fresh position would now allow him. The sight was better than he expected, forcing him to clear his throat in hopes of calming his damn libido. *Shit.* Her legs were parted enough for him to glimpse the coral shimmer of her labia and the darker mystery of her pussy. Just inches from that was the puckered ingress with which he'd just toyed...and had many more plans for tonight.

The conclusion was an ideal companion to his next movements. As he spread her ass cheeks again, he felt and observed the tension in her muscles. "Take a breath. Relax, baby."

She complied without hesitation, making it easy for him to get a generous squeeze of lube into her back hole. He used the lubrication to penetrate her deeper with a finger while spreading his thumb to rub the tender ridge of her clit at the same time.

"Oh!" she cried. "Oh, my!"

Despite the stimulation in her tone, tension still gripped her whole body. "You'll answer me honestly, sunshine," he directed. "Is this the first time you'll have a man in your ass?"

Not surprisingly, she went still. "Y-Yes, Sir."

Ethan stroked her back with soothing pressure. "Thank you."

As he observed her melting into the motion, even rolling her hips with it, he went ahead and optimized the advantage in front of him—by rolling the plug in some lube and sliding it into her.

"*Ay!*" she exclaimed. "Ethan! Didn't I just say this was new for me?"

She bucked and strained, but he turned the caress on her back into a controlling hold, exhilarated by it, pulling her through the portal of new awakening with firm, sensual surety. "And haven't I asked you to trust me, sunshine? Ssshhh. Calm down. Breathe again. A little training goes a long way."

Though her hard breaths still rocked her frame, she

shifted back into position. He leaned deeper over her, rubbing the fingers that now clawed at the bed. Her arms tensed beneath his, her shoulders hunched near her ears. He nudged his lips against her nape and kissed it. Nipped his way down to her shoulder blades. Continued the length of her spine until he got to her ass again, where he continued to work the plug in and out, letting her get used to the fullness of it, making sure the tender membranes at the edge got plentifully stimulated.

"How does it feel now, sunshine?"

Ava took a long second to reply. "Tight." Her shoulders tightened again. "It's so much..."

He shifted back, ordering himself to focus on everything she was feeling instead of the blood that banged up and down his cock, shouting a huge *Let's roll, already!* into his whole body. He compelled himself to focus on a higher goal. The nirvana he was going to reach in fucking an ass that burned with the welts he'd just dealt.

With that picture splashed in his head, he reached for the crop. As he started tapping at the sweet swells of her backside with it, he murmured, "Maybe a distraction will help."

Ava emitted an unsteady whimper, though her fingers uncurled and her hips writhed, giving in to her submissive instinct to process the little stings with movement. Not for the first time this week, Ethan shook his head in wonderment. How another Dom hadn't snatched her up, with her eagerness for all this so evident in her willing eyes and her acquiescent body, was beyond his comprehension. Maybe the sunshine in LA had a wonky gamma effect on its men. If that was the case, he hoped the city had a long, sundrenched summer. And fall. And winter.

She changed her movements as he put a little more

muscle into the taps. She lunged forward instead of swirling her hips. He began timing the hits farther apart, giving her time to absorb and process the pain. At the same time, he listened to her harsh gasps, accepting every blow eagerly. He knew her endorphin pumps were grinding at full speed now, warming her skin, racing her heart. Her fast breathing told him she was on her way to a thick haze of pleasure. Her glistening pussy showed him she was on fire with sexual need.

He couldn't resist having a touch.

Giving her a reassuring growl, he cupped his fingers between her thighs. Sure enough, the folds of her labia welcomed him with tight heat. She groaned and thrust it all harder into his hand. Her desire surged his to greater heights, driving the strength behind his blows and marking her flesh with incredible crimson ribbons. His marks. Yes. *Yes*, damn it, she was his—and he needed to seal that possession by driving himself into her most forbidden entrance.

With a snarl that sliced the air, he hurled aside the crop. He saw a shiver take over her from that alone, and it made him even harder. The process of freeing himself from the leathers seemed to take forever. After several urgent yanks, his dick surged out, shimmering with the evidence of just how ready he was for this, filled with more blood by the second thanks to the arousal roaring in his balls. It was an additional torment to grab at the stack of foil squares Hudsy had also left, tear one open with his teeth, and roll it over his thundering shaft. Then came the lube. Lots and lots of lube.

He grabbed Ava by the thighs and positioned her in front of him. The dark-purple head of his cock tapped against the clear tip of the anal plug. He worked the plug inside her once more while adding lube to the contact, working the slick liquid into her tight channel that way. She winced a little, though it turned into a full moan when he teased the stiff nub of her clit again.

"I'm going to pull it out now, baby," he said.

"Ok-k-kay."

"And I'm going to replace the plug with my cock."

He heard her swallow hard. "Y-Yes, Sir."

"You wanted this, Ava. You wanted my discipline."

She nodded slowly. "I want to make you happy, Ethan."

He gripped the sides of her ass, widening the opening at their apex. "You already do, sunshine. But this is a gift I'm not going to forget."

She didn't say anything as he eased the plug from her body.

She let out a high cry as he pressed his penis in.

"Push out." He gave it as a solid command. "Bear down against me, sunshine. We're almost there." The sound of the lube inside her body, the feeling of her ass clenching around him... It made his senses swim with sheer ecstasy. "Fuck. *Fuck*, Ava, you feel so good."

"Mmmm." It wasn't a moan reflecting her own pleasure. Not yet. But when she spoke again, there were wisps of arousal in her voice that gave him hope. "*Mierda.* It's...you're...it's so much..."

"Yeah." He didn't hold back from letting her hear every rough, hoarse note of his spiraling need. "It is, isn't it? I'm everywhere, aren't I? Conquering you, filling you, stretching you...making you wetter, hotter." Damn. His balls tucked in against her ass cheeks. He was in to the hilt, and it felt so fucking good.

"Ethan...oh God..."

"Let me fill you, Ava. Let me fuck you deep like this."

"Y-Yes. Ahhh!"

"It's setting you on fire, isn't it? I can feel it in your clit, Ava. You're ready to explode, just like me. And I want you to. Holy fuck, do I want you to."

"*Ay dios mio,*" she uttered. "Oh, my God!"

He pressed against her, raking his teeth against her shoulder, reveling in the lusty appeal he now heard in her voice. "What is it, baby? What do you need?"

"H-Harder." Her response barely carried volume because of her passion. "Fuck my ass harder. Faster. Claim me. Fill me. Hurt me. Heal me. P-Please..."

"Yes." His mind reeled into a world where fulfillment and feeling merged, where his soul was shifted...and his spirit was finally unleashed. "Yes, baby. *Yes.*"

A strangled huff left him as the comprehension blasted, hot and huge and magnificent. He shoved the hair from her neck and bit the back of it as he kept possessing her ass with his cock and her pussy with his fingers. The world wasn't just her anymore. The universe was. He was living the miracle he never thought he'd find. The exposed, perfect passion. The open, brutal openness. The connection he'd sought from BDSM yet had given up on discovering.

Ava's exclamation vibrated through them both. "I need to come, Ethan. Please...please!"

He smacked his body hard against hers, plunging into her with all the force his thighs would give. "Give it to me, sunshine. Give it all to me!"

Her scream filled the room as her body jerked and rocked. The walls of her ass fisted him tighter, doubling the friction of every pump he got in until the switch finally got thrown and his balls ignited. He climaxed like a goddamn fireworks show, his senses flying, his body consumed by color and fire and heat. He wanted it to go on forever, and thank fuck his load was a big one because Ava stiffened again, convulsing through another orgasm that rocked her so hard, she began sobbing before it was done.

"Baby." He rasped it into her ear, infusing it with every ounce of reverence and gratitude that warmed him.

"I'm okay," she squeaked.

"I know."

After a few minutes of holding her, he made short work of pulling his cock out of her body and her wrists out of the cuffs. "Don't move," he instructed, getting up to dispose of the condom and grab a blanket out of a nearby warmer. Hudsy really did run a class act here.

When he returned to the bed and wrapped the covering around Ava, he was careful yet cautious about his moves, partly due to resisting the urge to haul her back close. He'd just dominated her to the point of inducing tears. From experience, he knew that prompted some subs to withdraw into their own space for recovery. Others just wanted a hand to hold or someone nearby with a bottle of water. He couldn't read anything into Ava's bent head and curled posture, and he sure as hell wasn't going to start striking assumptions.

"Sunshine? Can I get you anyth—"

She drove the air from his lungs as she turned and lunged into his lap. "This," she whispered, burrowing closer as he folded his arms around her. "You can get me this."

Ethan rolled to his back, bringing her along with him. As the scent of their passion clung to the air and her heartbeat bumped against his, he murmured with total satisfaction,

"Anytime you need it, baby. Anytime at all."

★ ★ ★ ★ ★

When he looked at his watch again, he grumbled in irritation. Until he rubbed the sleep from his eyes and looked again. "Holy shit!"

"Hmmm?" Ava stirred and snuggled against his chest again. "What? No. Come here. You're warm."

"Sunshine, we fell asleep."

"I know," she mumbled. "Want more."

He smiled and kissed her forehead. "'Fraid not. It's five a.m. I'd better get you dressed and out of here. Your life is about to jump into warp speed."

Especially because her show might be losing its producer any minute.

Fuck, he hoped that wasn't the case. They'd chased down batshit intel before, and from the looks of things, they were either onto something huge here with Lor or something they could condense, contain, and hand over to the DEA for proper follow-up.

Either way, he was now hung balls-out over a barrel about it. Did he follow the damn rules and continue to keep Ava in the dark about their subterfuge involving Lor? Though she'd be insulated from the danger of that track, how would she react when he got back to the studio and renewed the kissy-la-la act with Bella, if she bought it at all after what they'd just shared? At that point, she'd likely confront him for a confession anyway. The woman was as smart as she was beautiful. It was why she made such a mesmerizing submissive—and the hardest lover he'd ever be recovering from, come a week's time.

There were more important things to think about right now.

Choice number one in that category hinged on how she rubbed the sleek ribbon of her leg against the inside of his. *Hell.* If she slid any higher, she'd be teasing his balls with that silken skin and would find herself thoroughly fucked as a wake-up call. Choice number two was how she tucked herself tighter into the crook of his shoulder and explored the breadth of his chest with her fingertips. Her touch, soothing and soft, had turned into the gift she'd given him all night, a treat he hadn't enjoyed in a very long time. Complete peace.

"Mmmm." She issued it as a wistful whine of protest as she began a tracing a figure eight with her pointer finger. "You're probably right. Bella's likely wondering where you were all night."

He clamped back a chuckle. Her not-so-subtle fishing expedition was pretty cute. He couldn't resist lifting her face and then kissing her until they both gasped for breath. At last he drawled, "She's not going to wonder shit."

"Oh?"

"For the record, I'm not fucking Bella either."

"Oh."

She went to reinsert her head against his shoulder, but he fastened a hand back on her head and forced her gaze back up. "You really sound surprised at that."

She flung a little frown. "Shouldn't I be? The two of you have been a walking tribute to moony and cuddly for the last five days."

Her sarcasm, a thin excuse for her hurt, knotted his gut. It sealed the deal on the words he deliberately chose next. "Yeah. Remember me when the Oscar ballots roll around."

She sat up a little. "Huh?"

Shutting out the tempting sight of her cleavage, he took a deep breath before moving on. "The Romeo act with Bella has been just that. An act."

"*Huh?*"

He fingered away some of her hair from her face so he could gaze deeper into her eyes. "Rhett, Rebel, and I aren't really on the set as consultants. We're working. On a mission. We're chasing a very credible lead in partnership with the CIA and the FBI. It links communication from a major crime cartel to an end source here in LA."

Ava blinked, taking in his words carefully. "Somebody in our crew?"

"You could say that." When she raised her face in silent query, he pulled in another measured breath. "Enzo Lemare."

She skittered backward while clutching the blanket around herself, reacting to the informational landmine he'd just detonated. "What the hell?" Her exclamation hung in the air for a long minute. Her shoulders rose and fell as her body struggled to keep up with her brain. "What the *hell*, Ethan?"

"I know it's a shock."

"*Tu piensas?* You think?"

He scooted up to lean against the headboard. He hadn't pictured ever having to have this exchange with her, but if he had, being buck naked on a bondage bed wouldn't have been his first choice for settings. Maybe the fresh positioning would help. "What I'm about to tell you is classified. It goes nowhere outside this room, right?" After she gave him a solemn nod, he went on, "His real name is Ephraim Lor, and he spent the better part of his life with radical extremists. When I was texted away from your place by Franzen last week, it was

to attend a briefing where we found out that an encrypted communication out of Mexico made its way into the country, with Lor as its likely recipient."

Her eyes darkened. "What did it say?"

"We didn't know for several days. The intel was parked on a laptop, with a USB key needed to unlock it. We banked on the assumption that Enzo had that stick, which was why they inserted Rhett, Rebel, and me into things at the *Dress Blues* set."

At that, she actually smiled. "They told you to get closer to Bella, in hopes that you'd get closer to Enzo." Relief visibly flooded her face as doors of understanding clearly began to open. But a second later, her features darkened again. "So did you find it? The memory stick?"

"Late on Friday." He tossed a lopsided grin. "Remember the *accountant* who came by the photo shoot at the Huntington?"

"The one who screamed *bee* and stopped my pulse for a full minute?" she snapped. "*Sí*, I remember her well. How could I—" Her eyes and mouth went wide. "*Caramba*. That was an act? She was there to grab the stick? She's one of you?"

"In a way. She's FBI special task force."

He decided she didn't need to know that the "bee girl" was also the woman who'd collaborated with the lunatic who'd attempted to kidnap Ava's cousin back to Thailand. Besides, at the moment, silence was a friend. The enormity of what he'd just disclosed hadn't lessened its weight on his mind. "A lot of people have been working for months on this intel," he asserted, letting her see his gravely serious side again. "Lor doesn't just cover his tracks. He erases the damn things from the face of the earth. In short, he's a sneaky fuck." His voice dipped into

a growl, and he didn't care. "Needless to say, watching him set his radar on you has been a goddamn torture session."

Ava's face crumpled in adoration and admonishment in the same sweep. She crawled closer and twined her fingers into his. "So did the stick unlock anything on the laptop?"

He scowled. "Only another code, which we've only nicked the surface on decoding. On top of that, we learned there was a second laptop that the Aragons sent, only we haven't been able to locate the damn thing. We've kept a constant vigil on the fucker, and he hasn't received any shipments except vitamin supplements and a couple of new ties from Italy." He squeezed her hand harder while using the other to scrub his face in frustration. "The asshat has to be working with someone. We just can't figure out who the hell it is."

A palpable wave of energy flowed off Ava. It was accompanied by her tighter grip in his, along with the total drain of color from her face. "Sunshine?" He leaned and gripped her by the elbow. *Damn it.* He'd been a hawk about watching her for signs of sub drop—except for the last ten minutes, in which he'd drop-kicked a wall of stunning new information on her. "Come here." He added to his command by thrusting a bottle of water at her. "Drink. Now. Let me see if the toy cabinet has any candy in it. Your blood sugar is likely whacked, and—"

"I know." She practically choked the words. Her hand clutched at him, forcing him to sit back down.

"You know what, baby?"

She lifted her face. It was twisted with distress, as if she'd just witnessed a murder. "I...I know who Enzo's working with."

Guess all the bombs of shock hadn't been dropped in here yet. "What?" he blurted. "How?"

Between frightened gasps and nervous fidgets, she

recounted a phone conversation of Lor's that she'd overheard the night of the wounded vets benefit. She told about the man's provoked tone at "Mateo," likely the elder Aragon brother. There were his references to "keeping one's enemies close" and accepting nothing less than a hundred percent on their "mission."

But most terrifying were the comments about Cameron Stock. About the man "handling" things like "relevant specialists" in preparation for a "triumph" that was going to happen on Tuesday night.

Tomorrow night.

"Holy fuck," Ethan finally muttered. Lightbulbs began popping to life in his mind—only to illuminate new corners of this maze that were maddeningly impenetrable, no matter how hard he tried to see. Important corners.

Next to him, Ava shivered beneath the blanket. "What does it all mean?"

He swallowed and grimaced at the sick acid that churned in his gut. "It means Colton was right," he grated.

"About what?"

He didn't look at her for a long second. Damn it, he didn't want to tell her this part, but silence wasn't an option anymore. He'd chosen to trust her with the truth. In return, she'd given him the Mack Daddy of all revelations. Excluding her in the name of protecting her wasn't a goddamn option anymore. "The information we did recover off the first laptop was a map. It detailed hundreds of locations over the whole West Coast, plus parts of Idaho, Nevada, and Arizona. Colton thought it was a target grid." He shook his head, inwardly flogging himself. "I told him he was a pecan short of a nut bowl."

"Then you need to call him, right?"

Three minutes later, after locating his street clothes and his cell, he punched in Dan Colton's number on his speed dial. Ava had dressed and stood next to him in the dungeon's small kitchen area. She picked at the sandwich he'd swiped from the leftovers in the fridge and shoved in front of her with an order to eat.

The agent didn't pick up the call.

Ethan growled an oath and called Franzen. The call also dropped into voice mail.

With a silent but fervent prayer, he dialed Colton's desk line at the Los Angeles CIA offices. Maybe the guy had decided to go in early. Colton was a huge fan of fresh coffee.

Pay dirt. Sort of. After three rings, the line was answered—by a woman. "Yes?"

Ethan quickly shoved back his surprise. "So sorry for bothering you, ma'am." Some habits from cotillion classes never died. "I think I misdialed."

"Are you looking for Dan Colton?"

"Yeah." He didn't try to hide the wonder this time. "Luna?"

"Bingo. His desk line is being forwarded to me." The pause from her end denoted her own mental dot connecting. "Archer?"

"Right." Now that they had the meaningless formalities handled, he hardened his voice back to on-duty mode. "Listen, I need to reach him. Do you know where he is? Can I still get him at home?"

"Negative. Have you tried his cell?"

"That was my first call." He huffed. "I've got fresh intel. Game-changing shit."

"Then let's hear it."

He glanced at Ava, relieved to see she didn't suspect this

Agent Luna was *the* Luna who was still supposed to be in jail back home. "We've been running blind about Lor's partner because I'm pretty damn certain it's Cameron Stock."

There was a tense stretch of silence on the line. "Wh-What?" she sputtered at last. "Ethan, are you fucking sure?"

"Affirmative." He quickly ran down the details Ava had just given him. When he concluded, Luna was eerily silent. "Hey? You still there?" he finally prompted.

"Yes." Her answer was clipped short by a harsh hiss. "*Shit.*"

"Shit?" he echoed. "Shit...what?"

"Where are you at?" she demanded, tripling his confusion. "Are you at the hotel? The Hilton?"

"No. I'm...umm...not."

"That's where Dan's going now."

"I know."

The five-alarm fire really blared through her voice now. "Ethan, he's on his way to an urgent meeting that Stock called for your team. He said it couldn't wait, that it was a matter of life and death."

"Fuck!"

"I'll meet you there. Use the hotel's loading dock, not the lobby entrance. We both need to keep trying Dan's cell."

"Roger."

He snapped the phone shut and then looked at Ava. Goddamn, how he wanted to draw her back next to him, envelop her in his arms, and never let her go. Her rich curls fell around her shoulders in a sexed-up mess. Her neck still bore the burn of his beard. Her cheeks were rosy and her indigo eyes were mesmerizing, even in the midst of the concern she directed at him now. She was his oasis in this suddenly shitty jungle of an op.

"What's going on? What is it, Ethan?"

"We think Stock's made a move." He cupped her nape and kissed her hard. He longed to plunge at her a second time but knew if he did, there'd be no way of dodging the damn doomsday thoughts. No escape from thinking this could be the last time he held her like this, gazing at the evidence of their intimacy on her body, breathing in her incredible scent of jasmine and orange blossoms... Instead, he pecked her forehead and muttered, "I have to go."

She straightened into a posture that could pass most musters. "You mean *we* have to go."

"No." He threw it at her with the same unshakable resolve. "No way. Ava—"

She grabbed his arm, digging her nails into his skin. When he wrenched up his glare, hers was waiting, shimmering with tears above lips that shook in her attempt at composure. "You want me to come with you, Sergeant, or you want me to simply follow you? Because I'm doing this." She curled her hold tighter. "You talked to me once about banishing the ghosts of Colin and Flynn. Well, help me do it, right now—because if I lose you to this mission, their ghosts will be cute Halloween props compared to the damage yours will wreak."

★ ★ ★ ★ ★

Fifteen minutes later, Ethan made a sharp right to go up the steep hill to the Hilton Universal City, peeling a strip of rubber off the tires of Ava's Mercedes in the doing. He followed the signs for truck deliveries to the hotel, knowing that would take them to the loading dock. The road led past a hallway that had walls of glass, apparently leading to the property's meeting rooms. At this hour of the morning, the corridor was filled mostly with uniformed hotel service staff—which made Colton and Franzen even more easy to spot. Even from behind, Ethan knew the two men. Their purposeful strides, as well as the way they elbowed each other trying to slosh one another's coffee, were defining flags.

"Christ." He used a loading curb to drive the car up onto the sidewalk and throw it into park. "There they are."

"Ethan! *Anda la osa!* What the hell are you—"

"Stay here," he ordered. "Stay. Here!" But before he got three steps, his nerves clenched at the *whump* of the car's passenger door and the patter of her feet behind him. As he yanked open the hotel's big glass portal, he growled, "For a woman who doesn't want a military hand in her life, baby, you are fast ensuring my palm and your ass are going to have a party soon."

"Promises, promises." She rushed past him and then jogged down the hall in which they'd spotted Franz and Colton.

Ethan caught her, impaled her with a glare, and then whipped her behind him as they rounded a corner and spotted the two men again. Franzen and Colton were already halfway across a foyer that led to a small, glass-domed atrium. He got a glimpse of the rest of the guys through the glass, sitting and shooting the shit, everyone thinking they'd been summoned to a meeting with an ally. "Fuck," he bit out. Garrett and Zeke had Sage and Rayna there, too. The women were wearing beach outfits and looked like they were saying goodbyes to their men before a day at the shore.

He and Ava had to move. *Now.*

Squeezing her hand with command, he sprinted across the foyer. They caught up to Franz and Colton as the men pulled on the glass door to the enclosed garden area. "Hey there, Runway," Franz offered. After giving a pleasant wave to Ava, he went on, "Sorry for the fuck-of-dawn team call, but Cameron has to be on the set early due to the script changes, and—"

"Cameron's the reason we're here." He hoped his terse interruption, delivered between his heavy breaths, conveyed the urgent subtext clear enough.

Thank God it did. Without veering his stare at Ethan, Franz reached and grabbed Colton's shoulder. "What've you got, Archer?"

Before he could get one syllable out, a defined *clack* filled the air. The sound of a round being loaded into a pistol.

Ethan pivoted to focus on that gun. It rested in Cameron Stock's big hand. The man's smirk was as steady as his grip on the weapon. "What has he 'got,' Captain?" said the director. "Think I can supply the answer to that one. How about an offer to join the rest of your team in this nice, cozy atrium?"

Ethan didn't release his grasp on Ava and was damn glad Stock didn't ask him to. After he stepped into the atrium at the end of the man's gun, he discerned the reason behind Stock's magnanimity. He was now backed by another ten soldiers who materialized out of the heavy foliage lining three sides of the atrium. Each one of them carried a damn fine firearm and had a facemask parked atop their head.

One of them carried something besides his rifle. A canister the size of a hairspray can. Ethan caught a glimpse of the label—and the skull and crossbones on it. Every drop of his blood went to ice. The shit was *not* hair product or even tear gas. Best-case scenario, it would simply make them all go to sleep. But he knew, along with every guy on the team, that

ANGEL PAYNE

"best-case scenario" didn't always hold true with sleeping gas.

He looked into the grim faces of both Hawkins and Hayes, who clutched their women as tightly as he grabbed Ava. His gut wrenched especially hard for Garrett, who spread one hand across Sage's extremely swollen belly.

"Fuck," Zeke spat.

"Ditto," Garrett choked.

"Get down," Ethan ordered Ava. After she complied, curling herself into a fetal ball, he draped himself across her and smiled as he inhaled the jasmine sweetness of her in the seconds before he fell into a black, mindless sleep.

CHAPTER TWENTY

Technically, this didn't qualify as stalker behavior.

Tait nodded his head, confident with the conclusion, as the sun started to burn off the June mist across the parking lot of the Los Angeles branch of the CIA. He hadn't followed her home, wherever the hell that was these days. He hadn't left her a single annoying text and only tried to call her at the desk once a day. All he'd done this morning was borrow the team's rental van to buy her coffee and a chocolate croissant and then park here for a few to wait for her to roll into work. She'd been working insane hours; he knew that because all the spooks were on an all-hands-on-deck status that didn't seem to be changing anytime soon. As soon as he gave her the sustenance, said a quick *hi*, and then maybe grabbed a fast kiss, he'd get his ass and the vehicle back to the hotel before Franz poked an eye open.

He kept a close eye on a few people who arrived. Three guys and a couple of women, though none of them was Luna. Everyone appeared like they'd gotten just a few hours of sleep and would be hitting the caffeine IV in a few mikes. After six years in Special Forces, he knew that look well.

While vowing he'd give this stunt only fifteen more minutes, he got out of the van and leaned against it. *Not* the wisest move in a parking lot where even the trash was likely given X-ray scrutiny, but he was oddly restless and couldn't keep still.

"Damn it, Luna." He fought off the disgruntlement with himself once more. How had she drawn him here, standing in line for the Insanity Coaster once again? He knew how this worked. He'd love every twist, turn, and drop of the ride, only to stumble off and puke on his shoes afterward.

But he couldn't stop himself and didn't want to. *Crazy Luna.* That's what she'd called herself. The trouble was, he liked crazy. Who on earth was he kidding? He adored crazy, especially when it was working so damn hard to show the world that cray-cray could be okay too. That crazy didn't mean it couldn't atone for its missteps and try to make the world a better place again.

But why the hell was crazy bolting *out* of the building now, black-and-lavender hair flying, ID badge twisted, knee-high boots clattering in a mad pace on the pavement?

Tait pushed off the van and called to her. "Luna?"

She whipped around with one emotion claiming her face. Fear. "Weasley! Shit! Y-You're *here.*"

He held his hands out. "I'm not pulling anything creepy, okay? Just brought you some coffee and—oof!"

A full-body check was the last thing he expected from her. His nose tangled in her hair as she pythoned his neck with her elbows. "Thank God," she uttered. "Thank fucking God."

If her face was permeated in terror, her voice swam in the stuff. He pulled away to get a good look into her eyes. "What is it?" he demanded. "What do you need?"

"Stock is Lor's bitch. He double-teamed us. And he's called an 'emergency' meeting for everyone at the hotel, not the studio, apparently for an urgent matter."

He choked on the ice bucket of shock she'd just dumped on him. "When?"

"Right now."

"Right *now*?"

He was genuinely shocked and her gaze narrowed, clearly believing him. "Franzen sent out the text about it an hour ago. Haven't you been checking your phone?"

"I took the rental van without asking. What do you think?"

Brandishing her second shock of the morning, Luna gave him a hard and fervent kiss. "For the first time, I'm damn glad you bend the rules, buddy." Alarm sparked anew in her eyes. "We have to get to the hotel. Now!"

He reached back and wrenched the driver's-side door open. Before Luna could get a step off toward the passenger side, he swept her up and threw her onto the bench seat. She'd crawled across and buckled up before he fired up the ignition. That was a good thing, because T-Bomb was in the driver's seat now.

★ ★ ★ ★ ★

"What the hell?" Luna blurted it as he guided the van toward the hotel's loading dock and they noticed a white C-Class Mercedes that'd been driven up a curb and left on one of the hotel's sidewalks with its hazards blinking.

Tait growled and stated, "You got it about right. That's Ava Chestain's car."

"Shit." During their fifteen-minute speed ride over here, she'd filled him in on the phone call she'd gotten from Ethan, in which he'd not only cited Ava as his source about Stock but had confirmed many of the details directly with the woman. They could imply she and Ethan had come here together. "That doesn't look like Archer made it to the loading dock."

ANGEL PAYNE

He braced his forearms against the steering wheel and considered his next move. Follow the trail from here, where Runway had obviously entered the building, or stick to the plan Luna had set and proceed to the loading dock?

When he looked up, his decision got sealed for him.

"Fuck."

"Wha—" Luna cut herself short when she followed his line of sight and took in the same incongruous thing he did. "What the hell?"

Part of the hotel had been built out with a domed atrium. The top was glass, meaning they should be able to see straight through to the sky on the other side. That wasn't the case. There was a thick cloud of smoke pushing up against that curved roof.

"That's a whole lotta hookah," he muttered in tight suspicion.

"Get this thing parked where we can get to it fast if we need to." Luna flashed him a look full of trepidation. "I don't feel good about this."

They tucked the van against the back side of the kitchens. Before Tait climbed out, he reached under the seat and was relieved to feel the reassuring steel of a SIG P226. After checking the chamber and the safety and pocketing the extra rounds Franz had also left behind, he swung out of the van, tucked the pistol into the middle of his back, and ran to catch up with Luna.

She waited for him at a corner that opened onto a lawn that adjoined the atrium. As he neared, she peeked around the corner. When she pulled back around, it looked as if there'd been a giant rubber stamp waiting for her around the corner—and it'd been dipped in ink made of mortification.

"Oh, my God!" She slumped against the wall.

"Oh, my God." Tait's version was different. Lower. Grittier. But resonant with just as much horror.

He looked out again across the lawn—to where his unconscious battalion mates, along with Rayna, Ava, and even the very pregnant Sage, were being carried out of the atrium on stretchers into what looked like a huge medical bus. Cameron Stock, with a grimace on his face, calmly supervised the mass kidnapping. Tait heard someone snarling at the duplicitous bastard and suddenly realized it was him.

"Sleeping gas." Luna's grief-stricken whisper came behind him. "Th-They're not dead, are they?"

He squeezed her hand. "I don't think so, beautiful." He watched Stock step over to consult with one of his camouflage-wearing minions. "Those dildos are probably the mercenaries Galvaz told us about," he ventured. "Looks like the one he's talking to is their captain. Damn it, they're talking too low for me to hear. I have to get closer."

Luna yanked him back. "No, you don't!" she seethed. "Tait, if they see you— *Tait!*"

He pulled the comfort of her voice, even if it was banded in terror, around him through every step he gained around the perimeter of the lawn. After less than a minute, he'd made significant progress using the pillars and hedges as shields. He was finally close enough to hear the exchange between Stock and camo asshole *numero uno*.

"So all their vital signs are within normal, with the exception of the one?" Stock asked it as he scrutinized a clipboard full of pages.

"Affirmative," the soldier answered in a thick Spanish accent. "We've ventilated him for now. He may pull through with that extra help."

Tait called on every ounce of his training to keep his breaths quiet and even. Ventilated *who*, goddamnit? And what did he mean by *may pull through*? Dealing with the death of a battalion mate was a disgusting part of this job, but when it came from being senselessly gassed in the name of terrorism, he had a serious fucking problem with activating the healthy coping thing.

"All right," Stock replied, "keep me posted. If our demands for safe passage out of the country aren't met, that may be a ventilator we decide we don't need."

"Understood."

He ground down a layer of tooth enamel as he clenched his jaw. The monster was asking for a forty-caliber "decision" in his skull right now. *Dial it back, T-Bomb. There's still a second laptop out there, getting prepped for God knows what kind of fuckery thanks to this traitor.*

"Did the missing one show up yet?" Stock prodded. "Our friend Sergeant Bommer?"

"Negative," the soldier supplied. "The team's rental van isn't in the lot, either. We are following up on your guess that he's involved with the special agent, Ms. Lawrence, and that they may be together. Her car is in the parking lot at the agency's building, but she isn't answering her desk line or her cell phone. We have three men watching the entrances and exits."

Stock's face hardened. It wasn't a scowl, merely an impassive look that reminded Tait of how his Uncle Jonah appeared whenever they went out hunting and the man pondered how to outwit a cunning whitetail. On the director's all-American features, it was a chilling visage. "What about her apartment?"

"Classified information. She's on a special task force, right?"

"Right. I don't know a lot about her, except that her undercover skills are exceptional." One side of the man's mouth quirked up. "Too bad. In a different world, I could hire her for the show. Probably much easier to direct than that plastic fish who calls herself my leading lady."

"Well, her apartment is registered under another name. It will take us a while to hack the proper channels into the CIA's database and get the address."

"Fine, fine. Hop on it as soon as you get it. In the meantime, track the van through the rental company."

"Yes, sir."

The soldier said it as they rolled out what looked like the last stretcher. They'd laid the guy's arm across the blanket as if wanting to make it look like a rescue instead of an abduction, and Tait knew by the sleeve of pirate-themed tattoos that it was Rebel. He swallowed his fury and sorrow in time to glance over at the perimeter the hotel staff was now taping off around the atrium. Shit. That was exactly what Stock had done, staging this thing as some kind of abnormal chemical spill.

Somebody started up the big bus. As the motor revved to life, Tait took advantage of Stock's temporary distraction to sneak his way back to Luna. Without wasting time for words, he scooped her up by a hand and raced back to the van.

"Where are they headed?" she charged as he flipped the ignition.

"Don't know." The words bit at his mouth like acid.

"So we're following them?"

"No." Now it was acid stirred with thumbtacks. "They're going to put a trace on the car through the rental company.

We'll need to ditch it. They're looking for loose ends right now, and I'm the biggest item on that list." He left the car in neutral for a moment longer, swinging a rueful stare her way. "They've also figured out I'm a little sweet on you, flower."

She lifted the generous curves of her lips at him. "Nothing I can't handle, wizard boy."

Though he tied back the physical urge to kiss her, he let her read the intent in his eyes. The next second, hard logistics dictated his words again. "They're watching your car and your office, and it'll only be a matter of time before they find your apartment address, Luna." He reached for her hand, feeling solemnity wash over his face. "Who else knows your Wonder Woman origin story? Is there anyone at LA's CIA or FBI besides Colton who knows where you really came from? And, more importantly, about the tracking chip in your neck?"

She went still. He didn't blame her for the shock, or the fresh fear that glittered in her eyes. "I...I don't think so," she replied.

"Good. We'll hope that stays the case, because I'm not letting you out of my sight."

Her response might as well have been a wallop with a two-by-four. Nevertheless, he wouldn't have traded the gentle touch she lifted to his face for anything. "And I'm not letting you out of mine."

He luxuriated in one more moment of elation before letting desperation crash in again. As he turned and watched the "medical bus" leave the hotel with red lights whirling and siren blaring, he whacked a hand on the steering wheel. "We need a fucking plan," he snarled. "Trouble is, I don't have one."

For the second time in as many minutes, Luna's calm fingers, now on his hunched shoulder, pulled him back to sanity. "I do, Weasley."

★ ★ ★ ★ ★

If his stress level wasn't pegging its needle in the red right now, he would have a serious boner of appreciation for what this woman called a plan.

The luxury condo, located on the top floor of a tower in Wilshire Boulevard's swankiest section, was pulled from a damn movie. The sprawling granite kitchen had a fully stocked pantry of nonperishables and a wet bar that rotated with a button push. Two bedrooms contained plush California-king beds piled high with pillows in gray, red, and black. In the bathroom, there were at least three ways to get clean, including a glass stall shower, whirlpool tub, and a eucalyptus "wet room," whatever the hell that was.

But the real shit that was worth the hard-on were the audio and video systems in the living room. Tait ran a hand along the sixteen-channel mixer, the sleek spheres of the Cabasse speakers, and the ledge beneath the massive image monitor—and mustered at least one "holy shit" of reverence.

Wasn't happening. All he could think about were his teammates, being locked and loaded into a phony medical transport, bound for God knew where.

The acid and thumbtack cocktail coursed through his whole body now. He paced, trying to escape it and chase it at once. Frustration pounded at his brain. Restlessness clawed his limbs.

"I found some soup," Luna called from the kitchen. "There might be crackers in here too. I know it's only seven in the morning, but you have to eat something."

He stopped only to dash off a burning glare. "I *need* to find my teammates. I *need* a goddamn phone."

She huffed. "I guarantee you Stock's boys had your phone thirty minutes ago and are scouring the SIM card as we speak. Making you toss it into the riverbed was one of the best decisions I've made all day."

He increased his pacing route to include a loop around the couch. That made it easier to slam a frustrated palm against the long marble bar that separated them. "Right up there with making me ditch the van for a Fiat and then telling me to circle the block six times before pulling in here?"

The woman braced hands to her black denim-covered hips. "The backup car was Dan's choice, not mine, and you sure as hell weren't minding its speed on the curves, so I'd seal the hole on that one, soldier. As for the ring-around-the-rosy, my first instinct was to go for ten rounds, but I was feeling generous. You got off easy. Now thank me."

He wanted to maintain his glare, but it was damn hard when she stood there looking so bossy and sexy. "You're lucky I like you." Grudgingly, he added, "Thanks, Mamma Mercy."

"Anytime, Daddy Grump."

He halted as he cleared the couch for the third time and stared over the cityscape that stretched for miles. Everything was brilliant in the midmorning sunshine, another golden LA day. "What is this place, anyway? This is too nice to be a safe house."

"But in a way, it is." She stepped out of the kitchen and hitched a hip on the edge of the couch. "As you probably already know, Dan's sister is Secret Service. But the ultra-down-low is that she moonlights on *unique* assignments from time to time, likely CIA Special Activities Division stuff."

"Hmm." It was a speculative grunt. "Wonder if I've met her."

"Maybe." She shrugged out of the bolero-style leather jacket she'd had on, which covered a pale-pink tank top. The color, lighter than the deep reds and purples she usually wore, lent her skin a glow he'd never noticed before. "Anyhow, Dan is convinced she's going to be in a situation someday requiring her to *disappear* for a while, so he used a chunk of his stock dividends to buy this crib and make it nearly invisible—at least electronically—to the outside world."

He turned fully toward her, drawn by curiosity. "Stock dividends?"

She tilted her head and flashed a little smile. "Colton Steel? Maybe you've heard of it?"

"Fuck," he muttered. "Uhhh, yeah. If he's one of *those* Coltons, why is he running around in bad suits, a worse haircut, and collecting a spook's piddly paycheck?"

"Same reason they found Prince Harry on the front lines in Afghanistan. Believe it or not, a few of the privileged remember why they have such good fortune and want to give back."

There was a hassock near the couch. He straddled it as he asked, "Is that the same story for his sister too?"

"Oh, no." Her lips took on an amused slant. "Devyn just fancies herself as a keen little mix of Nancy Drew, Sydney Bristow, and Lara Croft and wants to eat bad guys for breakfast every morning, no matter what it does to her big brother's blood pressure."

He rolled his shoulders, battling the distinct green pang that joined the tumult of his senses. It didn't mean anything that she knew all that about Colton's sister. It also didn't mean anything that every time she said the guy's name, the silk in her voice wrapped possessively around the syllable. *Dan.* Shit. He wasn't imagining it. *Come here and cuddle with me, Dan. Will you zip up my dress, Dan?*

"So how do you know about this place?" He tried to be civil about it. He probably didn't succeed. If Luna noticed, she bypassed it.

"As soon as Dan's team linked up with mine last week, he told me he was worried about the shit getting thick with Lor. He was also concerned that, as the *unconventional* agent, I had a place to go that was completely safe. Off the books, you know? He brought me up here and made me memorize the security codes, 'just in case.'"

"Didn't that work out hunky dory?"

He hated himself the moment it flew out. Jealousy was an item on his useless indulgences list, something he sure as fuck didn't have time for, especially now. But even thinking of Colton in here alone with Luna just a week ago flicked that needle of tension deep back into his mental red zone.

Goddamnit, she was *his.*

He'd planned on standing and moving out to the terrace for some air. Fuck if that was happening now, with that thought locking his brain in its crosshairs. As if he had a choice to escape it. As if he could run from that chamber in his soul that the woman had occupied from the moment he'd held her in his lap all those months ago at Bastille and again in that palm grove a few miles away. The woman she'd shown only to him. The tender girl who hurt and ached, who cried for Mexican informants she'd never met and had a touch that turned his cocky-ass attitude into a smitten puppy at her feet.

He was certain if the woman had a newspaper with which

to smack him right now, she would. With hands back on her hips and a new glower on her face, she charged, "What the hell is that supposed to mean?"

"Nothing." He looked away. "Nothing, okay?" *Everything.* Tension rushed his veins again, forcing him to his feet. The room swam, and he didn't care. It wasn't like he had anything to be solid for. "God*damn*it." He raised both fists and pounded the slider to the patio. Even the fucking glass wouldn't cooperate, only shuddering beneath the blow instead of joining his spirit in the whole shattering-to-pieces thing. "They're all out there, being held somewhere, and I'm sitting here in a palace instead of helping them!"

Luna's reply was filled with maddening calm. "You can't do anything to help them with those assholes stomping through the city searching for us." The *crunch* of her leather boots came closer. "You told me that Lor and Stock plan on using the guys as leverage for passage out of the country. They can't do that with dead people, okay? Based on what Ethan told me this morning, everything indicates that their plan is somehow connected to the show's live broadcast tomorrow night. That gives us tonight to try to figure all this out." She curled her hands, long and gentle and tapered, around the fists he still had clenched at his sides. "And we *will* figure it out, Weasley."

He shook with the effort of resisting her. Clinging to his rage was the last thing he had any control over in this giant goat fuck of a situation. "I can't stand this," he grated. "I need to be doing something. I'm a spotter for one of the best goddamn snipers in the world, and right now he's been turned into a half-dead Sleeping Beauty who needs me to *find* him, wake his ass up, and—"

"I know." She stepped in front of him. "I *know*." She ran her hands up his arms and over his shoulders before flattening them to the sides of his face. "Look at me, Tait."

He stiffened his jaw and shut his eyes.

No.

"Look. At. Me."

No!

He hated her for this. Hated that this was the one damn moment he'd been craving for the last week, except for now. He hated her for the velvet compassion in her words, the soft strength in her fingers. He *really* hated her for stepping in with such surety, daring him to fill his arms with her. She was so close. Her scent, that heady clash of smoke and roses, wrapped around him. Her hands, steady and determined, moved up to burrow in his hair.

Her lips, perfect and pleading, grazed his.

"Then just take me," she whispered.

It was so simple, like the tiny thread that yanked the whole sweater apart. And damn, did he unravel for her. He plunged his mouth on hers in a fever of need, lust, longing. When she opened for him, whimpering in passion, he pushed his tongue deep inside, demanding every flicker of the desire he'd seen in full bloom when monitoring the scene between her and Z those many months ago. He wanted all of it and more. Not just her submission but her desire. Not just her body but her mind. Not just her spark but her whole damn fire. It was nothing less than what she'd get from him in return.

The resolve surged through him, powering into his arms as he hauled her off her feet. Her gaze, dark and magnetic, was waiting when he opened his eyes. She smiled and cupped a hand to his face again, like some medieval princess thanking her knight for sweeping her from a dark tower. Didn't she get it? *She'd* rescued *him*...

And now freely offered up all that power back to him. She knew he needed something to control right now and offered herself as that something.

He twisted his head to kiss her fingers. Like no other woman in his life, she moved him. Humbled him. And turned him on so much, he wondered if he'd get them to the bedroom without coming in his jeans.

Thankfully, he managed the feat. After stomping into the nearest chamber, he turned and let her fall to the mattress, following her down a second later. He didn't give her a choice about what came next. Holding her jaw in one of his hands, he leveraged her for the deepest dive of his lips and tongue, possessing her mouth with the force of his. He didn't let her go until she all but churned beneath him, bunching her hands in his shirt, mewling and sighing.

He yanked the cotton free from his torso and grunted in pleasure as she trailed her fingers over his burning skin. That didn't stop him from making her bend both knees so he could rip down the zippers on her boots and jerk both things off. As soon as he had her feet bared, he bit into the edge of one and then the other, making Luna laugh and sigh in the same breath. He let her legs fall as he kneaded his way from her knees to her waist and then made short work of unfastening her jeans but not removing them. It had been his intent, but he wasn't opposed to switching a mission plan for a good cause. And right now, the sight of her lace-trimmed, powder-pink panties contrasted by her black jeans was too incredible to pass up. He jerked her pants wider to get a more complete view. God*damn*. Through the semisheer fabric, he could see the shadow of her close-trimmed pubic patch...a dark treasure veiled behind a color of innocence. He was going to claim that fortune soon, so soon...

But first, the thrill of getting to the bounty.

He caught one of her hands. Lowered it to the sweet triangle that captivated him so much. "Touch yourself," he ordered. "Put your hand under your panties and stroke your pussy for me. Make yourself wet for my cock."

"Yes, Sir."

Fuck, that sounded good on her lips. It was even better because it was meant for *him*. Tait let out a long growl, telling her how much she'd pleased him with her trust, her vulnerability, and the courage it took to perform such an intimate act for his eyes. He watched, hands on her hips, as she slipped her fingers inside the pink covering and found her sensitive hub of nerves. As she rubbed, her head fell back, her neck strained, her body writhed. Tait's ass clenched as his hips jerked forward from pure instinct, his body drawn to merge with hers.

Merge? Screw that. Goddamnit, he wanted to fuck this woman. In fifteen different ways. With her wild tigress screams filling the air as he did.

As the conclusion rocked his mind, it shocked him that his dick didn't laser-blast its way out of his pants. He feverishly worked the button and zipper in order to save the denim *and* his sanity, groaning hard as his erection sprang free. He shoved the pants and his briefs to his knees before returning a hand to fist himself, loving the reaction in Luna's eyes as he spread his precome down the length of his throbbing shaft.

"Something tells me you don't want soup anymore, flower."

Luna's mouth swept upward. "No, Sir."

"Maybe I can find something else to fill up your mouth."

She grinned a little bigger. "Please, Sir."

He didn't return the look. Instead, with his face somber and his eyes steady, he told her, "Slide to the other side of the bed. Let your head hang back, over the side."

She didn't even bother with the *Yes, Sir*. Her eager compliance perfectly coincided with Tait's need to unsheathe her body from the black pants. As she scooted away, he tugged down, letting the opposing forces work their magic on baring her long, smooth legs. And oh yeah...her gleaming, aroused pussy.

He kicked himself free from his own pants before circling the bed to where she dutifully waited for him. But before he knelt to align his erection with her lips, he stripped her from her top and bra too. Though he'd seen her completely naked before, the sight of her tits and nipples, now angled perfectly at him due to the drop of her head, made his knees feel like they'd been shot off. Good thing he was lowering to them already. Before he got fully into position, he had both hands on her generous mounds, fingers tugging their erect tips into stiffer attention. She cried out a little as he did, though her ass and hips ground against the bed, proving he aroused her in the midst of the pain.

"Someone a little sensitive?" he asked, watching the little grooves of her nipples become more pronounced as he flicked them with his thumbs.

Luna sighed. "Someone hasn't had this in a long while... so yes. Ahhh!" Her exclamation came when he joined his forefinger and thumb and pinched hard.

"You want more?"

She moaned as he added twists to the pinches. "God, *yes*.

Please, Sir."

"Even while my cock is deep in your throat?"

"Especially then."

He teased her with the slick knob of his erection, tracing the length of her parted lips. "I can't tie you down, so if you need to stop, you safe word by rolling away and stopping. Understood?"

She licked his head with a provocative sweep. "I'm not going to safe word."

"I wouldn't bet on that."

She whimpered in approval of that—until Tait dominated her mouth with his penis in one commanding stroke. She choked a little, and he withdrew by an inch, only to enter her again a second later.

"Use your nose to breathe, flower. You know how to do this." He shuddered as she obeyed, allowing him access to the deepest regions of her mouth. "Good Christ, you feel so good," he praised, watching the thick veins of his body disappear inside the soft depths of hers. "Yes. Yesssss."

His balls already surged and swelled, banging with his come, aching for release. To hold off the flood, he focused on giving Luna what she needed. He pulled relentlessly on her nipples, turning them into lush, engorged strawberries before alternating his approach to lightly slap her breasts, a torment that made her spread her thighs and swipe faster at the blood-filled ridge of her hottest need.

"Do it," Tait encouraged. "Come for me, Luna. Show me how you'll scream when my cock is in your gorgeous cunt instead of your mouth."

She breathed harder. Sucked him in deeper. Stroked herself faster. Her back arched. Her muscles tightened. With a high, guttural shriek, she tumbled over the ledge into a paroxysm of bliss, using her free hand to grab the back of his thigh while the waves of orgasm washed through her again and again.

It took a Herculean effort not to sink into the back of her throat and shoot his seed into her then and there. Instead, gritting his teeth with the effort, he helped her up to the pillows and lay beside her while her equilibrium returned. He leaned in to kiss her, but tasting himself on her tongue didn't help when it came to self-control. Not a hell of a lot *was* helping at this point—with the woman herself leading that brigade a moment later.

"You going soft on me, Weasley?" she taunted before biting his lower lip. "You told me you know what I need."

"Damn. *Damn.*" His growled repetition came as she grazed his balls with her fingernails. "Luna..."

"You remember that, don't you?"

"Yes. Shit, woman!"

"Well, it's time to pay up," she whispered. "Fill me, Tait—with every inch of you. Please."

"Yes, Ma'am, Agent Lawrence, ma'am." He kissed her again, fast and feverishly, before leaning to the nightstand and wrenching the drawer open. Nothing there except an old cough drop, a small LED flashlight, and a dog-eared Shayla Black novel. Great. If LA got hit by a major earthquake while he had a cold and wanted to read the adventures of Hunter and Kata, he was set.

"Doesn't Colton stash condoms around here?"

"How the hell should I know?"

Her answer was a braid of good and bad news. Her perplexity proved that when Colton brought her up here last week, it had been strictly business. But now he was naked and horizontal with the woman of his dreams and couldn't do anything about it—a dilemma that twisted its way across his face and made him wonder just how cold that eucalyptus wet room could get.

"Tait—"

"What?" He almost sliced her head off with the severity of it but made a mental note to apologize after breathing down his erection.

"I'm clean. They test us every other minute in prison."

He gave her a sardonic smile. "It's once a year in SOF. I just got my all-clear." He added extra meaning to his stare. "But I haven't touched anyone in months."

Her own eyes darkened. She lowered back to the pillows, pulling him with her this time. "Hmmm. Imagine that. Neither have I. Which means if you don't fuck me now, I'm liable to become crazy Luna for real."

"*Unnh-uh.*" Sometimes a guy had to let out his inner caveman in order to get the point across. But in case she wasn't clear, he whipped the pillows out from beneath her head. The next moment, he had her wrists locked to the mattress on either side of it. "No cray-cray on my watch, beautiful." He edged forward, letting the crown of his cock dance with her slick, hot folds. "Just well-fucked, very magical little witches."

"Yes..." Her eyes fluttered closed. "Yes!" They flung back open as he thrust deeper. On the third lunge, his balls hit her ass as he seated himself all the way in. Heaven. He was finally in heaven.

She kept her gaze on him, mesmerizing as a twilight sky, as he retreated and plunged, rocked and slid, over and over again. In the work he did for this country, getting lost wasn't an option—but right now, it was the only choice. Her eyes and her body pulled him into a wilderness of heat, of need, of beauty... and the magic of her submission.

"Raise your legs," he ordered, not wavering his gaze either. How could he, when her face bore so many marks of his possession? Her cheeks, flagged by his stubble burn. Her lips, swollen from sucking on him. Her skin, glowing with the sheen of her arousal. She was a thousand times more breathtaking than anything his fantasies had conjured. "Now wrap them around my neck."

As soon as she complied, a long moan spilled from her. As he suspected, the openly naughty position awakened the darkest side of her submissiveness, turning his jungle into hers as well. It also locked him closer to her, pressing his chest against hers, securing his stare into hers. He watched as she shook beneath him, the new angle ensuring that his cock filled every tight corner of her pussy.

He couldn't hold out any longer. The wilderness rose up and surrounded him. Oh yeah, was he lost...yet had never been so found.

Everything turned silver and white as his senses spun and his cock exploded. Somewhere in that chaos, an inner voice shrieked that he needed to pull out, to cut the chances of planting his seed significantly, but Luna's cries, climbing higher as another orgasm twined through her, kept him buried inside her pulsing walls. While her body wrung every drop of his seed, her face held every inch of his focus. With her dark hair tangled on the mattress, her forehead furrowed in sensual bliss, and her teeth digging into her delectable bottom lip, she stopped his heart and made him vow to imprint this moment on his memory forever. The first of so many he planned to have with her.

He finally forced himself to withdraw, though he clutched her close while rolling to his back. All the while, he inhaled deeply to bring his heart rate back to normal. After trotting to the bathroom and back with clean towels for them both, he cracked, "Why did we wait so long to make that happen?"

Her reply came quicker and filled with more regret than he expected. "Because of me." She pulled her towel against her chest. "Because I didn't trust that you were for real...that you meant all those things you kept telling me." She tucked her hair behind an ear, actually looking a little sheepish. "You... see me differently than the rest of the world does, Tait. You've always believed in me." Her forehead scrunched once more as if she still couldn't believe the promise of the words.

He knelt on the bed in front of her. Cupped her face and lifted it. "And I always will."

The conflict didn't leave her eyes. She sat in expectant silence as if thinking he was about to drop the "just kidding" disclaimer. Tait let her look. Though he longed to press her back down and kiss the truth into her, he held back. Pushing this woman would send her running. *Easy does it.* Some of the most important battles were won by gaining small but steady ground, not blowing up the whole countryside.

"Hey," he finally murmured, "how about some of that soup now?"

"You bet." The purple sparks returned to her eyes, and she gave him a soft smile. But before she turned to search for her clothes, Tait caught her by the elbow and dipped one more earnest stare down at her.

"Luna...if what we did today gets you pregnant—"

"*Psshhh.* Weasley! Seriously? Now?"

He reeled her close again, clutching her other elbow. "Yeah, seriously. And yeah, now."

She rolled her eyes. "Morning-after pills come over-the-counter now. I'll just go to the drugstore—"

"Which is six blocks away." He squared his shoulders and slipped his hands around both of hers. "Sorry, flower. Sleeping with a Special Ops guy means you get the photographic memory too—the same recall that'll also remind you how Stock's boys are searching for you as much as me." He kissed her forehead. "So no dice on the drugstore. *Now* will you listen to me?"

She skipped the eye roll in favor of averting her gaze completely. "Fine. *What?*"

He lifted one hand to the side of her face. "I just need you to know." He slipped a soft kiss to her lips. "It'd make me the happiest guy on the planet."

She shook her head. Uncertainty tangled her features again. "So you're going to slam a ring on my finger, find us a house in the suburbs, build the kid a jungle gym, and let me make casseroles from Pinterest recipes?"

The bloom of warmth in his chest shot its way right up to his lips. He couldn't resist planting a harder kiss on her. "Fuck yeah."

That got her to forget about the insecurity, at least. Her lips twitched as she shoved against his chest. "I'm going to make your soup, dork."

He laughed and pulled his pants back on while she sashayed out toward the kitchen, deciding to leave the top button undone when her backside mesmerized him with its typical hypnotic powers. Dear Christ, he'd never get tired of that sight. He couldn't wait for this cluster of a mission to be

ANGEL PAYNE

over so he could get back to the fantasies of waiting for her prison term to be over and treating her to a nice long session at Bastille to celebrate...

Time for a change of mindset. He was going to be rock hard and very frustrated if he didn't think of something else. *Now.*

While Luna puttered in the kitchen, he fired up the television and instantly regretted the move. It was one of those late-morning "women's" talk shows where the set looked like a patio from the Hamptons and everyone had a coffee mug with the show's name on it.

He hovered his thumb over the buttons, ready to hunt for *SportsCenter*, when he heard the studio audience on the talk show break out in screams and applause. Since the volume was turned low, that was saying something. He watched for a moment longer in curiosity.

He gaped for longer than that in open shock. "What the hell?"

Luna's gasp confirmed he wasn't alone in the feeling, joining him to watch as the show's perky hostesses escorted their new guests to a fake Hamptons seating area.

Bella Lanza. Cameron Stock.

And Ethan Archer.

CHAPTER TWENTY-ONE

So this is what it felt like to be brought back from the dead.

Memories of the morning had returned to Ethan in agonizing flashes, starting with the one that brought him back to consciousness. He'd gone from darkness to light inside a minute, thanks to the epinephrine vial that came into view once he could focus his vision again. The artificial adrenaline got a giant helping hand when he realized it was Cameron Stock who'd jammed it into his thigh. He remembered glaring at the asshole across one of the studio's dressing trailers. He'd been stripped naked but considered bolting anyway. After the getups forced on him by Grant Fulsom, streaking bare-assed across the back lot wasn't an unthinkable follow-up. And the idiots hadn't even bothered to zip tie him.

That was when his scrutiny had widened to the other corner of the trailer—and fell on Ava, passed out cold in a chair, clad only in her bra and panties. Her purse lay at her feet with its empty epi pen pouch on top. Next to that was a gallon-sized jar that trembled—from the force of the thousand agitated bees inside.

Cameron had smiled with slow confidence, just as he did now beneath the glaring TV studio lights. Ethan had clenched his jaw against a cold river of bile, recognizing why they hadn't bothered to cuff him. If he complied with their plan, the bees would stay cooped up. Otherwise, Ava would die in horrific and painful circumstances.

Thinking of her was the only thing that kept the fake smile plastered on his face now. He sat next to Bella on a hanging love seat in his dress blues, steeling himself against the images that played havoc with his head. One second, he drowned in helplessness while remembering the hotel's atrium with the soldiers surrounding them, the canister clanking, and the air thickening with deceptive sweetness. The next, he floundered in panic as more recent recollections hit. The windowless room in the back of the trailer that held his captain, battalion mates, Sage, and Rayna, all passed out and chained. The order from Stock to get his ass up and don his dress uniform. The sickening recognition, during the golf cart trip across the back lot, that calling Stock out as a terrorist on live TV was only going to get him labeled as a "poor, traumatized soldier who'd succumbed to the stress of his Special Forces duties." Not only would Lor and Stock still be free and primed to carry out the plan that still remained a mystery, but he'd be tossed into a padded room faster than anyone could say *the lunatics are taking over the asylum.*

He had to put it all away. Scour it all from his mind. Leave a fresh slate for focusing on the materials he had to work with on accomplishing the goals. Lor and Stock had to be taken down. His teammates had to be set free before being used as terrorist bargaining chips.

He telescoped his mind on a small opening of hope. It was just a pinhole, but it was all he had.

T-Bomb hadn't been at Stock's Kumbaya-fest this morning.

He had to assume that Tait had somehow been warned off and was watching this somewhere. *Right. Because the guy's so excited for the summer mimosa tips coming up in the next segment, right?*

Fuck it. Even if T-Bomb wasn't watching, maybe one of Colton's spook friends was. Maybe Luna had fed them enough details to start piecing things together, and they were in the audience now, hoping they'd get a hint of what Stock had done with Dan and the others.

Maybe he could give them a little more than a hint.

"...and he's been just wonderful, sharing all kinds of stories that are going to help this live broadcast be a special experience for our viewers." Bella paused for a breath along with the chance to wiggle closer to him, twining their hands together. "Nothing classified, of course." She playfully nudged him. "Right, dear?"

"Umm, yeah. Right."

All the ladies, and Cameron for that matter, joined in teasing laughter at his expense. Like he cared. The longer they laughed, the more he could peer around for "props" to help him divulge the team's location. And the sooner his battalion was secured, the sooner he could redirect his efforts on putting Lor and Stock into prison jumpsuits forever.

The show hostess across the coffee table from them, a leggy, mocha-skinned model he recognized but couldn't name, leaned forward and queried, "I imagine this has all been an interesting change of pace for you, hmm, Sergeant? You Special Forces boys travel the world, but I'll bet you've never been anywhere like Hollywood."

He tilted his head a little, appearing to weigh out his answer, though he was actually taking time to thank the Creator for plopping this opportunity in his lap. Who needed props when he could get creative with words?

"That's an interesting question," he began. "There've been

some days, like today for instance, where I've seen nothing but the studio's back lot."

The model beamed a commiserating grin. "They're working you hard, hmm? Beginning to wish for a deployment again?"

"Well, the food's much better here."

The model giggled. A lot. "Oh, my goodness, that face *and* that wit." She glanced at the audience and was answered with a round of squeals that made him squirm. "Tell us more," she encouraged.

That he could deal with. What else would help Colton's team find them? "I really like the dressing-room trailers. I've heard that people sleep like babies in them, even in the middle of a studio back lot."

The model tittered again. He managed a convincing grin in return until Bella cleared her throat and draped her free hand around his knee. That didn't shift the other woman an inch toward a yellow light, much less a red.

"Have you been sleeping in *your* trailer, Sergeant Archer?"

He let a meaningful beat go by. "Perhaps."

"In your uniform, or out of it?"

With deceiving calm, Stock rose to his feet. This flummoxed all four of the hostesses so much, they sloshed their coffee in an effort to match his move. The action clearly hadn't been discussed before the broadcast. Though this was live TV, a general sense of choreography was followed as closely as scripted material. Stock's impromptu move ensured he had the full attention of everyone on set—except Bella, who was busy sliding a minx's grin at Ethan. She was definitely "in" on whatever the man had up his sleeve.

Ethan's mind responded with only one word, coming right

after a thousand cords of tension gripped his muscles. The same cords that the team had termed "Runway's shitstorm sensors."

Fuck.

"As fascinating as we all find the subject of Sergeant Archer's sleep apparel"—he let everyone in the studio react with hearty laughs—"I am excited to ask him and my leading lady to join me over here for an even more exciting announcement."

The shitstorm alarms pealed through him now. Using mind over matter, he got to his feet along with Bella and let her drag him by one hand to Stock's side.

"Tell them already!" she urged the director, bouncing in her stilt-high heels.

"Patience, patience," Stock soothed back.

"Tell us already!" The four hostesses belted it together. One of them motioned at Bella for a high-five on the deal, but she was so riveted on Stock, she didn't notice.

Fuck. It gonged through Ethan again, making Stock's relaxed confidence feel like a goddamn kick in the teeth.

"All right, all right." The man held out his hands, milking the moment, making all the woman wail again. At last he continued, "A while ago, we heard that a special celebrity would be rolling through town today. We asked him if we could secure approval from the network to shift the *Dress Blues* live episode to tonight, if he'd be open to doing a special cameo on the show. To our excitement, he agreed. He's here now to talk a little about it with all of you too."

As Stock finished that, he swept an arm out toward the entranceway, accompanied by a musical swell that turned Ethan's bloodstream to ice and his heartbeat into a scream.

Hail to the Chief.

He slammed his shaking hand to his sweating brow as President Craig Nichols walked onto the stage.

CHAPTER TWENTY-TWO

Ava moaned. What the hell had she drunk last night? And with how many kinds of hooch? *Qué paso?* She hadn't been hung over like this for years. Her head hammered. Her throat felt like the Mojave, cacti plants intact. Hadn't she already learned this lesson? Who the hell had she been out with last night? She couldn't remember anything past the beautiful way she'd started the day, in Ethan's arms at Ricochet.

Maybe she needed to roll over and sleep off the rest of it.

A woman's scream ensured that wasn't going to happen. It was sad. Horrified. Grieving.

And oh hell...was she naked?

She forced her eyes open. She still had her underthings on, thank God. And now that blessed silence surrounded her again...

Except for the buzzing. Lots of it. Too angry and animalistic to be her inner ears resisting her headache.

Slowly, she turned her head.

"Ave Maria!"

She skittered back in the chair. The large jar of pissed-off bees, anxious to find their queen again, was less than three feet from her toes. If even one of those shits got to her, the situation would be—

She cut into that thought with a horror-stricken sob.

"Ssshhh." A man in desert camouflage, who'd be the poster guy for smoky handsomeness if it wasn't for the automatic rifle in his grip, issued it. "*Cálmate, mija.* You're safe and so is your man, as long as you stay put."

Inside seconds, the missing memories rushed back. Ethan on the phone with Luna Lawrence. Their insane drive to the hotel. Ethan spotting Franzen and Colton inside and then parking her car on the sidewalk. And then—

Holy shit. She wasn't hung over. She'd been hit by industrial-strength sleeping gas. They all had.

"I'm not your *mija*," she snarled.

The soldier shrugged. "Fair enough. As long as you stay there with your little *amigos*, we don't have a problem."

"Where's Ethan?" From the moment the man had referenced him, her heartbeat had spiked into a new realm of terror. What the hell had they done with him?

"He is fine as long as you are obedient." He cocked his head, looking even more like a magazine spread as his black hair fell into his eyes. "You do know how to obey a man, don't you?"

She huddled her legs against her chest, shuddering at how the guy raked his stare over her near nakedness. She chose to believe that Lor and Stock had threatened his balls if they got anywhere near her. And if not, she knew plenty of ways to hurt an asshole simply by watching the show's stunt experts teach the moves to Bella.

She had to focus. She had to try to think.

First priority was a quick assessment of her surroundings. She recognized things at once. They were in one of the trailers the studio reserved for guest stars of the show. It had the basics: a couple of couches and chairs, makeup mirror and vanity, kitchenette with a fridge and sink, widescreen TV, and a short hallway into a windowless bedroom. She sensed they weren't in the structure alone and hoped that instinct was right.

"Wh-Where are the others?" she asked the soldier. "The ones you and your boss decided to *put down* along with me?"

He jerked his chin toward the bedroom. "They are safe."

A hurricane in the form of a five-foot-three blond burst from that direction in retaliation. "The hell we are, asshole." Sage's face was streaked with tears, fear, and desperation. Her hand shook on top of her protruding belly. "We are *not* safe! And you aren't fucking doing anything about it!"

The guard responded with an impassive stare. Sage sobbed, grimaced, and then sank into the chair next to Ava. Moments later, Rayna appeared. After locking hands with Ava, openly grateful to see her alive, Ray kneeled next to her friend. As she did, Sage's face contorted harder. "Sweetie," she whispered, "you have to try to stay calm. Breathe, Sage. Please breathe."

"Good advice," the soldier stated.

Rayna snapped a glower at him. "Shut up. Can't you see what this is doing to her? She's nearly eight months along, asshat. Do the math. If you don't radio out and at least try to get a doctor in here, this might get really messy."

"Wh-What's wrong?" Ava reached to Sage. "Are you okay? Is it the baby?"

Rayna gave the answer since the question seemed to worsen Sage's distress. "Not yet," she murmured, "but if Garrett doesn't get attention soon—"

"Garrett?" Ava blinked in confusion. "How? Why?"

Rayna gulped. Her dark-green eyes gained a gloss of tears too. "He's still out."

"Out where?"

"*Out*, cuz. Asleep. He and Sage were closest to the

sleeping-gas canister when it went off, but he covered her head with his jacket and his own body. He took the brunt of it for all of us. They supposedly ventilated him for a while, but when Stock snapped his fingers and rallied the minions up, nobody was designated to stay and monitor Garrett."

Ava processed the revelation as calmly as she could. "But he's still alive, right?"

Sage started trembling from head to toe. She pushed Ava's hand away before baring her teeth in a snarl at the guard. "Depends on what you call alive."

Rayna explained, "His pulse is thready and his pupils won't respond to light. And his spinal reflexes are really slow."

Ava nodded softly but didn't push her cousin for anything more. None of that sounded good, and she figured both the women, who were medical corps, had already started guessing at diagnoses. Sage looked awful. Her pale profile was a picture of consuming anguish, except for the spasms that made her grimace with such regularity, Rayna started noting them with quiet glances at her watch.

Ava's heart panged. This wasn't fair. Two years ago, Sage had been presumed dead by the world until Garrett rescued her from a slave-trader's den in Thailand. Now her body swelled with new life, a miracle that had turned Garrett as giddy as a flute-playing minstrel dancing in a meadow. Thinking of him beneath that imaginary meadow instead, dead before ever seeing his child...

No. She couldn't go there. She wouldn't.

Taking care to keep her feet tucked beneath her, she pressed toward the guard as far as she dared. "*Amigo,*" she implored. "*Por favor*, you must listen—"

He chopped her short by lifting his rifle. "I'm not your

amigo, remember?" he retorted. "Probably for the best, anyway. Shit's gonna go down soon, and I don't wanna be on your side, honey."

Rayna bared her teeth at the bastard. "This has nothing to do with sides! This has everything to do with decency. Do you want a man's death on your conscience?"

The guy unfurled a wide, lethal smile. "Just add it to the stack, *mijita.*"

Ava squeezed her eyes shut to activate the kill switch on looking at him anymore. It was better than killing *him,* which every cell in her body begged her for. If she popped open her bra, how many seconds of distraction would that get her? Certainly it wouldn't take any longer than that to lunge the few feet to him, grab the rifle, and—

The plan was ripped off the table in the next moment. Her eyes flew wide as the trailer's door was yanked back. But after the panel traveled a few inches, seemingly tugged by a ghost, it shut again. The guard peered, blatantly curious. His frown deepened when the motion happened again. The third time, he got to his feet with the rifle poised in front of him.

Less than a second later, with less sound than a wisp of wind, Tait Bommer filled the space between the soldier and the door. He'd brought a pair of helpful accessories. Each of the pistols filled one of his big, steady hands. Their muzzles, nicely fitted with specialty suppressors, were a perfect fit on top of the guard's eyebrows.

"You willing to die for your mission today, asshole? If not, secure the safety on that stick and let it down nice and slow."

Without a word, the soldier complied. Tait pushed him farther into the trailer while kicking open the door behind him, allowing someone to climb inside. Astonishment jumped into her mosh pit of emotions now. It was Luna Lawrence, the nutcase who'd helped that Mua monster to nearly recapture Rayna last year. The woman was the same—but not. She still wore head-to-toe black, accented now by a matching backpack, and the lavender streaks in her hair still matched her fingernails. But the torment in her eyes was gone. And even in this insane situation, the creases of anger had been erased from the corners of her mouth.

That was when the mosh pit came to a stunned stop. Ava's gape stretched wider. The woman to whom Ethan had talked this morning, when he called from Ricochet seeking the CIA guy, had been named Luna. And if someone stuck a brown wig, pencil skirt, and heels on this woman, she could pass for a saucy studio accountant...

What the hell?

"Hi." The woman herself broke into that rumination with deliberate friendliness. "It's Ava, right? You okay? Hey, cute naughty nothings. Freddy's of Hollywood or Vicky's Sec—holy shit!" She gingerly pushed the bee jar away with her booted toe. "What bozo thought that would be funny?"

Tait grunted. "Hey, flower?"

Luna's lips quirked. "Yes, dear?"

"As much as I love listening to you talk about panties and shit, I could use some of your bondage expertise over here."

"Oh, yes, Sir!" She set down the backpack but not before reaching behind the chair and pulling out Ava's clothes. "You probably want these now."

Since Rayna seemed just as excited to see Luna as Tait, Ava decided her bewilderment about the woman could go on hold. She gratefully accepted the wad from Luna before watching as the woman unloaded her pack. Out came four more pistols, a steel box labeled Breaching Kit, a handful of sheathed Bowie knives, a couple of hand scopes, and two filled water bottles. It looked like there was a bunch more, but that was the point when the woman reached a pack of plastic zip ties and a large roll of duct tape.

Finally, Ava found her voice again. "How did you two know where we were?"

Luna smiled. "You can thank Ethan. That man of yours can think on his feet." She yanked out a long swath of the tape and nicked it for a tear with her teeth. "Is my boy toy ready for me, Weasley?"

"Damn straight, baby," Tait drawled.

"Have...have you seen Ethan?" Ava stammered. "Where is he? What's happening?"

Luna bobbled her head for a second. "There's a really interesting answer for that."

"Tell me." She backed the demand by shooting to her feet but was forced to sit back down, clutching her clothes in front of her, as Rhett. Rebel, and Kellan stumbled out of the bedroom at that moment. With them was another guy who had the potential of being a life-size Ken doll, though right now, the four of them looked more like the toys some kid had dragged through the backyard one too many times. When Luna jogged her chin toward the guy and cracked something about "Dan the man, back in action," Ava made the connection that this was the CIA agent Ethan had been looking for this morning.

"Ava." Kellan stepped forward to address her but respectfully dropped his head so she could at least get into her T-shirt again. "I know this won't help much, but I don't think they're going to hurt Ethan soon. When they came and got him, I stayed coherent long enough to hear Stock ordering him into his Class As."

"Makes sense considering with whom he was doing the grip-and-grin a few hours after that."

As Tait stated that, Franzen staggered out to join the party. He looked worse than the others combined, blue polo shirt clinging to his sweat-soaked torso, eyes bloodshot, skin sallow. "That sucked worse than fast-roping on those Afghan gun pirates in the middle of that gnarly sandstorm."

Tait crossed to his captain with grim purpose. "Sorry to be the messenger, Cap, but there won't be spa time yet. We have to get our shit together. Something major is coming down the line, and soon."

"That's exactly what our friend kindly shared." Ava was busy yanking up her jeans, so she just dipped her head at Mr. Gorgeous and Evil, who glared as Luna wound the tape to his ankles in an intricate figure eight.

Franzen wrenched open the trailer's refrigerator. He went straight for the freezer section, hauling out the bucket under the automatic icemaker. As soon as he plopped the thing in the sink, he rammed his face into it. After drying off with a paper towel, he told Tait, "First things first. Did you and Luna bring wheels?"

"Affirmative. We've stashed the vehicle between soundstages eighteen and nineteen. It's quiet over there; take it from the guy who's kept tabs on most of this place for the last week." He circled his stare to the others as he hoisted the goodie bag of weaponry onto the counter next to the sink. "But we won't need it. This fox is hiding right in the backyard."

Colton flashed a knowing smirk at Luna. "I see you remembered where the fun room was."

She grinned back. "Memorized the code for that before

the front door."

"Nice work. And the car you brought? It's the Fiat?" After her confirming nod, he beamed his confident look at Franzen. "It's not big, but it's fast. It'll get the job done."

"Outstanding," Franzen replied.

"What job?" Tait asked.

The captain's jaw clenched. "Hawkins isn't in great shape. Still in lullaby land with a set of vitals that isn't pretty."

Rayna stood. "And I'm fairly certain that Sage is in the early stages of labor, too."

"I heard that." Right after she flung the accusation, Sage whimpered, grabbed her stomach, and rolled her head back in pain. "And I'm...officially...refuting it."

Rayna folded her arms. "Uh-huh."

"Ray, please. I can't have this baby without Garrett!"

Rayna dropped back down to her friend's side and clasped their hands. "Look at me. *Listen* to me. You've slept in jungles. Scared off cobras. Slogged through swamps lined in worms. Don't you dare wimp out on me now, Sergeant Sage Hawkins. Garrett has to get the attention he needs. While he does, I'm not leaving your side."

Franzen nodded decisively. "That settles it. Z and Rayna will take Garrett and Sage to the hospital. Everyone else, huddle up so T-Bomb can fill us in on what we missed during our nap." He turned his nearly black gaze straight toward Ava. "Ms. Chestain, you're not on my payroll. I can't order you to do this, but damn, we could use your help. Nobody knows the lay of the land around here better than you."

She stepped forward until she stood next to the other guys, feeling like a sapling in a grove of sequoias but returning Franzen's stare without hesitation. "Nobody cares about getting Ethan away from those shits more than me, either. So yes, Captain. I'm in."

Way, way in.

Deeper than she could bring herself to admit.

CHAPTER TWENTY-THREE

"Cut! Great work!"

Cameron's command boomed through the set, followed by a wild burst of applause from the crew and support staff. Today even Charlie Jenkow himself, normally too busy running things to applaud them, joined the ovation. Ethan supposed that was what happened when the leader of the free world was the guy in the shot with Bella.

The woman herself clapped ecstatically before hugging President Nichols. "You are so damn good!" She cut her gushing short by slapping a hand over her mouth. "Oh, no. I just swore in front of the president."

Nichols tossed back his head, full of its famous thick hair, on the laugh that had charmed millions of women into voting for him. Hell, even Ethan had voted for him, but not for the laugh or the hair. The man was a worthy leader. It made the necessity of watching his every move, not to mention those around him, that much more important. The Secret Service detail, bumped to ten agents because of the unusual circumstances, had already acknowledged his diligence with respectful nods.

They still had no idea about the reason for his extra attention: the opportunity to get at least one of them alone for thirty seconds. He'd rehearsed his briefing well. It was the only refrain that kept filling his head.

Cameron Stock is in collusion with a paramilitary radical

named Ephraim Lor, who isn't on set today because he knew you'd run a security check. The two have been developing a plot involving hundreds of targets across six states, and the CIA has reason to believe that it's going down soon. You have to get the president out of here now!

"What do *you* think, Sergeant Archer?"

He hadn't thought to pray for a face-to-face with Nichols, but the man himself filled the bill, strolling over with an expectant smile on his face.

"About what, Mr. President?"

Nichols chuckled. "Well, am I ready for primetime now? Are my *subterfuge moves* filled with enough sexy stealth to satisfy you SOF boys?"

"Looks pretty good from where I'm standing," Charlie murmured.

"Ooooo, baby. Presidential hotness!" Bella swiveled her head in one of those *oh yeah, girl* moves that only women could pull off until interrupting herself with a giggle. "*Mamma mia.* Now I just *flirted* with the president. Thank God the press isn't here yet."

Ethan took advantage of everyone getting distracted by the mirth to dare a step closer to Nichols. He was conscious of Stock's eyes on him, though none of the mercenaries from earlier seemed to be here. That was either really good or really bad. Right now, he had to bet on the latter.

"Mr. President, please listen." He issued it fast and low. "Things here aren't what they seem. You might be in—"

"Mr. President, we're ready to run through the next part of the scene," Stock called.

You might be in danger. I have nothing to back up that allegation except a map of the western states rendered in rainbow dots, along with a phony TV producer who isn't even here and a whole battalion full of comrades who'd back me up on this if they could, but they're still passed out on sleeping gas and—

Shit. Maybe it was better that he couldn't babble to his heart's content.

Nichols, thank fuck, wasn't a stupid man. He studied Ethan for another second, his face reflecting concern. "Why don't we sit down and talk after I run this next shot with Cameron?"

A sliver of pressure slid off his chest. "That would be great. Thank you."

He drew in a long breath. Okay, all he had to do was sit tight for a few more minutes. Maybe that would be the extra cushion T-Bomb needed to get here too. Or any of Colton's teams. Or even a junior ROTC troop who'd made a wrong turn while out on maneuvers. He'd work with what he could get.

They'd moved to a set depicting a fictional command center. Ethan gave a bittersweet grunt. The set-design team had made some upgrades to the computer consoles based on Rhett's recommendations. His teammate would've been proud to see them.

Stock approached the president and his leading lady. "At this point in the plot, you two have made your way to the main missile deployment tower inside Vandenberg Air Force Base."

"That's just north of Santa Barbara." Bella recited it like a dutiful schoolgirl. "Where my character, Raven Ryder, has spent the week working with horses traumatized by the war."

Nichols earned another tick of respect from Ethan for reacting to that with a serious nod. Several people, Ethan included, had tried telling Bella that unless the world had decided to start fighting wars with ceremonial parades, horses were now safe from PTSD. Nothing had worked; the detail had stayed.

"Okay," Stock went on, "we've already scripted the setup into early scenes of the show. To recap, terrorists have gotten in, knowing that an arsenal of warheads is parked beneath the base, stockpiled there by the military in case thwarting a nuclear attack by North Korea ever becomes a necessity. But they've also learned that a second round of firepower is in place, designed to launch after the first warheads have been deployed, enough to take out all of North Korea and half of China if need be."

Nichols shook his head and laughed. "Your writers are very creative, Mr. Stock. I'll give you that."

Only from years of controlling his emotions did Ethan not act on what he observed next. While Stock walked Bella and him through the first steps in the scene, Nichols turned his head and threw a furtive glance at the floor. It lasted three seconds, but it spoke three thousand volumes of meaning.

It said that the plot was more real than anyone thought. That there really was a nuclear stockpile beneath Vandenberg.

If that wasn't enough to grab his heart and strangle it, the next moment would get the job done.

Stock punched a button in the "fake" computer console, igniting the large monitor on the wall with a "fake" image. That picture was the same layout that Franzen and Colton had shown Ethan last night, the map showing damn near everything west of the Rockies covered in multicolored dots.

Raw dread drove him forward by a silent but steady step. All ten of the POTUS protectors shifted with him. He caught the eye of the one nearest to him, letting his clenched jaw do the talking for him. Something wasn't right—but if he gave them the high sign and made them shuttle off Nichols now, no matter what the plausible reason, Stock would jam in on his own alarms. God only knew what shit that would rain on Franzen and the guys, let alone whatever scheme Stock and Lor were mixing.

He had to keep his fucking wits about him. Had to watch and listen. The appearance of the colored candy map, here and now, led him to believe that the second laptop was going to make an appearance soon. If the two were linked, he had to learn how. And if that link meant the success of Lor and Stock's plans, he had to shatter it, with or without help.

"Ooohhh, look how pretty that is," Bella murmured.

"The scariest things often are," Nichols answered. Without knowing the entire scope of what he looked at, the man already sensed the danger of the "plotline" Cameron proposed. "All right, so...the story is, the bastards have gotten in and redirected the missiles *at* the country instead of away from it."

"And the sexy-ass president is here to save it all!" Bella did a girlish victory dance and then shrugged. "Hey, I'm already going to hell. I might as well enjoy it."

Nichols carved an approving nod through the air. "Okay. That works."

Stock's light-blue gaze twinkled. "Figured you'd approve, Mr. President."

Nichols braced his hands on the set's large, round map table. "So brief me on how that happens."

Stock wiggled a couple of fingers, motioning a prop handler forward. As Ethan watched the guy approach, he thought the staffer looked more like one of the minion soldiers

352

in civvies. When he saw what the guy carried, he realized his impression wasn't wrong.

Holy shit.

The second laptop?

Stock took the leather case from his man, hoisted it onto the table, and unzipped it. Inside, there was another case. Industrial. Aluminum. So distinct, even Nichols let out a guttural "Goddamn" of awe.

"Are you sure that's a prop?" the president charged. "It looks exactly like the real thing."

Stock nodded. "Pretty good, eh? I keep thinking the same thing myself. But once you get inside..." He filled in the rest of the sentence with an appreciative whistle.

"The real thing of what?" Bella asked.

Stock draped an affectionate arm around her shoulders. "The slang term for it is 'the football.'" He lifted expectant eyebrows back at Nichols. "They *do* still call it that, right?"

Nichols managed a shrug. He was considered a handsome guy—a job hindrance more than a help, which Ethan really understood—but right now, every inch of his face was taut with tension. Ethan also commiserated on that front right now. "Uh, yeah," Nichols finally answered. "It's as good a word as any."

"A football?" Bella darted a glance between them, expecting someone to cave and let her in on their tease. "Even *I* know that's not a football, gentlemen."

"It's called that because of its portability," Nichols explained. "The real one travels with me most of the time, though it stays in a secure location, guarded twenty-four seven, because it gives me access to our nuclear arsenal from wherever I'm at in the world." He swiveled his gaze to the

Secret Service guy with whom Ethan had shared a cautious glance a minute ago. "And Rob is about to confirm to me that the real one is still safe so I'm not forced to have your boss arrested for treason."

After the agent nodded at Nichols to confirm the real football was where it should be, the president visibly chilled and traded a fresh smile with Stock.

"I think you'll appreciate the bells and whistles on our special version of the pigskin," the man said. He opened the aluminum lid, reached inside, and pulled out yet another console, showing that the unit wasn't a laptop but instead a bulletproof case for a sleek tablet. Ethan moved a little closer, feigning curiosity, until Stock's glare of warning froze him. He got near enough to see that the console resembled a bigger, marginally more sophisticated version of the handheld gaming devices Rhett and Rebel were always battling each other on.

Stock unplugged the unit from the case and walked it over to a "workstation" in the set. Unlike the other workspaces, there was no keyboard at the spot. The director hit a button that made the surface slide back, revealing a docking station beneath. Once he parked the tablet in the dock, two things happened. A map of the country, with major cities detailed, flashed onto the large screen overhead. On the pad itself, a handprint identification cue appeared.

"Well, well, well," the president murmured.

"Nice, eh?" Stock concurred.

"Shit," Ethan muttered. *Shit, shit, shit.* The gut that had helped steer his team out of harm's way on countless occasions, that growled at him when situations were wonky, let out a full roar now. His logic backed up the warning, beating at his brain so hard that it vibrated down to the base of his throat.

If all of these consoles weren't props...

If Lor and Stock had managed to recreate the nuclear football in tablet form...

Holy fuck.

Stock pulled the pad back out, making both screens go black again before telling Nichols, "You'll have visuals tonight during the show. Some of them might not sync up, but don't worry. We can fix them to look right in postproduction."

"I'll bet you will," Ethan spat under his breath.

"Right now we need you to practice handling all of this as if you really know it. Get comfortable with the feel of things and—"

"Nobody's getting comfortable with anything, Stock!"

Dan Colton's voice, coming from overhead, was a Godlike bellow through the cavernous building. But if the command was the Almighty, the outbreak of *chicks* and *chooks*, a chamber-loading party from on high, was the most angelic sound Ethan had ever heard. His chest swelled with emotion, and a shit-eating grin danced on his lips. *The wild boys of the First SFG are awake, dickwads. And they've come to play. Hard.*

"Put the tablet on the table—slowly—and then raise your hands and step away from the president." Colton still used the God voice.

"What the hell?" Nichols charged as three of his men ran toward him. On the way, they grabbed Bella and flung her back. Now off-balance in her heels, she shrieked and tumbled to her knees but was able to skitter into the shadows along with crewmembers who'd found safe corners.

Ethan breathed deep to calm his heart rate and refocus his attention. As much as he ached to join the agents, he held back. Unarmed and untrained in their protocol, he'd be dead weight, perhaps literally. As much as it sucked ass, he could do more good where he stood, with his hands up. "Mr. President, let them get you out of here. Now!"

"I'm afraid I can't let that happen."

Every God voice needed a Satanic sneer. It just blew chunks when the voice had an asshole monster attached to it. The King of Hell made his entrance now, emerging from the shadows in the form of Ephraim Lor. He moved with such sleek grace, Ethan wondered if any of the guys even saw him yet. Since there wasn't a single step from above, he assumed he was the only one with a clear visual of the bastard, dressed completely in black—including the custom CZ pistol in his hand.

"Down, down, down!" Ethan yelled, hitting the floor himself.

Not fast enough. *Fuck!*

Three shots exploded. Three bodies thudded to the floor.

"What the fuck?" The stunned mutter belonged to Charlie, who'd smacked the deck a few feet away.

"Stay down," Ethan told him.

"Dear God." The stunned mutter came from Nichols.

Lor cocked his pistol again. "My apologies, sir. I am sure they were good men." He paused and drew in a deep, long breath. "If anyone moves again, the next bullet I shoot shall be through the president's skull. I presume that is clear to everyone?"

Nichols took a breath too, but his shook with fury. "Who the hell are you, and what do you want?"

Lor tsked. "Where have my manners fled? My name is Ephraim Lor, Mr. President. You probably know me better as Enzo Lemare. I've produced this show for two years and helmed several more before that." He spread out his free hand. "In short, I have had plenty of opportunities to walk the gilded sidewalks of this country, to drive its golden roads, to consort with its most pampered few—who over the years have certainly become the *few*." The man's stance stiffened. "It is time to, how do you all say it here, *level the playing field* once more. It is time, Mr. President, for America to start over. When the people of this country watch six of its states decimated at the hand of their own leader, with the cities of his strongest opponents targeted, it will not be long before the rest of the land falls into chaos."

Ethan was glad he was already on the floor. His senses became a bread pudding of stunned. When he, Colton, and Franz were talking last night, looking for a deeper commonality to the dots on the map, politics had never entered the discussion—nor, he bet, any of their minds. "God*damn*," he uttered.

Nichols gave a more eloquent reaction. "Are you insane?"

"Sometimes burning the forest is the only way to save it, my friend."

Lor finished that with a sad smile as five of his soldiers appeared and locked on to Nichols from behind. Ethan spat a dozen *fucks* beneath his breath as the assholes forced Nichols to kneel in front of the missile-launch station. It would've been more, but Ethan and Charlie were grabbed too. Four of the mercenaries hauled them up, twisted them around, and slammed them facedown onto the table. The left side of Ethan's face erupted in pain, though it didn't prevent him from picking out a new cry that erupted amidst the frightened voices in the shadows. Ava.

Shit!

While his chest cramped from the thought of her near any of this chaos, his head reconciled the sense of it. His headstrong little hellfire had likely been the one who'd guided Franz and the guys in here. She had the passkeys, codes, and layout knowledge they'd needed to get to the building and infiltrate it from above. That didn't mean Ethan had to approve one goddamn bit of the decision. That didn't mean he wasn't hoping that the subtle movements from the catwalks would morph into his teammates descending on fast ropes any second. But as long as Lor's gun was parked on the president's face, they were as trapped as he was.

He prayed like hell that Kellan was somewhere up there. And that he had some decent sniper firepower in his hands.

"Can we warm up the set a little more?" Lor shouted. "Seems a little dim for our purposes. And Cameron, my friend, after you get the tablet locked back into the console and reconnected to Vandenberg, I believe we'll need to fire up that camera. Or do you think we should try for two angles for this?"

Ethan listened to the director stroll over to Lor. "Sure; what the hell? I own these guys for a minimum eight-hour call today. Not that there'll be much for them to spend the money on around here later."

Breathe. Focus. The second one of these asswads lets up on the pressure, you have to get free and haul ass to the president.

Nichols was proving his own backbone—and capacity for steely defiance. "Thought this thing looked a little too sophisticated for a prop," he seethed.

"You are not a stupid man," Lor countered. "Everyone, even your political opponents, knows that. It is why nobody will give a flinch of doubt when watching the footage of you *taking over* our rehearsal to enact your scheme. It was why we activated five cells at once upon learning you'd be coming to this area for a visit. We worked together to manipulate the show's scripts toward this plot finale, to get the necessary communication going with your office, and to build the station that would interface with the tablet."

Nichols's voice thickened with bewilderment. "So you've had the tablet complete for a while?"

Lor chuckled. "With our resources, that was the easy part. For the harder pieces, such as the plausibility and GPS locations of all the targets, as well as selling off the tablet to an advantageous buyer when we're done, required some third-party partners and a great deal of patience." He released a pleased hum. "Today, I can confirm that patience has its rewards. Yes, my friend?"

Stock's grunt officially outed him as the bastard's accomplice. "Right on. Sure. Whatever you say."

"Stock?" Nichols's amazement saturated his voice. "*You're* drinking this Kool-Aid too?"

"Pfft." The director stressed it with a sharp chortle. "Hell, no. I'm just a selfish sonofabitch who negotiated the business behind all this. I'm going to have fun watching the show from my secure condo in Bora Bora. I'll drop you a postcard if you want."

There was a significant pause from Nichols—but not a dormant one. Ethan felt the furnace of the man's rage from where he stood, roiling hotter by the second. "So Lor, my *friend*, you despise the excessive ways of our people yet have used that for every inch of your gain, even now. To paraphrase my teenager, I call bullshit on your hairy, hypocritical ass."

A sickening *whomp* filled the air. Nichols's stiff groan followed. As disgusted as Ethan was that Lor had pistol-whipped his president, the sound was a goddamn sonata to his ears. For a few precious seconds, that separated the president's face from the muzzle of that pistol.

A few seconds was all Franz and the guys needed.

Sure enough, a throng of heavy ropes were unfurled from the catwalks. As his teammates skimmed down them faster than tree monkeys on crack, Ethan opened the gates on his dammed-up adrenaline, letting it fire both his elbows back. His guards, distracted by the shouts, gunfire, and disorder, were easy to wrench from now. He was able to incapacitate the first with a knee to the gut, but as he grabbed for the guy's rifle, he was knocked down with the butt of another gun. As he went down, he was reassured to see Charlie getting away safely. The guy had pulled a slick cold-cock on one of his guards and then paralyzed the second into shock by kissing him.

Ethan lifted his head far enough off the floor to shake the equilibrium back into it. As long as he could see, he was still good to crawl. A lot of damage could be done on an effective crawl. He already had a direction. Rhett, Tait, and two members of Nichols's detail were struggling to hold their own against half a dozen of Lor's burliest men, with a seventh running to join the goons.

But the seventh soldier had...something of a handicap.

In the form of an auburn-haired wild woman latched onto his back, firing what sounded like gutter-grade Spanish as she tried to scratch his eyes out.

"Shit!" Screw the equilibrium. He pushed to his feet, ran straight for Ava, and hauled her off the guy's back—

And then he was thrown to the floor too. With Ava on his right side, Tait on his left, and the black hole of a rifle muzzle staring at him from straight ahead.

Just as a savage howl erupted from the president.

Ethan locked his fingers into Ava's and squeezed hard as she gasped. The horror in her eruption reflected what everyone felt while watching Lor, assisted by his soldiers, flatten the president's palm to the handprint recognition pad. After five seconds, the large screen over the console fired to life.

Loading Target Coordinates — Launch Sequence verification in 00:5:00.

As Nichols roared again, Lor pushed away with a triumphant smile. "Hope you got all of that, Stock. I don't think the president wants to reshoot."

Stock shrugged. "We can fix what we need to in editing."

"Perfect. And thank you, Mr. President, for your cooperation. It was a bit rough in the beginning, but since this is only the phase of redirecting the missiles at new targets, you'll get a chance to give us your better side in five minutes."

Ethan couldn't see clearly to Nichols due to the guards still hovering over him. The president remained on his knees, probably held there by the bastards. That made everyone's new directive pretty fucking clear. He eyed Franz, Colton, and the others, confirming his conclusion in each of their faces.

Get to the president. Get him as far away from that launcher as possible in the time they had left. Four minutes, thirty seconds.

If lives had to be given in the process, so be it.

Franzen gave a subtle but affirming nod. Ethan knew what it meant. He'd dip it again three times. On the third, they'd all move as one and pray like fuck for the element of surprise on these dickwads.

Priceless seconds. God, it wasn't enough. Not the hours

he needed to look at Ava and tell her everything she'd come to mean to him, all the ways she now filled his life, his heart. Not even enough to utter the three words that now resonated in his soul for her. All he had time to do was try to save her from the venom and fire they were about to unleash on this crackpot crew.

"Listen to me." He whispered it without moving his lips. "When we move, you move. *Far* away. Do *not* disobey me."

Franzen nodded another time. Then another.

Before he got his head down the third time, Nichols bellowed again in fury. "This is sick! *You're* sick, Lor! I'll order my soldiers to kill me first. I won't participate in this!"

Lor rocked back on his heels and rolled his eyes. "I really loathe the word *won't.*"

"Really? And I really loathe guys who drink like fish at my bar, gawk at my tits for hours, and then only tip me a buck."

The tense silence that followed was broken by two words. They came from Tait, and they were thick with fear. "Fuck. No."

Lor's face contorted with confusion. He almost laughed as he took a few steps toward the darkness between the set flats. "Laudia?"

He reappeared a second later, blown back by six feet with a rifle hole in his chest.

The woman who followed him reloaded the weapon in don't-fuck-with-me determination. "The name's Luna, you crazy anus, and that'll teach you to mess with the FBI." She rotated her bright-purple gaze around to the rest of Lor's guys, including Stock. "Anyone else want a sample of my specialty cocktail for the day?"

In seconds, the assholes scattered. Franzen motioned

everyone on the team to stay put just as the foam-covered walls let in a faint peal of sirens from outside. "They're not going to get far. LAPD's already on alert."

Even if that wasn't the case, chasing minions wasn't their immediate priority. Getting the president out of here and averting nuclear disaster across six states? That was clear at the top of everyone's to-do list.

"Bogeys have officially bugged," Franzen announced.

Colton threw a fast grin at Luna. "Excellent work, Agent Lawrence."

"Right," Tait added with a snort, "Though it earned your ass a few kisses from my palm once we're out of here."

Franzen's forehead tightened. He looked over to the launch console, where Nichols was now surrounded by three of his own men. "Hey, guys," he called to the agents. "Coast is clear. We're good to go."

The riposte to that came from Nichols himself. "No, we're not."

The president's men stepped back to reveal Nichols hadn't moved from his knees. More troubling was the position of his hand, still flattened to the electronic recognition pad— because it had been tightly cuffed into place there.

"Fuck." Ethan led the stampede over to the console. Rhett was his wingman, though Ava formed a reassuring presence on his other side.

"Oh, my God," she blurted. "There's four minutes left." Like he needed a reminder.

"What the hell?" Rebel queried.

"Everyone hold your panties," Franzen ordered. "It's an altered smart pad, right? We saw Stock click it in there, so just pull it back out."

"No!"

The protest came in tandem from Rhett and one of the Secret Service guys.

"It was our first thought too," the agent explained, "but the second we started to budge the brick, their failsafe lit up the whole damn screen."

"Yeah," Rhett muttered. "Why the fuck do bad guys have to be so brilliant too?"

Ethan moved another step closer. His chance to observe Craig Nichols in a huge variety of situations today, including the rare pistol-jammed-at-the-skull conundrum, had knocked his protectiveness about the guy into something more than just duty. Now, Rhett's stress officially prodded his. "What the hell kind of failsafe?"

Rhett grimaced. "If the unit gets pulled, it'll blow up inside ninety seconds."

"Sons of smack house bitches." Franzen's lips took on a malicious curl. Several of the guys chimed in with their creative titles on the situation.

"Three minutes," Ava said on a sob.

Ethan wasn't surprised when the most composed voice in the crowd came from the kneeling man in front of them. "Well, we have a couple of options." Nichols raised his steady gray gaze. "I stay locked to this thing, which launches the missiles and kills millions across six states."

Colton crouched in front of the president. "With all due respect, sir, removing the football isn't an option, either. If you're blown up at the hands of maniacal terrorists, Lor still gets his way. Fear and insecurity will balloon into distrust and paranoia. The country will still implode from the inside out."

Nichols scowled but nodded. "I reluctantly agree." He

dragged in a long breath to precede his next assertion. "So we can do this another way."

Colton tilted his head. "Sir?"

Nichols firmed his jaw. As soon as he did, the answer nearly wrote itself for Ethan across the rest of the man's face. The stony set of his mouth, the harsh hollows of his cheeks, the resigned terror in his eyes...

"Awww, shit," Ethan muttered. When Nichols looked up to him, the color draining from his face in confirmation, the oath spilled out again.

Franzen sprang toward Ava. "Bolt cutters. Sheez, why didn't I think—" He clutched Ava by the shoulders. "They have bolt cutters for all kinds of stuff here, right, hon? Where can we find them?"

"Engineering," she answered. "They're next to the Wardrobe department."

Franzen looked to Rebel. "Moonstormer, you're our fastest runner. Go now!"

"Strike that," Nichols countermanded. "There's not enough time."

Ethan pivoted toward his captain, starting to unbutton his jacket with its fresh sergeant stripe now added. His every movement was defined by the eerie calm he now felt. The surety of knowing his choice was completely right and that his commander-in-chief had his six on it. "He's shooting true on this one, Franz." He looked from his leader to his battalion mates. "Somebody's packing a Bowie knife, right?"

As if choreographed, they all dropped their jaws and narrowed their eyes. "Runway, what the fuck are you—"

"He's going to take the goddamn hand." Nichols channeled the God boom better than Colton. "Now one of you highly trained warriors has to grow a pair fast and give him the damn knife. We have a minute and a half!"

Kellan, who'd come downstairs after Luna took out Lor, stepped forward and unsheathed his knife. He quietly locked his stare to Ethan's as he pushed the weapon into his grip. "Don't hesitate once you know it's right. And follow through to the end."

Ethan gave him a brief nod. As he did, Ava and Luna hurried forward. "We're going to be your OR nurses." Ava didn't phrase it as a question. "Luna's the best thing we have for medical staff right now because she studied anatomy in her art classes."

He arched a questioning brow at her. "And you...?"

"Refuse to let you go through this alone."

He let the brow fall. Stared at her with intensity. "In my mind, I'm ramming my tongue down your throat right now."

Ava's gaze, strong and bold, and beautiful as the woman behind it, glistened for just a moment. "I love you too."

CHAPTER TWENTY-FOUR

It was worse than she'd thought it would be. Much worse.

By the time the three of them rushed over to President Nichols, only forty-five seconds remained on the launch clock. It was barely enough time for Ethan to mumble an apology, try to angle the man's hand for a clean cut, and then let out a battle cry to power him through the massive slice.

Until the day Ava died, she'd never forget the sound of Craig Nichols's agonized scream.

Until hell froze over, she wouldn't feel this sick again. Probably not even then.

"Ava. *Ava!*"

Luna's command drilled into her brain, jarring her back. She gawked at the woman's blood-spattered face. How the hell did Luna keep her shit together like this? And was she willing to share the training video?

"Wh-What's up?" she managed.

Luna shoved something into her hands. It was warm, wet, and wrapped in a big cloth. "Take this over there and give it to Franzen. Walk *carefully*. The cops are here, and he had them call for an ambulance. Tell him that Ethan's working on stabilizing the president as best as he can and—"

"*Ay dios mio!*"

Luna had given her the president's hand. It looked powerful, stately. A circle of patterned gold was still lodged on the ring finger.

She made sure to follow the woman's order to the letter. "Walk carefully," she muttered. "Walk carefully. Walk carefully."

Seeing Franzen stomp back in was almost as good as the moment Luna had cleared the bees from her side. "Ava," he boomed, "the paramedics and ambulance are here."

"As Ethan would say," she said with a dark laugh, "thank fuck."

After gratefully letting the paramedics take possession of President Nichols's hand, she followed Franzen back toward the set. Along the way, they ran into Tait and Ethan. She rushed to her sergeant, needing to feel him against her like the magnet who matched her poles. His arms engulfed her, one hand clamped to the back of her head, his face pressed into her neck. "Is the president going to be okay?"

"I'd lay a certain bet on it." His baritone, filled with the same steady strength as his massive arms, made her feel even more locked into him. More completed by him.

She tugged away so she could take in his incredible cobalt eyes. They were surrounded by blood smears, sweat streaks, and grooves of exhaustion, but they'd never been more stunning to her. Or more brilliant with the soul she wanted to take care of for the rest of their lives.

"Ethan," she whispered, "I love you so much."

He kissed her tenderly. "As I've loved you since the second I laid eyes on you."

"Egghhh." Tait's open sarcasm was delivered with a smirk. "You two want to wait until *everyone* here can eat at that table?" He peered around. "Where the hell *is* Luna, anyhow?"

As if cued to be the answer to his question, all hell broke loose.

Ava joined her gasp to Ethan's bite on the F-word as the paramedics bolted from the set as fast as they'd stormed toward it. This time they had the president on a rolling stretcher—and raw panic in their eyes.

"Everybody clear out!" they yelled. "Clear out; clear out!"

"What the hell?" Tait snapped before jogging toward the set. Though the paramedics' reaction made her blood pulse with fear, Ava let Ethan tug her along as he followed his friend.

They skidded to a stop when they saw Luna again. Though her back was to them, everything seemed completely normal. *She* seemed completely normal. But that was the problem. Luna and "normal" were a kinkster and a minister. A match meant for fiasco.

Tait had obviously gotten that memo too. He walked toward her, reaching for her. "Luna? Hey, flower? What's going—"

She cut him off by finally turning around.

With the missile-launch unit in her hand.

"I had to." Her voice shook as she stared at Tait, who'd instinctively backed up at seeing what was now a live bomb in her grip. "I'm sorry, Weasley. I had to."

"What?" Tait almost snarled it. Ava shook and squeezed her hand harder to Ethan's, unable to blame the guy for his horrified shock. "Why? Why the *fuck*, Luna?"

"A-After Ethan got Nichols d-disconnected...nobody watched the hand pad anymore. We all figured it was over, right?" The woman's classic features crumpled in grief. She shook her head "It wasn't. The...the pad..."

Ethan prompted her, "What about the pad?"

"It...it must've been because Nichols's hand was on it for so long. It k-kept a heat signature."

"Oh, God!" Ava cried. "It kept the launch timer going."

The tension drained from Tait's jaw. He looked back to Luna with his chest pumping hard, reading her intent a full two seconds before Ava and Ethan did. "Give it to me, Luna."

The woman backed away, every move replete with feline grace though she visibly trembled. "No."

"Luna!" Tait matched her every step. "I'm not going to let you do this!"

"Yes, you are." As she nodded, the set lights played along the salty tracks that poured from her eyes. "You're going to let me because you're a good man, Tait Bommer. You fly into danger every day to protect your country. You take care of the bad guys, and you teach the good ones how to make their countries better. You do good things. And I'm...I'm..."

"Luna! Stop!"

"I'm just...crazy Luna. Lost, crazy Luna." She finished it with a tight sob. When she turned her gaze back up, her eyes were rimmed in the red of her sorrow and the mushy kohl of her makeup. "But for a while, you made me believe I could be good too. And now I'm going to live up to that. For you. And for me too. I'm going to do good, Tait. I *want* to do good."

"No! *No!*"

"I love you, Weasley."

Tait tore after her as she turned and ran into the shadows. Ethan caught his friend in half of a desperate chokehold. "T-Bomb, what the *fuck* are you—"

"Let me go. I swear to God, Archer, I'll shoot your arm off if you don't!"

"Tait? Shit!"

"*Go.* Get out of here. Get the hell off me, take Ava and go, damn you!"

With a vicious roar, Ethan granted his teammate's wish. Ava struggled to swipe the tears off her face in order to watch where she ran as Ethan snatched her by the hand and tugged her the other way.

He heaved the door open and dragged her out into the controlled pandemonium that now reigned over the back lot. It was a sea of emergency vehicles, Secret Service personnel, and studio security. Before Ava joined him in waving everyone back from the building, she swore she heard a bellow that filled every corner of the soundstage with its horror and anguish.

"*Luna!*"

Seconds later, a deafening *boom* rocked the air—and all she heard for a long while was the stunned ringing of her ears.

CHAPTER TWENTY-FIVE

"Sergeant Archer! Over here! Over here, please. Just one more shot. Ms. Chestain, can you get him to look back over here? We're from *People*. We want this one for the cover. Good. Good! Yeah, make this the money shot!"

The money shot?

Ethan couldn't take it anymore. With a polite but brusque wave, he turned and ran up the steps past the two marines standing sentry at the door of Air Force One. Thankfully, Ava followed him. A hostess welcomed him on behalf of President Nichols and then led him into a swanky conference room surrounded by cushy leather chairs, four of which were occupied by Franzen, Rhett, Rebel, and Kellan. The table was already set with five huge trays of assorted food, everything from fried chicken, gourmet pizza, and chili fries to assorted cupcakes and cheesecake slices.

Ethan ran an admiring gaze over the dining choices. The spread looked amazing. But the best thing about this space was how it cut the din of the press throng to nearly nothing. Thank fuck.

"Hey there, Runway." Franz cracked a grin that split his tanned cheeks, lifting a bottle of something that looked dark, imported, and cold. "Nice of you to wave goodbye to your groupies and join us for the special shuttle home, courtesy of your new buddy."

He leaned forward. "No, no, no, Captain. I'm Runway, not

Zsycho. *He's* the one with the groupies, remember?"

Rhett snickered. "Groupies, yes. But President Nichols on speed dial and a ride in Big Bird One?" He waggled both pointer fingers across the table, a hipster in Class As. "It's all you, baby. It's all you."

Ethan cringed. "Is that your New York side talking, your London side talking, or your dork-on-a-stick side talking?" He peered around. "Speaking of the big groupie magnet, where the hell is he?"

"Z took a few extra days of leave," Franz explained. "He and Rayna decided to stay so they can help Sage and Garrett with little Racer Joseph during the drive back up the coast."

Rhett snorted. "Racer Hawkins. That fits, considering the kid's rush to get here."

Franzen took another swig on his beer and came out of the quaff more somber. "He was still big as a house. Looks just like Garrett too. Guess the kid just knew his mama needed him around. We really didn't know if Hawk was going to pull through."

"Thank God he did." The soft murmur came from the woman who sat next to him. Ava was more gorgeous today than he ever remembered, her lush curls falling over a little black sweater that covered the top of a white sundress with a full skirt, with the curves of her legs shown off by a classy pair of black patent pumps. But her beauty was about more than her wardrobe. It began in the satiny glow of her skin, shined from her entrancing eyes, captivated him in every inch of her joyous smile and especially the sweet words that spilled from it.

After they took off from LAX, he accepted a glass of Scotch from the flight attendant and made sure Ava had some light wine and then leaned his head back and closed his eyes. It had been three days since the insanity at the soundstage. Sometimes it felt like only three minutes, sometimes three years—especially when he relented and gave an interview, only to be hounded by the journalist to give up details about the episode that had been ordered as classified. No, he couldn't talk about the terrorists or what they'd wanted. No, he couldn't talk about who'd been killed or how. Yes, he really did cut off the president's hand to save his life. Yes, Bella Lanza was really that gorgeous in real life. Not quite the truth? Maybe some bubbles were best left unbroken.

Yeah...life needed a few more bubbles, period. If the last ten days had illuminated a lesson for him on top of schmoozing with Hollywood's elite, spending an unforgettable day with the president, and hitching a ride home on Air Force One, it was that life, and love, are made up of bubbles—precious pieces of beauty too often popped in the name of something as stupid as pride, fear, prejudice...or emotional baggage. Bubbles needed to be cherished. Bubbles needed to be defended, guarded, and fought for with all the valiance in a guy's soul, all the love in his heart.

Rebel's soft bayou twang tugged at the edges of Ethan's reverie.

"Franz? Did you get an update about T-Bomb too?"

Their captain's features tightened from serious to grim. "Hospital's keeping him for a while longer. The fucker refuses to stay in bed. He sneaks to Luna's side every chance he can get. They're still amazed he walked away from the blast with just a snapped collarbone and a shit ton of bruises. Runway, you probably saved his life by trying to pull him back. Those few seconds made the difference."

"*Psshh.*" Rhett loaded his plate with another slice of pizza. "First the president, then T-Bomb. Do we have to get him a cape and a magic ring now?"

Ethan glared. "Stuff that pie into your hole before I give you something else for it."

"In your dreams, pretty boy."

"And Luna?" Rhett asked after giving them both a dismissive eye roll. "How's she doing?"

Franz gave him a look that declared the answer wouldn't be pretty. "No change. The blast fucked her up something fierce. The docs won't bring her out of the medically induced coma yet. They're hopeful her brain and body will heal from the rest. She's a fighter, and all the signs are there that she'll pull through, but there just won't be a definitive answer for another few days. As we speak, Tait's brother is flying to LA so he won't be alone in all this."

"Shay's a good man," Kellan commented. "Is he still with the seventh, out of Florida?"

Franz nodded. "Good memory. But you know how deep into the shit they still are overseas. Took them a while to find them, even longer to procure the right paperwork for his leave."

Ethan quietly excused himself, making a beeline for the little hallway that led, if he remembered right, to the president's senior staffers' meeting room. As always, the talk about Tait made him restless. Both he and T-Bomb had been the fucking lucky ones during the insanity in LA, each finding the woman who perfectly snagged their heart. He still couldn't accept the monkey wrench fate had decided to hurl at Tait and Luna on the way to their happy ending. On the other hand, he knew few soldiers who had stronger spirits than Tait Bommer. If anyone could fight for Luna like this and win, it would be him.

"Damn," he muttered. The staffers' room was even nicer than the dining room. The couches were leather, the cup holders were backlit, and there was a huge flat screen on the wall.

"Sergeant Archer?" The flight attendant appeared in the doorway carrying more beers and a plate full of jalapeño poppers. Sheez. Hadn't someone told the woman this flight was only two and a half hours long? "Is there something I can help you with?"

"Sorry," he mumbled. "Just feeling restless." Her kind brown eyes and understanding smile gave him a surge of boldness. "Hey, is the president up and about?" He guessed that was how they said it in the rarified air of the Oval Office, even if it was airborne right now.

"Well, he is," she answered slowly, "but the doctors have only cleared him for six hours of work a day while his hand heals. He's lucky they were able to reattach it, and he needs to take it easy." She laughed a little. "The conference call he's on right now will officially push him into seven, meaning I'm gonna have to get on my bitch broom."

"Not that," Ethan teased. He spread his hands. "No worries. And...sorry. I wasn't snooping. Just—"

"Restless," she finished amiably. "I get it. My husband's on a SWAT team in DC. He gets like this after a shitty op, and he's never had to cut off the president's hand before."

On his way back to the dining room, Ethan concluded that Mr. SWAT Team Husband was a seriously lucky man.

The next second, he counted himself even luckier.

As he walked past the women's bathroom, he heard soft singing. In Spanish. He felt a smile curling his lips as he braced his hands to either side of the doorway. Without another word, he patiently waited.

It didn't take her too long to finish up. When she slid back the door and confronted him there, a very startled and damn cute *dios mio!* popped out of her mouth. Unable to resist, Ethan caught the last of it with his lips.

And as it happened so many times when he kissed her, he couldn't settle for just a tiny taste. Or just a gentle greeting. He had to have her fire. Her desire. Her passion. Her gasps.

Her surrender.

It involved the work of three steps to get her back into the little compartment. It was bigger than a normal airline bathroom, but not by much, meaning he had to be near her anyway. While dipping his mouth to hers again, fusing their connection with the open thrust of his tongue, he dug his hands into her waist and hiked her onto the little counter next to the sink. As her little squeal of surprise tickled his ear, his dick surged to full attention.

When they dragged free to catch their breaths, he smiled into her face and murmured, "Hello, sunshine."

Ava giggled, the sound an intoxicating mix of husky and sweet. "I wondered where you'd gone."

"I was restless."

"I can tell."

He dipped his head to lick the sensitive spot below her ear. Ava retaliated by grabbing him by the nape and scoring his scalp with her slender nails. "Fuck!" He hissed as she did it again. "Do you *know* what that does to my cock, baby?"

She drew up the pointer finger of her other hand and wobbled it in front of his lips. "Uh, uh, uh." Her singsong was even more maddening when she tugged her bottom lip between her teeth. "The President of the United States is twenty feet away, Sergeant Archer. No inductees to the mile-high club on Air Force One."

He answered that by rolling the tip of his tongue along her lip, coaxing her to set it free for him. When she released a longing sigh, he sucked it in via a long, tantalizing kiss. By the time he let her go again, her limbs were limp, her eyes heavy...

And her pussy soaking wet.

"Oh!" Her lazy gaze vanished at the first flick of his thumb against her clit. With wide eyes and parted lips, she fumed as he continued to play, clearly ramping up her arousal not in spite of their surroundings but because of them. "Ethan! *Quitaté!* We can't!"

"Your mouth is telling me one thing, but your body is telling me another, sunshine." He pushed back her thighs another inch, spreading her wider for him before he made fast work of his fly, releasing his penis so its crown helped his fingers tug aside her soaked panties. "Why don't we let it have a chat with mine?"

"Ohhh." Her moan was long, tormented, and sexy as hell. "Dear God, you're a heathen. N-Nobody does this on the president's plane!"

He rolled his hips, knowing the movement stimulated the entire ring of quivering tissues at her entrance. "I can guarantee you, baby, Craig and the First Lady have definitely given it a whirl."

"That's...that's different."

"How? Why?" He slid in a little deeper, letting her hear his own pleased groan. Fuck, she felt so good. So right. So perfect. So his.

"They're the president and First Lady. They're married!"

He was only halfway in, but he paused right where he was.

"And you're *my* first lady." He lifted a hand to her face. "So say you'll be my wife too."

Her indigo eyes went wide. She gripped his neck harder. "Are you— Do you know what you just—"

"I know exactly what I said. I love you, Ava. And I need you in my life." He dipped his head and kissed her soundly but sweetly. Since his cock was already buried halfway inside her, he needed to keep something about this on the level of chaste and serious. "I know we have some things to work out. I'm stationed in Tacoma, but I don't have to live there. I like LA— as long as you're there with me." He softly nipped the corner of her jaw. "We can even talk about that little house with the swing set...if you want."

She moaned once more, but this time it vibrated with conflict. "I...I don't know what to say."

He ran his mouth over her lips again. Her nose. The lids of her eyes. "Say yes. Surrender to me, Ava. Surrender to *us*."

He showered her with more soft kisses. In more of his wordless, boundless love. In the caresses that showed her how he yearned to cherish her for the rest of their lives.

At last, a sigh spilled from her that echoed straight into his soul. Ethan surged his body into hers, turning them into one being. She finished her breath with the word that changed his world the same way she'd connected to his soul, consumed his heart, and captured his love forever.

"Yes."

Continue the Honor Bound Series with Book Four

Wild

Coming January 2018!

ALSO BY ANGEL PAYNE

The Misadventures Series:
Misadventures with a Super Hero
Misadventures of a Time Traveler

Honor Bound:
Saved
Cuffed
Seduced
Wild (January 2018)
Wet (February 2018)
Hot (February 2018)
Masked (February 2018)
Mastered (Coming Soon)
Conquered (Coming Soon)
Ruled (Coming Soon)

**For a full list of Angel's other titles,
visit her at www.angelpayne.com**

ACKNOWLEDGMENTS

Dear Reader,

Thank you for coming along on Ethan and Ava's very wild ride of a journey! I truly hope you enjoyed it. The story was definitely an "E ticket" experience, for which I've received both rave reviews and eye-popping criticism since first writing the book. But I have to say, getting the special experience of getting to work on the book again for this new Waterhouse Press edition was just as much a blast as it was when first creating and editing this couple's special adventure.

I've never made it a secret that my plot twists usually stem from my fangirl stalkings of fiction's best, and never does that tenet hold more true than in the Honor Bound books. When I was first conceiving this part of the saga, I was loving on Lexi Blake, Diana Gabaldon, and Lee Child in literary form and binging on TV such as *24* and *Buffy* in my spare time. Needless to say, I was soaring all over the place for plot ideas and loving the fictional wildness I encountered in the doing. But it's always awesome, in all these forms, to see creative geniuses being bold and outrageous about their plotting choices. Fiction is for the fantastical: to make us sigh and gasp and drop our jaws; to pop those OMGs off our lips and elicit all the feels from our vulnerable and beautiful hearts. So if I made you do any of those things, my purpose in life has been served—and I hope you'll join the guys of the First Special Forces on more of their adventures soon!

I am always, *always* grateful and stunned and humbled by all the support and encouragement from all of *you*. Thanks so much for enjoying all the books—and for reaching out to let me know when you do. It truly means the world.

Thank you!

ABOUT ANGEL PAYNE

USA Today bestselling romance author Angel Payne loves to focus on high-heat romance starring memorable alpha men and the women who love them. She has numerous book series to her credit, including the Suited for Sin series, the Cimarron Saga, the Temptation Court series, the Secrets of Stone series, the Lords of Sin historicals, and the popular Honor Bound series, as well as several standalone titles.

Angel is a native Southern Californian, leading to her love of being in the outdoors, where she often reads and writes. She still lives in Southern California with her soul-mate husband and beautiful daughter, to whom she is a proud cosplay/culture con mom. Her passions also include whisky tasting, shoe shopping, and travel.

Visit her here:
www.angelpayne.com